PENGUIN BOOKS

THE HOUSE WITCH

and the Enchanting of the Hearth

ABOUT THE AUTHOR

Delemhach is the Canadian author of the popular series The House Witch and is already hard at work on the sequel series, The Burning Witch. When they aren't following the whims of their unfortunately intelligent cats, Kraken and Pina Colada, they are teaching music privately to their students. In their spare time outside of writing and work, they enjoy cooking, reading, hiking, spending time with family, and trying not to remember their socially awkward moments.

THE HOUSE WITCH

*and the Enchanting
of the Hearth*

DELEMHACH
Emilie Nikota

PENGUIN BOOKS

PENGUIN BOOKS

UK | USA | Canada | Ireland | Australia
India | New Zealand | South Africa

Penguin Books is part of the Penguin Random House group of companies
whose addresses can be found at global.penguinrandomhouse.com.

First published by Podium Publishing ULC, 2022
First published in Penguin Books, 2024
007

Printed and bound in Great Britain by Clays Ltd, Elcograf S.p.A.

The authorized representative in the EEA is Penguin Random House Ireland,
Morrison Chambers, 32 Nassau Street, Dublin D02 YH68

A CIP catalogue record for this book is available from the British Library

ISBN: 978–1–405–96711–2

www.greenpenguin.co.uk

MIX
Paper | Supporting
responsible forestry
FSC® C018179

Penguin Random House is committed to a
sustainable future for our business, our readers
and our planet. This book is made from Forest
Stewardship Council® certified paper.

This story is dedicated to Sigs and to my parents.

Sigs, for your support and help in making a longtime dream a reality. For helping me think outside the box on how to get there and letting me interrupt you whenever I got excited or ran into a roadblock and needed to share it. I love you and hope you can bear with me on all my future works!

My parents, for giving me a wholesome upbringing and a love of fantasy, wonder, and of course food. Your unconditional love and patience through the years has been a fantastic source of magic that I can't thank you enough for.

I am a very lucky person to be surrounded by so many brilliant people.

CHAPTER 1
FIN

The loyal citizens of the kingdom of Daxaria described their homeland as a lovable mess. The enemy kingdom Troivack, lying beyond the Alcide Sea, preferred to refer to the continent as a "mess of fools." This was in large part due to the tangle of nonsensical roads and villages smattered across its grassy fields, which seemed to spring up with the same amount of forethought a sheep would give to cartwheels. However, despite the majority of the land existing in geographical nonsense, Daxaria's four cities lay sensibly along the north, east, west, and south borders.

The reigning King and Queen of Daxaria primarily resided just west of the well-protected northern city of Austice. The couple had earned adoration and respect from their citizens during their near fifteen-year rule.

It was on a particularly lovely, sunny early spring day that the King of Daxaria was meeting with his advisors regarding the rumors of an attack coming from Troivack. He was entirely unaware that the first of his new employees for the castle had arrived.

A wooden cart clacked its way to the edge of the kitchen gardens. The short, hairy driver stumbled down out of his seat with a less than pleased grunt. He then immediately began chucking the soft sacks his passenger had stowed aboard down onto the emerald-green grass.

"I will unload them myself," the passenger, a tall young man, called out as he leapt nimbly from the back of the cart and caught one of the sacks before it hit the grass.

"Make it quick then. What kind of freak brings a broom when travelling?" The driver hiked up his stained tan trousers and leaned against his aging donkey impatiently.

"You don't happen to live in the castle, do you?" the young man queried.

The driver squinted against the high sun as he tried to glimpse the stranger's face, scowling.

"Do I look like I live in this hoity-toity mass o' stones?"

"I've had enough unpleasant surprises in my life. I didn't want another one," the passenger muttered aloud, more to himself than the driver, as he retrieved the last of his bags.

"Now see here, you—!" The infuriated retort was cut off as a plump maid in a white apron and cream wool dress came rushing down the garden path, interrupting the exchange.

"Are you Finlay Ashowan, the new cook?" she called out, slightly out of breath as she wiped her hands on her apron and squinted against the sun to try and glimpse the newcomer's face.

"Call me Fin, and yes, I am. You are Head of Housekeeping, I presume?"

"By the Gods you sound young! Yes, I am Ruby."

The new cook hoisted three of his bags over his shoulders and hefted the fourth in his right hand with the broom easily. There were still a couple sacks lying on the ground, but he didn't seem concerned about them as he addressed the driver over his shoulder.

"Goodbye, Kip. May we never have to speak again."

"You weird lookin' bastard, I hope you shit bricks!" came Kip's angry response at the fellow's back.

Fin's response was the middle finger of the hand carrying three bags, raised straight in the air.

Another slew of obscenities left the driver's mouth as his former passenger disappeared amongst the muddy vegetable and herb garden patches, where only a few shoots of green had broken through the surface.

When Fin stepped across the threshold into the castle kitchens, it took his eyes a few minutes to adjust to the darkness and discern the chaos that met him.

People were all talking over one another, and everyone seemed to be performing tasks out of sync with the other occupants of the room.

There were two maids in rose-colored wool dresses and pale blue aprons filling a bucket of water with vegetables, clutching paring knives and gossiping amongst themselves. A group of knights were huddled around a long wooden table nearly half a foot taller than a dining table located in front of the hearth. All of them were simultaneously heckling the young woman, who trembled as she tried to peel the pile of ruby red apples in front of her.

The squires of the knights were playing catch with what looked like a potato, laughing and chattering amongst themselves.

A trio of elderly maids clucked to each other as they piled sacks of flour against the only wall, where a large round window lit the sizable stone room. The window illuminated long wooden beams stretching across the stone arched ceiling, as well as the faces of the odd group of people. Not that the details of these faces bore any meaning to the newcomer.

It was then that Fin laid eyes on the only still person amongst the commotion.

A woman wearing a purple sheath gown stared at him from the corner beside an arched door he assumed led to a castle corridor. Her thick black hair was half pulled back, with the rest left to softly fall behind her shoulders. Her equally dark eyes were fixed on him as the twisted gold of her studded earrings caught the pale spring light. She was giving him a small smile, and had a single eyebrow raised as she studied him with undisguised interest. Her expression indicated she was caught between amusement and judgment.

Dropping his bags to the floor and folding his arms across his chest, the new cook looked down at the Head of Housekeeping. She turned and blinked in surprise at the man in front of her, as her eyes had also adjusted to the dimmer lighting.

"I *thought* you sounded young!" she gasped slightly as she finally saw the man's features.

Her exclamation effectively silenced the room, and every eye swiveled to stare at the new arrival.

He had bright red hair only a few inches long, half swept to the side. His slanted, bright blue eyes, flecked with gold, surveyed everyone levelly before he began tapping his index finger on the faint freckles on his forearm.

He was tall, lithe, and not even thirty years of age.

"There has to be a mistake, you couldn't possibly be—" Ruby started, clearly flustered that the cook for the King of Daxaria could be so young and … *pretty.*

"I will show you the letter signed and sealed by your former cook. Then I want everyone but the Head of Housekeeping *out* of my kitchen." The words were ground out as though he were fighting the urge to shout.

This tone resulted in everyone gaping at him with a mixture of awe and humor.

With a grunt, he reached into the sack in his right hand and pulled out a scroll.

"Now see here, young man, you cannot order around my staff, or the knights, for Gods' sake—"

He wielded the scroll in Ruby's face and waited as she spluttered to a stop and snatched it from him.

She unfurled it in angry silence, her mouth moving as she read. Her face paled as she perused the former cook's positive reference on behalf of the young man, and adamant declaration of his hire.

She rolled the scroll closed again and cleared her throat awkwardly.

"My lady, and sirs, this is Finlay Ashowan, our new Royal Cook." Ruby turned, and curtsied to the woman sitting near the window, then to the knights.

"Welcome, cook. Let's see what you can do about the piss-poor ale here, hm?" The largest of the knights stood up, his barrel chest donned in plate armor. As he tilted back his mug, ale trickled down into his black and white beard.

The young maid who was still trembling at the table stood to his left, and she visibly shrunk away from him as he stood.

Fin frowned but bowed his head, first to the mysterious lady in purple, then to the knights.

"If you could all leave the kitchen, I need to confer with the Head of Housekeeping to begin preparing His Majesty's meals," he remarked tersely, eyeing the knight. "You there." He pointed at the maid, who was about to slice her finger open while peeling the apples. "Please go out to the garden and fetch me peppermint, sage, and chamomile."

The maid dropped the knife and apple with a clatter and scurried as quickly as possible around the table. She flew past the new cook, and out the open door behind him, without a second glance.

There were no plants past sprouts this early in the season, but no one thought to point that out.

The knights all laughed and teased one another about the maid's obvious distress as they paraded out of the kitchen with their squires, thanks to the lack of their "toy." The maids also began to leave, casting uncertain glances toward the Head of Housekeeping and whispering hurriedly amongst themselves.

The lady was the last to stand, and once it was only herself, Fin, and Ruby in the room, she floated over to him.

He was surprised to see that though she had been introduced as a lady, she didn't wear a scrap of finery other than her earrings. Her olive toned skin was smooth and flawless, her dark eyes intense, her smile mystifying, and she was beginning to prick Fin's already sensitive nerves.

As a result, he only remembered to bow when she stood nearly toe-to-toe with him.

"I am Viscountess Annika Jenoure. I am pleased to make your acquaintance," she explained, giving a regal nod of her head.

Fin said nothing, and was wondering why she was still hanging around, when she suddenly smiled brilliantly up at him. Instead of becoming dazed, as most men did when faced with her beauty, Fin frowned.

"Have I said something to upset you?" she asked lightly, her eyes sweeping over the coppery red of his hair.

"No. Not to be rude, my lady, but I need to begin immediately if the king is to have a proper dinner this evening."

The lady's face became momentarily shuttered before she smiled in a far more restrained manner and gave a small nod before turning and leaving.

Once her footsteps had faded from earshot, Ruby rounded on him. "What on *earth* is wrong with you?!" she demanded noisily, right as the young maid burst in through the door behind Fin. He didn't move, despite the noise, and continued to stare down at the Head of Housekeeping with narrowed eyes.

"Cook, I've retrieved the herbs for you—though they were from some sacks on the back lawn!" the maid gasped, her long blond hair falling over her shoulders.

"Good. Please take the peppermint and chamomile and brew a pot of tea. We will now begin discussing the king's dietary preferences, and the numbers of nobility and staff within the castle."

The two women glanced at each other before turning to stare at him. "W-what of the sage you asked for?" the young maid asked tentatively

"I will take care of that later." Finally uncrossing his arms, he gestured to the cluttered cooking table. Both women wordlessly drew around the surface, despite having thousands of questions and thoughts.

An hour after the conclusion of the castle staff meeting, the Head of Housekeeping, Ruby, had rushed off to greet three new footmen and one new handmaiden for the queen, all of whom had arrived nearly an hour after Fin.

The young maid that had sat in on the new cook's instruction was Fin's first recruit, named Hannah. She was sent to polish the goblets for dinner and did so with a small skip in her step, thanks to her workspace being cleared of certain knights.

Fin was in a decent mood himself. After arguing for nearly half an hour, he had won the debate on how many servants he would require as aides. Cooking for the two hundred staff members and one hundred royals that lived in the castle, he required no more than four, yet had conceded to five when he began growing tired of hearing Ruby's dubious exclamations.

Fin would not, however, back down when it came to *who* was allowed in his kitchen, or how *he* would pick his aides. Hannah would be one, that had already been decided, and he would pick the rest by the end of the week.

The dinner for that evening had been nearly completed upon his arrival, and so he declared that he alone would complete the meal. Ruby had left, muttering a slew of grievances and the occasional curse word. Hannah had followed nervously behind her, shooting the new cook apologetic looks.

Fin began lifting pot lids and checking pans to stare at the food already on its way to completion, and he wrinkled his nose in dissatisfaction. Turning to stare at the now empty haphazard kitchen, he sighed.

There was a lot of work to do.

"Best get going. The coast is clear!" He directed the order toward his bags. With a shudder, the broom suddenly rose straight up, and began sweeping up the dirt that had been trekked in by the numerous people only an hour earlier.

Fin turned to the open kitchen door and shut it firmly. Should anyone touch its surface, all magic would cease in the room. He commanded this of the door with a small poke of his finger on its wrought iron handle.

When he turned back to the disorganized and grubby kitchen, he placed his hands on his hips and grit his teeth. He hadn't anticipated this level of inefficiency.

With a snap of his fingers, every knife in the room sprang to attention, and began peeling the abandoned pile of apples with inhuman speed. Fin strode over to his bags and pulled out an armful of carefully wrapped dried herbs.

He placed most of them on the ledge that ran along the entire kitchen, where some cooking bowls and plates resided. These stacked dishes hurriedly rose into the air and clattered off to the shelves down below their previous resting place. They did so of their own volition, after a stern eyebrow raise from Fin.

He laid out the remainder of the herbs, selected two of them, and then turned to a cast iron pot that held a bubbling mystery stew. After giving another disgusted sniff, Fin wielded a wooden spoon. Giving the abomination a few perfectly timed stirs, he turned his attention to the window, and gave his head a firm shake. He should've charmed that when he had done the door. Why was he being so forgetful of his precautions?

With another small prod against the cool glass, Fin commanded it to darken should anyone try to peer in while magic thrived in its presence.

He nodded in satisfaction and turned back to the kitchen that was rapidly gaining the order he preferred. Two ends of the red thread tying together the broom's bristles had snaked upward into the air as though it had sprouted arms, then wrapped around the bags that had remained on the floor and moved them to the corner of the room before setting itself upon a new task.

Soon there wasn't a single item out of place, and the most wondrous smells began filling the kitchen as Fin began creating more and more dishes. Despite the sky darkening outside, the kitchen began to look cozy and welcoming, with the fire well stoked and the food nearing completion.

With a flourish of his wrist, Fin sprinkled the last garnish of chives over the soup, and just as he had anticipated, the first of the serving staff entered the kitchen.

However, the sight that befuddled them wasn't floating dishware, or self-sufficient brooms whisking about on their own. It was the transformed kitchen that had become so unrecognizable that for a moment they all believed they had entered a different building entirely.

Instead of the lovable mess of permanent stains on the floors and tables with mystery smells hanging in clouds of smoke, the staff walked into a clean kitchen. The room had an inviting warmth that could only be compared to the feeling one got when walking into the arms of a loved one. The sight and feeling alone was baffling, but then came the most mouth-watering aromas any of them had ever smelled before.

Each person stopped in turn upon the threshold. They were all dazed for a moment as the waves of comfort washed over them soothingly, lulling them immediately into a relaxed state.

The overwhelming knowledge that they were home settled over them, and there were several moments of prolonged silence before Fin broke the spell.

With a clap of his hands, he drew every eye to his crisp clean white tunic and glittering eyes.

"Let us begin with the first course, shall we?"

CHAPTER 2
MANDATORY HELPERS

King Norman of Daxaria rubbed his temples wearily as the last of his vassals exited the counsel room, leaving him feeling older and more deflated than ever before. His eyes were closed against the headache that pulsed against his skull, and he was on the verge of falling asleep in his chair, when the unmistakable knock of his Head of Housekeeping broke through the silence.

"Enter, Ruby," he called slowly, drawing himself up slightly straighter.

The stout woman was brisk and forthcoming with her thoughts and feelings to a fault. She was also the best at organizing the rest of the staff, which in turn helped the castle run far more efficiently than it had before. It may have been as chaotic and haphazard as the rest of the continent, but things at least got done.

Ruby dropped into a deep curtsy, then straightened hastily with her hands already gripped together—a sign that something was on her mind.

"Did the new staff settle in well?" he asked, making an educated guess at what was troubling her.

"The footmen are young scamps, but Devon will sort them out in no time. The new handmaiden is a klutz, but that is due to her awkward feet still growing," she explained in a single breath. The woman hesitated all too suddenly at the end of the list.

"How is the cook?" The king stifled a yawn. He sincerely hoped the new fellow hadn't done something foolish like set the kitchen on fire.

"He acts as though he owns the place!" Ruby blurted as her round cheeks deepened in color. Norman's eyes snapped open, and a small, amused smile touched his lips.

"Please explain, Ruby," he asked quietly after a moment, clearly not taking too much heed of her agitation. While effective in managing the staff, the woman often had very rigid ideas on how things were to be done. It would not be the first time she butted heads with someone …

"Well, first of all, he seemed to be on bad terms with the driver that took him here. Which should've been my first sign that he was going to be an issue! Then he crosses the threshold to the kitchen and tells everyone save for myself and a lowly maid to get out! Sirs Taylor, Lewis, and Andrews were present, as was Lady Jenoure. He barely even acknowledged them before dismissing them! He refuses more than five helpers and insists that he picks them regardless of their previous positions. He also wants to limit who comes and goes through '*his*' kitchen."

By the time Ruby was finished with her summary she was even more worked up and clearly fighting the urge to pace in anger over her new colleague.

King Norman rested his head in the three fingers of his hand as his elbow rested on the armrest of his chair. "Is there more?" His voice was calm, but he was paying closer attention. The familiar shine in his hazel eyes reappeared as his mind began to clear away the fog of exhaustion.

"He asked about your dietary restrictions, then asked many more strange questions about yourself, the queen, the young prince and—"

"What kind of questions?" The voice that came from Norman was no longer casual or complacent. Instead, there was the commanding bite in his tone of someone with a good deal of sense and power.

Ruby balked at hearing the change in her ruler and took a shaky step back.

"He asked about what your favorite foods were, then asked about the wine and ale you drank. He wanted to know when you drank it, how you slept, what time you rose, and more questions I didn't want to answer but he—"

The king stood up forcefully. The mustard yellow silk coat buttoned to his throat straightened over his average frame, but the point of his beard exuded a stately aura.

He was about to speak again, when there was a soft knock on the door.

Too consumed with the conclusions he was drawing about his new cook, he didn't realize he had allowed entry to the individual behind it. The door opened to reveal none other than Lady Annika Jenoure—who was exactly the person he had been about to summon.

"You are excused, Ruby." The king didn't shift his gaze from Annika. The lady remained as calm and cool as always. She wore a dinner gown of deep navy blue with silver thread lining the V-shaped neckline. Sapphires that matched her dress dripped around her neck. She was a vision of dark beauty, and she smiled warmly at Ruby, who passed by her, still red in the face from her rant.

As soon as the door closed, Annika turned to the king with a serious expression.

"I have been hearing concerning things about the new cook," he started immediately, his voice low and his shoulders straight.

"He isn't a spy." Annika stated indifferently. She was unmoved by the urgency in the ruler before her.

The king's surprise was obvious.

"No one that looks like he does would have survived in Troivack. Even if he were a mage," she explained with a small shrug of her shoulders.

"I have enemies from this continent too, as well you know," King Norman gravely reminded her as he stepped out from behind the long rectangular meeting table and took measured steps toward her.

"None of them would bother having someone forge the recommendation of former cook Luca to gain access here. They would've sent in someone in the lower ranks, such as a maid or page, and they wouldn't have drawn so much … attention to themselves upon their arrival." Annika folded her hands in front of her and met the king's shining stare directly.

The king's expression morphed to one of wonder and bewilderment. "He truly looks and acts so strangely?"

"The new cook is incredibly fine featured for a man. Though somehow … elegant. Not at all like one of the round-bellied, red-faced cooks that we are all used to." At this, Annika gave a small laugh.

"Fine, fine. However, I will have my mage take a look at him to be safe. At least we don't have to worry about eating his own food until tomorrow evening—"

"Actually, Your Majesty, he took over the minute he walked in the door. You will be trying his food in the next few minutes, unless I am mistaken about the dining hour." She smiled prettily as the king sighed, and slumped, his posture defeated.

A knock rapped on the door for the third time that evening, and Annika hastily but gracefully gathered her skirts in her hands. She dipped herself down to the floor in a deep curtsy as the king summoned in a serving boy.

"Yes, Lady Annika, I will see that your horse is prepared for a ride tomorrow morning. The queen will sadly have to forgo the delight of your company as she is currently feeling under the weather."

Annika thanked the king and rose back to her feet. She shot the serving boy a wink that nearly had him spilling the contents of the small bowl he was holding.

"My king, the new cook has sent this broth to you to consume before the meal, along with this glass of spiced milk."

The king masked his expression, and while casting a sideways glance at the tray, asked, "Did my tasters try this first?"

"Yes, Your Majesty, both of them. They said the milk tasted terrible, but he informed them that it was medicinal. The broth they said tastes unlike anything they have had before, but that it was delicious." The serving boy couldn't have been more than sixteen years of age and wore his footman uniform of burgundy cap and matching vest proudly. The obvious meticulous care of the items stated the fact.

The king resigned himself to an early grave as the boy waited for him to consume the food.

The milk tasted terrible, as he had been warned, but his tasters had not been sugarcoating their review of the broth. It was unlike anything he had ever tasted before in his life. It was delicious, but it was more than that. It was somehow … deeply satisfying. It was as though there were parts of his stomach that had never really been sated before that moment.

As the king watched the young man clear away the dishes mere minutes later, he began to look forward to his next meal with far more curiosity and interest than he had before.

Fin continued rolling out dough across the large cooking table, the faint light of dawn gently smudging itself across the kitchen through the large round window.

Ruby stood towering over the table, her fists clenched at her sides. She looked as though she were about to explode at any moment as the vein in her right temple pulsed, and her clear blue eyes flashed brightly against her red face.

"Why did you rearrange the kitchen and demand ten buckets of water to be brought in?" Her voice rasped in her effort to contain her ire.

"Every dish, cloth, pot, pan, piece of cutlery—everything—is going to be washed with the soap I put in those pails. The kitchen is rearranged to its maximum efficiency for me. How is any of that your concern?" he asked calmly as he dribbled melted butter over the flat rectangle of dough.

"WHY?! BECAUSE I AM THE HEAD OF HOUSEKEEPING, THAT'S BLOODY WHY!" she screeched, pounding her palms against the table.

Unperturbed, Fin spread out a thick cream over the rectangle of dough, and then deftly began slicing strawberries over the surface.

"I need to know where everything is if I am to have meals prepared on time. I am doing the majority of cooking from sunup to sundown, and it is better if I can move as quickly as possible. Do you see the sense in this?" he explained tonelessly. He then slipped his fingertips under the edge of the dough and began rolling it over the cream and berries until it formed a thick log.

There was a moment of silence when Fin briefly wondered if the woman had had a stroke from rage, as his eyes were glued to his work.

When he eventually spared her a glance, his eyes widened briefly at the deranged look in the Head of Housekeeping's expression.

He waited patiently for her reply.

"I … can see … what you mean. *Though*," she spat, the explosion barely contained. "If you allowed more *staff* to *help you*, you wouldn't need to *rearrange* the kitchen."

"What a waste of workers. You now have extra help in the castle due to my reorganizing the kitchen. You are most welcome." Fin drew out a long knife and in a blur of movement, had sliced the entire log and turned each slice on its side to reveal the pretty spirals.

He lifted his gaze back to Ruby's, who was momentarily stunned at the speed of which he had executed the move.

"So who will be washing your hundreds of dishware, pots, and pans?" she demanded acidly after she regained her composure.

"Well, the five helpers you insisted I have shouldn't be completely bored this morning, I think," Fin supplied as he set the spirals on a thin pan and drizzled the last of the butter over them. He then turned and placed them in the great oven above the hearth.

As he did so, he pulled out a skillet from the oven that held what looked like a golden pie of egg, with some leafy green vegetable mixed in it. He seasoned it with a strange, rust-colored spice and cut the circle precisely into eight even slices.

He then poured a steaming cup of tea and placed two slices of the egg pie concoction on separate plates. He handed one to Ruby and placed the cup of tea in front of her.

"Eat. Drink. Then please allow me to view your staff so that I can select my mandatory five helpers." The request sounded more like an order, and were Ruby not staring confused at the food in front of her, she would've remembered she was angry with him.

"What is this?" she asked as she slowly took the fork he was offering her.

Fin rubbed his right hand over his face, and wearily leaned his elbows down onto the table. He hoped he wouldn't have to battle the woman every morning. She was more wearisome than his mother, or at the very least, just as much.

"It's good food. Enjoy," he ordered again as he himself began eating and sipping from a cup of black liquid.

After a few bites of food and downing half of her cup of tea, Ruby finally spoke again, this time her voice far quieter.

"What are those spirals for?"

"Teatime."

"You haven't prepared breakfast?!" Ruby straightened immediately in alarm.

"I will. Breakfast takes me an hour to make for everyone. Meat and fruit are easy. Speaking of which ..." He walked over to a sack leaning against the wall under the window and returned carrying two pears.

Ruby sighed as she watched him cut both pieces of fruit in less than a minute.

"How did you become so talented at such a young age?" she asked half to herself, as the young man fanned the pear slices artfully on her half-empty plate.

Fin raised an eyebrow, surprised. It wasn't a question he was used to getting. Or lying about, for that matter ...

"My mother informed me I just always had this skill. A few lessons helped me fine tune some recipes and techniques, but mostly I am self-taught." He drank deeply from his cup.

"What are you drinking?" Ruby queried as she drained the last of her tea.

"Something you shouldn't ever have," he muttered so that she couldn't hear while he finished the drink.

"Pardon me?"

"A special medicine for … for my heart," he lied lamely, not having the energy to be more convincing.

He was not one for early morning conversations before his second cup of coffee.

"Now, Ruby, if you could from now on please refrain from interrupting me in the mornings, I will be able to prepare the meals without delay."

The Head of Housekeeping frowned darkly. "Do you not care for *any* company?"

"I like being alone."

Fin cleared both their dishes over to the buckets and dropped the plates in. He pointedly ignored the *tsk*ing sounds his visitor was making.

"Shall we go look at the staff now?"

"What about preparing breakfast?" she demanded, bewildered.

"I will be able to prepare breakfast after selecting the staff. The royals won't be up for at least three more hours," he added as he headed to the door and opened it, then gestured for Ruby to exit.

The Head of Housekeeping shook her head as she strolled over him. "You are the strangest man I have ever met."

"I'd rather be the strangest than the worst."

"You might be that too."

In front of Fin, in the servants' dining hall, stood four long rows of maids and footmen. Many of them still had sleep crusted in their eyes, while others were barely stifling yawns.

None of that bothered Fin, though.

"Everyone, I want your hands out, palms down," he ordered, his voice ringing out clearly.

The entire staff shared puzzled expressions as they all obeyed and ogled the striking new cook that everyone had heard about.

He perused each set of hands carefully, and occasionally then studied the rest of the person.

When he reached the end of the final line, he began walking back through them. He proceeded to point and beckon three women (one of them being Hannah from the day before) to follow him, and two men.

"Wait a moment! You cannot take Claire! She is one of the best seamstresses in the entire castle!" Ruby grabbed the woman's arm and jerked her back sharply.

"Then I will make do with these four." Fin shrugged and turned to exit the servant's dining hall. It was a short passage that would take him a few feet down to the end of the hallway, where the kitchen door stood on the righthand side.

"You chose her on purpose!" Ruby snapped, crossing her arms over her chest, ready to once again square off with him.

"Of course I did. You saw me point at her face."

"No! You knew I would never part with her and wanted me to put up with you having only four helpers!"

Fin had finally had enough resistance for one morning. He turned and walked with his hands clasped behind his back, until he was directly over Ruby staring down at her. "I chose the people with the cleanest fingernails, and who appeared to bathe regularly. I do not know who they are, or what their duties have been before. If you continue to make demands that make no sense, then throw a fit when I compromise, I will walk out of the castle before lunch. I do not tell you how to run the staff unless it affects my work. I know how to run my kitchen, just like you know your own job."

Ruby's breathing was coming out in small gasps, but she didn't say another word. Satisfied, Fin turned back around and led out the five servants.

"Claire will only work for you part-time! She will continue being the queen's aid during her hours of—"

"Great!" Fin shouted back swiftly, too irked to turn around.

From outside the hall, leaning back in the shadows, stood Lady Annika Jenoure. She listened to the entire scene with growing interest. Her arms were folded across her chest, her ankles crossed, and a small smile grew on her face.

That is quite the arrogant ass.

CHAPTER 3
CAUSING A FUSS

Annika threw open the kitchen door, and smiled brightly, fully prepared to greet the five overworked servants that Finlay Ashowan had selected, only to find that the room was completely empty, save for the man himself. He threw a casual glance at her with a small nod of his head, instead of the customary bow, before turning back to what he was working on. His white tunic sleeves were rolled up, and he was in the process of tossing a salad of what looked to be green beans, peppers, and cheese.

"Where are your aides?" Annika questioned as she strolled to the front of the cooking table and placed her riding crop down along with her gloves.

She wore a rust-colored vest with matching trousers, and a snowy white ruffled lace cravat at her throat. She had her hair piled high atop her head, with the only piece of finery being an emerald brooch at her throat that glimmered darkly. Lady Jenoure was well aware of the smart figure she cut in it and raised an expectant eyebrow as she squared off in front of the cook.

"Outside washing dishes and cutlery," he answered, tightly glaring at the riding crop and gloves she had just placed down on his worktable. He remained oblivious to her charms, much to her chagrin.

"Why aren't they *inside* washing them?"

"Because the dishware will dry faster outside, and the staff will stay out of my way."

The lady laughed. Normally the sound of her laugh made men stop in delight and awe at its enchanting notes, but Fin only shot her a sardonic glance as he set the salad aside, then picked up a black loaf of bread, which he sliced in a blur.

"Wow, you really do move quickly."

"When I'm not interrupted," he uttered tersely under his breath.

Annika folded her arms over her chest and jutted her hip out.

"You have no fear of reprimand for speaking so rudely to a member of nobility?"

Fin clapped his hands together as he dusted his floured hands off, not caring that the cloud drifted onto Annika's impeccable riding gear. He then placed his hands on his hips and gazed at her levelly.

"You won't do anything to me until you get what you want." He didn't shy away from her gaze, or show any sign of intimidation, which drew an incensed laugh from her.

"What could I possibly want from *you*?" Her eyes were bright, and Fin couldn't help but feel a small twinge in his chest when the spark appeared in their dark depths.

"Whatever it is, you've wanted it from me since you first smiled at me yesterday," he answered evenly.

"I smile at everyone."

"No. You were trying to be affable to me for no obvious reason."

"The word 'affable' is quite complex for a lowly cook."

"Would you like me to use shorter words for you?"

"Perhaps I was trying to appear friendly to a newcomer when I smiled," Annika fired back, ignoring his earlier insult.

"When someone doesn't smile with their eyes, it's because they want something, and or are hiding something." Fin leaned his head forward during his explanation and waited.

"You think I'm hiding something?" the viscountess demanded, her volume rising rapidly.

"… Or you want something, or both, really. You keep avoiding saying what it is, and I really do not have time to wait around for you to get to it." Fin continued staring and waiting in silence, as the lady gawked at him, trying to form words.

"I could have you rot in a cell for the rest of your life for the way you've just spoken to me," she pointed out, sounding somehow both impressed and appalled.

"Something tells me it'd take a lot more than a few words from a 'lowly cook' to really bother you."

Fin turned around, poured a cup of tea, then handed it to her.

"What is this?"

"A special tea too many people in this bloody castle need to drink."

"Why?"

"It's a Godsdamn sedative."

"I ... beg your pardon?" Annika managed, stunned.

"Peppermint and chamomile. Same ingredients used in a relaxing tea one commonly consumes before bed. Once the lavender comes in this year it will round out the flavor—good Gods, did you think I meant I was poisoning people?!" Fin demanded, looking disturbed and exasperated.

"No one you've met so far would be surprised," she snapped back defensively, slamming the cup down onto the table.

Fin didn't say anything to that, and instead waited a moment of silence before asking again, "So are you going to tell me?"

"Tell you what?"

"For the love of— *What do you want from me?*" While he didn't raise his voice, he didn't hide his impatience in the least.

"I don't think I will! I think I will just *take* what I want." Turning on her heel, Annika gracefully strode toward the door.

Then, she did something she had never done before.

She glanced over her shoulder to see the effect her words had had on him.

It was a great surprise and annoyance to her to find that he had resumed preparing the meal as though there hadn't been any interruption at all.

The king stroked his queen's hair lovingly as they sat in the slightly chilly early spring evening, watching their son rush about the gardens trying to catch fireflies.

"The roses in the maze will be spectacular this year," she said, looking at the plump blooms at the hedge to their backs.

"It seems so, love. Surprising, given the cold spring we've been having," the king murmured into her hair. "How have you been feeling?"

The question hung in tense silence for a moment before the queen answered.

"I ... I don't like getting our hopes up, Norman. We haven't had a successful pregnancy since Eric."

"That isn't what I asked, though," Norman pointed out, gently taking her white hand with its long artistic fingers into his own.

"I don't want to disappoint you, I—"

Norman kissed her lips, silencing the choked words coming from his wife.

"Ainsley, you haven't disappointed me a day in your life. Having Eric nearly killed you, and if we are only meant to have one handsome—albeit spoilt—child, then so be it."

The tears welled in the queen's eyes as she bent over her lap and broke down weeping.

"I want—" she started, then hiccupped. "I want to admit I'm feeling good. But I'm scared. I'm scared that I'll be wrong again."

The king pulled her into his chest and continued stroking her gray-streaked hair without speaking. He simply allowed his pregnant wife to sob out her fear, while holding his own hammering terror away.

He didn't want to lose her.

Ever.

"You know." The king pulled away, forcing the strong emotions back down. "The new cook has all the maids attentive in ... womanly ways I'm told."

She laughed; her sharp bark of a joy never failed to make him smile.

"He's handsome? Or is it that he has a sonorous voice, like Lord Martin's?" she asked leaning her head on his shoulder.

"I cannot say I have laid eyes on him, but shall I arrange a formal introduction so we can see what all the fuss is about?"

She chortled, her watery eyes bright with fun, and the king's heart nearly exploded.

"You are far too busy for that frivolity," she managed as she wiped the last of her tears from her face.

"I might make an exception for this, as he has caused quite a stir. Ruby is beside herself, and even Lady Annika—I do not think I have ever seen that woman look so perturbed, but lo' and behold, I caught sight of her on her way back from her ride—"

"I'm sorry to interrupt you, my love, but speaking of Annika's ride, did she meet with *him*?" The queen impatiently distracted the king from the lighter topic.

"No. *He* wasn't able to meet her this time. Besides, I do not want her far from your side until I am more confident about the new staff additions. We cannot be too careful with these rumors circulating."

The queen nodded solemnly, then turned the topic back to the subject of the peculiar new staff member.

"So this cook managed to even rattle the unflappable Lady Annika Jenoure?"

"He did! It's incredible. Those who work under him appear happy and relaxed, but anyone who tries to tell him what to do leaves half-mad." The king chuckled to himself at recalling Ruby's latest rant about the cook.

"Best be cautious with dealing with him, then. We can't have the leader of this continent losing any part of his bright mind." The queen tapped a finger to the king's forehead before continuing.

"I must admit … he seems to be quite controlling for his position. He has already insisted I eat specific foods that differ from everyone else. He even threatened the poor pitcher boy to never serve me a drop of ale or wine," the queen remarked with a thoughtful expression.

The king frowned.

"What were his reasons?"

"Apparently his mother was a healer back home, and she claimed that these substances were harmful to expectant women—especially if they were already risky pregnancies. I checked with the court physician, and he said that this is a part of newer beliefs and studies, but he applauds the extra caution."

The king shared his surprised expression with his wife.

"I must say that the lad just earned a little more of my gratitude. If he is doing everything possible to protect you and our babe, I am inclined to give him the benefit of the doubt despite his brusque tendencies. Though even just making the best food I've ever tasted has earned a good deal of credit from me."

"I know. You have never slept better than last night after that meal. You slept half the day away and awoke a new man!" the queen teased, poking a knuckle into his side.

Norman smiled and kissed the top of his wife's head.

The peace he felt in that moment, he knew he shouldn't fall into. He knew it was only a simple evening with his family, and that larger threats and evils lurked around, but … he held on to the passing minutes as long as he could.

In the future days should they grow dark, then at least …

At least he'd have this memory.

Fin lay on his pallet in front of a kitchen hearth that barely glowed aside from its orange coals. He was beginning to fall into a doze, the smell of freshly baked loaves still wafting over him for the next day's luncheon, and was welcoming his descent into warm nothingness.

In the silence, the kitchen door leading to the gardens suddenly burst open, and in stumbled a cloaked stranger, who was muttering quietly to themselves.

"Good Gods, do these people never sleep?" Fin groaned as he slowly sat up, then used the table to finish pulling himself into a slumped but standing position.

The cloaked figure stumbled over a potato sack a few feet into the room and cursed.

"Kitchen is closed. Please show yourself out," Fin croaked rubbing his eyes.

Another curse came from the figure, and that was when Fin saw the knife appear.

Now wide awake, he automatically opened his palm, and the iron skillet that rested cleaned and cooled on the nearby ledge flew into his hand, while his broom sprang to life from beside the garden door and swept the legs out from under the assailant.

The stranger threw the knife at Fin's face during their fall, which he blocked with the frying pan.

The figure was knocked down for only a second before they leapt nimbly back onto their feet. Fin immediately launched the pan toward the shadowed hood, but they easily dodged from its path, and even managed to duck its return as it flew back into his hand.

In the silence, there was only the gentle panting of the two opponents' breaths, until a soft mewl broke the tense silence. Fin waved the hand not holding a frying pan, and suddenly every candle burst into flame, illuminating the room in a warm glow.

The figure placed something black down on the outer ledge of the kitchen and dashed out the door before Fin could decide what to do with them. He ran to the doorway to try and glimpse or stop them before they got too far out of his reach, but the mysterious assailant had disappeared into the darkness.

With an aggravated sigh, he began to ponder what the attacker wanted, and begrudgingly admitted to himself that he would need to address the incident with Ruby in the morning. Another soft mew broke through his thoughts.

Walking slowly over to where the figure had placed something down, Fin stared with a frown at the black shadow. He didn't understand what he was looking at until a pair of tiny green eyes suddenly popped up, along with a pair of distinct ears.

"A ... kitten?"

The tiny creature mewed once more.

Fin blinked, stunned, and before he registered what he was doing, went and retrieved some clean water from the kettle he had boiled before going to bed and had already cooled.

As soon as he placed the dish down, the little creature dunked its fluffy black paws in and immediately began to lap it up.

"They ... that person brought you here because you needed help," he reasoned slowly, his mind still trying to piece together the sequence of events that had happened in the past ten minutes.

When the kitten appeared to have had its fill, Fin carefully lifted it up, and checked as his mother had taught him to discover the gender.

"Well, *sir*, you are too young to be away from your parents," he announced after putting the tail back down and offering his palm as support for the tiny paws.

The kitten immediately nestled against Fin's chest, his tiny face turned into the rough wool tunic.

Fin gave him an absent-minded scratch along his chin, when a sudden jolt in his chest froze the movement.

He glanced down immediately as the kitten looked up, just as surprised.

"So. I must have made the right decision coming here if you, my familiar, have appeared."

The kitten mewed again, as though in agreement.

"I guess I will have to figure out a name for you tomorrow." Fin yawned, then walked over to the open kitchen door, and closed it.

There was much he had to think about with the intrusion into the kitchen, and the strange behavior of the individual.

Why be in disguise when delivering a kitten? Why attack someone if there was no ill intent?

Fin rubbed his face with his free hand before gazing back down into the tiny green eyes that blinked sleepily up at him.

He couldn't deny the strange sense of peace that had formed after he had recognized his familiar. Somehow the connection made any concerns or worries feel distant to him ...

His mother *had* always said that finding one's familiar would be of significant comfort.

It was strange.

The feeling of responsibility for a life that was not his own, and one that was completely helpless without him ...

It should have been a nuisance, but instead it brought a strange sense of being grounded, and important.

Fin lay back down on the floor in front of the hearth, so completely soothed that he even forgot to charm the kitchen door to the outside to remain locked until he opened it the next day.

Instead, he fell into a deep peaceful sleep, with the kitten curled up beside him, and he couldn't remember ever feeling more at one with the world.

In the haze of tranquility, he forgot another important detail of the evening that would later cause him great anxiety and stress ...

Someone nearby knew he had magic.

CHAPTER 4
CAT AND MOUSE

Fin had just finished sending out breakfast for the nobles and was leaning against the hearth with a sandwich in his hand, when his peaceful kitchen was infiltrated.

The door to the hallway flew open, and Ruby entered holding the clean rags Fin had requested the previous day, along with a blond-haired boy, perhaps only seven years old, on her heels reading from a tome that appeared to weigh more than himself.

"... And they eat people!" the boy exclaimed, staring up at Ruby's back with shining eyes. The lad was clad in a smart royal blue velvet jacket, tan shorts, high white knee socks, and a large burgundy bow tied around his neck that nearly swallowed his chin.

"Prince Eric, have you met our new cook?" Ruby plopped the rags down on the table, her cheeks their customary shade of red, and her expression desperate as she stared pleadingly at Fin who looked like a deer caught in torchlight.

"Then there's another monst— Oh! No, I haven't. Hello!" The boy smiled and waved at Fin, then promptly dropped the book as it toppled out of his small hand.

Ruby winced and mouthed an apology to Fin as the future ruler of the kingdom bent to pick up the novella. Taking a bite from his sandwich, he chose to remain expressionless.

When the boy righted himself, he was beaming up at the grown-ups.

"Your Highness." Fin gave a slight dip of his head, then awkwardly continued eating while Ruby scowled disapprovingly.

"My name's Eric! What is your name?" The child hefted the book in his arms as he openly peered at the unfamiliar face.

"Finlay Ashowan, Your Highness," he answered, slowly straightening and placing his sandwich on the table as he poured himself a goblet of water. "Please feel free to call me Fin."

"You look too young to be a cook! Our old cook, Luca, he was old and fat!" With a great huff, the boy hefted the book onto Fin's table, and Ruby shot him a warning look when she noticed the twitch in his right eye.

"Your Highness," Fin began, clearly trying not to lecture the boy.

"Please call me Eric!" The boy beamed.

"That is not proper, Your High—" Ruby began.

"Eric, this table isn't very clean, your book may become dirty," Fin cut her off, his tone surprisingly gentle.

"Oh, that's okay! I keep dropping it, so it isn't very clean anyway. Did you know that no one has seen a dragon in two hundred years?!" Eric slapped his palms on the table around his book, his hazel eyes the size of saucers.

"One hundred and fifty years, actually. They say the golden dragon still hides in the mountains, but no one knows if they are in the mountains here in Daxaria along the western border, or if he perhaps rests in the northern mountains of Troivack." As he spoke, Fin began pulling pears out of the wooden bowl in the corner of the table, along with the smaller of the two knives he kept clipped to his belt while cooking.

"Woah! Really? I bet he is just waiting for a princess to steal! I hear the king in Troivack doesn't have any girls, but *eleven boys*!" The innocent enthusiasm and seriousness until that moment had made it hard for Ruby to interrupt the lad.

"Your Highness, the Troivackian king has two boys, not eleven. The maids and I were saying how it is not uncommon for Troivackians to have large families with eleven children," Ruby explained with a small hint of guilt in her expression.

A corner of Fin's mouth twitched upward, and a soft chuckle left his lips as he sliced up the pear at a more leisurely pace than he normally would.

He failed to see the stunned look on the Head of Housekeeping's face, however, as she saw a glimpse of what her female staff had been twittering about.

When the cook smiled, he was …

"Well now, Eric, why do you think the dragon isn't here in Daxaria?" Fin handed the prince a pear slice, unknowingly interrupting Ruby's thoughts.

"Because my dad wouldn't let him live here! He'd get rid of him! Especially because my mom might have a girl, and we don't want a dragon stealing my sister," Eric explained wisely.

Fin smiled more openly at the child.

Out of the corner of his eye he noticed Ruby quietly backing out of the room, an unfamiliar kind smile on her face.

"What makes you think dragons are bad? What if they just want to have a nice home and family?"

"They burn down villages and eat all the sheep, though!" the prince managed through a mouthful of pear, his etiquette lessons completely forgotten.

"Ever wonder why?" Fin handed Eric another pear slice once the first was swallowed, and Ruby backed out of the room unnoticed.

"Roasted lamb is delicious?" Eric shrugged. "I read about another monster that lives in the sea, and JUMPS out of the water, *and* eats whole ships!" he explained while leaping into the air as he mimicked his idea of the beast.

"Ahh. The Kraken." Fin leaned on the table, nodding in understanding.

It was then a soft mew was heard.

"What was that?!" The energetic prince spun around, searching the room for the source of sound.

Fin slowly walked around the table and gestured for the prince to come closer.

"Can you keep a secret, Eric?"

The little boy nodded excitedly.

"This little kitten happened to find me last night, and I'm going to keep him as my official mouse hunter." Fin lifted an empty potato sack, which he had weighed down at the top of the kitchen ledge to act as a curtain, to reveal a wooden box where the fluffy black kitten with a dab of white on his chest sat up and peered at the two onlookers curiously.

The prince's eyes went wide as saucers.

"What's her name?" the little boy whispered. He was clearly trying not to scare the kitten, despite his obvious excitement.

"I haven't picked one yet. Would you like to help me name him?"

"It's a boy?" Eric turned to stare at Fin, who was crouched beside the box, already picking up the little mass of adorable fur.

"It is indeed."

"Can I ... Can I pet him?"

Fin smiled. "You sure can, but gently. He is too young to not have his mother."

The little boy reached out and stroked the downy fur shakily. He looked as though he were holding his breath as the tiny kitten began to purr at his careful caresses.

"Can we name him Kraken? He could be the sea monster, but for mice."

Fin lifted the kitten and looked into the tiny green eyes. "What do you say, is your name Kraken?"

The kitten mewed again, suddenly seeming more animated, as though excited for such a fearsome and respectable name.

"Well, you must be wonderful at naming things, because I think he likes it. He shall be known as Kraken the Kitchen Cat. Has a nice ring to it, don't you think?"

The prince giggled, beaming proudly that his name was approved.

"Maybe you should be the one to tell Ruby that there's another staff member in here. I think she'll be more accepting of his presence if it comes from you, Your Highness." Annika stood in the doorway with her arms folded across her chest. She wore a burgundy gown that looked far more expensive than anything Fin had seen her in thus far, and had pearls wound into her hair, while her hands glittered with golden rings. She didn't usually wear so much finery ...

"Lady Jenoure! You can't tell her! It's a secret!" The prince's panicked face warranted a strained expression from the woman as she tried to hide her smile.

"For now it is, but she will find out once Kraken decides he's ready to begin earning his keep." Annika strode into the room then bent down to scratch the kitten's head.

"Well ... I'll tell her when he starts hunting," Eric conceded with a firm nod of his head.

"Your Highness, I'm here to tell you that the queen is looking for you." Annika smiled with genuine affection down at the boy, who grinned back. Not that he had ever stopped smiling—the child would outshine the sun at the rate he exuded unbridled excitement and happiness.

The prince leapt to his knees, rushed over to the table to grab his book, and then staggered to the doorway.

"Don't worry Fin! I won't tell anyone! Bye Kraken!" The prince gave him an enthusiastic wave, and once again dropped the book. He scrambled to pick it up before darting down the hallway away from the kitchens, leaving both Fin and Annika crouched by the wooden box, with Kraken patting a curious paw on the lady's golden rings.

"Was the queen actually looking for him? Or are you finally going to tell me what it is you want from me?" Fin stood up after putting Kraken back in his box, his face back to its usual dry expression.

"She was looking for him ever since he ran off without eating breakfast." Annika straightened herself and strode over to the window to peer out at the brilliantly sunny day.

Fin slowly walked back over to his worktable, and resumed eating his sandwich, leaning an elbow on its surface facing the hearth.

"Good day to you then, Lady Jenoure." Fin didn't bother turning around to dismiss her.

"Where are you from, Fin?" she asked casually, turning to stare at him with the glow of daylight behind her, making her appear all the more angelic.

He slowly placed his sandwich down and turned to face the woman with his arms crossed. He didn't want to tell her anything. If he lied and got caught, however, that could have an unfortunate outcome.

"The southern islands."

"Which one?"

"The Isle of Quildon."

"Do you have family there still?" she asked, tilting her head to the left, a mysteriously pleasant smile on her face.

Fin placed his hands on his hips, then slowly walked until he stood less than two feet in front of the lady and stared down into her upturned face with his own odd expression.

"You know, Lady Jenoure, there was a mysterious stranger who delivered Kraken to me," he began innocently as theories began to form in his mind as to why the woman was suddenly incredibly interested in him.

She didn't bat an eye as she smiled a little wider. "Oh? What a kind stranger. Now, what were you saying about your family?"

Fin frowned slightly but didn't move out of her personal space.

"I wasn't saying anything about them. Might I ask why you are interested in my kin?"

"I'm curious! A man with your talents is incredible, given your youth."

"It is also curious how a noblewoman is unmarried at your age," he replied evenly.

She paused and swallowed. "My husband died."

Fin took a step back in surprise.

"Oh … I'm sorry to hear that." He looked incredibly sheepish, which surprised Annika immensely.

"It's fine. It was a year ago, and we had only been married a few months. He was more than forty years my senior."

Fin's hands moved to his pockets as he listened. "Even so, I'm sorry for your loss."

She shrugged, but Fin could see that the man's death had meant more to her than she wanted to let on.

"What about yourself? No wife or children waiting for you back home?"

His expression became guarded. "No."

Fin turned, stepped back to his food, finished his sandwich, then placed the plate in a bucket of water on the floor beside the table. His "helpers" were tasked with the dishes and cutlery every day, and given the cook's insistence on them being washed with hot water, his aides spent most of their days outside with a large boiling cauldron of water.

Annika still wasn't leaving, and so Fin began pulling out ingredients for the soup he was planning on serving for the midday meal, hoping she took the hint.

"Is there anything else, Lady Jenoure?" he asked pointedly as he began deftly peeling the carrots.

"Why do you insist on an empty kitchen?"

His gaze cut to her sharply. He was almost completely certain he knew who the knife-wielding intruder had been the previous night. Prior to that morning, she had only been interested in taunting, and trying to manipulate him. Now, out of nowhere, she wanted his life story?

"I am good at my job, and people tend to get in my way or make a mess. I also have strong opinions regarding certain behavior between the knights and serving staff," he replied tersely.

"I was surprised how good you were with the prince. You do not seem like you would be the type to be tolerant of children." She switched her approach swiftly at hearing his irritable tone, and Fin was back to staring at her appraisingly.

"I prefer children to adults most days. They generally follow orders and are usually honest to a fault."

Annika smiled coolly, and sidled casually over to Fin, only this time she was the one to invade his space. As he turned to face her, placing down his knife and carrot, she stood close enough that if she bowed her head, it would touch his chest.

"You need to watch what you say, Fin. One of these days that frank opinion of yours is going to get you in trouble."

"Another excellent reason for me to avoid people," he said, trying not to focus on the faint smell of spices coming from her.

Didn't most women smell like flowers?

Why did she smell like a spiced oil, or …

She laughed.

It wasn't her dainty fake laugh she had tried on him before, but an honest chuckle.

"I like talking to you, though." She smiled up at him and shrugged her right shoulder.

"No, you don't. I annoy you, so why not end your misery and tell me what you want? Then you could kindly take your noble company else-where." He was not going to allow her to trick himself into believing she was devoid of guile.

"I want something different now." She managed to look sincere, but Fin still wasn't buying it.

"Will you tell me what this new thing is?"

The lady did a dramatic pause as she feigned considering his suggestion.

"What I want …" she trailed off and tapped her finger against her lips in exaggerated thought. "I want answers." Annika smiled up at him, then abruptly turned, and walked over to the door.

Fin rolled his eyes to the ceiling, annoyed. This woman and her games …

"As long as you don't pry into my privacy, I'll be glad to give them to you. Oh, and Lady Jenoure?" Annika turned, feeling confident, until she saw what was in Fin's hand.

"Maybe knock instead of throwing knives at me next time, hm?" The black handle of a superiorly crafted blade was pointed toward her to take, and while she blanched for a single second, she lifted her gaze with a concerned frown.

"That isn't mine. Though it is good to know you're making new friends."

Then without a second glance back, she left.

Fin shook his head after the door clacked shut, and he placed the blade on the table.

He still didn't believe that it wasn't her, but if by some act of the Gods it hadn't been … Why in the world was she asking him so many questions?

The cloaked figure stood on the ribbon of lawn that ran between the king's forest and the royal rose maze in the chilled May evening. Their black cloak shielded their face, while they waited without moving a muscle until the glint of plate armor caught their eye coming through the mist amongst the trees. Despite the overcast night, the large man wasn't hard to spot … or hear, for that matter.

"Idiot," the figure hissed quietly before their guest could hear.

When the tall muscular man stood eight feet away, they called out, "I must say, I am enjoying these cooler evening temperatures."

The cloaked figure was struggling not to stab him. It took the lunk-head another moment to realize he had not issued the code.

"Oh, right! Tomorrow the roses might bloom, unless the bats eat them."

The cloaked figure briefly pinched the bridge of their nose under their hood, before slowly lowering their hand.

"What news is there, Corey?"

"There has been confirmation that the King of Troivack intends to declare war on Daxaria."

The figure stiffened. "What are their numbers?"

"That I do not know. You will have to wait for—"

"Do not speak his name!" the figure snapped.

"Shit, right. Sorry, Dragon."

"Just keep your mouth *shut*. I won't be able to meet with you until after Beltane."

"I understand." Corey bowed, the long wavy hair of his ponytail bristling in the wind.

The Dragon turned after giving one final disapproving head shake, and disappeared into the mists, leaving Corey to straighten and sigh alone.

He needed better pay than the mere promise of knighthood if he was going to keep spying on the underbelly of Austice.

CHAPTER 5
KEEP YOUR DISTANCE

Fin sat outside the open garden door, atop a grain barrel that happened to be holding said door wide open. He rested with his eyes closed, holding a cup of water and relishing the breeze that began to dry the sweat on his face. The cold front the kingdom had been experiencing through the first weeks of spring had finally broken, but in its stead came a wrathful heat that was the bane of the cook's existence in front of the hearth.

He had plenty on his plate as it was, with the Beltane festival taking place on the final day of the month, and preparations had already begun for the large celebration on top of his daily duties. The added threat of constantly having to avoid heat stroke was making Fin begin to feel weak with weariness.

It was especially frustrating with the constant flow of people parading in and out of the kitchens for food and ale deliveries. The steady stream of people meant any magical aid Fin could conjure to combat the high temperatures was limited.

Despite the aggravations, he had managed to avoid anyone discovering his abilities thus far and was pleased that Ruby had grown to begrudgingly accept his ruling of the kitchen. Both accomplishments were deserving of a relaxing evening with a pint of ale, and solitude—save for Kraken. Alas, despite all this, the Royal Cook would not be able to congratulate himself until after the festival.

The hooded figure had not reappeared, and Lady Jenoure had only popped in to see him a couple of times. Both visits, she had been surprised to see the kitchen full of merchants angrily bartering with the new cook about their wares and prices.

That particular day, however, during his rest, the sound of rapidly approaching feet forced Fin to crack open an eye. He could see the pretty blond locks belonging to Hannah barreling around the gardens that were showing plenty of green promises of delicious vegetables and herbs to come.

The girl was red in the face and had her beige skirts and blue apron hiked up in her hands as she rounded the main garden path. She didn't slow down until she was mere feet from the doorway, and noticed Fin.

"Is something wrong?" he asked, bringing her to a halt beside him as she avoided his gaze.

"N-No. I'm just going to count … count potato bags behind the door," she stammered, and tried to rush over the threshold.

Fin's arm shot out, and gently pressed her back a step so that he could study her. "Hannah, you're shaking." He observed her trembling hands, and was about to ask another question, when he heard a loud, boisterous laugh nearing the gardens.

He glanced over his shoulder, toward the nearest turret of the castle on his right-hand side where Hannah had come from, and saw Sirs Taylor, Andrews, and Lewis drawing closer.

Standing straighter and blocking Hannah from their view, he looked down at her and noted a few tears had begun to fall down her face.

It took a great deal of control for Fin to keep his voice gentle as a black rage pulsed through him.

"Hannah, please crouch under the ledge behind the doorway. I'll let you know when it's safe."

She nodded wordlessly and darted inside.

Fin finished his cup of water, placed it down atop the barrel, and casually stood in front of the open door as the knights set foot on the path before him.

"*Youareincontrolyouareincontrolyoucannotlet*them*findout*," Fin thought to himself over and over as he fought the swelling magic in his being that wanted to protect Hannah at all costs.

"Ohh, the cook's slackin' off!" Sir Andrews slurred as he looked up at Sir Taylor with a grin.

"No wonder we haven't seen Hannah around—she hasta pick up his slack!" Sir Lewis mocked, his unfocused blue eyes trying to stare down the cook, who, while not nearly as bulky or muscular as the knights, towered over nearly all three of them.

"Sirs, I was just opening the kitchen door." Fin's voice was hard as he negated any bowing from his addressing of the men.

"We don't wanna be in your stupid kitchen anyway," Sir Lewis snarled while trying to peer around him.

Fin wasn't budging, nor was he bothering to look at the knights that flanked Sir Taylor. He knew who the real threat was.

The largest of everyone present flashed his perfectly white teeth, and leaned forward, the smell of ale evident on his breath despite it not being long past the luncheon hour.

"Move aside, beanpole," he teased as the other knights burst out in enthusiastic laughter.

"I don't allow non-personnel in my kitchen."

"You see … it's funny how I don't recall anyone giving *you* the *authority* to ban *me* from the kitchen."

The plates and cutlery had begun rattling, and a certain iron pan's handle whipped around as though standing at attention from within the kitchen. The knights failed to notice the lively dishware behind the cook, but Hannah sure did, and she wondered if there was an earthquake, or a great beast storming toward the castle, as she tried to make herself even smaller in her hiding place.

"Then you may ask the king for confirmation." Fin had not once spoken to the king, but he hoped it would be enough to reroute the louse.

"The king granted *you* that kinda say? I don't think so." Sir Taylor grabbed the front of the cook's sweaty tunic and yanked him a few inches closer to his face.

"You know what kinda trouble you can get for lyin' to me?"

"Less trouble than you defying the king's order," Fin countered, his hands curled into fists at his sides.

The knights had to leave.

Immediately.

There was a distinct possibility he was about to blast them straight into the Alcide Sea several leagues from shore, at the rate they were infuriating him.

Sir Taylor glared at him in silence, his clear blue eyes searching the lanky man's expression for any sign of a bluff.

Fin knew he would never see any. He had learned from a young age how to betray nothing of the rage he held inside of him when faced with men like this.

"Guess I'll go ask right now. Anyone ever tell you that you look like a fairy bitch?" The lackeys were beside themselves with laughter as Sir Taylor released Fin.

The men turned around, and promptly fell over a wide array of rakes, hoes, and shovels, that had until moments before been propped against the garden fences.

In their inebriated stupors, they had failed to notice the tools gathering in a pile (seemingly on their own) at their heels.

Sir Lewis received the worst injury of the trio, with a rake having scraped his forehead and cheek thanks to his face-plant. Sir Andrews received a badly bruised right temple with a shovel, and sadly, Sir Taylor had his fall broken by his two friends.

All was not lost, however, as Fin noticed that the man winced and had to shift his weight off of his right knee once he had managed to stand back up with a grunt.

"When the hell did those get here?" Sir Taylor barked glaring openly at the cook.

"You lot knocked them over. You should pick them up before the gardener comes back from tending the flower beds by the entrance." Fin turned his back on the knights, pushed his hands into his pockets, and stepped into the kitchen. He could hear the men curse and swear at him as they made their way back down the path.

He knew it was far from over, but he was prepared for that.

Once he was certain they had disappeared from view, he ensured the tools danced back from where they had originated.

"Hannah, it's safe to come out," he called out quietly.

Fin strolled farther into the kitchen, and was beginning to round his cooking table, when he realized the girl hadn't moved from under the ledge. The soft gasps of her crying were easy to hear in the renewed silence.

Walking over slowly to her hiding spot, he moved the bag of potatoes obscuring her petite form and seated himself down on the ground so that he was facing her.

"I've been thinking, and I want you working at the end of the garden path peeling vegetables from now on."

The girl, who couldn't have been older than nineteen years, gave a small nod into her lap.

His heart ached in his chest, and so Fin added to his statement.

"If you are ever in trouble, come see me. I want you to think of this kitchen as safe as your own room or home, alright?"

Hannah slowly raised her teary face, and quickly wiped away the various fluids she was leaking with the back of her hand.

"Wash up and grab a stump to sit on. I'll bring out the vegetables. If you need a cup of water or tea first, just let me know."

Awkwardly, he stood back up, grabbed a large wooden bowl, and began filling it with potatoes and carrots.

Hannah sniffed a few more times, and slowly shifted out from under the ledge. With her shoulders hunched and her hands still trembling in front of her, she neared the kitchen table warily.

"They ..." her voice rasped, and Fin without looking up from his work, poured a cup of water, and handed it to her. She drank thankfully and took another few deep gulps of air before attempting to speak again.

"They will come back after they find out you lied."

"Not today."

Hannah looked at him worriedly.

"I happen to know excessive day drinking is frowned upon amongst the knights. If they are dumb enough to try approaching the captain about this right now, they will be punished."

"They won't just let this go," she noted anxiously.

"No, they won't. That isn't for you to worry about, though." At long last, Fin raised his gold-flecked blue eyes to hers.

"Why aren't you scared of them? I mean, you don't seem scared of anyone!" Hannah observed with obvious awe.

Fin did his best to appear nonchalant. "I *was* scared of them—I'm pretty sure Sir Taylor's body odor could count as a weapon."

The adrenaline-filled laugh that erupted out of Hannah startled him, but also made him grow a small half-smile of his own. When she had settled down again and finished wiping her face with the back of her hand, she let out a long shaky breath.

"Hannah, everyone gets frightened at times. I just hide it better because I've known worse men than those three in my life."

Her look of sad anxiety on his behalf made Fin begin to blush.

"I had an ... unpleasant father. He's gone now, and we will leave it at that. Now." He handed the nearly overflowing bowl of vegetables to Hannah, who gripped it firmly while giving him a firm nod to show her resolve and compliance.

As she made her way back down the garden path, she couldn't help but notice that whatever had made all three of the knights fall over had already been completely eradicated. However, she was feeling far too grateful, and perhaps a little in awe of the cook, to ponder it much further.

The evening brought with it a blissfully merciful breeze that cooled the earth, and Fin was finally able to close the garden door as he bid the last of his aides farewell for the night. It had been another productive day, despite the run-in with the three pricks.

He eyed one of the ale barrels wistfully and wondered if he would be able to keep himself awake long enough to enjoy a pint. Kraken poked his head out from the potatoes as if on cue and mewed while staring up at him encouragingly.

Fin felt bad that he had been too busy to give the kitten much attention, but at the very least the prince had come by every morning to play with him for nearly an hour before having to disappear for his lessons.

He had just bent down and picked up the rapidly growing ball of fluff, when the handle of the door that led to the castle corridor turned and wedged itself open slowly.

Fin was hasty and silent in stowing Kraken back behind the potatoes, as the new intruder finished opening the door, and laid eyes on the young cook, who stood expectantly.

A man in his late fifties stepped into the room slowly, leaning heavily on a staff made of oak, with a clear crystal at its top.

The Royal Mage.

"Good evening." The mage smiled softly, his already gray hair falling in waves down to his shoulders, and matching his beard, which remained trimmed neatly close to his face.

"Er … hi." Fin had no idea if he had to bow to the man or not.

The mage finished entering the kitchen, staring around at the surroundings with a bit of surprise.

"This isn't the same kitchen I last saw here in the castle," he announced pleasantly.

Fin cleared his throat awkwardly and stepped farther away from the man, as though he were a leper.

The last thing he needed was a *mage* figuring him out.

He barely resisted the urge to cringe.

"My name is Lee. I am pleased to make the acquaintance of the one responsible for my delicious meals." Lee smiled and bobbed his head.

"I'm Fin. Did you need something?" He knew that the mage only had to stand a few feet from him to discern he had magic, and he also knew he would never live it down if the fraud outed him.

Lee chuckled, which interrupted his spiraling thoughts.

"I see Lady Jenoure wasn't jesting about your straightforward attitude."

"Does Lady Jenoure often jest?"

Lee's eyes actually twinkled, and Fin's gaze grew even more wary. Kindly old mages were good at getting people's defenses down.

Witch wannabes, the lot of 'em, he thought to himself, accusatory of the man before him.

"Lady Jenoure has remarkable intelligence and wit. You are lucky indeed that she has developed such a unique opinion of you."

"Lucky. Cursed. Same thing, depending on the person."

Lee laughed.

"I see. While I do not recommend wagging that tongue of yours to everyone here in the castle, I humbly request to see you and the lady banter sometime. I can foresee it being quite entertaining."

Lee had just taken a step closer to Fin, and he responded by moving back another pace.

"I don't bite, lad." Lee stopped and leaned on his staff as though tired.

Attempting to convince me you are weak? Not bloody likely!

"I am particular about who is in my kitchen. If there is nothing else for this evening, sir, I would like to go to sleep."

Lee squinted at him, not even bothering to hide what he was obviously doing as a faint white glow came from his powder blue eyes.

"Is something in your eyes, *sir*?" Fin snipped, accidentally making a cup topple off the ledge behind the elder.

Lee blinked, and the light disappeared as he shook his head. "Ahh, cataracts. Getting old is a thankless task, I wouldn't recommend it to you." He gave another warm smile.

Is this sod with a stick telling me to kill myself?!

Fin decided to respond appropriately to disperse any tensions. "I prefer aging to the alternative, thanks."

Lee chuckled again and turned toward the door.

"Well, I will leave you to sleep." He slowly moved away, and Fin took tentative steps in his wake, while being sure to maintain the distance, when the old man abruptly whirled around, and took a step closer.

Fin leapt back as far as he could and instinctively leaned back as well.

Exactly what one should expect from a friggin' mage, Fin snapped internally, his heart pounding in his chest.

"Sorry to startle you, I just wanted to let you know that your secret is safe with me."

Fin's poker face appeared so promptly that Lee retreated a step in surprise.

"I'm not sure I know what you mean. You also haven't mentioned what brought you down to my kitchen."

Lee nodded, the tiniest of frowns forming between his eyebrows.

"Ah yes. One reason was that I was hoping you might spare me the recipe for those tiny flat cakes you made earlier with the unforgettable spice. My son and wife I'm certain would adore them as much as I did."

"Oh, you mean cinnamon sugar cookies? I can give it to you, but the spice is expensive. It's shipped from the kingdom of Zinfera from their islands in the south."

"You don't say? Too bad …"

Lee turned to leave again, only this time, Fin folded his arms stubbornly across his chest. He wouldn't move anywhere near the nincompoop until his shuffling footsteps were long gone.

"The actual reason I came was the king wondered why you did not utilize the cottage assigned to you for your position. It's only a five- or ten-minute walk from the castle."

Liar. Something or someone tipped him off that I might have magic.

"I start earlier and finish later than everyone. I'd rather get the few extra minutes of sleep. My own personal time is quite sparse as is."

Fin didn't even try to mask the hint.

Lee's eyebrows shot up at his tone, but as a result became fully committed to finding his way out of the kitchen. When both feet were beyond the threshold, Lee once again turned, though this time far more slowly.

"Oh, and I meant I wouldn't tell Ruby about your secret pet. Good evening, Finlay Ashowan."

Fin glared as Lee closed the door and remained rooted to the spot for several more minutes until he was certain the minion of Satan's anus wouldn't return.

At long last, he blinked and relished the sound of the door bolting itself and shielding the room from any further attack. This time, he also double checked that he had done the same with the garden door and window before once again picking up Kraken, who seemed slightly ruffled by being blown off earlier.

"I'm sorry; blame the mage."

Kraken mewed, and Fin took that to mean the kitten not only forgave him, but full-heartedly agreed. "One day, Kraken, you are going to help me ward off unwanted guests, and I will pay you with the finest cooked fish in the kingdom."

Kraken mewed twice in a row.

"Glad you agree. Now, let's get some sleep. The festival is nearly a week away, and I have a strange feeling things are only going to get more chaotic around here."

CHAPTER 6
WITCHES AND MAGES

Annika sat in the inner courtyard of the castle, sipping her tea, which happened to be generously spiked with Troivackian moonshine. She had been casually enjoying it far more regularly since the death of her husband, and was building an annoying tolerance to the liquor, which had a reputation of making cows faint from the fumes.

"Lady Jenoure!" Annika's mask of pleasantry became briefly strained at the sound of Lady Emily Gauva.

She took a deep gulp of her "tea," then stood and faced the woman with a closed mouth smile. Baroness Emily Gauva was a short blond woman only a couple of years younger than Annika. She had married the Baron Gauva, a decent enough man, months before Annika had first arrived in Daxaria.

"Good afternoon, Lady Gauva." Annika briefly nodded her head while thanking the Gods for the millionth time she was technically above the baroness, as she was a viscountess.

"Mind if I join you for tea? You look so lonely here by yourself." Emily eyed the full-tiered cake stand on the table, before casting her deep blue eyes back to Lady Jenoure.

"Sadly, today will not do, as I am awaiting Her Majesty the Queen this afternoon for a private meeting. Another time, perhaps?"

Annika secretly feasted on the obvious look of annoyance on the lady's face. However, Emily Gauva quickly resumed her sickeningly sweet smile while gently clasping her hands in front of her gold gown.

"Of course! How is Her Majesty fairing these days?"

"Well as always." Annika continued staring unwaveringly at the lady with a heart-shaped face. She loved how direct eye contact made the woman squirm.

"That is certainly wonderful to hear. I shall see you at the Beltane celebration … ?"

"Perhaps. I find the crowds unpleasant."

"Oh, but you should still come! At least for a short time!"

Annika laughed prettily.

"Such eves are for young maidens looking for a beau. I sadly lost my great love already, but I do hope you and Baron Gauva enjoy yourselves." Annika adopted the expression of the heartbroken woman.

"Lady Jenoure, I am sure your husband, Gods rest him peacefully, would wish you to find joy in the remaining life you have ahead of you." Emily Gauva reached out and grabbed both of Annika's hands. "My! What calluses you have! I must give you some of my ointment, it will help soften your hands to the ladylike tenderness you deserve," she chirped, forcing Annika to muster every nerve in her body in order to stop herself from gritting her teeth.

"Presenting, Her Majesty, Queen Ainsley."

The manservant had entered from the main north doors to the courtyard, and Annika continued to take perverse pleasure as Lady Emily shrank back, gradually disappearing into the shadows of the west courtyard exit. The queen was known to be short and to the point with those outside of her inner circle, and for some, it was incredibly intimidating.

Ainsley's face lit up in a warm smile at seeing Annika. The queen wore a pale green gown, with her gray-streaked light brown hair piled atop her head. Gold dangled from her ears, and glinted on her hands, while a simple circlet rested on her head, declaring her importance.

When she reached Annika, she embraced her, and kissed each of her cheeks, making sure to linger on the last kiss to whisper in her ear.

"Is that woman being a tad vexing?"

"She's a vapid turkey."

"Ah. Has she run *afowl* again?" Ainsley laughed gleefully at her pun, while Annika gave her a look of exasperated amusement, but eventually let out a sigh and smiled.

The queen wrinkled her nose as the strong smell that originated from her companion reached her. She gave Annika a knowing eyebrow raise.

Annika responded with a shrug and a smile. "I need to train myself for the day I find myself in a drinking competition."

"My dear, those events are reserved for the blockheaded knights, and women are seldom welcome."

"I'd rather be overprepared than underprepared."

The pair of friends then seated themselves and waited politely as the serving staff brought out the teacakes.

Both women sighed in unison when they bit into the fluffy pastry stuffed with blueberries and a cheesy cream.

"Despite the numerous complaints I've received about the new cook, I am quite taken with him." The queen smiled, her brown eyes dazed in pleasure.

"You finally saw him?" For some reason Annika suddenly looked strained.

"No, I haven't. Though, do tell, why are you giving me that reaction?"

Lady Jenoure let out a small breath as she reached for her teacup and lifted it to her lips.

"No reason. I was worried you were yet another victim of his charms."

The queen laughed, and watched as Annika emptied her cup, suppressing a smile.

"Norman said that the female staff were quite enthralled with him, and I must admit I'm growing curious."

"I wouldn't waste your time. The only thing remarkable about him is his lack of manners or sense."

A slow smile began to spread on Ainsley's face.

"My dear Lady Jenoure ... are *you* perhaps taken with him?"

Annika snorted.

"I'm suspicious of him. I've not met someone so damn private since coming here from Troivack."

"Sounds like you when you first came to marry Hank."

Annika's good-humored expression faded then, and the queen immediately rushed to apologize.

"Oh, my dear, I'm so sorry. I know how much you miss him."

"He was my good friend. I cannot mourn him forever." Annika drew out a small leather flask from a hidden pocket in her bright red dress, which the queen sighed upon seeing. Ignoring her, Annika topped up her tea before a servant refilled her cup with the nonalcoholic portion of the drink and stepped back out of earshot once finished.

Her deceased husband's warm smile, and somehow perfect laugh, seared through her memory. His kind eyes twinkled at her even when she snapped at him the first time they met …

"Have you heard anything more about the war from your family?" Ainsley's voice dropped as she glanced around casually.

Annika blinked, hastily bringing herself back to the present—falling into thoughts of the past was not a good idea.

"Nothing yet, but hopefully in early June before the solstice I will hear from one of my brothers."

The queen nodded.

"How are the preparations for the festival coming along? I hear you and your ladies in waiting have been sewing up a storm."

"Oh, it has been absolutely back breaking work, but we will be finished with time to spare before the parade." The queen glowed with pride as she sipped her tea.

"That's good. Though I can't imagine His Majesty being thrilled about you working so hard in your current condition."

Ainsley shook her head while placing the porcelain cup back on its saucer with a small *clink*. "He isn't, of course, but after this I'll rest more." Her hand absentmindedly drew down to the bump she had recently begun to show.

"How have you been feeling?"

The queen laughed, though more out of weariness than amusement.

"You sound like Norman." She looked at her lap for a moment before raising her gaze, both her fierceness and vulnerability shining through. "I'm alright. To declare more would be taunting the Gods."

Annika swallowed and nodded. She couldn't imagine what her friend was going through.

"MOMMOMMOMOMOMOM!" The unmistakable voice of the young prince rang out through the courtyard.

Both women's heads turned to see Eric barreling out of the southern doorway to the courtyard.

When the little boy had finally arrived at the tea table, he was out of breath and grabbing the queen's hand eagerly.

"Captain Antonio says I can start learning how to use a sword!" The boy then began jumping up and down on the spot.

Annika smiled as she sipped her "tea," and the queen blinked in surprise.

"He … he thinks you're big enough?" The hesitancy in her voice went unnoticed by her son.

"Yes! He does! I'm going to learn how to fight!"

The queen opened and closed her mouth a couple of times before catching Annika's amused expression and sending a glare.

"My love, you forgot to greet Lady Jenoure."

Eric turned to the lady and waved while still jumping. "Lady Jenoure, I'm going to become a knight!"

"I heard! I'm sure you will make a marvelous one, Your Highness."

The little boy squealed and then skipped around the tall tower of glass in the middle of the courtyard, singing, "I'm going to be a kniiight, I'm going to be a kniiiight …"

Ainsley turned to face Annika again. "Once this babe is born, I am going to need a healthy dose of that moonshine," she whispered.

"The prince had to grow up eventually," Annika reminded her with a playful smile.

"It's too quick," the queen lamented sorrowfully.

"Don't worry, you'll have another to worry about soon enough."

The queen's expression became gravely serious as she glanced down, then over to her healthy son who was about to start bouncing off the walls.

"I hope so."

The king stared out at the distant glittering city of Austice from the window of his study, swirling the red wine in his goblet thoughtfully. The castle was quiet, as most of its occupants had tucked themselves into bed, and the new heat of the day had once again dissolved under the inky night sky.

The study was in the front right tower of the castle, its walls lined with shelves holding books, scrolls, maps, and trinkets. A tapestry depicting a man and woman in a lush garden hung over the hearth, with two plush armchairs facing the now cool grate. There was a small square table in the center of the room, and a desk along the same wall as the door.

The king allowed very few individuals into the room, and was waiting for one of those privileged few, when he heard their knock.

"Come in, Lee."

The mage strode in, his cloak and staff not on his person, instead wearing a dark blue short-sleeved tunic showing his powerful arms and broad shoulders.

Yes, it was a well-hidden secret that the mage was in fact incredibly strong and healthy despite being in his sixties (though often mistaken for his fifties), but he preferred that people remain unaware of the fact. He believed it tarnished the sacred image mages were to uphold.

"Good evening, Your Majesty." Lee bowed gracefully after closing the door behind himself.

"Has the well water problem been fixed in town?"

"It has. Some birds had nested down on one of the stones, and their excrement was poisoning the well."

The king didn't hide his look of disgust.

"Thank you for handling that. Would you like a nightcap?"

"No thank you, my liege. I will have the full report on your desk by lunchtime tomorrow."

Norman nodded in understanding as he cast his eyes down and sipped from his goblet.

"About the new cook ..." Lee started slowly, and Norman immediately straightened his posture.

"He's a witch."

The king blinked in surprise. "A male witch? Aren't those quite rare?"

"They are. Perhaps only twenty percent of the witch population is men."

"What element is he aligned with?"

"I do not know, but I suspect air," Lee declared carefully.

The king frowned and placed his goblet down on the square table while gesturing for Lee to sit.

"How is it you do not know his element when you discovered he was a witch? I thought your identifying spell could tell both?"

"It can, but he wouldn't let me close enough to see," Lee explained, lowering himself into the chair at the king's right side.

"Then how is it you know he is a witch?"

"He knew not to let me come closer and was openly hostile toward me."

Norman's expression fell as he shook his head, unconvinced. "He could just be particular about his personal space, and to be honest, I have been receiving a few complaints about his temperament. I do not think we should get ahead of ourselves in our assumptions."

"Most people are either a little in awe or fearful of me when we meet. Only witches are disdainful." There was a dip in his tone at the word *witches*, which made one of Norman's eyebrows quirk upward.

"I know there have been many misconceptions about witches, but you are an open-minded man, Lee. What is it about them you dislike?"

Lee let out a breath and touched his forehead briefly before attempting to explain.

"Mages and witches have never gotten along. Witches are born with magic as a part of them as their blood or bones. Mages have to *work*, and study for years to master what a witch can sometimes do from the time they can walk, depending on their strengths. Mages are better, of course, because we are not limited to a single element, but against a powerful witch, even the best of us might have some troubles. Some witches are still … bitter about our involvement in their persecution fifty years ago, but we've already issued apologies about that so it's been put to rest."

Norman noticed that his friend sounded a tad biased.

"Lee, I heard somewhere recently that there have been witches with mutated abilities … what does this mean?"

"It means that their powers are branching out from their elements, though are still rooted in them. For example, one well-known mutation was a woman who could speak to and be understood by animals. It is rooted in air as a means of moving and understanding sound."

"Ah. That explains that witch in the south being an already legendary healer. If magic is a part of her proficiency, it makes sense. How many varied mutations have been reported?"

"That I know of? Perhaps ten. However, they are atypical."

The king nodded sagely as he pondered the new information. Witches were an infrequent enough phenomenon that he hadn't really given them any thought. Norman had been suspecting the cook as a spy for Troivack, despite Annika's doubts, but if the man was a witch *and* a spy? He could be a real threat.

"Why do witches still dislike mages?" he asked offhandedly as his worries began to climb.

Lee looked as though he wanted to go on a tirade as his eyes welled with thousands of emotions—the largest one being annoyance. However, he managed to calm himself before speaking.

"They dislike us because of how we came to be. The first mage was a man who resented not having any means to use magic, and so he badgered the Gods his entire life. A year before his death, the Green Man decided he would reward his tenacity, despite it being against the wishes of the Goddess. He gave the dying man the archaic language and knowledge of magic that would flow power from the Green Man himself to us. To help amplify this connection, he even guided us to crystals that would allow us to amplify this power. The first mage then passed the sacred practice and crystals on to his sons, who carried on his legacy."

"Why does that bother the witches?" Norman shook his head, perplexed at hearing the tale.

"Witches came to be by the creation of the Goddess, which is why even male witches are "witches," instead of warlocks. Their powers come from the feminine half of the Gods. They believe the mages (or "wizards," as some call us), to be tyrants who have gone against the natural order and laws of life. It has been an ancient feud that I am ashamed to admit I am a part of."

The king let silence settle between the two of them as he continued processing the information and dwelling on the problem of a powerful foe being under the same roof.

"While I do not like him as a witch or a man, I do not believe he is a spy."

The king's eyes snapped up. How had Lee known his thoughts?

"Why not?"

"A spy would be pestering people for information. This witch alienates nearly everyone and wants to be left alone. While I agree we should be wary of him, I believe he is a witch that wants to peacefully exist while making a living. Which is the truth of most of their kind."

Norman leaned back in his chair, and picked up his goblet, deep in thought.

"Should I contact the Coven of Wittica? As a civilian under my rule, he would have had to register with them."

"You can, though they are incredibly difficult to get any information from unless it is of the utmost importance. If he has committed no crimes, they will not share anything about him."

"Knowing if he has a criminal background is still worthwhile. I will send them a messenger pigeon tomorrow."

Lee nodded in acknowledgment and leaned back in his own chair.

Quiet crept up once more between the two men as they sat with their own thoughts over the matter.

"His cooking is incredible, I will give him that," Lee uttered after several minutes had ticked by.

"The steak tonight nearly made me weep. I have never had meat fall apart in my mouth like that," the king responded immediately, his eyes glimmering at the memory.

"I agree. I wonder how in the world he gets the potatoes so creamy ..." Lee was unaware of the awe that had entered his voice.

"Not to mention the dill sauce?" Norman gently touched his mouth at the memory.

Lee half-groaned, half-moaned as he recalled the creamy sauce that he would have eaten straight out of the pitcher, it was so diabolically delicious.

The two continued discussing their favorite meals made by Fin for at least another hour before they retired to their own chambers, each one already hungry for breakfast the next day.

Fin scratched under Kraken's chin as he lay on the cool ground of his kitchen.

"What an oddly uneventful day ..."

The kitten's reply was "booping" Fin's nose without opening his eyes, signaling that it was time for a restful sleep, and the chatter needed to end.

CHAPTER 7
A ROYAL VISIT

Fin popped the oil-coated asparagus with lemon and garlic into the oven, then turned to address the precocious seven-year-old seated facing him in one of the three tall chairs that had been brought down by the boy's governess.

The lad was currently taking a large gulp of sweet milk tea, with a bowl of freshly cut fruit in front of him. As he set the cup down with a satisfied sigh, he began peering into the bowl of cut grapes, apples, and strawberries as though trying to decide which one he wanted to eat.

"Thank you for waiting so patiently, Eric, what was it you wanted to ask me?"

Hastily shoving a handful of fruit into his mouth and rapidly chewing and swallowing, Eric watched as Fin drew out the longer of the two knives from his belt and began slicing fillets off of the salmon on the table in front of him.

"I want to know if I should become a knight or a mage," he lamented, as though the weight of the world rested on his shoulders.

"A knight."

The little boy's eyes widened as he stared up at Fin's serious expression.

"You didn't even think about it!"

"I don't need to think about it. A knight is a more honorable position. They don't defy the laws of nature, and it will help you become a better king."

Eric thought carefully before forming his next question.

"Why aren't mages honorable?"

Fin wisely hesitated as he considered how he should explain this tough truth to the lad.

"Imagine a dog decides he wants to be like Kraken." At the sound of his name, the fast-growing kitten's head popped up from the prince's lap. "The mutt badgers Kraken and his owner its entire life to become not just a cat, but the *best* cat. Our smart kitten here knows that sadly, the dog cannot ever be a cat. Despite telling the dog the truth, the canine refuses to accept this, and the dog's master feels so bad for the dog, that he gives him a pair of fake cat ears, and even teaches the dog to meow a little bit. The dog thinks he is now a cat."

Eric was already giggling at the story.

"So, is the dog a cat?" Fin asked patiently.

"No!"

"But the dog says he is the best cat now—even better than Kraken," Fin pointed out, raising an eyebrow expectantly.

"He still isn't a real cat though!"

"Exactly. Mages are the dogs."

"Who are the cats?"

"Witches."

The little boy's eyes bugged outside of his head in shock, before looking down at Kraken, who was craning his neck up to bump noses with him.

"Kraken's a witch?"

"The very best."

Eric tried to stay serious, but Kraken was repeatedly bumping his head against the boy's chin impatiently, and so he broke down in laughter. After a minute, Kraken jumped down, disinterested at the lack of attention, and began prowling near the open garden door for wayward ants that dared to cross his threshold.

"Okay, I think I get it. I'll be the best knight ever!"

"A sensible decision," Fin agreed.

Eric's expression of determination suddenly melted away, and instead a defeated slump curved his shoulders.

"Being a knight is hard, though … I got knocked down a lot on my first day yesterday. My friend Morgan is already ten times better than me."

The look of embarrassed sadness tugged every heartstring Fin possessed, and so he made a resolution.

"It will get easier. The beginning is always tough, but I need you to do something for me." Fin had finished slicing up the fish and rested his hands on his slim hips.

Eric looked up at him with such a determined expression that he had a hard time keeping a straight face.

"I need you to tell me all about becoming a knight so that I know how great it is, and in return, I will make you a special treat on the days of your training."

Eric beamed and extended his hand eagerly.

"Deal!"

Fin shook the small hand and grabbed his skillet to begin sautéing the fish. Eric decided to investigate Kraken's hunt, and so leapt down from the chair, and was crouched by a sack of potatoes, trying to point out to the kitten where the ants were escaping Kraken's notice.

It was then that the kitchen door leading to the castle banged open, and in stepped none other than Sirs Lewis, Andrews, and Taylor.

Fin's grip tightened on the pan he had just placed on the fire grate, but otherwise didn't convey his apprehension.

Hannah was sitting at the end of the garden path, washing a heaping pile of green beans before snapping their ends off, and had luckily not heard the commotion.

"So we happened to ask the captain if we *were* banned from this kitchen, and you know what he said?" Sir Lewis sneered. The scab from the rake injury looked painful.

"He probably wondered why you were wasting your time bothering a cook?" Fin continued tilting the pan as the butter quickly bubbled and released the mouth-watering aromas of rosemary, garlic, and dried cranberries.

The knights were momentarily distracted as the smell overwhelmed their focus. All three sets of eyes became glued to the hearth as their mouths began to collectively water.

Sir Taylor was the first to regain his sense of the present. "No. He said he didn't know if it was true, but that it was strange Luca had never banned us!"

Fin had known Luca the former cook for a few months and knew that the man had been bullied horribly by the knights, though the kind soul never held it against them.

"So you want to gamble breaking the king's order for some petty ego crusade?"

All three knights blinked. It took them a moment to identify what each of the words meant.

"What crusade? We're just making sure a lowly *cook* knows his place," Sir Taylor growled, taking another step closer to the redhead.

Wordlessly, Fin turned and picked up the filleted fish strips, and added them to the pan.

The seductive smell tripled as the knights once again fought to remain focused.

Giving the pan a few shakes to make sure the butter was distributed evenly, Fin then began to flip each fillet.

A large *clunk* behind him drew a very slow turning of his head, to see that the three knights had seated themselves at his cooking table, and Sir Taylor had laid his sword across its surface. The sword had dirt and dust covering its scabbard, and Sir Taylor stared smugly at Fin, leaning back in the seat.

"We'll watch. Might as well wait for that pretty helper you have to come around."

Fin picked up the pan from the flames, the salmon already finished.

He gazed coolly at the knights, then shifted his gaze to Eric, who was watching unnoticed by the invaders near the door with a pursed mouth.

Fin gave the smallest jerk of his chin, enough of a communication for the boy to understand he was to remain quiet. Eric slowly backed out of the door and fled down the garden path. Kraken remained by the door, now sitting at attention facing the knights.

"Sirs, you will leave my kitchen the moment you finish removing your sword and wiping down this table."

All three knights began laughing, when Fin began flipping his large cooking knife casually in the air and catching it, ceasing their amusement.

"Is that meant to scare us?" Sir Andrews snorted.

"Not at all. I don't rely on fear to get things done." Fin caught the knife by the handle, then plunged the tip down into the table with enough force that the blade remained embedded in the surface, with the handle waving upright. In the blink of an eye, Fin had a cleaver in his hand as he beheaded another fish.

There was a small spray of blood that made the knights twitch, but Fin continued expertly cutting the animal up in no time at all. He switched quickly to the thinner blade better suited for slicing away thin pieces.

"Are you upset that your little bluff didn't work on us?" Sir Lewis demanded, significantly less jovial than before.

Fin drew out the knife that had been in the process of removing innards with a flick of his wrist, purposefully spraying the knight with guts.

"Oops," he exclaimed flatly.

All three men stood.

Sir Taylor reached over and grabbed Fin by the front of his shirt, yanking him forward. Sir Lewis began to draw back his fist, and Sir Andrews's hand was darting toward the dagger in his belt.

Fin's expression remained stoic as he grabbed the skillet that had until seconds before been in the flames of the fire, and casually pressed it into Sir Andrew's hand still resting on his table, making the man yelp.

The knife Fin had stuck into the table was flipped into his left hand and pointed at Sir Lewis's eye.

Sir Taylor growled, then wrapped his hand around Fin's throat.

Everything shifted.

Without knowing why, cold dread suddenly filled Sir Taylor's mind.

It was the same feeling of poking a small critter, only to look up and realize that the runt had merely been a tiny toe of a terrifying monster that was now *pissed*.

Blue lightning was beginning to crackle in Fin's eyes, and the fire behind him was beginning to rise to a dull roar.

"WHAT IS THE MEANING OF THIS?" The millisecond it took for the captain's voice to reach Fin's ears, the fire died down to the friendly flicker it had been before, and there wasn't a trace of lightning anywhere.

Sir Taylor's hand dropped from Fin's throat shakily, though it hadn't been doing any damage anyway, having been too petrified by the sudden terror to do much more.

The three knights turned slowly to see Captain Antonio standing, wearing his full plate armor, his royal blue cape pinned at his shoulders and his helmet under his left arm.

The man had shoulder length white hair, and one icy blue eye that rested in the middle of a long deep scar that ran from his forehead down to his jaw. The other eye was covered with a black eyepatch that added a rather menacing touch. Despite the man's advanced age, he looked powerfully built, and while not as thick in muscle as Sir Taylor, he matched him in height.

Behind him stood a far more averagely built fellow, wearing a dark blue silk tunic, a black leather vest, and matching gloves. The most remarkable things about him, besides the shape of his beard, was the blaze in his hazel eyes and regal bearing.

It didn't take Fin long to guess who he was. Eric stood beside the man, holding his hand, with his tiny fist curled at his right side.

"All of you will go to the training ring *this instant* while I discuss your punishment with the king."

Sir Andrews was too busy cradling his burnt hand to bother arguing, and Sir Taylor still seemed rattled, but Sir Lewis remained the most clear-headed.

"Captain, the cook said he had the authority to ban us from the kitchen, and when we refused to leave, he attacked us!"

The knights stepped aside to reveal Fin, who was still holding the knife he had been wielding at Sir Lewis, though it was flopped over in a more innocent position.

"Captain, Your Majesty, Your Highness." Fin bowed his head, and when he lifted his chin again, shot a brief dark look at Sir Taylor, who visibly winced.

"Dad, they made a mess of Fin's table! He tells everyone dirt can get in the food!" The knights all gaped at the young prince, who was pointing at them with an accusatory glare.

"Eric, please let me hear the Royal Cook's side of the story." The king's voice wasn't harsh, but firm, as he stepped into the room, and all knights present dropped onto a single knee, save for the captain. The prince stayed by the door.

"Speak your tale." The king fiercely stared at the cook, who stood a few inches taller.

"Your Majesty, these knights have been harassing my aides and making it impossible for them to do their jobs. I banned the knights as they show complete disregard not only for the kitchen," Fin gestured angrily at the dirty sword on the table, "but for those in it. I want all here to feel safe while they serve you, Your Majesty, and I want them to do their jobs without having to clean up unnecessary messes made by the knights."

The king cast an icy glance over Sirs Taylor, Lewis, and Andrews's bowed heads.

"Is it true you attacked these knights?"

"No, Your Majesty. I am preparing fish for lunch. The 'attack' was Sir Lewis being sprayed by fish guts, but if you look at myself, you will see it is a hazard of proximity."

The king's eyes swept down and noted the droplets of blood and guts on Fin's cream-colored tunic.

"That isn't true! You burned my hand!" Sir Andrews crowed from the floor, raising his head and showcasing the blistering skin of his left hand. The captain growled, and he quickly fell silent again.

"Only after Sir Taylor grabbed me and the two others moved to join him in assaulting me."

Fin held the king's gaze, doing his utmost to ignore his racing heart. He knew he tended to speak at great speed and at great length when he was nervous.

"Why is it, Finlay Ashowan, that my former cook did not have these problems?" the king wondered, clasping his hands behind his back.

"I believe Luca was often intimidated by the knights, sire."

The silence that followed was crushing, and the only one that dared to move was Eric, who had bent down, picked Kraken up, and begun petting him while watching the scene unfold.

The captain shot a tender look at the young boy, as he seemed to be petting the kitten to calm his own nerves. Somehow, that small show of affection made Fin feel braver.

The king seemed deep in thought, but no one dared to interrupt him until …

"Y-Your Majesty?"

Everyone either turned or looked to the doorway, where Hannah stood shaking and crying quietly, with her hands clasped in front of herself. "T-The Royal Cook w-was just … was just trying to p-protect me."

Her shaking continued to worsen, until Eric stepped forward and clasped her hand with his left, continuing to hold Kraken in his right.

She squeezed back.

"Please speak freely." The king's voice had turned gentle, and the captain stepped away from the doorway to give her more room.

While still holding on to Eric's hand, she stepped into the room, her knees practically knocking together.

"Th-The Sirs have been … have been …" She began crying harder when she saw all three knights look up and glare at her.

When the captain noticed, his expression turned murderous, and all color drained from the trio's faces before they quickly bowed their heads again.

"Hannah," Fin called out softly. "Remember, I promise you're safe here."

The king's features became unreadable as Fin suddenly rounded the table, passed by him, and handed a cup of water to Hannah. He remained at her side, gave the king another small bow of his head, and stood waiting.

"They've made many ... ad-advances t-t-toward me, and d-don't listen when I tell them t-to stop. They follow me when I-I leave. C-Cook keeps them a-away."

"*Is that so?*"

Every eye but Hannah's jumped up to see the queen with Lady Jenoure at her side in the doorway to the kitchen.

When the queen stepped into the room, the captain dropped to his knee, and Eric released Hannah's hand to run to his mother's side. At seeing the captain's show of respect, Fin slowly knelt down, and wondered why there was a difference in the two monarchs when it came to the captain.

The queen strolled forward into the kitchen with Eric behind her skirts, her head held high until she was glowering down at the knights.

"You three mark my words, you will rue the day you *dared* to think you could throw your weight around this castle, as though you had any right to. You will not *sully* this kingdom with your behavior. Is that understood?" she seethed down at them, making them wince and murmur their apologies at the same time.

The king stepped forward then, giving his wife a short nod that somehow communicated everything he needed to. The queen lowered her gaze briefly in response, her eyes burning, but then stood at her husband's side without saying more.

"All of you will kneel in the pig slop pile until the captain and I decide on your punishments. You are dismissed this instant."

All three knights stood and filed out of the room. Hannah continued to tremble and hunch her shoulders to avoid being noticed, as Fin laid a gentle reassuring hand on her shoulder.

"Royal Cook Finlay Ashowan, and you, lass, rise," the king commanded, his boots coming into their views on the stone floor.

Fin stood slowly while helping Hannah to stand as well.

"My dear, if you could please come with me." The queen was at Hannah's side instantly, her arm wrapped around her shoulders, as Lady Jenoure stepped forward to help.

"Hannah." Fin leaned down to her ear so that only she might hear before being ushered outside. "Thank you for defending me. You were very brave."

The young woman managed a weak smile up at him, sniffling.

"I-I just thought you might be scared t-too," she whispered to him, and the look on Fin's face was one of such heartbreaking surprise and appreciation, that everyone who saw it was instantly moved without knowing what was said.

"Come on Hannah! Kraken hasn't ever seen the end of the garden path!" Eric marched past the ladies, carrying the kitten, who mewed boldly as though heralding them to follow.

Once the women had left, the king and captain both stared at each other, then at Fin.

"I must admit, I do not know exactly what I expected of you, Finlay Ashowan, but it certainly wasn't this."

Fin hung his head, his hands twitching at his sides. He immediately began packing in his mind.

"I have been hearing of your disrespectful behavior, your bluntness, and your fearlessness of any consequences. I have not heard a word of the kindness I just witnessed. Are you and the servant Hannah courting?"

"No, Your Majesty. There is no interest from either of us, she is merely my aide," he replied, stiffening in surprise over the king's words.

For some reason he felt as though he were babbling again.

"I see. The crown prince also seems quite taken with you and your cat."

"The prince is bright and kind."

"I'm aware."

Fin winced. He couldn't tell if he were about to be fired or not.

"Lift your head."

He did so.

"Ruby was not lying when she said you were surprisingly young for your talents. Tell me, what is your age?"

"I am twenty-eight years, Your Majesty."

"Not as young as I had thought." The king glanced at Antonio, who raised the eyebrow of his good eye in response. "You sound well educated, tell me, can you read and write?"

"Yes, Your Majesty."

"You can cook the best things I've ever eaten in my life."

"Uh …"

"No need to answer that. It was a statement."

"Thank you for the compliment, Your Majesty." Fin bobbed his head.

"Mr. Ashowan, have you met Captain Antonio before?" The king gestured to the warrior, who stepped forward while casting an appraising eye over the cook.

"I have not, pleased to make your acquaintance." Fin bowed.

"It would seem that you are better educated than a quarter of the knights in my employ, why is that?" the captain demanded, his voice slightly less threatening than a bear's growl.

Fin's mouth opened and closed twice before he cleared his throat.

"My mother had a friend who was a tutor. She herself was also literate, and well-read."

The king raised an eyebrow, glanced at Antonio, then back to the cook.

"As one of the victims of the knights' misuse of power, what punishment do you believe would be befitting for their crimes?"

"Demotion to squires for a year and serve part-time to the queen and her ladies-in-waiting." Fin realized he probably should not have given such a truthful answer … He probably should have deferred to the *ruler of the entire continent* on that one.

The snort of laughter drew the king and Fin's attention to Captain Antonio. The incredibly serious, incredibly intimidating man, had his mouth squeezed and wrinkled into a bud, his eyes bulging and his face turning red.

"Antonio," the king began, but that was all the captain could take before the man was roaring with laughter.

"M-make … th-them act as ladies-in-waiting?!" He was doubled over and slapping his knee.

The king appeared to have trouble keeping a straight face of his own at the sight, but he managed to remain in control as the captain briefly excused himself to step outdoors.

"Mr. Ashowan, to demote the knights is no small feat. Their comrades will not let them suffer silently should they be forced to serve the queen and her ladies."

"With all due respect, Your Majesty, that is the point. Those men made Hannah feel weak, powerless, and terrified. They stopped her from seeking help, and when she came to me, they attempted to do the same to myself." Fin's heart was going to explode at any moment from the stress, but Hannah's scared, crying face kept flashing in his mind.

"They need to be stripped of their power because they abused it, and their dignity needs to be challenged because they need to repent for the one they infringed upon. If you suspend their titles, it negates the process of a full demotion," Fin suggested firmly, somehow remaining outwardly calm.

The king looked slightly disturbed and uncomfortable at how well-spoken, and how blunt the cook truly was.

At times he sounded even more educated and intelligent than some of the nobles in his court ... though he had some pretty radical notions ...

"I think serving women will give the knights more respect for the gender as well. They need to mend the wounded party," Fin continued while the king stared at him appraisingly.

After several long moments where the only sound was the captain's fading guffaws beyond the threshold, the king turned to the garden door, where the warrior was only just beginning to regain control.

"Antonio, I'm going to have a private word with the cook. I will be out in a few minutes."

After closing the garden door, the king walked over to the castle door-way and closed that one as well, ignoring the stifling heat of the room.

"I am becoming greatly concerned, and I need truthful answers from the source, namely you, this instant."

The king's expression was severe, his tone forceful, and Fin felt his stomach drop as dread flooded his body at what was about to happen.

"Finlay Ashowan, I am aware that you are a witch, and I have questions."

CHAPTER 8
SOMETHING FISHY

Fin's eyes went wide, and his hands balled into fists at his side.

"That friggin' mage," he couldn't help but mutter, earning a cold look from the king.

"Your insolence will be excused only *once* as I understand there is some bad blood between your kinds, and you appear to be caught off guard."

Fin looked sheepish at being chastened, and he nodded in acceptance.

"I am certain that you can imagine my concern, as very little is known about your kind. Aside from the fact you all were hunted until nearly fifty years ago, and your abilities are based in the elements. While my mage does not think you are here as a threat to my people or the kingdom, I prefer to err on the side of caution. I am going to request you answer my questions for you truthfully. Failure to do so will result in your immediate termination."

Fin swallowed with great difficulty.

"Your Majesty, might I please beg a small favor prior to this discussion?"

The king leveled him with his gaze.

"That would depend on the favor, Mr. Ashowan."

"Would it be possible if this conversation remains confidential?" The trepidation on Fin's face made the king narrow his gaze.

"Why would people knowing be problematic?"

"While hunting, burning, and decapitating witches has been made illegal, Your Majesty, there are still many who feel hostile toward our kind. The ones that are not hostile come to us asking to use our magic on their behalf. I would be concerned not only for my safety, but for my ability to perform my job if word got out."

The king studied him with a stony expression, and after several moments, gave a short nod.

"Very well. You have my oath as king that I will not expose the information you share with me without your consent. Unless, of course, extenuating circumstances require it."

Fin didn't like the last part of the oath, but figured he was not in the best position to bargain at the moment. He slowly let out a breath and braced himself despite his stomach roiling.

"What is your element?" the king questioned shortly.

"Erm. I suppose earth. However, I am what is called a 'mutant' or 'deficient' witch."

Norman's eyes widened a fraction at the news, but otherwise kept his emotions in check.

"You know what those are, don't you?" Fin looked pained as he stated, more than questioned, the king.

"What is it you can do?" came the even reply from the king.

Fin was already blushing as he reached up and rubbed the back of his neck self-consciously.

"I am called a house witch."

The king blanched.

"I beg your pardon?"

"A house witch. Or hearth witch if you prefer. My powers are centered around the home. Food, protection, so on and so forth; I can do a lot of things to make life comfier, and homier."

"Such as?" Norman's voice sounded distant to his own ears. The young man had to be jesting.

Fin's shy smile was mysterious, as he then snapped his fingers.

The king took a step back in shock as dishes and cups floated into the air all around them, knives started to resume prepping the food that lay on the table, and a nearby broom sprung up and began sweeping the floor. He watched frozen for a long while, and when he finally blinked himself back to reality, turned abruptly to the garden door, marched over, and wrenched it open.

Fin immediately stopped all magic and returned the floating dishware to their previous locations.

"Antonio, inform my assistant to clear my next appointment." Without waiting for a reply, he closed the door, and turned back to Fin, who had the knives continue working on the food.

"You could have easily killed those knights," he stated, staring at the witch with a raised eyebrow and flat tone.

"No, I couldn't have. That is against my ability. Magic in witches is fused with their personalities, and the elements they are aligned with— and each one has limitations. I am not a killer by nature. I am a protector, and a nurturer. I could have erected a barrier that would have immediately blown the knights clear off the grounds, but they wouldn't be killed. The only other way I could've bested them would've been by knocking them out in the name of self-defense."

"You are able to create a barrier?" The king sounded keenly interested, which made Fin swallow in reluctance. He knew how useful such a skill could be to a ruler, however …

"I can create a shield around 'my home.'" Fin gestured around the kitchen.

"Does that tax you in any way?" The king seated himself at the cooking table and gestured for Fin to do the same.

"Conjuring a shield that blows people away from me? Absolutely. I would need to fall asleep probably within a couple of hours. Moving parts of the home isn't too taxing—especially if it promotes the feeling of 'safety,' and 'home.' The more people that share my 'home,' the more power, or energy that returns to me. Though at most, it would only rejuvenate me about half my normal stamina. I still need rest like any other person."

The king stared at the fish being cooked and plated without any human assistance in front of him as Fin spoke. "I understand now why you didn't want any aides," he declared before turning his gaze back to the cook.

"This all generally seems … non-threatening," the king continued slowly as he began to absorb the information. "Aside from the blasting attackers away."

Fin nodded.

"Are all witches powerful like this?"

Fin laughed and waved his hand to summon a tankard, which then zipped over to the ale barrel and filled itself. It settled in front of the king, who stared in awe at it for a few more moments before picking it up and drinking.

"I am not deemed powerful in comparison to other witches."

The king choked briefly.

"Fire, water, and air witches *can* kill and hurt people. If in a battle, they can do brutal damage. Air witches can do most of what I am doing right now, but they aren't limited like I am to the house. If I were to step off Your Majesty's grounds, I'd become powerless. Right now, I only identify the kitchen and perhaps the gardens as my home. I probably couldn't even float a spoon in the dining hall, unless I frequented there more often."

The king considered the information and found himself somewhat relieved that there were limits to the abilities.

"How many witches are in this kingdom?"

"I don't know exactly, but, not including those that reside on the Isle of Wittica, I would say less than five hundred. I have a very narrow view of the world, given that I have not traveled much, so I am not the best person to ask." Fin bowed apologetically, then continued as the king continued to openly study him

"There are a good chunk of witches that aren't powerful at all," Fin continued as he succumbed to his tendency of nervous ranting. "Some fire witches can only light small bonfires and candles. Some water witches can only fill a goblet."

"Can you tell me percentages of how many harmful witches there are in my kingdom?"

"You don't have *any* harmful witches, because the Coven of Wittica holds us all to the law." Fin frowned while staring at the table, clearly displeased at the inference that there was a bunch of magical murdering witches loose but knowing he could not challenge the king.

"Witches who, if they abused their powers, would be dangerous," the king corrected carefully, eyeing Fin.

"Again, I cannot say, as I do not know the exact numbers of my kind. I too would be interested to know—witches are usually wary about making themselves known."

"Are you able to recognize them when you meet them?"

"Only if we shake hands or touch somehow, and even then, their abilities would have to be potent enough to be sensed. In short, not easily."

The king pondered the discussion over, then stroked his beard tip thrice before speaking again.

"Why did you come here to the castle?"

Fin straightened his shoulders, as his eyebrows knit together out of concern for the direction of the discussion:

"I grew up on one of the Southern Isles, and found my island confining ... Everyone there knew who and what I was, and I didn't want that. I had wanted to learn more about myself and my abilities my entire life, and then your former cook Luca came across our path. He stayed with my mother and I for a few months, and when he figured out what I could do ... recommended me for the job here."

"Is your mother also a witch?" the king asked, hoping to humanize Fin in his mind.

"Yes. Though I'd rather not say what her abilities are, if it's all the same to you, Your Majesty."

The king debated ordering him to tell him, but decided it was better to keep the exchange on a far more amiable track.

"Did your father know?"

Fin's expression hardened, and the king sensed a surge of emotion in the cook.

"My father was a witch as well."

"Was he a mutated witch?"

"No."

There was something in the cook's tone that made it clear it was a deeply uncomfortable topic, and so he decided not to press the matter further.

"I will be sending a letter to the Coven of Wittica to verify everything you have told me today, and so if you have fabricated anything, now would be an excellent time to tell me."

Fin bowed his head but said nothing.

"I have one final matter I would like to query about, Mr. Ashowan."

"Yes, sire?"

"Captain Antonio and I were not giving you false praise concerning your level of education. How is it that you are so well-read, and yet come from so little?"

Fin smiled: at last, an easier question.

"The Coven of Wittica enforces education upon all registered witches. They believe that an educated witch is a witch that will make educated decisions—especially when it comes to wielding their power."

"You said that you have to learn about your ability on your own; wouldn't the Coven's instructors guide you?"

"If I simply had pure elemental magic, yes, they would. However, I am the only one of my kind on official records. There was a witch more than a century ago who, some records indicate, had the same abilities, but it was before the current Coven's time."

The king made a slight *hmm*, and stood, forcing Fin to his feet hastily as well.

"As of this moment, I believe what you have told me to be the truth. I will have you informed of when the Coven confirms what you have said. Until then, continue performing your duties."

The king strode toward the garden door, while Fin began rubbing the back of his neck again.

"Oh, and Mr. Ashowan?"

Fin had his head bowed and his hands back at his sides by the time the king swung around, raising a finger in the air.

"Yes, Your Majesty?"

"Your punishment for inflicting a burn wound on Sir Andrews will be helping our Royal Botanist every Sunday for an hour over lunch, for the next four months."

Fin bowed and fought the urge to sigh. He was already busy enough as it were … adding more to his workload was getting insane, but he understood he couldn't get off without consequences, either.

"I understand, sire. Oh, uh …"

The king raised an expectant eyebrow as Fin's hand gently curled into fists and released several times over.

"Could the knights please retrieve their sword and wipe down my table? I can do it myself, obviously, but it's the principle of it all." Fin was blushing at the request, knowing that he was already most likely considered incredibly lucky.

"I see. Captain Antonio and I will decide for their punishment, but we will take your suggestion under consideration. Though I do not recommend you letting it be known that you had any hand in the matter."

"Yes, Your Majesty, and … thank you for the opportunity to work here."

The king nodded once in acknowledgment, then exited the sweltering kitchen toward the garden with his head held high.

Once the crowned head had disappeared around the huddle of women at the end of the garden pathway, Fin let out a breath while half-collapsing half-sitting in one of the chairs. Kraken had returned to the kitchen, having been waiting outside the door worriedly.

"Alright, Kraken, that's now three people who know I'm a witch: the strange, hooded figure, the king, and … that mage. Don't tell anyone else, okay?" Fin looked down at the kitten, who gazed back up at him and remained silent with his tail swishing on the floor playfully.

"Well, time to get cooking."

~~~~~~~

The three knights had come in wordlessly, their ears burning red from hearing about their punishment, and cleaned the table. They promptly left without once glancing at the bustling cook, not wanting to risk another confrontation.

Fin was using his own manpower to send off the lunch dishes with the last of the servants at the time, so paid them little mind. Once the kitchen was cleared of everyone but the cook, Lady Jenoure stepped over the garden door threshold.

"Lunch is served in the banquet hall. I suggest you go now so that the food is still hot," Fin informed her, nodding toward the open door leading to the castle.

"That was impressive, what you did before." She stepped closer to the cook's table, ignoring his previous statement.

"I serve three meals a day. There isn't anything spec—"

"I meant with the knights."

"Oh."

Fin began compiling a plate of his own lunch without lifting his face to Annika, though she stopped to pet Kraken as he brushed himself against her emerald skirts.

"That was Hannah's doing. I merely offered support."

Annika stood in front of the table as Fin picked up his utensils and began divvying up the vegetables on his plate.

"I think you did a lot more than that. While those knights have the collective intelligence of a fruit fly, they are not weak. I'm relatively certain a single slap from Sir Taylor would render you unconscious."

"It wouldn't. If you will excuse me, Lady Jenoure, I would like to eat my meal now." Fin moved over to the side of the table with the chairs and seated himself with his back to his visitor.

Annika said nothing as he began to eat his food. Instead, she wandered over slowly to the nearby shelf, and picked up a cup. She drew out a flask from her skirts, poured in a strong-smelling liquor, then walked back over to Fin's side and took a seat.

"Isn't it a little early in the day to be drinking?" Fin asked as Kraken, smelling the fish, leapt up onto his lap.

"Was it not you who said that everyone in this castle needs a sedative?"

"I have a tea for that."

"While your tea may help Ruby from exploding some days, it will not stop me from strangling a few of the ladies at court. This stuff is a failsafe method that I remain agreeable."

Fin raised an eyebrow and shot a sidelong look at her.

"Do you rank beneath these ladies?"

Annika looked at him, only mildly stunned by his words.

"My dear cook, don't you know that it is considered a terrible social blunder to ask such a question?"

"I thought you said you were sedated?" Fin was in the middle of a struggle between the cat and himself. Kraken, it would seem, was ambitious in his goal of eating from Fin's plate.

He picked up the hastily growing feline and stared into the animal's eyes. "I will set some aside for you, but I am not giving you some from my plate," he explained sternly before putting Kraken back on the floor, then turning back to see Lady Jenoure fighting against a smile.

"You talk to that animal as though it understands."

"Animals understand more than you think. Especially cats, they just don't want to be bothered with people—save for a few they like."

Annika drank her liquor, her expression a strange mix of anxious and unreadable.

Fin observed this out of the corner of his eye as he continued eating his meal without saying a word. He didn't trust that the woman wasn't playing games with him again. He knew that in uncertain social circumstances, the quieter he was, the more his opponent was forced to reveal.

"They rank beneath me, but that doesn't mean I can tell them to take their backhanded compliments and shove them up—"

"Ah. Is that why you hide in the kitchens? To avoid them?" Fin cut her off, taking a sip of water from his cup.

Annika went still, but a slow smile grew on her face as her finger traced the lip of the pottery mug.

"Not quite. It is an added bonus, though."

"You should go upstairs and eat your food on proper dishware," Fin announced as he forked the last of his asparagus into his mouth.

"I don't like fish. Or any seafood, for that matter." She drained her mug, and Fin eyed it suspiciously.

"What have you eaten today?"

"I had one of your incredible scones with some clotted cream and jam, and some grapes."

Fin shook his head and stood.

He loosely grasped a loaf of thick white bread that had only just cooled from the oven, then took a knife with a serrated blade, and carved three thick slices. He set the end crusty bit to the side and dusted off his hands.

He then buttered both sides of two of the slices and drew out his skillet. Placing another dollop of butter in the cast iron, Fin moved it over the fire. Once there was a golden puddle in the pan, he lay down a single slice of the bread, and rested the pan on a small grate.

Walking over to a small hatch in the ground in the upper left corner of the kitchen, Fin drew out two separate cheeses: one a brick of bright orange cheddar, and the other a wheel of brie. After setting them both on his table, and cutting thin pieces from each block, he rested them on the bread in the pan, then capped it with the remaining buttered bread.

Annika's mouth was already salivating. The smell of the toasting bread and butter had never been so scintillating.

In a matter of minutes, Fin slid from the pan a golden sandwich with dripping gooey cheese between its slices onto a plate in front of her.

"It isn't fancy, but it is delicious."

She eyed the sandwich skeptically.

"This doesn't look very … tidy."

Fin rolled his eyes to the ceiling before snatching a knife and fork from the cups that held the lesser quality cutlery. He handed them to her gingerly, and then proceeded to dump his own dishes into the soapy bucket beside the cooking table.

He turned back toward the heaping bowls of prepped green beans and began to empty the contents onto the table.

Annika sliced off a corner of the steaming sandwich, and using the fork he had given her, tentatively bit into the golden perfection.

Instinctively, her eyes closed, and a breath of pure satisfaction left her body. Which was when Fin stole a look at her face and dared a smile before she could open her eyes to see.

By the time she came out of the spiritual experience, the sandwich was gone.

She looked at Fin with dazed surprise.

"That should be illegal," Annika announced while catching herself already considering licking the plate.

"I am glad you enjoyed it. Now please leave my kitchen." Despite the abrupt wording of his request, Fin's tone was softer as he cast her a single bemused glance before returning to the spinach.

Annika stood, and slowly stepped toward the door, still somewhat out of sorts from the experience.

"Thank you, Fin. I think that dish has earned a place as one of my favorites." She smiled at him, and for the first time he saw … her. No masks, no games … just Annika Jenoure. She looked as though she had been fighting in darkness on her own for far too long, and that smile …

That smile told him that the grilled cheese sandwich he'd made had made a single moment of her life a little easier.

The spell was broken as movement in the corner of his eye drew Fin's attention, and he saw Kraken eating the leftover salmon he had set aside.

"KRAKEN, DOWN!"

CHAPTER 9
RUFFLING A FEW
FEATHERS

It was three days before the Beltane festival, and the kitchen was as busy as every other nook and cranny of the castle. Foreign diplomats had arrived, vendors had begun setting up their stalls along the road between the castle and Austice, and the sheer volume of food required to feed everyone was staggering.

Fin was running out of room to store his supplies, so he requested the use of the servant's dining hall for extra surface area from Ruby. She hadn't known how to process the inquiry, as three to five people were bombarding her every minute of the day. Fin's voice had been layered in between a maid asking which guest rooms were to be prepared next, a footman asking who he could take to help unload a particular noble carriage, and a squire asking for bandages for a wound that had occurred in the training ring.

Knowing that there was little chance of the hectic activity quieting down anytime soon, Fin began sectioning off tables of the room without waiting for a reply and hoped the Head of Housekeeping wouldn't comment.

As he returned to the kitchens to finish prepping lunch, and then start carrying out some of the supplies to allow his team more space to work, he watched with masked joy at the aides that were lined up to help him.

Sirs Lewis, Andrews, and Taylor stood by the garden door as Hannah handed them heavy buckets filled with silverware and dishes to be washed.

The knights had been flung to the bottom of the pecking order—even beneath the newest addition of sirs that had been knighted at the Winter Solstice. Though not as lowly as a squire, they had fallen far, and would remain buried for the next six months.

The icing on the cake, however: they were ordered to serve under Hannah during that time, and therefore, fell under Fin's command. While he had been worried that she would be too terrified to accept the role, she had agreed on the condition that she never be left alone with them.

When Fin approached his cooking table, he drew out his chef's knife in the direction of the five pheasants laid before him. After giving the knights a flat expression, Sirs Andrews and Lewis scowled, and Sir Taylor winced.

The leader of the three had developed a newfound caginess regarding the cook, for reasons he would not share with his lackeys.

Once the knights had left to lug the heavy buckets down to the river, where a massive cauldron of boiling water awaited, the remaining two people turned to him.

Peter and Hannah were his only original aides remaining after the knights had been assigned to the kitchens: with the other three being relieved of duties, much to Ruby's sincere relief.

"Where should we set up the spits for the lambs and pigs?" Peter asked in his usual quiet manner.

Fin thought about it for a while before directing them to set up in between the dishwashing station by the river along the castle's west side, and the kitchens. They needed to be close enough for him to check, but far enough that he could use magic to complete the rest of the cooking and baking without being caught.

They nodded, and immediately set out to work.

Peter was a quiet man in his mid-forties, with mousy brown hair and brown eyes. His face was slightly pocked from his youth, but he carried himself confidently. He had a stern "do not mess around" manner about him, which was probably the reason Hannah had asked Fin to keep him on with the knights joining them. The man seemed to only soften around the petite blond woman, and Fin couldn't help but wonder in what capacity he cared for her—he would have to talk with Peter and find out subtly.

Fin stopped himself suddenly and shook his head. What was wrong with him? More people around him in his space, talking with him …

These were bad things. He didn't want to risk any more people finding out he was a witch.

Not wanting to share the secret of his abilities and history, which meant he could never really be honest, or create genuine relationships with people, and he didn't think it fair for friendships to be so one-sided.

No, Peter was better off keeping his opinion of Hannah to himself.

As Fin began preparing the pheasants, Kraken jumped up onto the chair in front of him and began sniffing the birds awaiting preparation. The kitten's velvety black nose twitched, and his eyes closed slightly as he took in the delicious scent of fresh meat.

"Do not even think about taking a bite out of one of these birds. You are not to set a single paw on this table, understood?" Fin informed the feline without hesitating in his chopping.

Kraken straightened, and allowed his pupils to fill his eyes, creating the most adorable wide-eyed kitten face that was normally reserved for nightly cuddles.

"… That isn't fair."

Fin could feel the pleading coming from his familiar, could almost hear the young voice wanting to barter for just a nibble or five from the food …

"What in the world is that stray doing in here!"

Fin's eyes bulged as he slowly turned to look at Ruby, who was staring at the kitten with disgust written all over her face. She stepped into the kitchen, and it was clear what her intent was as she began to make a bee-line for the animal.

"He's mine, don't touch him." The command was mixed with a tint of desperation as Fin ceased his work.

Ruby turned slowly to face him while glaring.

"I did not authorize an animal in—"

"… In *my* kitchen?" Fin challenged back, drawing the woman's attention enough for Kraken to make a stealthy escape from her range of reach.

"Reorganizing the kitchen, fine. I've accepted the change. Limiting the personnel in here I … begrudgingly … admit was a good decision that I hadn't fully understood at the time. *This*, however, is a different matter entirely!" Her face was beginning to deepen in color, and Fin wordlessly cursed the warm weather for ruling out his tea as a calming solution.

"Ruby, cats are excellent at keeping away bugs and rodents. This one showed up on my doorstep and has been a great help in minimizing the ant invasions," he tried, grabbing a clean knife and a scone from the pan where he had set them to cool.

"They bury their poop, and then have their paws all over the food!"

"The only food that he has any kind of access to are the potatoes, and they are in bags before they are *cooked*."

While Fin was maintaining a calm voice and facial expression, his hands worked swiftly in lathering the scone in clotted cream and jam. Ruby's eyes darted to his hands, and she narrowed her gaze at him, but he saw her swallow.

"They jump up everywhere! I bet you he has already had his paws all over this table." She pointed her index finger down into the wooden surface, bending her fingertip as she did so.

Fin set the food on a plate, placed it in front of her, then poured her a glass of chilled mint lavender tea that she had failed to notice had levitated an inch off the ground from the cooling hole beneath the small trap door, to then raise up into Fin's dangling right arm beneath the table's surface.

He set the teacup in front of her and placed his hands on his hips.

"I am in here twenty-four hours of the day, Ruby. He has not set a paw on this table, and if he had during the night, it wouldn't matter, as I scrub this table down before I go to bed and after I rise every morning."

Ruby didn't know when she had picked up the scone; all she knew was the burst of flavor in her mouth when she took the first bite. The world melted away as swiftly as the cream melted in her mouth, and when her hands clasped around the pleasantly cool goblet, and she drank, she felt more of her worries fade away.

"You need to remember to save time to eat," Fin reminded gently.

When Ruby slowly opened her eyes, her coloring had returned to normal, and her heart rate had slowed down. The overwhelming feeling of peace had settled under her bosom, and it took her a few prolonged minutes before remembering what they had been talking about.

"No cats," she reiterated, though her voice had become far softer than it had been before.

Fin sighed. He hadn't wanted to use his ace card, but he had no choice. There was no way she was taking his familiar from him.

"The prince comes to the kitchens every morning after his lessons and plays with him. He will be sorely upset if the cat is suddenly banished."

Ruby blinked rapidly as her mouth opened and closed several times. A small blush began returning to her round cheeks.

"He does not."

"He does. If you weren't so busy, I would recommend you wait around to see. He normally comes after his lessons with the mage."

"Well then he should be down any minute now, if what you say is true!" Ruby indignantly seated herself in the chair on the far right of the table as she then tucked in for the rest of her meal.

"Why is it you wanted to see me right now, anyway?" Fin tried distracting her further.

"I wanted to ask what was going to be served for lunch, but I see my answer." She sniffed in the direction of the pheasants and resumed consuming her late breakfast.

He slowly picked up his knife again and thought, for the thousandth time since the blasted Beltane malarky had started, how he desperately wanted a pint.

Fin had just finished filling the oven with the stuffed pheasants, and was turning to begin making the dinner rolls, all under the narrowed gaze of Ruby. She had finished the scone, and the lavender mint drink, and had been waiting wordlessly for less than thirty minutes. Despite her silence, the woman's foot continued to quiver under the table endlessly—most likely thinking how no one knew where she was, and how she was needed in twenty places at once.

"If you want to see the prince play with Kraken after the festival, I'm sure—"

"I am fine waiting right here," Ruby cut him off while folding her arms across her chest stubbornly.

Fin let out a sigh, shook his head, and picked up his knife when the door burst open, and the prince rushed inside.

"Sorry I'm late! The dog wouldn't stop trying to tell me he was a cat— Hi, Fin!" Eric waved as he darted around the table, and froze at the sight of Ruby, who looked stunned.

"Oh … hullo, Ruby," Eric mumbled as Ruby stood up immediately and curtsied.

"Eric, it's okay, Ruby here just wants to know that you're helping me take care of Kraken," Fin said quietly, picking up fruit from the wooden bowl on his table and beginning to get the prince's snack ready.

Ruby's eyes were wide and unblinking as Eric bent down and picked up Kraken, who had been smartly hidden under the cooking table by Fin's feet until hearing his playmate's voice. The kitten immediately rubbed his face into Eric's cheek, and the little boy responded by nuzzling him back with a big smile before looking shyly back up at Ruby.

"I'm sorry we hid Kraken from you, but he's a really good cat! He's even a witch!"

Ruby's face paled, and looked at Fin, who remained looking innocent as he shrugged, then when the woman had her back to him, shot the young boy a wink that made him smile brighter.

"If Your Highness would like … this animal to … stay … Then, I suppose there is nothing I can—".

Eric rushed over to Ruby, and hugged her around her waist, immediately making Kraken leap down from his arms. The kitten was not a fan of group hugs.

Ruby shot Fin a dirty glare while he began humming inconspicuously and became keenly focused on cutting the tops off of the strawberries.

"If you will pardon me, Your Highness, I need to return to my duties." She managed to make her voice sound kind as the prince released her waist. Though as she exited the kitchen, she shot Fin another murderous scowl.

After letting out a breath of relief, he turned and smiled down at Eric, who was already climbing up into his favorite chair on the far righthand side in front of Fin that Ruby had been formerly occupying.

"Did I do well?" Eric asked with a sly smile.

Fin held up his hand and the little boy slapped his small one against the palm.

"Just like we practiced. I have to hand it to you, you saved Kraken's and my butts!"

Eric giggled triumphantly, and immediately began eating the strawberries Fin set out for him.

Then the two proceeded to catch each other up on their days thus far.

Fin was in the middle of wiping down his table post dinner hour, when the door flew open, and in rushed Annika, who hastily closed the door behind herself.

He was about to tell her to leave, but then saw her pale expression and wide eyes.

"I'm going to hide here," she informed him before dashing around his table to the other side of the fireplace, which was the same side where the trap door down to the cool hole was, and the ledge built in the wall began.

"How long will you be here?" Fin questioned, drying his hands with a white towel and turning to rest his bottom against the table edge.

"That depends. If someone comes in here looking for me, send them to the front gardens. Shortly after that, I will take my leave."

"I see, and who is it that might be looking for—"

The door banged open again, and in strode Lee with his staff clasped firmly in hand. Gone were the long robes and feeble visage, and instead stood a man that, while gray in his beard and hair, had bulging biceps in a short-sleeved red tunic, brown vest, and matching trousers. A crystal hung around his neck that matched his staff, and his wavy hair was partially tied back.

He looks more like a woodcutting gypsy than a mage. Typical buffoonery, trying to hide his true self ... Fin thought to himself scathingly.

"Alright you dirt magic monger, what in the world did you tell the prince?"

"Why, Mage Lee, what brings you to my kitchen?" Fin's eyes were wide and his fists clenched as he stared at the man who was unaware that Lady Jenoure was standing hidden behind the fireplace.

"You've been filling a seven-year-old prince's head up with nonsense that mages only 'borrow magic'!"

Fin said nothing for a long moment, biding his words carefully while placing the towel in his hands down onto the table.

"Tell me, were you by chance looking for Lady Jenoure just now?"

Lee pointed at Fin, igniting a flame on his fingertip as he glared at the cook.

"You will stop filling that boy's head with nonsense. If you think you can best me, then prove it!"

Fin reached up, and easily pinched out the flame on Lee's finger, looking strained.

Lee stared, startled at the steaming end of his finger. The mage fire should not have been so easily extinguished ...

"I think it's rude to embarrass the elderly. Let's put a pin in that, as we have comp—"

Lee muttered several guttural words, and *thunk*ed his staff against the stone floor once. A powerful wind swirled around them as his eyes glowed milky white.

"I will show you what it means to disparage my—"

Fin stood in the swirling winds, looking thoroughly exasperated and annoyed, and so without saying a word, his eyes momentarily flashed a brighter blue. The winds stopped, and the towel he had only just then abandoned on the table snapped itself around Lee's head and pulled him toward the door. Fortunately, Lee was still standing out of Lady Jenoure's eyeline by standing on the opposite side of the fireplace, and so she couldn't see what was happening.

"VGHJBJNOIGVKJ— STOP THIS!" Mage Lee finally managed after freeing his mouth and tearing the cloth from his head.

"How dare you—"

"How dare *I*?! How dare *you* try to use magic on a helpless commoner in his own kitchen, in the presence of *Lady Jenoure*."

Annika took that moment to step away from her hiding place, her eyes round as she dazedly lifted her hand in greeting. "Hello, Mage Lee."

The man found himself bereft of words, and Fin stared disapprovingly down at him.

Leave it to the mage to throw a tantrum.

CHAPTER 10
LORD PIEREVA

Mage Lee was beginning to stammer an apology, when the kitchen door slammed open for the third time that evening.

Both Royal Cook Fin and Royal Mage Lee looked to see a tall man with short thick curling black hair, a black beard, and intense brown eyes step into the kitchen, still brightly lit by the extended daylight hours. He wore plate armor and a black cape around his shoulders, and he surveyed the room coolly before turning to Lee, plainly ignoring Fin's presence.

"Have you seen Lady Pi—Lady Jenoure come this way?" he demanded gruffly.

Lee's blue eyes were bulging from his previous shock at discovering he was not alone in the room with Fin, and yet also calculating the new occupant of the kitchen, when Fin jumped in.

"We have not seen Lady Jenoure this evening, but I am sure if you ask her ladies-in-waiting, they will be happy to assist you in locating her. I believe I saw one of them heading toward the front gardens."

The man straightened at Fin's tone and annunciation and studied him for several moments before tilting his head over his right shoulder.

"You dare to address me so informally, cook?" His dark eyes glimmered, and his head weaved over to his left side toward Fin, reminding the witch of a snake, as though he were a rat to be hunted.

"Forgive him, Lord Piereva, this cook is from the country and is still learning how to properly address his betters." Lee gave a graceful bow, hunching his shoulders to appear smaller and shriveled. His biceps were a dead giveaway.

"Why is it that the court mage and cook are conversing when there are festivities happening in the banquet hall?" The stranger once again addressed Lee, and turned to block Fin.

"Royal Mage Lee is bringing to my attention that his meal was less than satisfactory," Fin replied despite clearly being unwelcome, giving a shallow bow.

He had never seen this man before, but it was incredibly obvious he was one of the diplomats from Troivack, due to his dark hair and tanned olive skin. Though his eyes ...

Fin recognized immediately.

"Really, mage? I saw you devouring your meal with your eyes closed you were so pleased with the food. I, on the other hand, found it to be ... unique," the newcomer pointed out shortly. Whether his comment was meant as a compliment or an insult remained unknown.

Mage Lee cast his eyes to the ground, leaned on his staff more noticeably, then spoke.

"The cook here was unaware how an excess of pepper can aggravate my bowels."

Fin bowed again. "A note I will take with great care toward meals to come."

The Troivackian man glanced between them, amused.

"Cook, you prepared a delectable meal this evening. I require more wine delivered to my rooms."

Fin remained bowed.

"Of course."

After a final derisive snort, the man left, and once his footfalls faded in the distance, Mage Lee turned to Fin, who had resumed his usual jaded expression standing fully upright.

"Why did we lie to Lady Jenoure's *brother*?" Lee demanded, outraged.

"She asked me to," Fin replied simply with a shrug as Annika stepped out from her hiding spot, startling Lee for the second time that evening.

During his lie, he had once again forgotten she was in the room.

"I thank you both for your help. I am sorry to place you two in this predicament." She bowed her head to both of them. "My eldest brother wishes to discuss my returning to my homeland since my husband has passed, and I do not wish to broach the matter at this time," she announced, her voice calm despite her face being several shades paler than usual.

While Fin turned to his cooking table and began his final wipe down for the evening, Lee became awkward.

"Lady Jenoure, I ... I will be most sorry to see you go."

"She hasn't said she's leaving." Fin's sharp reply drew both Lee and Annika's gaze as he continued his cleaning ritual.

"Sadly, unless the king finds me another marriage partner before the year is over, I will be sent back home," Annika answered, clearly still taken aback by Fin's outburst.

"Then marry some idiot that will let you continue acting as you please. What's the problem?" Fin managed to give a cavalier single shoulder shrug as he scrubbed the legs of the table.

Lee rounded on him.

"How dare you speak to Lady Jenoure disrespectfully! She will not settle for 'some idiot.' The king has been fielding offers since the new year from many prosperous noble families! You should be bowing to her shoes."

Annika winced at Lee's words, but the old man failed to see the action.

"So why has a pairing not been made?" Fin straightened and stared at Lee coolly.

"That is not our business, Finlay Ashowan! I think you have grown far too used to the leniency of our king with your terrible attitude and impertinence. I will be addressing this matter to the king and—"

"Mage Lee, please remember this man has been working nearly twenty-four hours every day for the past week to have the Beltane feast ready. He is sleep deprived, and earlier this week had that nasty business with the knights threatening him. Could you not see how that might make a man's wits be somewhat addled?" Lady Jenoure had stepped forward, her brown eyes wide with innocence and good intentions.

Fin didn't buy it for a moment.

He knew she was persuading Lee on his behalf, however, and so kept quiet.

"My lady, he was still discourteous, and he is *only* a cook—"

"*Only a cook?!*" Annika stepped in front of Fin, her hands clenched at her sides. "This man is in charge of food for *the entire royal family, court, and serving staff!*" she declared, her shoulders straightening, and her new posture raising her higher.

"He is the one to nourish our great leader, and to diminish his role as a protector of what His Majesty ingests is to—"

"I apologize, my lady, I did not mean to upset you." Mage Lee bowed frantically, his voice breathless.

"While Mr. Ashowan is not always the most *sensitive* of beings, he has always performed his duties with nothing less than perfection. He is now under the demand of several *hundreds* of commoners and nobility alike to deliver the same quality as always, can we not spare him an ounce of leniency?" she demanded, her voice rising.

Lee remained bowed and quiet, acknowledging a losing battle when he heard one.

"Of course, my lady. Royal Cook Finlay Ashowan, please do your best to mind your manners." When addressing Fin, Lee straightened, and his voice turned to a growl as Fin smiled cheekily at him behind Annika's back.

Lee looked as though he were debating incinerating him on the spot.

"I bid you good evening, Mage Lee. I'll be sure to include less pepper into your dishes from now on!" Fin called jovially as the man disappeared over the threshold with a frustrated grunt.

Annika turned to face Fin, wearing a half-smile as she stared up at his good-humored expression.

"Well, Finlay Ashowan, I believe I just earned full rights to come and go from your kitchen whenever I please."

Fin's face fell.

"No, you haven't. I would consider that payment for getting rid of your brother—speaking of, why is it you are hiding from him instead of just telling him this is your home now?"

Annika's smug appearance faded, and she shrank away from Fin.

"My brother is a powerful man, and with there being talk of war … it's complicated," she finished lamely while turning toward the door to the castle.

Fin sighed, and quietly shrugged to himself. It really wasn't his business.

"Before I retire for the evening, I was wondering what you told the prince that got Mage Lee so angry? The man is usually wrapped up in a cloak and mild mannered to a fault." Annika's tone indicated she was a mixture of impressed and concerned.

"Oh uh … I'm a little bit mistrustful and doubtful of mages overall, and I suppose I may have influenced the prince's opinion on the matter as well."

"You turned a seven-year-old against a mage?!"

The look of stunned horror and amazement on Annika's face made Fin awkwardly rub the back of his neck and cast his eyes to the floor.

"A royal seven-year-old. To be honest I would be more worried for the mage," he said, managing to keep his voice cavalier.

"That's what makes it worse! You taught him to be disrespectful of his teacher, a member of royalty shouldn't be looking down at anyone," she chastised, making Fin blush.

"I can … see your point. Though, I shouldn't have been able to sway him so easily. He probably had his own reserves even before I mentio—"

The flat expression on Annika's face made Fin stop talking.

"That child adores you. I do not know why, but you two have a weird friendship. He hasn't asked any other serving staff to call him by his first name—other than Hannah, I suppose, but that is different. This means you have a responsibility to be a good influence on him," she continued with a small smile and a raised eyebrow.

Fin scuffed his boot against the stone floor.

"Alright, I'll tell him to be respectful to everyone … even toward *mages*." The derision that dripped from his voice at the mere mention of Lee's ilk made Annika elicit a small snort.

He gave a sheepish smile and darted a small glance at her.

"You are a strange one, Finlay Ashowan."

With a final smile, she exited the kitchen, and as he waited for her soft footfalls to fade, Kraken poked his head out from under the table.

"She is a trying woman," Fin lamented as he bent down to pick up the kitten with a sigh. "But I suppose she has her good moments."

The banquet hall was boisterously loud, as it was packed with nobility, visitors, and serving staff. The drinks were flowing, the food disappearing, and it appeared everyone was dressed in their finest.

Fin stood before the king's long table at the back wall of the room, which ran widthwise, while two long tables ran parallel to one another against the length of the hall. It was crowded and hot, and despite the barrage of voices and minstrel music playing, the room gradually quieted, as eyes were drawn to the tall, red-headed man dressed in peasant garb standing before His Majesty alone.

The king cast his gaze around the room, and all too quickly, the remaining noise disappeared, which is when he then fixed his unreadable hazel eyes on his cook.

Fin's stomach was clenched as he bowed before the king, and then slowly straightened. He was keeping his emotions from his face, but he couldn't deny that his stress levels were making the magic in his skin begin to itch something terrible.

"Royal Cook Finlay Ashowan, I have summoned you here at the behest of Lord Piereva of the Troivackian kingdom." The king's voice rang out into the room, and Fin felt his toes curl in his boots at the lord's name. Something about Lady Jenoure's brother made him incredibly wary and agitated. The itch in his skin turned into a buzz as the earl stood and stooped to the king first before turning to the cook.

Fin bowed in turn, and when he rose, locked eyes with Lord Piereva, earning a small eyebrow twitch from the lord. Whether from amusement, or outrage at his brazenness, he wasn't sure …

"Cook, I have requested your presence from the King of Daxaria to offer my compliments on the meal you prepared for us all." Lord Piereva raised his goblet, and the room broke out in polite applause. Fin didn't bat an eye, however; he could sense that there was more to it.

"Thank you for your kind words." Fin bowed again, stiffly.

"I don't suppose our Troivackian court could persuade you to come serve us instead." The room shifted. There was an uncomfortable silence, despite Lord Piereva looking impervious to it, but Fin could feel rather than see the king's eyes sharpen on the earl.

"While you flatter me greatly, my heart and skill has always belonged to Daxaria." He bobbed his head, but did not avert his eyes, and he could feel his stomach twist as a small toying smile climbed up the lord's face.

"I understand, men from humble beginnings often latch on to the first master to show them interest."

Fin felt a small burst of magic escape his grasp and heard a glass shatter somewhere at the back of the banquet hall. No one seemed to notice, though, as all eyes were glued to the scene in front of them.

"I will hold on to the hope that my knowledge of the heart proves true, and that we will speak again soon."

The tension in the air was thick as Lord Piereva raised his goblet once more to Fin. He began to seat himself, but suddenly stood back up.

"I nearly forgot. Last night, I could not put my finger on it, but you reminded me greatly of a man in the Troivackian court. He was originally from Daxaria, and I wondered if there was any relation. His name is Aidan Helmer. Bright red hair, though turning quite silver, black eyes, about your height?"

Fin felt as though he were about to be sick but managed to turn his chin and shake his head loosely.

"I am afraid not, my lord."

"Pity."

Lord Piereva sat down, his eyes glittering as he continued to study Fin.

"Who is Aidan Helmer, if I may inquire, Lord Piereva?" The king stared coolly at the man, and Fin was relieved to see that the king didn't seem to be overly fond of the visitor either.

"Oh, he is our new chief of military. A fire witch, if you can believe that! First time a witch has ever been allowed a spot in the Troivackian court, but the magnitude of his abilities is too impressive to go unharnessed."

The fearful glances that ran around the room from Daxarian nobility only made Lord Piereva's smile wider. While still officially unconfirmed, the rumors of war had been growing fervently amongst the land, and the announcement only magnified the threat.

"I see. He sounds like an interesting man, to say the least," the king replied calmly, appearing completely unmoved by the news, despite Mage Lee shooting Fin a dark look from his corner seat at the table back where no one could see.

"Brother, I fear we have taken up enough of this cook's time. He has the Beltane feast to prepare for tomorrow, after all." Lady Jenoure somehow made her voice sound musical as she gently touched the earl's arm and directed the conversation back to more neutral ground.

Fin had been so focused on monitoring Lord Piereva that he had failed to notice Annika at the man's righthand side. She wore a black gown with silver thread, and silver chains woven through the loose braid that fell down her back.

What unnerved Fin further was that had never seen her look so ill at ease. Despite her smile and relaxed body language, there was a distance in her eyes that told him she was trying to skirt around the periphery of her brother's awareness.

Interesting ... he thought to himself though with a note of apprehension.

"Ah yes, my sister is correct, you're dismissed, cook." Lord Piereva waved his hand while turning his gaze to Annika, who continued to appear in control.

"I do not believe it is up to you to dismiss my staff." The king's voice chilled the room instantly, and Lord Piereva's head quickly swiveled around. He let a small, chesty chuckle leave his lips before slipping a mask of respectfulness over his amused expression.

"My apologies, Your Majesty, I meant no insult." He nodded his head toward the ruler indifferently.

Fin stared as the man reached under the table and gripped Annika's forearm tightly. No one could see unless they happened to be standing directly in front of the table, and while the lady's face remained pleasant, Fin knew that he was gripping her hard enough for it to hurt.

The table suddenly jerked violently, as though a team of large men had picked it up an inch with all the food and finery and then dropped it back on the ground. A few pieces of food dropped to the floor, and dishware clattered abruptly.

The king's jaw clenched despite remaining focused on the lord, and Lee's eyes bore into Fin, but he saw that the occurrence had made Lord Piereva release his sister, and that was all that mattered.

Lee stood. "Pardon me, Your Majesty, I was attempting to rise from my seat. These old feet seem to have fallen asleep," he announced, and after giving a withered bow, he sat back down.

The king acknowledged the apology before waving a hand in Fin's direction.

"You are excused."

Fin gave his respectful farewell, turned on his heel, and left the banquet hall swiftly.

Well, I've learned two valuable things that evening. The first: my abilities can extend the more rooms I visit connected to my "home." The second: my father, who I haven't seen since I was eight years old, is leading a war to Daxaria's doorstep.

CHAPTER 11
BLAST FROM THE PAST

Fin had exited the banquet hastily, not wanting to prolong his magical discomfort, and had nearly made it to the end of the long corridor with tapestries and suits of armor standing polished to a blinding gleam, when he heard the massive oak banquet doors opening and closing behind him.

"Fin!"

Turning warily, he peered around to see who was chasing him, half-expecting one of the footmen or serving staff. Instead, a tall, lithe man with flowing long black hair, beard, and mustache wearing long white silk robes glided over to him.

He blinked several times, then after several moments, the look of realization dawned on his face.

"It's been a few years!" The Zinferan man smiled at Fin warmly, and the cook's face broke out in an astonished grin.

"Holy Gods, you can say that again! How are you, Jiho?" Fin took the man's offered hand and gave it a firm shake, then folded his arms across his chest and stared down fondly at him.

"Been fit as a fiddle since I last saw you and your mother. How long has it been? Five years?"

"Sounds about right—you must be doing well if you're a guest here," Fin complimented as his old friend smiled and bowed his head slightly.

"Indeed, fortune has smiled fondly upon me since our time together. I am here on behalf of Zinfera, along with a few other associates of mine."

Fin nodded as he listened.

"I see that you have moved on and up if you are the cook for the king!" Jiho shook his head in amazement. "I never thought I would get to taste your food again, then lo and behold, I sit down to the best meal of my life, thinking I finally found someone who could best you in the culinary arts."

Fin laughed. "Don't worry, you'll find someone better than me someday."

Jiho glanced at the closed banquet doors over his shoulder briefly before turning slowly back to Fin and dropping his voice.

"I see that war may be imminent for your kingdom." His kind brown eyes suggested his sympathy as Fin gave a small shrug.

"Probably. Not that a lowly cook would know anything."

Jiho nodded slowly, as though considering something with great care.

"You know, if you ever wanted a job in Zinfera, you would only need to ask."

Fin laughed. "Apparently I need to ask for a raise—you're the second offer tonight!"

At the mention of Lord Piereva's recent show of force, Jiho's face became taut. "Yes, I witnessed his invitation … Finlay, be wary of that man. He is not one to be trifled with, nor is his chief of military, from what I've heard," Jiho whispered, ducking his head even closer to avoid anyone overhearing.

Fin frowned and leaned down. "Lord Piereva seems a bully, but there's no reason for me to cross his path," he reasoned seriously. His expression then shifted to one of minor apprehension. "Jiho, please do me a favor, though … and don't mention about my … *talents* to anyone while you're here."

Jiho's look of genuine surprise, followed by taking a step back from Fin, confused the cook for a moment. "You mean you got this job without them knowing?"

"The king knows now, but I got the position thanks to a referral from an old friend."

Jiho looked a strange mix of amazed and thoughtful. "I always said you were far more capable than anyone knew … I will be very interested to see what happens in your future."

Fin smiled again and held out his hand. "Hopefully only good things for the both of us. I need to get back to work, but in my next letter home, I will tell my mother you send your well wishes."

Jiho took his hand with a smile. "Please do. I owe the both of you everything I have." He then gave a small bow before turning and walking back to the banquet.

Jiho had given Fin a respectful farewell deemed for an esteemed equal, and this was not lost on him. While embarrassed, he was also flattered, making him rub the back of his neck self-consciously.

Unable to stop smiling to himself over getting to see an old friend, Fin turned and headed back to the kitchen. To think the man that had once been a poor dockworker had become a foreign diplomat …

The world really was full of wonder.

Fin stood stirring the pot over the fire, as his mother wound red twine around the bundle of broken willow twigs to form their new broom. It was a meager dinner that night, as had become the norm since his father had banned his mother from offering her magical help to anyone that wasn't a witch.

Hunger sucked at his stomach as the aroma of onion and fish clung to the air. The young boy, small and scrawny for his age, mentally divided the portions of the meal, and realized he would be lucky if he got half a bowl of his creation. His father would be home soon, and Fin already felt anxious enough without the knowledge that he would be going hungry for another stretch of time …

A heavy chilly mist coated the Isle of Quildon, the warm spring air soaking up the snow into the air and turning the thick grass a deep shade of emerald that ran over the entire island. There was near constant rain and storms that time of year as well, meaning it was a barrage of his father's anti-element.

It was the kind of weather that put his father in a bad mood … and Fin had already been awaiting his return with cold dread gnawing through him, making his skin itch every hour of the day.

His father had been out on one of his "scouting missions," and those had been garnering worse and worse results with each trip to the mainland. The "missions" were in reality his father's way of trying to claim followers that would agree to overrun the Coven of Wittica Elders.

Aidan Helmer was one of the witches that called themselves "purists." They believed that witches were meant to rule the continent as the middle ground between nature and people. They did not look favorably upon mutant witches, believing them to be damaged by growing divided from the original nature of their powers.

His father's efforts to recruit partners in his grand plan had not been well received, however, and his anger over his disappointment was often channeled toward his wife and son when he returned home after a month or more away on the mainland.

As Fin picked up the pot holding his stew, and carefully moved it out of the flames, he glanced at his mother.

Gaunt, pale, but resilient as always, with warm bright brown eyes and light sandy brown hair tied back with a white handkerchief that stood out against her faded floral dress.

Despite having a heart made of mush, Katelyn Ashowan always persevered. The bounce in her step was never gone, and even when its presence bordered on delusional, there was a hopeful pep to her at all times. Her sunny outlook infuriated Fin on occasion, though he never said so, as on other days, he also found comfort in the one positive constant of his life.

The young boy dropped his stare down to the pitiful supper he had mustered up, and that was when it dawned on him: he wanted to run away.

He wanted to run to a place where there was always good food, where he and his mom would always be safe …

The unmistakable sound of their squeaky front gate opening and closing made Fin's head snap up. He couldn't deny the tears that welled up when he saw his mother's hands begin to tremble at the sound.

Fin slunk back to the corner of the small cottage that he had been born and raised in. Aside from the single room where the small fireplace and table stood, there were two separate rooms off to the left of the front doorway, his bedroom, and his parents' bedroom, but they were too far to get to now.

The door opened, and Aidan Helmer stepped in.

While he didn't slam the door closed, there was a rigidness in his movements that indicated he already was a tightly wound coil ready to spring at any moment.

His eyes first rested on his wife, who gazed up at him with a blank expression as she assessed his mood.

"Dinner is on the table; you must be chilled." She rose slowly, making no sudden moves, and making sure not to look too long into his black eyes.

As she moved past him, he watched her go, a dead look in his eyes before he noticed his son standing with his back to the corner. Fin froze on the spot under the cold gaze that could swallow all of his pain, all of his anger, until there was nothing left of him. He did his best not to tremble, or shiver. He knew when the man was looking for an excuse to snap.

"Kate, don't beat around the bush. Did the boy find his element?" His voice was flat, and Fin felt the sinking horror he had felt a thousand times before as he saw his mother tense behind the table.

He glared at her, then strode over to the corner where Fin stood, desperately trying to fight off the tears in his eyes.

He wrapped his hand around the back of Fin's neck, making the boy cry out as the blistering heat in Aidan's fingers seared his neck.

"Why won't you show us your element? You're Godsdamn eight years old. Proper witches show their abilities before they can walk, so why are you deficient?"

The tears were spilling down Fin's cheeks as his hands balled at his sides.

"Aidan, let him go! You know it isn't a conscious decision!" Kate dared a step closer to the man, who turned his hard stare at her, making her wince.

"Perhaps it is your fault. I knew I shouldn't have risked a child with a mutant." He released Fin, who trembled and sobbed silently, not daring to touch the blistering skin around his neck.

The man glowered down at his wife, who shrank away from him.

"Y-Your stew is getting cold." She continued backing away from him.

Aidan turned to the pot and wrinkled his nose, then turned back to his son.

"Look at you. Sniveling uselessly in the corner. I think it's safe to say you aren't a fire witch. You would actually be a man and not be hiding from your failures if you were."

"I haven't failed anything! M-My magic could be b-b-better than yours!" Fin felt like vomiting the moment the words had finished coming out of his mouth.

The look on his father's face terrified him to his core, and he had the horrible premonition that he was about to die.

His father snatched his arm, and half-pulled, half-dragged him outside, where rain had once again began pounding the soaked ground.

"Let's see it then, hm? Show me your great power!"

Fin shook as the cold seeped into his bones from the water, while his father's hands steamed menacingly instead.

"Exactly what I thought. Your tutor is supposed to be here in three weeks, and what do you have to show for it? Nothing!" The backhand that struck across Fin's face made a roaring headache appear in his head, and he clutched his stinging cheek reflexively.

"Stop it! It isn't his fault!" His mother came charging out of the house, but as soon as she was within arm's reach of her husband, he grabbed her and threw her to the ground.

Fin heard the snap, and even in the pouring rain, saw that her wrist looked wrong. He felt bile rise in his throat as his father reached down and hauled his mom up to her feet.

"Did I tell you to intervene with the boy's discipline?" He shook her, and she yelped at the pain from her wrist.

"STOP IT!" Fin shouted as his tears continued running down his face with the rain.

When Aidan turned his blazing fury to his son, Fin couldn't help but weakly think …

A home is always supposed to be safe. It isn't supposed to be like this …

"If you want this to get better, Finlay, you will show me your magic!" his father taunted, giving his mother's body another small but firm shake. Her face was screwed tight in pain, but she didn't make a sound that time.

"I SAID STOP IT!"

The young boy sensed something explode in his heart, and then felt a strange crackling on his skin. He couldn't tell if he were imagining blue lightning in the air around his father, but he couldn't focus on anything but his fury toward the man.

"SHOW ME YOUR POWER FIRST!" Aidan bellowed, once again jerking Kate, this time making her give another small cry.

"LET GO OF MY MOM!"

The charge was building, and Fin, feeling that the buzz was going to make his brain explode, let out a wordless scream.

He screamed at his father's wretched face.

Fin felt the explosion from within himself and watched as blue lightning struck down all around them, watched the blue reflection in his father's widened black eyes, all in slow motion. Fin barely saw the ancient symbol appear in front of him in the lightning, the words in the inner circle foreign to him, and yet their truth somehow became burned in his heart and mind.

He watched the symbol pulse once, and as the wave of energy released, a shield of bright blue lightning extended over their yard and cottage. The symbol rushed through his father, and as it exited Aidan's body, dragged him into the air as though on a massive fishing hook pulling him high into the sky. Shock and ire burned in the man's eyes as he stared at his son's shrinking form on the ground, as he was thrown outside of the shield into the mists, where he disappeared from sight.

Fin's mother watched from the ground, shocked, at the blue lightning bubble surrounding their land, before she squinted through the rain, and saw her son's eyes aglow with electricity, his pale battered face stretched in his ringing scream as the rain hovered just a few inches above his frail body.

Kate felt the amount of power he was exuding, felt its indomitable force, and when she suddenly felt the magic pouring out of him begin to draw away his life as well, she snapped out of her astonishment, and jumped up. She rushed to her son, wrapping her arms around him and calling out his name over and over above the roar of the rain, the crackle of lightning, and the soul-shattering scream.

The young boy's cry faded off as thunder rumbled above them, and suddenly Fin felt heavy with exhaustion … heavier than he'd ever felt in his life. He collapsed in his mother's arms onto the ground with her. If it pained her to do so, she made no sound, and Fin's eyes were already unfocused.

"Mom … is he gone? … Are we safe? Did I … Did I do … it?" His words trailed off as his head rolled onto her shoulder, his eyes closed, and his body weakened.

Kate sat on the ground breathing heavily, her exhales coming out in mists with her son in her arms. Slowly, she raised her arm with the snapped wrist, and focused pointedly. Her right hand trembled in a green glow, and the bones slowly placed themselves back together, while she fought off the nausea at feeling her insides shift and mend.

Once that had been completed, she ran her repaired hand over Fin's neck, healing the burns.

Standing with great difficulty, she hefted her son in her arms, and stumbled back toward the cottage while eyeing the shield above them that, while fading, was still present and could be felt.

"Oh, my sweet boy," she whispered into his ear as she carried him back into the dry cottage that suddenly felt warmer, even though the fire had dwindled.

Kate managed to get him into his bed, before half-collapsing at his side, and grabbing his small cold hand.

"My darling sweet boy … I am so sorry."

After that day, Fin never again felt unsafe in his own home.

~~~~~~

He awoke gasping, his eyes alight with blue lightning and his body covered in a cold sweat. Kraken sat beside him, preening his damp forehead and hair- expressing his concern for his witch. With a trembling hand, Fin reached up and petted the silky fur of the kitten.

"It's rare for me to dream of a memory ... hopefully it means nothing." He tried to soothe his aching chest from the pain that gripped it by taking deep breaths.

Kraken, becoming more concerned for him, began rubbing his face against Fin's cheek as wayward tears fell down the human's face.

"Don't worry, Kraken, if I ever have to meet that man again, I will not think twice before blasting him into the sea."

The kitten mewed in agreement.

Slowly, Fin sat up, and stared around at his kitchen that was normally organized and tidy but was now stuffed to the brim with prepared dishes and uncooked food.

"Well, I knew I was only getting a couple hours of sleep anyway, best get cracking Kraken!"

The kitten mewed again, then crawled into Fin's lap, staring up at him expectantly.

"... I think we have different ideas of what's happening right now."

Kraken's claws extended enough that they punctured through the thin fabric of Fin's trousers, and grazed his skin *slowly*, in a gentle, loving threat.

"Then again, maybe a few minutes of hanging out together isn't such a bad idea," he declared wisely.

Kraken mewed once and closed his eyes.

It was important that his witch knew that the great Kraken didn't look after him without expecting a little bum and cheek scratch in return now and then.

CHAPTER 12
BLOOMING OF BELTANE

The day had finally arrived. The Beltane festival had been a back-breaking, laborious event that had sent Fin to the edge of his patience more times than he could count, but it had finally arrived. He relished the thought that by the end of the day, he could celebrate with a *well*-deserved pint … That is, if he managed to keep his eyes open after the feast was served.

As it was, over the past three days he had perhaps been able to obtain eight hours of sleep in total, and that was being generous.

Were it not for Kraken occasionally grooming him on the floor, Fin would not have been aware of himself passing out while in the middle of cooking in the heart of the night.

He braced himself with the reminders that the meat was completed on the spits outdoors, and all that was left were the potatoes and the vegetables. The nearby vendors for the fireworks show would serve the desserts, and Fin could not be more grateful for the small reprieve.

He had decided to do a combination of herbs for the vegetables, and to keep the roasted potatoes fairly simple in order to deliver quality side dishes in a timely fashion.

By the time the vegetables were prepped for the oven, Sirs Taylor, Lewis, and Andrews looked dead on their feet, while Hannah and Peter both looked worn, but resilient.

"We are six hours away from the end, once these courses go out, don't worry about the dishes. We will deal with them tomorrow, and I doubt the nobles will be up before noon after the festivities, so we can all sleep in," Fin informed them as each member of his team members swayed on the spot.

"Nnnnooo way. My body can't move another inch," Sir Lewis managed, his words slurring together as his knees buckled.

"I know you're all tired, and you've done very well. Take an hour to nap, eat, or whatever else you need to do, but then we need to do one final stretch," Fin's voice was strained, yet encouraging.

Hannah managed to give him a weak smile, Peter gave a barely visible nod, but the knights continued to rock on the spot, despite Fin knowing for a fact that they had not had anything to drink since under his command.

That was all he could offer them, however. The moment they disappeared from his view, he'd be able to take care of most of the prep with magic; however, even *he* knew it wouldn't be quite enough to cover all that needed to be done, especially given his low energy levels. If he had been given a few hours a day alone with the proper amount of sleep, he could have easily finished everything, but with everyone coming and going, there was no way he could do that.

The small group stumbled out the door, each carrying pails full of dirty dishware and cutlery, while Hannah and Peter traipsed out with piles of carrots to peel.

Fin blinked wearily at the pile of food in front of him.

Never before had he cooked such large quantities for so long. He could feel his eyelids closing, and was certain he had begun hallucinating periodically, when the kitchen door opened.

Ruby stepped in, her face red in anger, but after one look at the man's drawn face and fluttering eyelids, she clamped her mouth closed and shut the door behind her. It really wasn't all that important that her tea was slightly late. Fin wasn't sure if he had dreamed the Head of Housekeeping coming to the kitchen, but he decided not to allow his thoughts to linger too long on the growing possibility that he was losing his mind due to exhaustion.

When Lady Jenoure entered the room after the luncheon hour, she found him chopping cabbage at a significantly slower rate than was normal for him. His eyes were glossed over as though blind to the work before him, and each movement looked labored, despite maintaining the usual precision.

Stepping forward, Annika called out to him, but he failed to hear her.

With a smile, she stepped behind him, picked up a black kettle that was already filled with water, hung it carefully over the fire, and watched as he completed chopping one cabbage mechanically, then started on the next one, still oblivious to her presence.

Annika brewed an entire pot of tea and set out a steaming cup for him by his right hand while not being acknowledged once, and she left without Fin even knowing someone had been there with him. He sipped the mysterious cup of tea gratefully, and assumed his magic had made it for him … or maybe it had been Kraken …

The parade was celebrated with birdseed and rose petals being tossed joyously into the air as the procession of military knights marched past and carriages of the inner court passed by, along with the foreign diplomats and lastly the royal family themselves.

The slightly lesser nobility waited down by the docks to board family-owned vessels that would embark on a night sail for the firework display over the water.

Prince Eric tossed candy to the crowds, while the king and queen waved to their people under heavy guard. Were it not for the queen's condition, there would only be a guard or two, but the common people understood. If anything, it only reaffirmed the king's love for his queen that he should care so much for her and his unborn child's safety.

The parade had followed after the main feast, and as a result, the castle staff had the choice of joining in on the festivities or retiring for an early bedtime.

Hannah and Peter remained resolute in seeing the fireworks, while the knights, barely coherent at the end of the feast, opted for the luxury of a full night's rest in their beds.

Fin had been holding out for his single pint once the last of the dishes had been returned to the kitchen, despite every muscle in his body screaming for a reprieve.

He had just settled outside on the grass by the eastern gardens, which were around the corner from his kitchen, and up near the rose maze of the castle, when he could hear some of the castle maids giggling with their suitors for the night off in the shadows of the flowering shrubbery, earning themselves a disapproving grunt from him.

He stood and turned toward the somewhat forbidden rose maze. While servants weren't *really* allowed in there, it was rarely ever enforced, as the staff tended to pick nighttime to explore it, which was when most nobles were already asleep anyway.

The gardening wonder wrapped around the east wing of the castle and took up nearly the entire side. It had earned its fame throughout the land for its incorporated multiple rose colors that could be viewed while journeying toward the center of the maze. Fin had heard about its beauty his entire life and wanted to explore it while the roses were in their full bloom, but he decided that it would be better perhaps when he was less exhausted.

He decided to return to the kitchen gardens wearily, while planning on staring up at the night stars in peace, when he bumped into none other than Hannah and Peter.

"Fin! Have you seen the stalls?" Hannah called, her face aglow in the excitement of the evening, and a flower crown adorning her golden hair.

"I have not, I was going to have a drink and go to bed," Fin answered slowly as he lifted the steel tankard in his hand as proof.

"Oh, but you should! It's one of the most magical nights of the year," she gushed with rosy cheeks.

Fin glanced at Peter, who shrugged briefly, and gave him all the indication he needed.

"I am quite alright, Hannah, but you two enjoy. Thank you for thinking of me." Fin raised his pint and managed a tired smile.

"At least check out the farmers' stands near the front of the castle; they have fresh herbs and vegetables!" Hannah called over her shoulder as she skipped toward the festivities.

That caught Fin's attention.

After the feasts, he needed to replenish some of his stocks, and taking a look at some of the local produce wasn't a bad thing.

The streets were lined with twelve-foot torches, and the stalls all had their finest wares out for the crowd to pick through. Unfortunately, by the time

Fin had made it to the stalls nearest the castle, they had been mostly picked through, and there was very little left to choose from.

He had just decided his aching body couldn't take any more feeble resistance to sleep and had begun his trek back up the hill to the castle, when he became crowd locked due to a group of noblewomen walking arm in arm through the middle of the road. No one dared to tell them to move or that they were causing a traffic flow problem, however, and so most of the crowd heard their conversation without a problem.

"... I know!"

"She claimed she wanted nothing to do with the festival, but then she showed up in *that*?!"

The group of four noblewomen strolling down the long sloping road were heading down toward the docks. They were giggling behind their hands, their cheeks rosy and eyes glassy from the wines and meads that they had consumed during the day's festivities.

"I think she is just sleeping around with whomever she pleases, and that's why the king hasn't married her off—she is too much of a hussy for another noble to want her."

"She has really been exploiting the king's kindness if you ask me. I mean, *as if* she is actually upset to lose Viscount Jenoure. He was seventy-five when they married! She's probably cackling that she's inherited his fortune with no brats while she's still young."

"No one wants her because she's from Troivack!" one of the girls, a young brunette noblewoman with freckles, threw in almost absent-mindedly as she scanned the crowd, apparently looking for someone.

Fin rolled his eyes. Gossips were central figures in any community, but he didn't like being bothered with their nonsense.

He was shaking his head and rolling his eyes, when he caught the rustle of a bright blue teal silk disappearing between the stalls.

Why hadn't he thought of that? The spaces behind the stalls were green fields with no crowds! He blamed his mental fatigue, and swiftly made his escape.

When his eyes fixed on the figure in the significantly quieter darkness on the other side of the stalls, Fin saw the woman he had followed draw out a long black cloak in her arms and wrap it around her shoulders, then pull the hood up over long, slightly curled hair, and Fin knew exactly who he was staring at.

"Lady Jenoure," he called softly to her back.

She didn't show any sign of hearing him, so Fin quickened his step until his long strides fell in time beside her own.

"I wouldn't pay them any heed, you know," he remarked airily while pressing his hands into his pockets.

She shot him a sidelong glance and a raised eyebrow from under her hood, then continued on in silence.

When they had made it back to the castle grounds where the land was leveled out, Fin instinctively headed toward the east wing to meander past the maze. After growing warm from climbing up the hill in the balmy evening, Annika removed her cloak, and turned to get a better view of her company under the moonlight.

Fin's breath caught in his throat when he laid eyes on her attire for the evening.

Her bright teal silk gown was cut in a wide V, exposing her flawless chest with modest cleavage, and its sleeves clung the length of her arms. While the bodice was perfectly fitted to her curvy form, the skirts were bunched up, and fell in thick layers. Her lips had been painted a deep red, and her hair left unadorned, flowing down her back. For her jewelry, she only wore two gold rings, one on her right forefinger, and another on her left index finger.

"While I thank you for your companionship in walking me back to the castle, to continue being in my presence alone could spread rumors, so if you could please take your leave." She waved him away with her hand, ignoring that his mouth had come slightly ajar at seeing her dressed up.

Fin blinked twice before placing his hands on his hips and let out a single sarcastic "ha."

"I tell you thousands of times to leave my kitchen, and you don't listen to me a whit! Now you think I have to obey you?"

Annika rolled her bright brown eyes to the starry sky above them before she shook her head incredulously.

"You keep forgetting I am a lady, and you are a commoner. You are supposed to comply with my wishes."

"Is that the kind of lady you really want to be? Ordering around those 'lesser' than you?"

"Glad to see your righteous beliefs aren't just for the male nobility," Annika interjected flatly.

Fin shrugged. "Everyone is at the festival. I just wondered if you wanted to walk through the maze with me before I fall asleep on my feet. It's the only spare time I've had in nearly a month." He nodded at the bright yellow blooms behind them that arched widely over the maze entrance.

Annika glanced behind herself, then gave him a calculated glance.

"You know more ladies have compromised themselves in that maze than any bedchamber in the castle, right?"

Fin blushed brightly.

"I— Er— N-no. I don't mean anything like that I—"

"Something innocent can easily become the cannon fodder to any woman's virtue." She shook her head, clearly enjoying making him uncomfortable.

Fin sighed. He understood it was a bad idea, and to be perfectly honest, he wasn't even sure why he had made such a ludicrous request in the first place.

I must have gone crazier than I realized.

"Alright, alright. I don't have the energy to do battle with you. I will escort you to the castle then leave you be."

"I'm not ready to head in just yet, but have a good night." She turned toward the maze when he tapped her shoulder.

"It isn't safe for you to be out by yourself, especially when you look—"

Annika turned with a bright, delighted smile on her face, as she waited for him to finish the sentence, looking incredibly amused.

"How *do* I look, Finlay?" she asked slyly.

He cleared his throat and glared at her.

"Some might say they find you palatable."

"Oh stop, I'm blushing," she teased, waving her hand.

"Women have been attacked for less," Fin grumbled at her, not appreciating the condescension.

"Ah, so is that always your role? Protector of women? You always want to be their hero?"

Fin's hands clenched and unclenched at his side, and he stared down at the grass for a moment before speaking.

"My mother used to get horribly beaten by my father," he said, his heart beginning to pound in his chest.

Annika's mirthful expression fell.

"He finally left when I was eight or so, but I struggle with the idea of someone being preyed upon and no one helping them. I am sorry if I've insulted you."

Annika gripped her fingers in front of her skirts, feeling regretful for touching on a sad subject.

"I am sorry that you and your mother had to endure that," she replied softly.

Fin shrugged uncomfortably. He didn't need her pity, but she *did* need to be safe.

"However, not all women are the prey." Annika gave a tight smile. "I grew up in Troivack, and man or woman, you were supposed to take care of yourself. My mother was from Daxaria, and while doctors say she died in childbirth, the truth is she just gave up fighting to live."

Fin's eyebrows shot up in surprise.

"Your mother was a Daxarian? But neither you nor your brother show any signs of that—"

"That's because he's a half-brother. My mother was my father's second wife. He had three sons with his first, and just me with the second. My skin is slightly paler than other Troivackians, but that is the only way to tell, really."

She folded her arms across her body gracefully as she explained her family history.

"Is it because of your mother being Daxarian that your brother's an ass to you?"

Annika's jaw dropped.

"Fin! You cannot, and *should not*, EVER say something like that. You do not know how brutal Troivackian people can be. If my brother caught even the slightest hint of your insolence toward him, you would most likely go missing 'mysteriously.'"

What took Fin back the most was that he had never seen her look so serious or ... worried.

"I can take care of myself, don't lose sleep over me," Fin managed to tease quietly, leaning down slightly to smile gently at her in the darkness, hoping to ease some of her obvious anxiety.

Annika's eyes widened, and her mouth opened and closed once. For some reason at a loss for words ...

"Do you know how hard it is to find a good cook? Luca was gone nearly a year before you came along!" she snapped finally, a light blush cresting her cheeks.

Fin chuckled.

"You were the one a few moments ago telling me that some women can take care of themselves, and I believe it, but it is also possible some peasants can handle themselves as well."

She opened her mouth to retort, but Fin was already beginning to amble into the rose maze, his hands in his pockets as he struck a leisurely pace.

Picking up her skirts with a huff, she hurriedly followed after him.

"I am not jesting, Fin, you do not know the cruelty Troivackian nobles grow up with. It's easy for them to kill a person and not think twice about it."

"If your brother tries to kill me, I promise you, he'll have more than just two thoughts about it."

As Fin walked, he breathed in the cool night air, and relished in the sweet smells around him.

"You overestimate yourself," Annika snapped in frustration, unconsciously following him to continue their conversation.

"You underestimate me."

"Why are all men equally stupid?" she muttered, more to herself than to him.

"Why are all ladies equally overbearing?"

Fin didn't need to look to feel the glare he was receiving, but he continued smiling as he walked.

"Are you … are you saying these things to anger me on purpose?" she demanded, after a moment's breath.

"Not anger so much as distract," Fin replied while remaining aloof.

"Distract? What do you— Oh. You wanted to go on a walk with me that badly?" Annika quipped dryly when she looked around them and found the beautiful blooms.

"I haven't had a walk outside in months, and you happened across my path. I've taken it as a sign that we should have a nice stroll together."

She shook her head while making an aggravated *tsk*, but Fin saw out of the corner of his eye the noblewoman try to hide her smile.

"Have I grown that much on you, or is it that you think I was bothered by the other ladies?" she queried after a few moments of them rounding another bend in the maze where pink roses grew.

"… Or the third option of: I wanted to go for a walk through the maze and thought you might want to join me?"

Annika shot him a dubious expression.

After a tense moment, Fin dared to ask a more serious question. "It's true. They don't bother you, though? The ladies?"

"I don't like them, why should I care what they think?" Annika sounded genuinely unaffected.

Fin shrugged.

"Most people care about being liked, but I'm glad to hear you're the exception."

The pair continued to walk down the path of roses, pink blossoms gradually fading into peach. Annika stopped and sniffed one before resuming her position at Fin's side.

"Do you think I enjoy your company?" she asked after yet another turn in the maze.

"You spend a lot of time annoying me for someone who doesn't."

"You just are … different. I'm curious about you … we don't usually get new staff members here. Everyone is born and dies here, so you and the handful of people who arrived around the time you did are something of a novelty."

Fin stiffened slightly but didn't comment. Instead, they found themselves staring at a dead end, the hedge towering several feet above them cradling a stone bench.

"Would you like to rest?" he offered.

"We haven't found the center of the maze yet, let's keep going." Annika shrugged with a glint of determination in her eyes.

"Have you never been through this maze?"

"Only once before with … with Hank. It was the first time we met." Her steady voice faltered.

Fin reasoned "Hank" was her deceased husband. "You seem fond of him."

"He was a good man who … who showed me how a government and kingdom of good people could work." She let out a slow breath. "I haven't really spoken about him properly for a long time."

After several minutes of amicable silence, the duo reached the crimson roses. They walked along their beautiful blooms without a word, until the flowers suddenly turned to white.

"The center should be … here!" Annika announced with a satisfied smile.

When they turned the corner, Fin found himself staring at a square section of the garden where a beautiful marble gazebo stood brightly under the moon. Small sections of lattice and benches were set up in various locations, and there was even a three-tiered fountain standing proudly in the middle of the brick pathway.

"I think I've realized why I keep telling you things I don't normally tell people." Annika's uncharacteristically quiet voice made Fin's head turn as she stared sadly at the fountain, as though lost in a once happy memory.

"Because you can have me beheaded if I tell anyone?" he tried, hoping to break some of the somber mood.

She shook her head, not moving her gaze an inch. "You look as lonely and out of place as I feel."

She turned and smiled sadly up at him, then walked over to the fountain.

Fin rubbed the back of his neck as he watched Annika walk away, eventually letting his eyes fall to the ground as he felt something begin to stir in the pit of his stomach.

He was feeling something new ... and the slightly unnerving sensation of just not knowing what it was made him all the more rattled.

CHAPTER 13
THE KING'S ILLNESS

Fin's entire body ached as he sat on the chair at his cooking table. While he had slept a solid nine hours, he knew he needed more to make up for the long stretch of time he had been without a proper night's rest.

It was alright, though, because the Beltane festival was finally over. The diplomats would leave that very day, while most of the merchant ships remained docked due to the crews and captains having been up late.

He sat cradling his cup of coffee with Kraken asleep on the stool to his right, while the very last left stool, where the prince normally sat, remained empty.

Outside it looked as though everything were peaceful. A cloudless sunny day, a gentle breeze, birds chirping ... it was the polar opposite to Fin's insides.

He was in the middle of deciding what to eat for breakfast, when the door opened a crack, and in slipped the future ruler of the continent.

"Morning, Eric," Fin called out wearily, giving the child a brief smile. The lad looked bedraggled himself as he managed a grin, and climbed into the only unoccupied seat beside Fin.

"You're the first one up?" He asked, wondering if he cared about Eric learning he was a witch if it meant he didn't have to move to get the boy food.

"Yeah ... mom is up sick 'cause of the baby, but other than that no one else is awake. It's like this every year ... last year most of us didn't even wake up until dinner time," Eric explained as Fin slowly poured the boy some milk he had retrieved from the cold hole, then tossed a few pieces of bread in his skillet over the fire.

He began whisking some eggs as well and pulling out thick strawberry jam from the cooling hole on the table, while the boy used the back of his hands to wipe residual sleep from his eyes.

"Did you have fun?" Fin queried as he moved the golden toast out of the pan and poured in the scrambled eggs.

As he buttered the bread, the smell of the eggs filled the kitchen, and Eric began inhaling deeply through his nose.

"Why do those eggs smell different?" he wondered curiously.

"They smell different because I mixed in some dried dill with salt, pepper, and a tiny bit of dried garlic," Fin explained before turning with a wooden spoon to start making sure their breakfast cooked evenly.

The boy breathed in deeply, then let out a long, contented sigh.

"It smells sooo good!" His feet began swinging under his chair in anticipation.

Fin grinned, then pulled out two plates. He loaded them up with food, and as the eggs continued steaming on the wooden plates, Fin pulled out a cantaloupe from the fruit bowl, and had it cut into bite-size pieces in no time. He topped off their plates with a bundle of crisp green grapes each and joined the prince at the table.

"You didn't answer how the festival was," Fin pointed out, picking up his fork and leaning his forearms onto the table.

"MMMM!" Eric had taken his first bite of eggs and closed his eyes briefly before hastily chewing and shoveling another bite into his mouth.

Fin waited patiently, laughing slightly to himself.

"It was good! Morgan rode on the carriage in front of me, and we got to take turns throwing candy on different sides of the road. I had the better candy, though!" Eric grinned, his cheeks so stuffed full of food he resembled a chipmunk.

"Don't choke," Fin reminded him, taking a deep drink of his coffee.

The boy abided and took his time chewing—though it was evident he had more to say.

"Did you go to the festival?" Eric returned happily, once again filling his mouth with food.

"A little bit. By the time I got there, the fireworks were going to start and the stalls were closing down, but I … I walked through the rose maze." Fin hesitated a little, his fork hovering in front of his mouth for a moment as he remembered Annika Jenoure standing in the moonlight in her bright teal dress, and her almost … innocent, expectant expression.

"By yourself?" Eric sounded surprised as he turned to face Fin seriously. "Mom and dad say that's where people go to fall in love."

"I—uh—no, not by myself. I had a friend with me." Fin was blushing and trying to hide it by shoveling eggs into his mouth.

The slow-growing smile on Eric's face filled Fin with apprehension.

"Fiiiin, you like a giiiiiiiirl!"

He choked, and immediately reached for his coffee cup.

"No, it really was just a friend! A man friend," Fin tried, but Eric was giggling so much he had turned a lovely shade of radish red.

"Fin likes a giiiiiirl, Fin likes a giiiiiirl," the seven-year-old chanted while laughing so hard that milk had started dribbling out of his nose.

"Well do *you* like any girls?" Fin decided to change the subject as he sipped his coffee with watering eyes.

Eric's laughter died down and he looked at Fin as though he were an idiot.

"Of course I do."

He gave the prince a look of confusion, before the boy threw his hands up in the air.

"My mom! So I know all about girls. Have you tried giving her flowers? My mom loves it when I give her flowers."

Fin rubbed his face, then moved his hand to the back of his neck as he stared at the young royal and debated pouring himself a second cup of coffee.

"I don't have a girl I like, Eric, but if I did, you'd be the person I'd talk to about it. That is, if you don't mind."

The prince sighed in a way that made him sound wiser than his years, and he gave Fin a look of utter disbelief.

As Fin awkwardly turned back to his breakfast, he found an unwelcome image flash through his mind of Annika smiling down into a bouquet of various kinds of bright wildflowers.

He shook his head, clearing the image away.

Seven-year-olds had no idea what they were talking about.

~~~~~~~

King Norman stood at the top of the castle steps as he watched the carriages carrying away Lord Piereva and his aides grow smaller and smaller.

Ainsley had entered into an unpleasant phase of her pregnancy where she found herself horribly ill periodically throughout the day, meaning she was exempt from the happy occasion of getting rid of awful nobles.

The representative from Zinfera stepped forward, wearing blue silk robes and long ebony hair twisted into a bun atop his head.

"Your Majesty, as always, it is a pleasure to visit your land." The man named Jiho bowed deeply and rose with a polite smile.

"On behalf of my kingdom, thank you for gracing us with your attendance of Beltane." Norman bowed politely and was ready to bid the man his last farewell, when Jiho gave a small nod to his entourage behind him. Everyone but the diplomat stepped back, until it was only the king and himself at the top of the castle entryway. Captain Antonio's posture stiffened as he stood at the far end of the long step, and several other knights stood down the steps to the ground, ready to spring into action if the need arose.

"I hope Your Majesty knows what a rare, and fortunate blessing he has in his midst." Jiho's warm eyes made Norman relax, but instead made him furrow his brow in confusion. "I happen to be a friend of a certain cook you know since many years ago. He will bring nothing but happiness to your home." Jiho bowed again, and stepped back, leaving Norman looking completely stunned.

The king didn't stop the diplomat from leaving to explain further, however, and instead mulled over the message as he watched the carriage disembark.

When the king strolled back into a far quieter castle, he headed toward the kitchen. He had a few bones to pick with the witch in question anyway.

The king stood squarely in front of the cook, his legs braced, his hands clasped behind his back.

"Why did you use magic in the banquet hall the night you were summoned before me?" Norman demanded, eyeing Fin as the man lifted a plate off of a large bowl to reveal a marinated mess of raw meat.

The king wrinkled his nose, until the smell hit him.

The sauce … was unlike anything he had ever smelled before.

"Pardon my behavior, Your Majesty." Fin bowed, his hands falling to his sides, which drew the king's attention back to the task at hand.

"When … Lord Piereva … I-I responded strongly to his attitude toward his sister." Fin knew he had made no sense but hoped the king was perceptive enough to understand.

Sure enough, the noble's stern expression softened for a moment, which Fin was unable to see as he remained bowed.

"While I understand you were under a stressful situation, you will refrain from using your magic to meddle in affairs that are not your own."

"I understand, Your Majesty. I am still learning to control my abilities in this new environment."

The king said nothing for a moment, but the smell of the marinade was beginning to become too much of a distraction.

"You may rise. However, this is your last warning. Should you find yourself unable to control such outbursts, I will force you to apprentice with Mage Lee."

Fin's frozen, unblinking expression as he stared at the king succeeded in making the ruler of an entire continent concerned.

"Your Majesty, I will respect your wishes and orders to the best of my capabilities. However … mages do not know how our magic works," he attempted delicately.

"Mages are not simply taught magic, they are also taught control, awareness, and meditation to best hone their abilities," the king defended sternly.

"Is that why Mage Lee burst in here demanding a duel?"

Fin clamped his mouth shut.

He knew he had said too much.

The king's eyes widened, and his left hand casually rested on the dagger on his belt.

Fin did the only thing he could think to do. He grabbed his skillet, dropped a dollop of butter in the cast iron, then placed it over the flames while maintaining eye contact with the king.

The king was about to interrupt the process, when Fin magically floated the thin strips of steak into the pan, and a foreign aroma that made the ruler's mouth salivate filled the room.

"What is … What is that?"

"Sire, this here is a way of cooking beef that I learned from an old friend from Zinfera. I have not been able to recreate it for quite some time; however, your foreign diplomats gifted Your Majesty spices and pastes that are grown and made in their kingdom."

Norman said nothing as Fin waved his finger, and the meat flipped over to reveal golden-tinged, fully cooked beef.

"What is it called?" Norman demanded a little too hastily.

"Bulgogi beef, Your Highness." Fin removed the pan from the flames and gestured to a bundle of lettuce leaves that rested on a plate, as well as a bowl of what the king recognized as rice and a strange reddish pile of what looked like marinated cabbage or onions.

The king's eyes were glued to the food, making Fin give a small smile to himself as he noticed the similarities between Eric and his father.

He picked up a lettuce leaf, scooped up some of the rice into it, then the reddish mix, topped with a beautiful slice of meat.

"The red stuff is called kimchi. It is a form of fermented cabbage and other vegetables, sire. It is relatively similar to the sauerkraut that the Troivackian people are famous for." Fin proffered the filled lettuce leaf to the king and summoned a tankard of ale for him.

The king gave him a dubious expression, then bit into the wrap.

It was messy.

It was unusual.

It was the king's new favorite food.

The strong flavor of beef was complemented by others that the king had never fathomed existed, the crispy lettuce added texture, and the zip of the kimchi …

Suffice it to say, the first pan of beef was quickly cleared.

"Ah, Ruby! Have you seen His Majesty?" Queen Ainsley finally found someone who could potentially tell her where her husband had disappeared to in the middle of the day.

"I am not sure, Your Majesty. I seem to recall him discussing a matter with Royal Mage Lee after the diplomats left." Ruby gave a deep curtsy, and then resumed carrying the pile of crisply folded linens up to the guest chambers.

It took Ainsley another hour, but she finally found the mage sipping tea in the gardens with Lady Emily Gauva. They both hastily stood and paid their respects.

"Lady Gauva, please excuse me, I have need for Mage Lee for a moment."

The lady did a hasty curtsy and scurried away, her blond locks bouncing in the fading daylight.

"Lee, have you seen my husband anywhere? I haven't seen him since this morning."

For some reason unbeknownst to the queen, Lee looked … gleeful at the question.

"I heard he went downstairs to speak with the cook. He must have lots to say to him." There was a strange cackle in Lee's voice that immediately made the queen narrow her gaze suspiciously.

"I hope he is giving the Royal Cook Finlay his unrefined thanks. The food he prepared was so incredible that the foreign diplomats could not stop raving about it. The sheer amount of work he has given while under-staffed is nothing short of miraculous."

Lee's face slowly fell, to an expression that was far more subdued. "Yes. He is talented."

He sounded strained.

"If you will excuse me, I am going to go see if His Majesty is still there." Lee bowed once more as the queen left the courtyard swiftly.

As Ainsley neared the kitchens, she could hear loud voices, but they weren't shouting or distressed …

Slowly, she opened the door, and when she processed the sight before her, dropped her jaw.

"It'sss the Queeeen!" Norman announced brandishing his empty tankard up as Fin gave a quick bow, and an apologetic expression.

"Norm— Your Majesty, are you ill?" Ainsley's eyes darted between her husband and the cook.

The king stood and swayed on the spot. "I … AM!" he declared, his left hand slapping his chest. "I am sick … that you are *hic* sick!" he slurred. "You … are the love … of my *life*. So … sosoSO *important*. An' you … An' you do *too much*! Ansssnow! You feel sick!" The king slumped back down into his chair as Ainsley turned slowly toward the cook.

"What did you do to him?" she demanded softly.

Fin looked petrified. "I-I made His Majesty lunch, and he had an ale … then he had … more ale. I apologize, Your Majesty." He bowed hastily.

"I will discuss this with His Majesty when he is less … ill. For now, you are tasked with getting His Majesty to his chamber without—" The queen suddenly stopped talking.

Her eyes fixed on the kimchi bowl that was almost completely empty. "What is that?" she demanded. The scent awakened a powerful craving she hadn't known possible.

"Kimchi, Your Majesty, would you like—"

The queen hastily picked up the bowl and ate the remainder. The look of bliss on her face made Fin momentarily uncomfortable.

"Would you like more, Your—"

"Yes please." The queen had not been able to keep anything in her stomach for the past three days, but somehow, this magical mana from the Gods was not only sitting well, but also satiating her completely!

He placed the refreshed bowl in front of her and then rounded the table to her husband. "Pardon me, Your Majesty, I am going to carry you to your chamber."

"Do you know where his chamber is?" the queen asked after hastily gobbling up another forkful of kimchi.

"I do not, I was hoping Your Majesty might tell me."

"We are on the fourth floor in the north wing. If you take the east wing servant's staircase up, it will be the third door on your right." The queen resumed eating the kimchi as Fin wound the mostly unconscious royal's arm around his neck, and stood, effectively hauling the man, who was quite a bit shorter than himself, up to his feet.

"Remember, cook, no one can see." Her sharp tone earned another head bob from Fin, who was struggling to maintain his balance, as the king failed to decide whether or not he could remain upright on his own.

As the duo shuffled out of the room, Fin glanced once over his shoulder, and saw the queen begin sniffing the pan with the remainder of the bulgogi beef that the king had not yet attacked. She tentatively nibbled on a piece, her eyes widened, and she immediately dove for more.

Fin made a mental note to request more shipments of the Zinferan ingredients, and perhaps some of their special soybean recipes, as he saw the queen park herself in the chair on the far right and tuck into the meal.

As soon as the kitchen door had closed behind him, Fin let out a sigh.

"Your Majesty, permission to use magic to get you to your room?" Fin requested while attempting to take several more stumbling steps.

A garbled response was all that he managed to get, but he decided that it was resounding consent.

He summoned one of the nearby tapestries off the walls, and after creating a small levitating hammock, gently guided the king to lay back. While resistant at first, the king was gently snoring before they even reached the end of the hallway.

Most of the servants were busy stripping the linens off of the recently abandoned guest beds and cleaning up the messes in the banquet halls. The queen had shown great foresight in suggesting that they take the eastern servant's staircase, as it was dark and narrow. If someone else were coming down the stairs, they would have to retreat, and Fin would have time to make it seem as though he were attempting to move a recently dusted carpet back into the rooms upstairs as opposed to the most powerful man in the country, who happened to be passed out drunk in a tapestry.

Fortunately, it only happened twice that Fin had to use the excuse. Both times the servants had respectively retreated.

He poked his head out on the fourth-floor stairwell and let out a breath of relief. The windows that ran along the left side and lit the hallway overlooked the inner courtyard, while the doors to the chambers ran along the righthand side. Candelabras and ornate wooden chests decorated the space between the doors, and as Fin floated the king in his hammock to the third door, he accidentally knocked one of the candelabras to the ground.

"JADE, I SWEAR TO THE GODS, IF YOU BROKE SOMETHING ELSE—".

Fin flung himself and the king into his chambers.

The unmistakable sound of Ruby exiting one of the doors farther down the corridor and stomping down the hallway occurring only a moment later.

After hastily laying the king in his bed, he waited to hear Ruby leave, when to his horror, he heard her knock instead.

"Your Majesty? Is that you in there?" Fin immediately surveyed the room for a hiding spot.

He quickly decided the safest place was crouched behind the king's own bed, on the side that put him between it and the wall. He dove for cover just in time as the door creaked open, and Fin held his breath as he heard Ruby give a short gasp, then hastily close the door, clearly not wanting to disturb His Majesty's slumber.

After waiting in the silence for several heart pounding minutes, Fin stood and stretched. His back cracked in multiple places, and after a relieved sigh, he strolled back over to the exit to listen.

He was certain Ruby was gone.

Upon opening the door, however, he found himself staring down at Lady Annika Jenoure.

CHAPTER 14
STRESSFUL TIMES

Her arms were folded, and her hip jutted out, as she stared at him with wide brown eyes. Her long dark hair was tied in a loose braid, and she wore a cream-colored gown that fit loosely around her body.

"Why are you in the king's chamber?" Lady Annika Jenoure's tone was deceptively innocent and unassuming.

"I ... had a task given to me by Her Majesty the queen," Fin explained as his traitorous cheeks burned red.

"I see ..." Annika continued staring up at him calculatingly. "You were told to randomly deliver a carpet to His Majesty's chambers?" she pondered aloud.

How had she known? Unless she had heard him shouting his intentions while coming up the stairwell ...

Drat.

Fin knew she was tormenting him and enjoying every second of it.

"That is exactly what I was doing. You may ask Her Majesty." He knew the queen would corroborate his story.

Annika didn't seem phased by his confidence.

"I will. Shall we go speak with her together?" She gestured toward the vacant hallway casually.

"Why are *you* here?" Fin challenged suddenly, only mildly surprised when, despite the query, she smiled.

"Why, I heard the crash of the candelabra and Ruby's shouts." She laughed. Not her actual laugh—as Fin had learned. The pretty laugh she used when hiding things.

"My chambers are at the end of the hallway, after all," she pointed out casually.

Fin sighed, feigning exasperation.

"She should still be in the kitchens. We can go together—" Fin was abruptly interrupted as a door farther down the hallway opened, and Annika responded by covering his mouth and rushing them both into the king's chamber, closing the door behind her with her heel.

Fin stared down at the woman whose face had turned calm, yet serious. There wasn't an ounce of emotion as she very clearly listened to the sounds of the corridor while at the same time studying the chamber. She noted the king's sleeping form, and the tapestry that was under him, and remained still as her confusion set in.

While Annika pondered the mysterious sight, she failed to see Fin assessing *her* while in close proximity.

Her hand was warm over his mouth, and as he stared down at the significantly shorter viscountess, he found he didn't resist the closeness even a little. The rest of the world had gone completely quiet to him as he watched her think while inadvertently …

Protecting him? From Ruby?

After a moment, Annika realized his eyes were on her. She slowly turned to stare up into the pale blue, gold-flecked eyes that didn't seem alarmed or outraged at her show of force.

Annika kept her hand over his mouth, when suddenly he moved forward, backing her into the closed door and gazing down at her. A mysterious, tenacious force he couldn't explain, and felt overpowered by, pulled at Fin. He was leaning close to her and had her fully shielded as his right palm braced against the door above her head.

He found himself somehow wishing she would use her other hand to pull him closer …

Slowly, Annika lowered her hand from his mouth, and stared up into his eyes.

The intensity of the look they shared was interrupted, however, by another knock on the very door they leaned against.

"Your Majesty, I just heard your door open! Is everything alright?" Ruby's voice pierced the air, and Fin saw the resolution on Annika's face at hearing it, as though being reminded of their reality.

"MMMNSNSNjhSn *fine!*" The lazy reply from the king, who was miraculously roused by the sound, was enough. Thankfully.

"My apologies, Your Majesty!"

Both Fin and Annika let out quiet breaths, before tensing once again at the sight of one another. After a few more moments of nervous silence, Fin dared to speak again.

"Why'd you help me?" he demanded, his voice barely above a whisper.

For some reason, Lady Jenoure couldn't find any words. "I ... I ..."

Without understanding why, Fin felt his balance become skewed, and as a result, he rested his forearm on the door, which only brought himself closer to Annika.

A weighted gaze locked them into stillness, and an undeniable electricity running through every millimeter of their bodies consumed their minds.

"Sorry, I ... it was a lot of work bringing the king up." Fin pushed away from the door and Annika, feeling ashamed that he had invaded her space and had thoughts that were far from innocent.

"Don't be. You probably haven't even recovered from the festival." Annika sported a small blush in her cheeks as she briefly glanced away from him before masking her expression.

"Why did you have to bring the king up?"

"He ... caught a small flu. I happened to be nearby. We should leave him to rest." Fin reached for the handle, but Annika's hand snaked out and gently grasped his arm.

"We need to wait until Ruby is gone," she whispered hastily.

Fin slowly turned his head to stare at Annika. Her grasp was hot to the touch, the scent of the foreign spices heavy around her. He knew he was feeling ... far more than he should toward the woman. Taking several steps back, he nodded silently in agreement before turning to look out one of the windows to the chamber.

Annika stared at his back, wondering why in the world she felt disappointed that he wasn't still inches from her body. "So does the king have the flu, or is it the ale making him sick?"

Fin whirled around to stare at her, and she tapped her nose with a small, knowing smile. He sighed in defeat. "I don't know. He just kept

... drinking. He ate a lot but drank more." Fin's voice tightened, the worry evident.

Annika glanced at the king's slackened face as he snored, oblivious to the world around him.

"His country faces war. His wife has miscarried several times and even had two stillborns ... but is once again pregnant. I imagine he has been storing up all of his stress."

Fin's face tightened before glancing at the king who struck deep fear in him. Not because he was unfair or especially cruel ... but because if a good, intelligent man deemed Fin unworthy and monstrous, he was inclined to give the opinion some weight.

He rubbed his neck out of habit, and turned to gaze out the chamber windows, which overlooked the long road that led toward the city of Austice and the Alcide Sea. The distant waters sparkled under the sun.

"Did your brother respect your wishes to remain here in Daxaria?" he asked after a moment.

"You assume that is what I want?"

Fin's head snapped around to stare at Annika, who looked deceptively angelic in her cream-colored dress. "My apologies, my lady." Fin gave a small bow and turned back toward the window. He had been foolish to think he knew anything of her wishes, or of the intricacies of court.

"I do not want to leave, and I won't. I merely need time to finalize my plan to stay." Annika's soft yet determined voice met his back, but he did not turn around.

He felt a swell of hope that he promptly squashed. What was wrong with him? She was *several* levels of nobility above him, and the most he could honestly hope for was a passionate affair that would leave him with nothing—or the knowledge that some other man was raising *his* kin.

"I wish you success in your endeavors," Fin announced in a professional tone as he turned abruptly to the door, stepping past Lady Jenoure, and exited hastily, no longer caring if he were caught by Ruby.

Fortunately, he managed to breeze through the corridor to the servant stairwell without interruption, and as he began descending the stairs, he found himself picking up speed.

Fin needed distance from the strange draw he was feeling toward Annika. *Whatever this is, it's strong, surprising, and a pain in the ass.*

Norman awoke with a piercing headache that made him moan, clutching his overheated forehead.

"Serves you right." Ainsley's tight voice made his eyes open wide, and immediately wince at the effort.

"What … What happened?" His mind attempted to connect memories, but found they were as foggy and thick as the worst of bogs. The feeling of slogging through hazy recollections only made the nausea the king felt double.

"You went to talk to the cook, and were intoxicated by mid-afternoon," the queen reminded coolly from her place at the foot of the bed, her arms folded across her chest.

Norman clutched his aching head.

"Gods, Ainsley … I feel as though I'm falling apart."

The woman immediately softened.

Her husband *never* broke down.

"There is war coming, and we have a baby on the way, but I don't want you to stress …" the king announced while he rubbed his hands over his face in an uncharacteristic show of weariness.

"We have handled worse." Ainsley announced regally.

"We have?"

The queen walked over to her husband, reached for his hand, and interlaced her fingers with his as she seated herself beside him and rested her head on his shoulder.

"Out of twelve pregnancies, I have had only one successful child over the past fifteen years," she began, her voice wavering yet firm. "We have seen droughts, rebels, and even a group attempt to kidnap our son. We will rise to the threats, and we will crush them. The Gods have prepared us for these trials."

Ainsley then turned her bright eyes up to her husband, and as the evidence of her pregnancy showed in her rounded belly, her conviction blazed in her eyes.

Norman felt like vomiting and collapsing back into his pillows, but seeing his wife so fired up made those nasty little side effects shrink away to be slightly more tolerable.

"Ainsley, we don't know how quickly they've drafted soldiers. Annika hasn't been home in two years at least. Her knowledge of their military is most likely not up-to-date, and she still hasn't heard from—"

"She will get us the information. Of that, I have no doubt," the queen interrupted, giving his hand a small squeeze.

"What did the diplomat from Zinfera have to say?"

"Jiho? He said the Zinferan Emperor is open to assisting us should a war occur but would want to build good ties with us ahead of time."

"You mean increase their trades?"

"Trades and marriage," the king lamented, reaching for the goblet of water that had been placed on the small bedside table. "He wants us to increase the amount Zinferan merchants are able to sell on Daxarian land to thirty percent, and a marriage to either Duchess Iona's daughter, Marigold, or … Annika."

The queen tensed, saying nothing.

The king sighed and immediately kissed the top of her head.

"I know you and Annika have become quite close. However, if she marries one of the chosen partners for her from Zinfera, there is a possibility that they could spend part of their time here, and the rest there to maintain a strong relationship. I'm sure the Zinferan Emperor would actually prefer to have one of his own people here, to be honest." Norman managed to make his tone hopeful, but even so, he felt his wife's tears falling as he held her, and immediately chastised himself.

"Norman, don't worry about this I … I genuinely cannot help it. This pregnancy is making me a bit more emotional is all, please don't worry." She reached up and hugged him but could feel how reticent he was to be embraced.

"So … how is it you got as drunk as Hilda?" the queen tried teasing as she straightened her posture and hastily wiped away her tears.

The king smiled softly. Hilda was the infamous city drunk in Austice. She could drink *anyone* under the table, and it was rumored that no one had seen her sober for years. Despite maintaining a slovenly appearance, the old woman never seemed to be short of coin, so she was never really deemed a hazard aside from her angry rants at times, and instead was more so thought of as a local legend.

"The cook showed me this new recipe … I have never tried anything like it before, and—"

"You mean the beef and kimchi? Oh, I know! Norman, I could *eat* it!" His wife's eyes were wide, and her excited smile warmed the king's heart.

Norman's eyes crinkled as he grinned at Ainsley. *At least that is one less worry to manage. I was troubled how weak she was becoming without food …*

He gently brushed his thumb across her forehead before speaking. "Today in the kitchen … there was something about the food, not being surrounded by hundreds of nobles, not hearing people whisper about war, or seeing how scared and tense people are …" He looked down at the floor, ashamed of himself. "I haven't felt at ease for longer than I can recall, and I can't explain how it … How I—"

The king stopped. In the kitchen, he had felt as though he were in a safe space to put aside his burdens. He'd felt warm, well fed, free to be himself, and able to just let go of his anxieties and responsibilities for one afternoon. He was ashamed of getting drunk in the middle of the day, but he couldn't deny he got the distinct feeling that he had become slightly more rejuvenated, and peaceful as a result.

Was it a spell? the king wondered silently to himself, but as he stared into Ainsley's understanding face, decided he would think about it later; for now, he just wanted to lay in bed with his wife, and sleep until the next morning.

The hooded figure stood in the thick of the forest atop their mount; dusk had settled around them, casting shadows in the thick undergrowth, and the squeaks and snaps of the bats awaking for their hunt blended in with the owl calls.

At long last, the sound of another rider stealthily approaching made the horse's ears twitch, and the cloaked figure immediately turned their head toward the sound.

"They say you never see a dragon at night," the slender man atop the black stallion called out softly.

"Its fire would burn away the night, leaving the sun to shine every hour," the cloaked figure replied, sidling up to the visitor.

"How have you been?" The man atop the horse wore simple clothes befitting a middle-class peasant. A leather vest protected his back, and a dark burgundy shirt and black pants made him slip easily into the shadows along with his short black hair.

"The earl was here." The figure ignored the question.

"I heard … did he inform you about the new chief of military?"

"He did. The threat was very thinly veiled."

"You know how Phillip is." The man visibly shuddered.

"A fire witch, then? What about their military numbers?" the figure demanded.

"Yes, a fire witch. A powerful one at that … he agreed to help win the war and brought with him other powerful witches to increase the military power. In exchange, he wants the Coven of Wittica and Troivack's Coven of Aguas all under his leadership."

The cloaked figure stilled for a long time.

"Do the Covens know?"

"I doubt Wittica is aware, but it sounds as though Aguas may already be willing to agree to the new leadership of the fire witch if he succeeds in conquering this country and its Coven."

"How many troops?"

"At least fifty thousand."

"They have fifty thousand soldiers already mobilized?!"

"This has been in the works for more than a year."

The hidden rider swore colorfully.

"On what grounds do they wish to wage war?"

"They want to monopolize the fertile land and fresh water sources. They've depleted their soils due to the king's decision to tax the farmers higher, and as a result they haven't been able to properly care for their lands."

"So they aren't even bothering to hide behind some made-up grievance to lay claim? I suppose Troivack has never been known for its subtlety."

"Oh, they *are* going to try to hide it behind something inconsequential."

The hooded figure turned slowly to better face the young man.

"Charles," the figure's soft voice called over to the spy, making him wince.

"The ... The marriage. They want the late viscount's wealth ... King Matthias and Lord Piereva are angry that the viscountess has amassed so much wealth that remains solely under her control. They wish to find a means to seize these funds so that they can do what they see fit with it." The spy looked down at the pommel of his saddle, looking deeply uncomfortable.

"Charles, you don't need to soften the news by referring to me as though the viscountess is someone else." Slowly, the hood lowered, and Annika Jenoure stared at her brother with a mix of pity and love.

She reached out, and touched his arm, making his brown eyes snap up to hers.

"I'll figure something out, don't worry about me. Take care of your wife and my niece." Annika reached into her satchel and drew out a hefty bag of gold coins.

Charles accepted the funds without being able to look in her face. Once they were stowed away, his hands kept gripping the reins then relaxing repeatedly. A sure sign that he was working up the courage to say something.

"Don't come home. Whatever you do, don't let Phillip take you back. It's become worse since he inherited the title. Dad at least knew moderation, but Phillip is even more hot-headed, and wants more of everything. King Matthias keeps giving him more and more power … but I get the idea that … never mind. It's stupid." Charles shook his head, chastising himself.

"Haven't I told you that the family stupidity went to John? Then it's Phillip, then you."

A shy smile spread on his face despite the mention of their deceased eldest brother, John. Despite being almost two years older than Annika, Charles often felt like the younger brother to her.

"I was just thinking … if in the unlikely event that Daxaria wins," Annika cleared her throat loudly.

"Sorry—the odds really don't seem great." Charles looked sheepish but made an effort to continue regardless. "If I were the king … I could use Phillip as a scapegoat for most of the shady plans. If Troivack wins, His Majesty just needs to grant him a large plot of Daxarian land and can be rid of him that way."

"Assuming, of course, that Phillip doesn't turn around and try to become king."

"Also likely, however, betrayal has always been expected. I'm sure His Majesty has a plan for that inevitability."

Annika nodded. She did not miss the constant backstabbing of the Troivackian court, or the underhanded deals, and she'd be damned if she allowed that kind of group to taint Daxaria.

"Thank you, Charles. I will ask for your help only once more before the war. Please … I know it is a great risk, but *please* find out how many witches are fighting with the Troivackian army, and what their capabilities are. If you can find out when they intend to attack, I will ensure regardless of any involvement you have in the war that you become a Daxarian, safe from the Troivackian court."

Her brother looked petrified, but after a large gulp, nodded his head.

"Until next time." Annika offered her hand, and he shook it.

No one in Troivack was a "hugger."

Annika turned her steed to return to the castle, and rode silently while deep in thought.

Once through the final row of trees, she gazed up at her home, the backdrop of billions of glittering stars making it appear magical.

You only need to look up to see the best proof of endless possibilities.

Hank's voice rang out in her mind.

He had loved the stars and would tell her the stories of the constellations as they laid in their chamber preparing for sleep. Listening to his soft voice describe the battles between angels and demons, the tricks of the fey folk, the lovers …

One of Annika's greatest regrets was that she never bore him a child he could tell the legends of wonder to. She wished someone could have heard his tales and held them with the innocence and wholesomeness they deserved, instead of being wasted on her own cold heart that, prior to him, hadn't really loved anyone.

CHAPTER 15
DAXARIA'S CHIEF
OF MILITARY

It was a bright sunny day two weeks after the Beltane festival. The king had been spending every day in his counsel room poring over maps, and numbers pertaining to the cost of a war. He had also issued the call to arms to all the noble families and their communities with young men willing to volunteer themselves for the army. Many were wary about gathering their forces when word of Troivack's intentions were little more than rumors.

"Your Majesty, your chief of military is gravely ill again," the king's assistant, a man a decade younger than the king himself named Kevin Howard informed him. The sandy brown-haired fellow had dark blue eyes, was incredibly organized, and despite his penchant for aggravating noblewomen and conservative noblemen, was invaluable to the king.

"Again? Didn't the Royal Court Physician examine him and cure him?"

"It appears the illness has resurfaced. He keeps sending food back to the kitchens demanding nothing but whiskey, and now for some reason the cook wants to speak with him."

The king blinked slowly.

"The Royal Cook, Finlay Ashowan?" he clarified.

"Yes, Your Majesty. He believes he may have an idea of what pains the man."

Norman sat down heavily in his chair.

He wondered what he had done wrong in his life to inherit the curse hidden as a blessing that was the house witch. Nobles all around the table shared concerned expressions. The idea that an uneducated peasant was trying to take care of one of their esteemed selves was abrasive to them all. Not that they knew he was at the very least as educated as a baron.

"The cook's mother is a healer. I will allow *one* meeting between them under the supervision of the Royal Physician and Mr. Howard." The king nodded to his assistant, who was puzzled over why the king appeared aggrieved by a mere cook but thought nothing more of it.

This, of course, would change in the course of the afternoon, but he had no way of knowing it.

"So I can finally meet the man?" Fin questioned tightly, as he worked on sewing a stuffed pig shut to ready it for the spit outdoors.

"That *man* is an earl and the chief of military," Mr. Howard reminded calmly while raising a skeptical eyebrow at him.

"My apologies. He is called Lord … ?"

"Fuks," Mr. Howard replied hastily.

"I beg your pardon?" Fin straightened immediately.

Kevin's mouth tightened into a thin line.

"His name is Fuks. Lord Fuks."

The corner of the cook's mouth twitched as he fought to keep a straight face.

"I … I look forward to … meeting with Lord …" Fin breathed heavily with his mouth pressed closed. "Lord … Fuks."

Mr. Howard continued looking blankly at the cook. "Finlay Ashowan, I do not recommend any poor behavior in front of the chief of military," he warned, sensing what was giving him difficulties.

The explosion of laughter that came wasn't from Fin.

It came from Sirs Lewis, Andrews, and Taylor, who were wearing aprons while hauling out buckets of vegetables to peel beside Hannah.

"You three already know his name!" Mr. Howard shouted exasperatedly.

The trio kept howling until finally, while clutching his sides, Sir Lewis managed to speak.

"W-We know! I've just never seen the cook about to lose it!"

Fin's eyes were watering as Mr. Howard threw up his hands and stormed out of the room while shouting, "You're all imbeciles!"

Fin immediately was doubled over, pounding the table with the palm of his hand as his laughs wracked his body.

This only made the knights laugh harder alongside him.

Hannah poked her head in to see what the commotion was about and became thoroughly stunned to see the knights and Fin all laughing so gaily.

"What is happening?" she asked loudly over the din.

Fin straightened, wiping tears from his eyes. "Ah, sorry Hannah. I just uh ... I just heard the chief of military's name." He placed his hands on his hips and resisted with all his might the urge to laugh again.

"Oh, you mean Lord Fuks?"

The immediate snort that came out of Fin sent all of the men back into hysterics.

"Why are men all so childish!" Hannah turned and stormed out of the doorway, forcing Fin to attempt again, unsuccessfully, to straighten and apologize. She suddenly stopped and cast a sly smile over her shoulder. "Hard to believe you are laughing that much without even knowing his first name."

Fin was already wheezing, but managed to catch enough breath to ask, "W-what is his first name?"

"Richard. Though he goes by—"

"Dick, why are you allowing a *cook* to try to heal you?"

The chief of military glowered at his son, who stood at his bedside, exasperated.

"It's my business! Now go do something useful instead of tormenting me, and stop calling me by my first name! It's 'Father' to you!" the lord raged, doubling over from the pain in his stomach.

The younger man rolled his eyes, and stood, deciding to leave his feisty father to his own devices, despite the antics being more than likely to lead to more harm than good.

Fin had been outside the door, his hand suspended in the air ready to knock, when it swung open. He found himself blinking in surprise at a man in his early thirties with thin blond hair, round spectacles, and dark brown eyes.

He looked genuinely annoyed at the sight of Fin, who was flanked by the court physician and king's assistant.

"I cannot believe the court standards have fallen so low," he spat at them before storming off past the physician, who had already been in a poor mood over his esteemed position apparently being no better than a cook's.

Fin paid it little mind as he stepped over the chamber's threshold and gazed at the rich red silk coverlet that covered the frail elderly man. The chief of military was completely bald atop his head, but the hair along the sides were wiry and stuck straight out, making him look quite demented.

"My Lord." Fin bowed. "Thank you for trusting me to examine you, I doubt this will take a long time."

The chief of military glared at him.

"The king ordered me to comply! Why he listened to a commoner like you is beyond me." He huffed and winced as his stomach clenched painfully.

Fin tilted his head and studied the man for all of thirty seconds before nodding.

"You've developed alcohol intolerance,"

Every eye snapped to the cook.

"What … What malarkey are you spouting?!" the lord spluttered.

"During Beltane you indulged in excessive alcohol, so I'm guessing you started feeling ill shortly after the festivities. Since then, you've cut out all food and resorted to drinking whiskey for your meals."

The lord was turning redder and redder in the face, while the physician stared at Fin with a look of slow dawning horror, and the king's assistant began cringing.

"When you get older your body sometimes doesn't process foods the same. You're flushed, have nausea, stomach cramps, and diarrhea?"

"I SHOULD HAVE YOUR TONGUE!"

Fin fought off the urge to smile.

"It'd be healthier for you to consume my tongue than more whiskey at this point, my lord. The good news is it isn't serious. Stop drinking and eat some plain foods at first to get your strength back. I will have some sent to you." Fin bowed as the lord reached for the whiskey glass at his bedside and hurled it at the cook.

Fin swiftly dodged it, but all three men were splattered with its contents as the glass smashed against the stone floor.

"Lord Fuks, I will have a word with Royal Cook Finlay Ashowan outside to ascertain why he is under such an odd impression," the physician ground out, while Mr. Howard pinched the bridge of his nose wearily.

"You'll have that 'word' in here! I am no simpleton; I can decide for myself how valid his reasoning is!"

The physician, a man named Frederick Durand, was short but solidly built. He had a curling black and gray beard, and dark brown eyes. He wore his black physician's robe with the white sash around his shoulders, a mark of a man at the top of his field. He faced off with Fin, planting his feet firmly on the ground.

"Royal Cook, please explain your findings."

"His symptoms and his diet. I also have a ... keen instinct on what someone's body is craving. Call it a painfully accurate hunch."

Kevin Howard was unable to stop himself from rolling his eyes and crossing his arms.

Without looking away from the physician, Fin pointed a finger at the king's assistant behind him, while his other hand remained firmly on his hip.

"Mr. Howard *wants* a bottle of red wine and toast with cheese on it. What his body *needs* is a *glass* of red wine, with a mushroom cheese omelet, and maybe a few weeks without stress. He is actually quite well balanced compared to Lord ... Lord Fuks." Fin's right eye twitched as he fought with every ounce of self-control he possessed not to burst out laughing.

The physician looked unconvinced, while Mr. Howard looked all kinds of disturbed. "You, Mr. Durand, are craving crab and white port, you are ... incredibly well balanced, actually." Fin raised his eyebrows, impressed.

The physician blinked several times.

"Mr. Howard, I can only speak for myself, but that is exactly what I am craving."

Fin looked back at the assistant, who was staring at him with a suspicious grimace.

"Mine was right as well. At least about what I'm craving."

Fin nodded.

"Do me next!" Everyone turned to stare at the lord, who clearly didn't like being left out of the discussion.

"My lord, you want whiskey because you think it makes you feel better, but your body is so horribly off balance, it actually needs plain broths, ginger tea, and mashed apple for a few days to help you hydrate yourself. After that, keep eating what I serve at mealtimes. Maybe choose more of my salads, the dishes with beets, cabbage—"

"This is preposterous!"

Every eye turned to the lord's son, who had reappeared in the door, clearly unable to withhold his opinion and keep his distance.

"You cannot possibly think of trying the health instructions from a *cook*!"

"Les, I told you to bugger off!" Lord Fuks huffed, the color in his face climbing.

"With all due respect, my lord, what do you have to lose? It is non-invasive and—wait, did you say his lordship's son's name is ... Les?"

Sensing where this was going, Mr. Howard shot Fin a warning death glare that could have melted his face.

"I am the earl's only son, and heir to his titles and land!" The man stomped into the room glowering up at Fin's face, which only made it harder for him to remain expressionless.

"Of course, my lord, I was just wondering if 'Les' were short for something. My apologies, it is none of my business." Fin bobbed his head subserviently, desperately trying not to think about the name anymore.

"Royal Cook Finlay, was it?" Grateful for the distraction, Fin looked to the old man in his bed.

"Yes, my lord?"

"Is there something wrong with my son's name? Les Fuks?"

Fin pressed his lips together so tightly that all color drained from them.

"N-not at all." He took a quiet breath through his nose before adding on, "My lord."

The old chief of military threw his coverlet off of his ghostly white legs, and stood up in his sleep shirt, clearly unbothered by his disrobed state.

"Father, don't," his son spoke out while closing the door firmly behind himself. He sounded angry, but also desperate.

"Les Fuks, you will be proud of your name," the old man offhandedly ordered while he too neared Fin, glaring up at him.

Fin glanced at the son over his shoulder. "You should care *less* about what I think."

He didn't know why he did it.

Did *not* know *what* in the world possessed him, but the snort that escaped from the physician only made it worse.

"Alright there, Big Red, tell me, do you find *my* name humorous?" Lord Fuks demanded.

Fin's face paled.

It was torture.

He was being punished for every misdeed he ever committed.

*Please don't say it, please don't say it, please—*he begged internally over and over.

"Dick Fuks?"

Fin glued his eyes to the man's forehead and took several deep breaths through his nose.

"An ... esteemed name ... for an esteemed family," he managed, his cheeks aching from the effort of keeping still.

"I am glad to hear you think so! My father Gaylord certainly knew it to be true!"

"Your father was ... Lord Gaylord Fuks?" Fin deadpanned the question the best he could, while the chief of military stood inches too short, but close enough that he could smell the man's breath.

"Yes, he was a great man. His nickname—"

The physician seemed to explode in spasms between snorts as he turned and fled the room, while Fin remained rooted to the spot, the king's assistant glued by his elbow and watching in horror.

After a long minute, Fin finally locked eyes with the lord again.

"My lord, were you perhaps ... *trying* to garner a reaction?" Fin's voice was light, but distant.

The man grinned maniacally.

"You think we don't know how ridiculous our names are?!"

Les, to his credit, was remaining remarkably in control as he had one arm folded across his chest, and his forehead pressed into his other hand.

"Your names aren't ridiculous, my lord—"

"DICK FUKS!" the old man shouted, with pure lunacy glinting out of his eyes.

Fin lost it. He was doubled over wheezing and crying on the ground.

If he was executed for this, it was worth it.

When Fin had finally calmed down and the king's assistant had finally finished apologizing on his behalf, the elderly lord crouched down to the floor, where Fin was still working on wiping away tears.

"Now you see, lad, you have just walked into my trap. You now owe me a debt of servitude for your insolence, which I will collect on my terms," the Daxarian chief of military remarked proudly, before straightening up and continuing.

"For generations of our family, fathers have given their sons difficult names, and when asked why, would say: 'Become the type of man that regardless of how ludicrous your name is, when people meet you, they wouldn't dare laugh again.'"

The lord gripped his left hand behind his back with his right as he strolled toward his chamber window.

"Of course, it's important to let people get their titters all out in the first meeting, if it is obvious that they are too immature to handle it. It is also important in life to never take oneself too seriously. Ego easily gets in the way of true success—a skill I am still teaching my son." The lord turned suddenly, and frowned at his heir, who now had his mouth covered and was shaking his head shamefully without making eye contact with his father.

"No, you see these challenges given to you by life, and it gives you the chance to get stronger! You become better, you become worthy of respect, and take your triumphs knowing without a doubt you have *earned* them."

Fin slowly stood, listening to the man lecture. The lord halted his pacing and cast a sly look over his shoulder.

"Not to mention, I doubt anyone has ever forgotten meeting me. I have become a legend in my own time, and not only that!" He turned to be fully facing Fin again, his fist raised triumphantly to the heavens.

"I have inspired people not to settle. Take what life gives you, and grow with it!"

"My lord?" Fin asked, a pained expression wracking his face.

"What is it, Cook Finlay? Speak!"

"When you raise your fist, your shirt hitches and we can see your—"

"Well, Kraken ... Lord Dick Fuks agreed to try my idea to give up alcohol, and he was right. I will *never* forget him."

Kraken purred happily as Fin scratched his cat's neck, sipping his peppermint tea in front of the warm kitchen fire. A cool breeze rolled in through the open garden door, crickets serenaded the night, and the only other sound to be heard was the chortles of the redheaded witch.

CHAPTER 16
SORTING LIFE OUT

"Ouch!" Sir Andrews cursed under his breath as he sucked on his bleeding thumb.

"You're really terrible with knife handling," Sir Taylor observed, continuing to peel the ruby apples slowly. It was another warm lazy day out in the shade, with the usual insurmountable pile of food bowls mixed among the peel buckets the groundskeepers supplied them with, as the waste would later be fed to the animals.

"I am not! I just get bored with doing this day in and day out," he snapped.

Hannah wordlessly offered a clean handkerchief, and the knight snatched it rudely from her to quench the bleeding.

Since she had confronted the king regarding their behavior, the men had decided that pointedly ignoring her was the best method, except when she specifically addressed them to do a job.

"You should kiss it better," Sir Andrews jeered.

Hannah froze. She knew the tentative peace would be tested at some point, Fin had warned her as much, and she steeled herself for the response. Peter had excused himself to relieve his intestines of breakfast, and it was up to her to say something.

"I don't like it when you say those things to me. A 'thank you' will suffice." She turned back to the apples and continued peeling them.

The other two knights had fallen silent, but Sir Andrews was in as foul a mood as ever.

"We're your betters, we don't need to treat you like some bloody fancy lady."

"Why do it if I don't like it?" Hannah's cheeks were red, and her hands had started shaking again.

"We'll treat you as we see fit!"

"You didn't answer my question! *Why*?"

Sir Andrews glanced at his fellow knights for help, only to see them watching the outburst, stunned.

"Why?! Look at you! You're asking for it, looking like that."

"But I'm not asking for 'it'! I'm asking for 'it' to stop! I can't help how I look!" Hannah's eyes were growing increasingly moist.

"Well, you need to lighten up, it's funny." Sir Andrews rolled his eyes, shifting in his seat.

"It's only f-funny if everyone involved thinks so! Otherwise, it's just m-mean!" Tears had started rolling down Hannah's face, and she hated them. She hated how she was gasping and her hands were shaking.

She stood, turned, and fled.

Sir Andrews faced back toward the bowl of vegetables, and after a small snort, kicked it over.

When he glanced back to stare after Hannah's backside running off, he instead got a face full of Peter, who had appeared out of nowhere and then grabbed him by the front of his leather vest and wrenched him up with surprising strength so that they were nose to nose.

"Unhand me! You think—"

"SHUT UP!" The roar that came from the normally near mute man rattled the knight to his core, and he promptly closed his mouth, though Sir Lewis and Taylor both stood up, prepared to help him.

"What if *I* give you a kiss, hm?" Peter kissed Sir Andrews's lips roughly, before jerking himself away. "What if *I* grab your bottom?" He released Sir Andrews and snatched his right butt cheek.

"How firm. You must be asking for my *attention* with tasty buns like these. Fresh out of the oven!"

The knight stumbled back, horrified, while Peter looked infuriated to the point of appearing frighteningly deranged.

"There. Wasn't that funny?"

"Y-You can't treat me that way, I am—"

"YOU ARE UNDER *MINE* and the COOK'S COMMAND AS ORDERED BY THE CAPTAIN AND HIS MAJESTY!"

Sir Andrews shrank back.

"A *man* doesn't make good people cry and feel powerless! He doesn't bully those without authority! He *defends* these people. He is not their enemy; he is their ally! If you terrify that poor girl and make her cry, WHICH DO YOU THINK YOU ARE?" Peter bellowed, his voice echoing in the woods beside them.

Sir Andrews had stumbled back and tripped over another bowl of vegetables. Landing hard on his recently groped bottom, he continued to try and scoot away while Peter loomed over him.

Sir Taylor and Lewis came and stood beside their friend, who remained on the ground, but they made no move to help him up. They only came to stop Peter advancing.

"I suggest you sirs consider your past behaviors and ways of thinking *far* more seriously." The aide glowered at all three of them, the fire still burning brightly in his eyes.

"Sir Andrews, if you do not apologize to Hannah on your knees, begging for forgiveness before the dinner dishes are cleared, I will report you to Finlay Ashowan, who will in turn decide whether to report you to Captain Antonio or His Majesty for violating their orders." Peter gave the man one last withering look before turning on his heel and following the direction Hannah had disappeared.

Sir Andrews scrambled to his feet, his face still white as a sheet as he glanced briefly between his two friends.

"I did not know Peter of all people could be terrifying. Where the hell did he even come from?!"

"He's intimidating, but I still say Finlay is far more frightening." Sir Taylor shuddered.

"I think we can all agree that all the kitchen staff are a little insane," Sir Lewis pointed out, giving his head a small shake.

All three knights nodded, and then glanced at all the work they had left themselves with.

"Son of a—"

Fin stared at the three sets of eyes watching him uncomfortably closely as he precisely sliced the dough on his table into several thin strips.

In the three tall chairs sat, the queen, Mr. Howard, and Eric.

Each had a conundrum that day.

The queen had just learned that she had eaten the remainder of the kimchi, and they were waiting on the fresh batch to finish fermenting over the next few days. In the meantime, Fin was having her try different dishes to see if the babe would accept them.

Eric was trying to decide how he wanted to celebrate his birthday, caught between wanting to throw a ball, or to stick with the luncheon that was customary of young nobility.

The most surprising of the guests, however, was Mr. Howard, who sat with his arms folded stubbornly across his chest, determined in his mission to prove Fin wrong regarding what he was craving.

The queen made a face as she placed down the seasoned scrambled eggs.

"Alright, no eggs." Fin nodded and shifted the plate to the prince, who was happy to dig in. "Eric, why do you want a ball?" he asked with a genuinely curious tone.

"Well ... I feel like luncheons are for little kids, and I'm going to be eight this year!" Eric explained patiently. "But I would have to start learning dancing." He made a face as Fin placed a plate of steamed broccoli down in front of the queen.

"Eric, we have put off you learning how to dance for—" The queen's face turned a tragic shade of olive green, and she bolted in an unladylike fashion for the garden door immediately.

Fin shifted the plate of broccoli from her spot over to Mr. Howard.

"Ha! I am not craving this at all!" He brandished his finger at Fin.

"Of course you aren't. You are *always* craving cheese and bread. Sometimes blueberries. Wine if you're stressed. You're going to eat *this*, however, because it's good for you, and I hate to waste food."

Fin resumed his work as Eric stuck his tongue out at the king's assistant before beginning to slip his fork into the golden, garlicky, dill-seasoned eggs.

The man deftly swapped the plates before Eric could get a bite in.

"Hey!" The prince turned and scowled, but when he saw Mr. Howard's bitter expression, burst out giggling. "Fine, you look like you need them more than I do."

Fin shot Eric a wink as he continued slicing another sheet of thin dough.

When the queen returned to her seat, Fin had a cup of ginger peppermint tea with honey awaiting her. She sipped it, and he watched satisfied when color returned to her face.

"Why is it you cannot guess what the queen is craving?" Mr. Howard sneered between mouthfuls of the best egg he had ever eaten.

"Because the babe doesn't know what it likes yet."

At this, the queen froze, the cup of tea frozen at her lips.

She slowly lowered it back down to the table with her eyes round as saucers.

"Do you mean to say that you can … sense the babe?" Her voice was a whisper, and Mr. Howard suddenly paled.

"I—uh—a little. It's probably different than what you think. This hunch of mine … I sense what others are craving as I focus on them, and I get a gist of their overall well-being and, somehow crave what they crave for a moment. Does that make sense?"

"Not at all," Mr. Howard snapped indignantly.

The queen gave no indication of her own thoughts, but the way she was staring at Finlay made him continue.

"I can tell Your Majesty is craving meat. You want beef specifically. I will next have you try a dumpling soup that I normally only make in winter, but I think the fluids would be good for you. Your child, I believe, is the one to crave kimchi. A little bit of spice and tang."

"How can you discern between the two?" Mr. Howard demanded.

"One is quieter. A smaller feeling. Given how much the queen has been devouring kimchi, however, I believe that it would feel much bigger if it were solely her own. The two aren't separate, and yet they are. One feeds the other as they work together, but trying to maintain a balance can be tough."

Mr. Howard rolled his eyes, yet for some reason the queen started weeping.

"Your Highness! I-I am so sorry if I have said something to offend you! Honestly, this stuff is just old wives' tales, it just works for me," Fin rushed making it up, as Eric casually leapt down from his seat, and walked over to his mum who immediately was on her knees hugging him.

Eric looked up cheerfully at the two men, who were both on their feet in a panic.

"Mum just cries more these days. She's fine!"

Both men stared at each other, then back at the queen, uncertain of whether or not to summon the physician or the king …

After a moment of quiet sobs, the queen stood straight, with the prince holding her hand at her side.

"I apologize for my show of emotions—I am not myself as of late. I am alright, I just at times am overcome with …" She cleared her throat, slightly embarrassed. "Eric, you and I shall discuss the idea of a ball with your father this evening. Cook Finlay, thank you for your diligence and consideration for my condition. Mr. Howard, good day to you."

Fin bowed, as did Mr. Howard, as the mother and son left, leaving Fin alone with the slightly older man.

"You *had* to spout that nonsense." Mr. Howard began rubbing his eyes wearily.

"What did I say?" Fin asked with great alarm.

"The queen has had many pregnancies, and only one child lives, you do the math."

Fin's cheeks burned. He had forgotten what Lady Jenoure had told him, and he felt like a massive fool.

"Don't worry about it for now. Her Majesty is a kind and good soul. Strong and resilient … She truly never cried before this pregnancy. Aside from times of mourning, of course, but otherwise, she is always composed." The respect the man had for his king's wife was admirable.

"They are good people," Fin added on simply.

"They are the best." Mr. Howard sighed again and reached over to the plate of broccoli. "Sadly, even you cannot make this vegetable palatable."

Fin snorted. He snatched back the plate, lathered the vegetable with butter, added salt, pepper, and scraped a dusting of parmesan cheese over the florets, then planted it back down on the table.

Mr. Howard glanced dubiously down at the altered dish, and tentatively speared one into his mouth.

The man's shoulders visibly relaxed before breathily saying, "At last! Healthy food tastes right."

"With the amount of butter and cheese on there, it is nowhere near healthy, but at least it isn't wasted," Fin reminded glibly.

Mr. Howard glowered, but still cleaned his plate. He never had to wonder why he was no longer considered the most annoying man in the castle.

Finlay Ashowan had made it perfectly clear for everyone.

Fin had nearly finished slicing the sheet of dough on his table, when through the open garden door, he saw Hannah being hugged by Peter. Frowning, he slowly rounded the table, and walked over to the door. Fin couldn't hear what was being said from where he stood and was about to go out and ask what had happened, but he froze when he saw Sir Andrews strolling toward his fellow aides.

The knight looked resigned, his blond head hanging slightly lower, his shoulders hunched and his hands in his pockets.

Peter released Hannah, and as she turned her tear-stained face toward the man who had arrived in front of them, he wordlessly fell to his knees, his hands still in his pockets.

Fin leaned against the doorframe, and folded his arms across his chest, as Kraken stepped beside him and sat at attention. He couldn't hear the exchange, but he watched Hannah cross her arms over her chest and say only a few words.

By the end of her sentence, Fin locked eyes with Peter, and the man gave him a short nod, which he returned in understanding. He made his way back to his work at the table.

"What was that about?" Mr. Howard questioned as he poured himself a glass of red wine.

How he had procured the bottle in record time, Fin wasn't entirely sure … "Just some personnel matters." He brushed off without leaving room for questions.

Mr. Howard rolled his eyes as Fin then snatched the bottle off the table, retrieved a wooden goblet from the nearby ledge, and poured himself a glass.

"Is it common for you to drink on the job?" Mr. Howard guffawed as he crossed his legs and sipped from his own goblet.

"It is when you're in my kitchen."

Mr. Howard glared. "I don't like you."

"Then get out of my workplace," Fin countered dryly as he returned to his work.

"You know what I'm craving right now?"

"You're going to be craving some new ankles for yourself if you don't make yourself scarce."

"New ankles? Why in the world would I—" Kraken suddenly leapt up and latched on to Mr. Howard's ankles using his claws and teeth. While not drawing blood, the fast-growing kitten easily broke some skin.

With a yelp, the man leapt up, shaking off the cat. "Did you train him to do that?!" the assistant demanded, outraged.

"He's a cat. You really think I can *make* him do anything?"

Mr. Howard's eyes narrowed. "I'm going to be paying close attention to you, Mr. Ashowan."

Fin looked up with a flat expression. "Pay closer attention to your job. If you bother me, I will serve everything *but* what you crave at all mealtimes."

The look of horror on the man's face nearly made the witch laugh.

"Excellent. Now that we understand each other, goodbye."

As Mr. Howard began storming out of the room, the assistant suddenly paused. "Oh yes. The reason I came down here to begin with was because Lord Fuks is gifting you a window as thanks for helping him."

"A window?" Fin blinked in confusion as he stared at Mr. Howard, who did not look in any way pleased.

"Yes. One that opens."

Fin's jaw dropped. The world suddenly became a bright and beautiful place ... and that bright beautiful place would soon have a breeze in the normally stifling kitchen the witch called home.

CHAPTER 17
SUNDAY WOES

F in stared at the glass door with a wrought black iron frame and
handle, stunned.

Every Sunday afternoon he had gone to help the botanist of the
courtyard glass tower as ordered, and he had always found a sign on the
door telling him his services were not needed. Today, however, there
was no message.

Upon slowly entering the tower, having never set foot in it before, his
jaw immediately dropped.

Plants grew above him as tall as any forest. Some of them spanned the
entire height of the tower, which surpassed the highest turret of the castle
itself. Trees and other vegetation thrived in the warm, moist environment,
and as Fin stepped in farther, he saw insects buzzing around massive
flower blooms that he had never seen before. When he looked upward,
he saw the multiple rings of open balconies with wrought iron banisters
that climbed up the entire structure. Each floor appeared to carry various
different types of plant life.

The glass on the exterior of the tower was opaque, and while Fin had
expected pots of dirt and green shoots, and gardening tools, he could have
never fathomed its true wonder.

"Hello?" Fin called out, his voice echoing into nothing amongst the deep green leaves.

"Are you Finlay Ashowan?" The response was a male voice that Fin was unable to identify but that seemed to come from somewhere above him. There was something else in the air, though ... some kind of power ...

"I am. I was asked by the king to help for an hour on Sundays."

"Tsuk. Of course. I suppose I'll use you today." The man made a halfhearted tut.

Fin turned around fully, but still had no idea of where the voice was coming from.

"This place is incredible. Is that a lemon tree? I've only heard about them from—"

A figure thudded to his left while his back was turned, falling from one of the balconies above. Fin only saw the gleam of the blade, but sensed the vast power behind him, and automatically lightning flickered in his eyes.

As he faced off against the mysterious man, Fin found himself staring at a swell of green energy, and vines that moved of their own accord.

As they stared at each other, Fin studied the man at the center of the supernatural activity before him. He appeared to be in his late thirties, with ebony skin, long locs, a cream tunic shirt, tan pants, and bare feet, and was crouched down close to the ground with a dagger in his right hand, as though ready to spring into action.

Fin's lightning began striking down on the ground around them in the face of the obvious magic, but as they locked eyes, every threatening magical movement dissolved between the two men.

"You're a witch," the mysterious botanist announced, his tone indicating respect.

"I am. As are you. An earth witch, I take it," Fin replied, standing straighter and feeling himself become more wary.

The two men evaluated one another for a moment.

"A fire witch?" the botanist asked, his face a mask of tension.

"No. I'm a house witch."

The botanist wore a strange distant smile as he studied Fin with renewed interest.

"You are one of the chosen."

"Pardon?"

The botanist straightened and cracked his neck by first rotating it to the right, then the left.

"In my culture, we are of the belief that what Daxarian people call 'mutant' witches have come into existence due to the evolution of society and its changing needs. We call these pioneers the chosen ones. Witches are the ones responsible for maintaining balance in the world between nature, and people. Although now, there is more to it, especially as some traitors of our kind seek to destroy the balance."

"... I guess that's better than being called a deficient witch," Fin managed slowly. The botanist's power was palpable, and while his dark eyes seemed to glow, there was something wise about him.

"I have heard that is how most of your people in Daxaria think of your kind. However, back in my homeland, it is a very different story."

Fin could feel the immense power flowing from the man, and couldn't help but feel curious ...

"How did you end up here?" he asked, glancing around the impressive glass tower.

"A merchant tried to sell me to the king."

"Tried?"

"If you have met our ruler even once, you will know he does not ever accept slavery. The idiot merchant was hanged for his slave trading, and as a result, I offered my expertise to His Majesty."

"He knows you're a witch?!"

"No. I have kept that hidden during my fifteen years here. When I was captured and delivered here, I had been heavily drugged, so my abilities have not ever been apparent."

Fin felt ashamed. He had barely lasted a month before being discovered ...

"You aren't friends with Mage Lee, are you?" he asked feebly.

"The overpaid man who is more qualified to be an actor than a 'magician'?"

Fin let out a sigh of relief. "Oh, thank the Goddess. My name is Finlay Ashowan."

"Ashowan? Are you related to the great Katelyn Ashowan?"

"She's my mother, and you are?" Fin redirected the conversation pointedly.

"Please call me Kasim. Tell me, please, is it true you are the sole child of a mutated witch and a pure fire witch?"

He wanted to be sick. He liked the man in front of him already ... but he hated hearing his history recounted. Especially given how the details were often smudged.

"It is," Fin managed shortly, his voice hoarse as he tried to strategize how to end the conversation regarding his parentage.

"What is a house witch, exactly?" Kasim queried instead, his awe undisguised, which made Fin feel all the more discomforted.

"I ... I ..." He began clenching and unclenching his hands. He could hear the taunting of his peers from times past, could hear the ridiculing of the children on the island ...

His cheeks burned, and his shoulders hunched. He had come this far to avoid this kind of relationship.

"I would prefer to keep it private."

Kasim stared at him skeptically. "You act ashamed, friend. Why is that?" he pondered, inching closer.

"Please, I don't want to talk about that. The king assigned me as your aide, how can I help?"

Kasim continued to stare at him gravely, assessing the slightly younger man before him. "Why are you embarrassed as a chosen one?"

Fin could've cursed. The man was just not letting it go!

"I am not very powerful. Why are we dwelling on it?"

Kasim laughed, a hearty boom of a sound. "Finlay, I felt the *small* burst of your ability, you are *not* a weak witch. If you ever said that in front of my son, you'd be biting your tongue."

He didn't know why, but those simple words choked Fin.

"I am weak, though. I can only do things to promote peace."

"You think that is weakness?! Kingdoms go to war not because they are strong, but because they are weak! Peace is strength, Finlay. You are far stronger than you know. I feel it. I feel it in my chest, and in my belly," Kasim pounded his stomach with a firm fist. "Just as I feel my son and daughter will be fortunate. I feel you will have a great destiny, and I am never wrong. I feel the earth in its slow but strong movements every day, and I know when it will shift for greatness."

Fin didn't trust his new friend's words. Didn't trust the alleged "destiny" forecasted for him. He knew all he was was a peasant. A peasant that was a copper a dozen, with a skill for food, but no bearing on the land, and that was okay. To be normal was a greater wish than many knew.

"Come, you will help me with the lemon trees today." Kasim had at long last decided to move on from the discussion, as he strode forward confidently and beckoned Fin with his index finger.

"Believe it or not, somehow you are not the craziest person in this castle." Fin called out as he slowly snapped out of the stiffness of shock.

Kasim laughed. "I see you have met Lord Fuks already."

~~~~~~

Annika remained on her knees before the King and Queen of Daxaria as she gave them her report. They were in the king's bedchamber, with the noble couple standing with their backs to the windows as Annika knelt and informed them of what was to come.

"You are absolutely certain that it is fifty thousand soldiers?" the king inquired, attempting to keep his voice level.

"Yes, Your Majesty. According to my brother, this has been in the works for more than a year."

"Why is it we have not heard of it sooner?" the queen demanded.

"It is my guess that they trained these soldiers in several smaller groups throughout the land to not raise warning signs." Annika kept herself bowed to the couple.

"Can we manage this war, in your opinion, without Zinfera?"

Annika raised her eyes only slightly.

"Over-preparedness is better than under-preparedness," she worded delicately.

"In other words: you believe our armies ineffective against them?"

"That is not what I said," Annika remarked, bowing her head even closer to the floor before continuing.

"Troivackians will slaughter whatever stands in their way. They are remarkable soldiers and will not delay in their pursuit of what they want. Your Majesty's propensity for fairness and kindness will be used against you, so we will need a remarkable strategy." She raised her head slightly to gaze upon the king and her friend. "Sadly, we do not know at which port they will first attack, nor the extent of power they wield through their witches."

"We can rule out Sorlia City, as it is on the west side of our continent, and there is no way we wouldn't notice warships entering their waters. Rollom is too far from the castle in the south, not to mention navigating through the islands would be difficult. It is far more likely that they will attack Xava or Austice to wage war first," the queen reasoned aloud.

The king stroked his beard thoughtfully.

"We need Zinferans to cover Rollom, and Xava, while we focus sixty percent of our military on Austice. The remainder should watch Sorlia, just in case," Annika announced confidently.

Both the king and queen shared an uncertain look.

"That is relying heavily on the Zinferans. We are asking them to defend two out of four port cities."

"With all due respect, Your Majesties, my bet would be that the Troivackian king is too impatient to wait for ships to reach Sorlia, and while he may land a few ships in Rollom, he will focus his attack on Xava and Austice in order to capture Your Majesty and the castle."

The king didn't dare look at his wife, he couldn't bear it.

"Lady Jenoure, are you aware of what joining an alliance with Zinfera will cost?"

"Increased percentage of trades, Your Majesty?"

"Yes, and marriage contracts,"

The lady stiffened. "We made a deal, Your Majesty."

"I'm aware, viscountess. We either convince Lady Marigold to a marriage with a Zinferan, or you. They have two suitors they would like you to meet with."

Norman did his best to ignore the way his wife nervously gripped her hands over the bump of her belly. He knew there was no avoiding what needed to be said and done, but it didn't make the heartbreak any easier.

"I see ..."

Annika didn't know why, but the annoying face of Finlay Ashowan flashed through her mind. The way he had leaned forward and smiled at her in the darkness of the rose maze burned in her mind. Then there was the magical charge she had felt when he had been inches from her body in the king's chamber ...

"Annika?" The queen's voice broke through her distracted thoughts.

"I will go through the official marriage offers for the most advantageous choice. Wasn't the prince planning on throwing a ball?" Annika knew she was grasping at straws, but she needed time to think.

"He is, yes."

"I will make a decision afterward—assuming one of the suitors is acceptable. If I suspect anything suspicious of them, I will use the ball as an opportunity to ... investigate. If possible, Your Majesties, perhaps the prince's party could be a masquerade. It'd make it a little easier to hide in plain sight."

The king and queen shared another telling look.

"You are aware the flood of ... noble births that follow masquerades, yes?" Ainsley asked delicately.

"More noble births are a happy added consequence to my finding an advantageous marriage partner in time for the war, no?" Annika countered, feigning unawareness that the king was worried about the amount of bastards that were often conceived at such events.

The queen glanced at her husband, clearly stressed. She didn't like this one bit, but they had no choice.

Lady Marigold was a spoiled brat, and even if they forced her to marry, the odds were that she would insult her groom's family so severely that a whole other war would break out as a result.

"It is decided. The day after the masquerade, you will decide who you will marry."

"Not publicly, but to Your Majesties," Annika clarified carefully.

"Of course!" Ainsley exclaimed, earning a cautious expression from her husband.

"Annika, I know this is hard, but if there are any of the nobles here in Daxaria that could make you happy, please let us know," the queen encouraged, regardless of the king's apprehensive glances.

Annika stood, and immediately dipped into a graceful curtsey.

"I told you when Hank died, Your Majesty, there is little chance I will find luck in love again. I only wish to better serve the kingdom."

"Thank you, Lady Jenoure, you are excused." The king had an odd emotion on his face as he stared at the woman, and he continued to have an unreadable air as she exited their chambers.

"Please, Norman … Please don't force her into a loveless marriage," Ainsley begged. The queen knew she was being idealistic, and that she shouldn't have such lofty hopes. Yet she couldn't give up on the idea that her most treasured friend could find her own happiness.

"Whatever is meant to happen, my dear, will happen. We must simply accept what comes. However, if I have learned anything about Annika, it is that things will go in her favor if she has any say in it."

Fin was in the middle of preparing dinner, and he was enjoying being able to use his magic without restrictions, as his aides remained outside washing dishes.

Everything was just about set, when out of the corner of his eye, he noticed a dinner roll slowly inching off the table.

When he snapped his head to see what was happening, he saw Kraken with a dinner roll larger than his head in his mouth.

"KRAKEN! GET BACK HERE! SON OF A—" The garden door opened then, and in stepped a young man with long, tied-back blond hair and bright blue eyes, wearing gray robes and carrying a thick stick in his hand with a crystal embedded in its top.

"... Mage?"

"Hello, my name is Keith. I am the son of Royal Mage Lee; where might I find him?" Fin blinked several times, the theft of the dinner roll long forgotten as he stared at the young man before him.

"I will need more proof than that before I give you detailed information," Fin announced, despite not having a shred of a doubt that the young man in front of him was who he said he was. The eyes were the same as Mage Lee's, and he was very obviously trying to appear "mysterious" and "magical."

Fin already didn't like him.

"Very well. Send for him. While I wait, I will have a cup of water, and a tankard of ale. Your finest meat I expect as a side dish."

Fin stared at Keith blankly as he entered the kitchen and sat in one of the chairs in front of his table. "Only authorized personnel can sit there. You can wait in the garden until I hear that you are who you say you are."

"Come now, as a servant you should show proper etiquette for esteemed guests."

"Go to the front gates and ask the guards, then." Fin resumed cooking while waiting for the massive pain in the ass to leave.

The young man sighed as he rose and drew the stick with a rock out of his pocket.

Fin gave him a flat expression, and a large sigh. "Are you about to draw fire on a civilian in the *king's* own castle?" his lazy tone only aggravated the young man further.

"Cook, there is no need to be stressed by my greatness. As a prodigy of my craft, I make a point of being more understanding of lesser beings, I was merely going to alert my father myself that I have arrived."

... A prodigy of what? Being conceived and born? Because I cannot fathom how a woman was attracted to your father as a mage ...

"As a child of two mages, I have the natural inclination to—"

"... Make long-winded speeches that go nowhere, yes I'm aware. Either wait outside or go speak to the guards at the front." Fin chopped his blade over the bundle of herbs on his table loudly.

Child of two mages ... I never thought I would have to live to see the day ... Do I want to keep living now that I know such a creature exists?

"Look, you don't need to feel timid in my presence. I know what you're thinking."

He paused his intense chopping of herbs.

"You're thinking you would have never lived to see the day where two mages produced another one of their kind," Keith sighed knowingly.

Fin looked at the young man, alarmed. Had the mages learned how to read minds? He knew they were a blasphemous people but to go so far—

"I know that I can be intimidating, but you don't need to chase me away because you're afraid. I promise, if you gain the privilege of meeting my father, you will see we do not harm innocent people."

Fin's deadened, expressionless gaze made Keith shake his head in a way that was both an attempt to be humble and slightly ridiculing of the plebe before him.

"Tell me, how old are you?" Fin demanded as he put his knife down and placed his hands on his hips, his expression hard.

"Ahh, trying to humanize me as a performance of the archaic show of dominance through age. Either way, my age of twenty-four has no bearing on— What are you doing?"

Fin had rounded his cooking table, pinned Keith's shoulders to his sides, making his wand clatter to the floor, and began ushering him backward out of the kitchen.

"If you are twenty-four then that means you have at least one more year to complete your mage studies. Which means you are prohibited from using your magic outside of school unless under the supervision of a recognized mage by the Academy of Wilton. Just wanted to check that you were powerless to stop me escorting you out." Fin's steady stream of explanation didn't falter while the young man balked at being physically removed from the kitchen.

When they reached the threshold of the garden door, Keith tripped backward and landed flat on his back.

"Go around the castle until you reach the big doors. That's the entrance. And take your stick with you." The wand landed firmly on the mage's chest from within the kitchen. Then without any hesitation, the door closed in the young man's face as he sat up.

While spluttering on the ground, three massive men appeared over him. Keith visibly shrank back as the newcomers, who were *clearly* all hardened knights, as they all carried ... Peeled vegetables?

"You annoyed the cook, didn't you?" one of the men with brown eyes and blond hair stated more than asked.

None of them seemed at all surprised or interested in the stranger on the ground and instead carried on their way, entering the kitchen. They didn't even pause when they stepped over him and closed the door firmly behind themselves.

"I suppose he was a little too frightened by me ... mother did say this would happen. Uneducated folk resort to violence so quickly when faced with an unknown great power ..." Keith stood and dusted off his robes. "I will just have to help him understand." He sighed and redirected himself to the front doors. He would ask his father perhaps on some pointers to help educate the rude cook.

CHAPTER 18
UH OH

The castle was strangely quiet for once, with the king having left for a brief reprieve from planning for war to go out on a short hunt with most of the knights, Physician Frederick Durand, Mage Lee, and Mage Lee's idiot son, Keith. After packing the party some fruit, dried meats, and a few root vegetables that wouldn't rot quickly, Fin found himself having a significant amount of free time to himself. The mages, fortunately, had not reappeared since the day Keith had arrived. Fin guessed this was because Mage Lee had wisely steered his offspring away from him. As a result, Fin was more relieved than he could say.

The ladies in the castle ate significantly less than the men, and with the heat of summer rising, no one really wanted to feel bogged down with extra food.

Fin had started taking it upon himself to go down to the creek that ran by the east side of the castle in the woods and dip his bare feet in the cool waters. He did this once lunch was served and would spend an hour or two in the quiet shade, listening to the various bird calls and occasionally closing his eyes for sleep. Kraken would prowl around the undergrowth searching for mice and chipmunks to play with off farther down the beck, but would come when Fin called him.

On the third day of the hunt, Fin was preparing lunch and eagerly await-ing his hour of solitude, when in walked none other than Annika Jenoure.

Fin was in the middle of rolling out dough for a pie, his hands covered in flour, and a thin sheen of sweat settled on his brow despite the garden door being propped open. The new window that was to be installed wouldn't come until the following week, and he could hardly wait. Were it not for the plates magically fanning him all morning, he would've most likely needed to bathe several times a day from the heat.

The dishware, sadly, had returned to their shelves the moment Annika had stepped behind the kitchen door.

"Good morning, Fin," she greeted, giving him a tentative smile.

He stopped what he was doing and bowed.

"Good morning, Lady Jenoure."

He didn't see the look of shock and mild revulsion on her face as he did so. Once he straightened, she had schooled her features into a mostly blank expression, though the glint of worry in her eyes was still clear.

"I haven't seen you much lately, are you avoiding me?" she teased slightly, walking over to the mugs, picking up a cup, and then seating herself in the middle chair in front of Fin.

"No, my lady, I have been working here. I apologize if you feel as though I have slighted you."

"... You're scaring me with your proper manners," Annika declared with flat trepidation.

"I am sorry for causing you alarm." Fin bowed again.

Annika continued staring at him stunned before blinking several times and forcing herself to look away. She withdrew a flask from her emerald skirts and filled her cup eagerly. Her hair was loosely piled at the back of her head, and as usual, she wore little jewelry.

"Alright, who are you and what have you done with our beloved cook who can, in a single sentence, infuriate a room full of people to the point of violence?"

She took a deep drink from her cup when he didn't answer, and sud-denly began undoing the ties of her sleeves that attached them to the bodice of her gown.

Fin turned away from her, putting his back to Annika.

"Would you like me to leave my lady to provide you with privacy?"

"Good Gods, Fin, it's boiling in here, I was just going to remove my sleeves. Are you going to be as stuffy as the nobles about that?"

"My lady, it is improper for me to—"

"Knock it off. What in the name of the king's pointy beard has gotten into you?"

Fin didn't reply, and instead headed toward the closed castle door, still refusing to look at Annika.

She was suddenly in front of him, her palm pressed against the door behind her back, her brown eyes gazing up at him in an expression Fin couldn't understand any more than the speed with which she got to him.

"I'm sorry; if you want me to leave my sleeves on, I will. Is something wrong, though? You're acting really—"

His heart was racing with her standing so close, but if he reached for the handle, he would be even nearer to her. Yet if he stayed ... he wasn't sure what he would possibly betray.

He took the risk and snatched the handle; he saw in almost slow motion her eyes widen in surprise, and the immediate arrival of a faint blush on her cheeks as Fin was close enough that she could smell him.

He definitely smelled of sweat, and flour, but underneath all of that ... he smelled like herbs. He smelled like garlic, mint, rosemary, lavender ... How was that possible, and why did it smell good?!

The door opened a crack, but before Fin could finish opening it, Annika pushed it shut again, her mouth hardening.

"Stop it," she demanded. "I don't know what's wrong, but I thought we were becoming friends." The hurt in her tone struck at Fin, and it made resisting her all the harder.

"With all due respect, my lady, how can a viscountess be friends with a commoner? I would not want you to suffer hardship for having ties with myself."

"Isn't it more suspicious that you don't treat me like everyone else, and what does it matter if we're friends?"

Fin was going to lose control at the rate his heartbeats were rattling his mind, filling it with images and urges he hadn't ever experienced so potently.

"I don't want to be your friend," he finally said, his voice somehow sounding calm and in control. "Pardon my rudeness, my lady." He bowed.

"Oh." Annika looked stricken for a full moment, before she lowered her gaze, embarrassed. "I'm sorry. I didn't realize you had been serious all this time about my bothering you. I formally apologize, Royal Cook Finlay, for making your job more difficult." Without lifting her eyes to him, Annika curtsied, and promptly exited the room.

Fin straightened, and stared at the closed door for several minutes, lost in thought, then began rubbing his neck as he turned back to his work, only to find Kraken sitting in Annika's empty chair, glaring at him.

"I was going to bloody kiss her at that rate! It's for the best. It isn't like anything could happen, or that she's even interested in me. She's just a bored noble not used to someone not giving her her way."

Fin did his best not to stare at his cat, who remained rooted to the chair the rest of lunch, his judging stare relentlessly boring into his witch's face.

It was in the middle of the night when Fin's eyes snapped open.

Someone was in trouble.

He could feel their terror … their weakness …

Sitting up, he gazed around the room in a panic.

Calm down! Think … you can only sense those that also live in the space you call home. Your "home" has to be rooms you've visited or grounds you've visited in the castle … That means, the kitchen, the servants' hall, the banquet hall, the glass tower …

Fin began recalling all the places he had visited in the castle, and who could be in them at the late hour.

The rose maze? Possibly … perhaps Hannah is in trouble, or perhaps Lord Fuks, or …

Fin's blood ran cold.

The queen. The baby. The king's chambers.

Fin was on his feet and running.

He made it up to the fourth floor in record time, his heart pounding.

He stood in front of the door, ready to burst in, when he found himself petrified to the spot.

If I burst in there and the queen is fine … I could be imprisoned—or hanged. I would be seeing the queen in a disrobed state and bursting in on her while she is in a delicate state. It could be seen as an attack. Fin's hand hovered over the handle, caught in his indecision.

"Move and I will shove this knife through your heart."

He froze. He could feel a sharp point in his back, but he knew that voice. He knew he didn't need his magic.

"Lady Jenoure, thank the Gods. I think the queen is in trouble, could you please check on her." Fin breathed beyond grateful for her sudden appearance.

"Why in the world would you think that?" Annika hissed, the knife tip piercing his shirt and touching his skin, making the spot on his skin itch uncomfortably.

"I ... I had a dream. Please, I can turn around and head back to the stairs, but could you check on her?"

Annika didn't say anything for what felt like eternity as Fin's heart continued to race erratically.

"I want you to slowly raise your arms above your head, then turn to your right, and stand by the servant stairwell."

He did his best to move slowly, but it was difficult not to be more panicked.

He followed her directions, however, and at long last Fin turned and saw Annika in the moonlight that poured in through the windows, standing in a gauzy white chemise, her long hair unbound.

He gave his head a quick shake. It was not the time to notice these things ...

Annika pushed the chamber door open, and Fin could see from where he stood that there were still candles lighting the room, and in their light, he saw the look of terror on Annika's face.

"AINSLEY!" She ran into the room. Fin couldn't stand by anymore; he dashed into the chamber and took stock of the sight.

The queen was curled on her side on the floor, arms wrapped protectively over her belly. Her face was screwed in pain, and as Fin neared, he saw the blood. Annika was crouched over her friend, speaking softly and hurriedly to her.

Years of working with his mother snapped into focus in an instant. "Annika, go get the physician, I don't know where his chambers are." Fin rushed over to the pitcher of water on the bedside and snatched one of the clean white towels that were folded beside them.

"He's gone on the hunting trip and won't be back until tomorrow," she breathed, the fear in her voice rising.

"We need a physician immediately, get Ruby to send for someone in Austice. I don't know where her chambers are either." Fin dropped down beside the queen, who still hadn't said a word, and began applying the damp cloth to her head before he scooped her up in his arms, and with a strength he normally did not possess, carefully managed to get her into the bed.

Annika fled from the room, and once she was out of sight, Fin made every flame in the room a bit brighter. He gently began wiping up the blood that had somehow smeared on her cheek, and whispered prayers to the Goddess.

"Is ... the babe ... dead?" the hoarse, gentle voice of the queen asked, and Fin felt his chest constrict.

"I cannot say, Your Majesty."

"Can your magic save ..."

He froze. The king had told his wife his secret, and one of his many fears about people knowing came true in that moment as he stared down into the queen's desperate face. Right then, she wasn't the ruler of a country, she was just another petrified woman and mother, fearing for the life of her unborn, and it tortured Fin.

"I ... I can't do anything here. I've seen this before only because of my mother."

"Oh Gods ... Oh Gods," she whispered in agony as tears flowed under her closed eyes.

Fin dropped to his knees beside her and gripped her hand. "Your Majesty, we are going to get you help, I promise. It isn't over yet; you need to hang on to whatever hope you can."

"I-It's been too much. I can't lose ... another one ... what hope is there?"

"You have to. You have to for this baby." Fin could feel his magic flow to the queen. He knew all he *could* do ... was offer the feeling of warmth that came from being in a loving supportive place. He knew the value of being surrounded by peace, even when the moment felt anything but peaceful.

"I cannot, it's happened too many times," she wept, gripping harder on to Fin's hand as another wave of pain flooded through her.

"Then I'll help. You're not alone, Your Majesty, and I think there's a chance things could be alright. You and the king inspire more than enough hope in me, I can definitely share some."

For a moment, the queen cried harder, her free hand rising up to cover her eyes as she sobbed.

"Your Majesty, please don't distress too much if you can, it can make it worse," Fin pleaded not sure how else to say it. He couldn't fathom her fear and grief, but also had seen enough times on the island with his mother, how getting even more worked up could be the difference of success and failure.

"Ask me anything, and I will tell you the honest truth." Fin tried desperately trying to draw her away from the sinking pit of grief.

She gave a few small gasps and lowered her hand from her face.

"Please, if you are anywhere near as stubborn as Eric, we can do our best to hang on to any sliver of a chance that things could still turn around."

"He gets it from his father."

The knee-jerk response made Fin smile desperately.

The queen took a deep steadying breath and continued gripping his hand. "I wish Norman were here." Her voice broke, and Fin could tell she was about to dive deeper into a place he couldn't reach, unless he intervened.

"Ah, sorry, I know I am not as captivatingly charming as His Majesty, but I promise I do have a couple good stories at least."

The queen cast an accusing glare at him for his jesting at such a time, before softening her tense expression slightly. He saw the flicker of determination in her eyes revive itself, and he dared to breathe a little more.

"Tell me these stories, and let's see if they are as good as you seem to think."

Fin smiled, gently took the cloth from the queen's forehead, and dabbed her tear-ridden cheeks. "Well, there is the first time that Kraken stole an entire loaf of bread I'd made for Your Majesty's supper."

The adrenaline-fueled chuckle mixed with gasps that erupted from the queen made Fin smile, and so he continued his story.

"Finlay, did you say *the first* time?" the queen asked suddenly, turning her watery gaze to him.

"I did indeed."

"How many times has it been?" Her face suddenly screwed in pain again, and Fin allowed her to crush the bones in his hand, ignoring his own pain, and when it looked as though it had eased away, he answered.

"It's been four times, Your Majesty."

She laughed again. She was far weaker than her usual self, but at that moment it was the best they could ask for. Even so, Fin was asking the Goddess for a hell of a lot more …

CHAPTER 19
EVERY CAT HAS ITS DAY

The faint light of day permeated the corridor outside the queen's chamber, where Annika paced, wringing her hands. The physician had arrived two hours after the call had gone out. When he had entered the room, he allowed Fin to stay to help keep the queen calm, and since then, not a sound had left the chamber. The fastest messenger in the castle had also been sent to find the king's hunting party, perhaps a three-hour ride away.

Ruby had sprung into action and had the most capable maids take over for Fin's cooking, though she still wasn't clear how he had become involved in the whole ordeal. A constant stream of boiling water and towels had come and gone into the queen's chamber as Annika continued waiting for the king to come.

It was a cloudy day outside, and the threat of a storm seemed imminent, forcing Annika's worry that the king's delay in returning would triple.

The first roll of thunder outside was nearly completely drowned out, however, by the commotion Annika heard coming from the end of the corridor. She thanked the Gods as she heard the unmistakable voice of the king approaching.

When he came into view, she could see that he had ridden hard to get to his wife's side; he was splattered with mud and his hair remained in complete disarray.

"What's happened?" he demanded once he was in front of Annika, his eyes flashing.

"We found her on the ground, and—"

"Who is 'we'?"

"Fin—Finlay Ashowan the cook. We found her when we did because of him."

The king remained silent as he turned to the door, and the cook himself stepped outside.

Dark bags were under his eyes, and his face was pale, but it was the sight of blood on his white shirt that drew the king's eyes.

"Lady Jenoure, you are dismissed. Finlay, you will explain everything this instant." The man looked terrifying, but Fin was the picture of calm as he gave a quick bow, and Annika hastily made herself scarce.

Once she was out of earshot, Fin spoke.

"I can sense if someone that shares my home is in serious danger. It has to be serious for me to even notice, and it has to be in a place I have been. I woke up last night because I knew someone was in trouble, and I immediately worried for Her Majesty's safety. I came up to her chamber and met with Lady Jenoure outside her door. Lady Jenoure entered the chamber while I waited a ways back, and when it was clear there was trouble, went inside to offer my assistance."

He explained everything rationally, but there was a stress in his tone that betrayed some larger emotion.

"Why is it *you* are in the queen's chamber with the physician?"

"Her Majesty requested that I stay, and the physician required my help in keeping her distracted. Sire, if you could please now see to the queen, I believe the physician would like to speak with you." Fin bowed.

The king gave one last icy look to the cook, threw open the door, saw the bloody pile of sheets and towels, and then laid eyes on the pale sleeping form of his wife. The physician appeared to be finished packing up his leather satchel and was rolling down his sleeves when he turned around.

The scene was too familiar.

The king felt despair crush his heart.

The physician that approached him appeared to be in his late forties, with dark brown and gray hair, and bright green eyes. He bowed deeply.

"Your Majesty, perhaps we should talk outside, while the queen rests," he requested softly.

The king gave a short, brisk nod, and promptly turned back around and exited.

Once the door was softly closed behind them, the physician addressed the king.

"The babe still lives," he began, earning a heavy escape of breath from the king before he composed himself again, and waited for the rest of the report.

"The queen is not out of the woods yet, Your Majesty. Her Majesty will need to remain in bed for the remainder of her pregnancy and is not to be stressed or burdened at this time. I cannot say that the child will survive until the full term. However, for now, I can still hear the heart." He bowed again as the king blinked rapidly, attempting to hold back his tears from a mixture of relief and fear.

"It was fortunate she was found when she was and that Finlay calmed her down. Were it not for him helping her to relax, I fear I may have had to deliver very different news." The physician bowed again and excused himself to give his findings to the court physician, who would be arriving shortly following the king. The man received generous thanks and payment for his care and attention to the queen and would not be forgotten in troubling times to come.

The king stared at the closed door between himself and his wife, feeling completely at a loss as to what to do. His world felt as though it were crumbling around him, and that any moment of relief or reprieve was going to disappear at any time.

I cannot change these things. So I must focus on what can be done. Regardless of Norman's inner monologue reaching such a conclusion, he remained rooted to the spot, staring at the door.

After the light shifted in the corridor, he wiped the tears from his cheeks, and turned away. He decided to speak with the cook. He owed the man his thanks, and perhaps a small pay bump …

The king found Fin sitting with his back against the castle wall around the corner of the kitchen, crouched on the ground with his forehead pressed into his palms. It had taken His Majesty two hours of searching and he was ready to pummel the witch by the end of it, but seeing the dejected state of him softened the king considerably.

"Royal Cook Finlay Ashowan, please rise."

Fin's shoulders visibly stiffened at the king's voice, and as he slowly stood and bowed once again, Norman saw the hard set of his jaw.

"I have come to give you my thanks in aiding the queen. You played an integral part in her safety, as well as my child's. You have my sincere gratitude." The king gave a small bow of his head to Fin, but the witch only continued to look somewhat … angry?

"Your Majesty, permission to speak freely." Fin's tight tone gave the king pause.

"Permission granted."

Fin's expression turned dark. "You broke your promise. You told the queen about my abilities, and I would like to know why you would breach my trust and your own honor."

The king felt as though he had been struck. He felt fury rise in him.

He was upset because of something so trivial at a time like this?

"Finlay Ashowan, I informed Her Majesty because she is my wife, and deserves to know of something of such significance under her own roof!"

"Then why didn't you tell me you would be doing that! If you had, I could have spoken to Her Majesty myself, and—"

"And what? Why in the world is this important, Mr. Ashowan? I believe you are forgetting—"

"Because I couldn't help her!" Fin bellowed, making the king take a step back.

"Your Majesty, did you ever stop to consider what it is like when someone is dying or in pain, and they think just because you are a witch you can help? The queen, while in pain and bleeding, asked me to help her, and I couldn't! I cannot stop death; I cannot heal the body!" Fin's face became rife with sadness and grief. "You yourself would have probably blamed me if something had happened to them, and I hadn't been able to do anything. I wanted to help, but instead I gave her more pain when I had to say that I couldn't make any difference," he accused, tears rising in his bright blue eyes.

Norman stood still and said nothing.

He was right.

He would've expected Fin to be able to do *something* … even though the witch *had* said he wasn't powerful … the king still would have expected … some kind of magical miracle.

"Finlay, I am sorry for breaking my oath. For not having the foresight of how misunderstanding your abilities could lead to such pain." The king paused as Fin rested his hands on his hips and looked away with hunched shoulders, breathing in and out sharply.

"However, believe me when I say, I know what it feels like for there to be unending high expectations of you. I know what it is to feel helpless and powerless." The softness of the king's voice broke Fin.

He sobbed, and immediately, without hesitation, Norman wrapped him in an embrace, which he accepted as the stress and fear of the night filled him in an overwhelming wave. It was only for a few moments, but when they parted, Fin was once again composed.

"You need to sleep. I heard you were up most of the night." The king clapped him on the shoulder and turned to leave.

"Your Majesty?" Fin called out to the royal's back while resisting the urge to rub the back of his neck. "You have always exceeded my expectations, if that is worth anything."

The king didn't turn around, didn't say anything, but if Fin had seen the man's expression, he would have seen the intense flicker of emotion cross his face as he reentered the castle and left Fin in peace outdoors as thunder rumbled above them.

Fin slept as the storm raged outside. The kitchen had been bustling with several maids and footmen as they tried to make up for Fin's absence, so he was forced to visit the cottage assigned to him for his post to sleep, but it had not been used since Luca's time.

Upon arriving, he managed to hastily dust the space using magic and set his broom to work sweeping out the dead insects and dirt on the ground. Next, he started a fire in the grate as the rain outside pounded down on the ground. Once the fire was crackling, he lay down on his mat, and fell into a comatose sleep, lulled by the sound of the rain pounding the ground outside.

Fin didn't awake until evening, and when he did, was shocked to see the small cottage had been completely transformed.

He knew his broom was capable of simple tasks, but it had somehow turned the entire space into a warm and welcoming home. Slowly, he began to explore his surroundings.

There was a single large room when one first walked in, and a table and chairs positioned a few feet from the fireplace, which Fin recalled before falling asleep had been overturned and leaning against a cobweb-filled corner. There were three large windows, two on either side of the door when one first entered, and one on the back wall. Soft blue curtains had been hung in the windows, a steel tankard had been filled with wildflowers in the middle of the table, and there was a pile of fresh cut wood beside the fireplace.

A rocking chair that had previously been gathering spider nests had been polished off in the far back corner, along with other shelves that stood holding various pots and pans that now gleamed in the otherwise empty room.

Beside the fireplace was a doorway into a bedchamber that Fin hadn't even bothered to inspect prior to falling asleep.

Inside the room was a double bed and a small chest of drawers along the back wall, where the only window overlooked the line of trees that marked the beginning of the king's forest at the back of the building. The fireplace apparently was open to the room on the other side of the wall as well, meaning the bedroom would be incredibly cozy in the winter months.

There was a quilt over crisp white sheets on the bed, and Fin noticed that the wood of the bed and chest of drawers had been dusted and polished to a loving gleam. His broom stood in the corner, made inactive by the presence of others ... someone had done all of this work while he had slept through it.

Slowly, he turned to the exit, and pressed the latch open.

"Woahwoahwoahwoah!"

Upon opening the door, Fin found himself staring down stunned at Sir Lewis, who was holding a paintbrush in his right hand, a can of what looked like green paint beside him on the ground.

"Careful of the paint!" the knight chided, while standing with a small groan.

"What ... what is going on?" Fin asked, ducking under the low doorway to step outside into the warm rays of sunset that glinted off of raindrops over the lush green grass. Sir Lewis backed up to give him room.

"You protected the queen. So, Sirs Taylor and Andrews, and both Hannah and Peter, came up with the idea to ... tidy up. Plus, with you gone, we kinda saw how much you do. It took four people to do what you manage to do on your own." Sir Lewis shrugged.

Fin was speechless. He noticed the window boxes had been painted green to match the door, and fresh, cheery yellow pansies had been planted.

He turned his stare back at Sir Lewis, who was grinning with pride.

"Th-Thank you. Where are the others?"

"Well, Hannah and Peter are grabbing us all some food, while Sirs Taylor and Andrews are grabbing a few bottles of wine and some ale. We figured you might exempt our drinking ban to celebrate tonight." Sir Lewis looked a bit sheepish and gave a nervous smile.

"They … you … all are … we're all going to eat together?"

"Well, I mean if you need to rest more, I guess we'd all understand."

"I'd be worried that you lot would re-thatch the roof if I so much as blink." Fin couldn't hide the awe in his tone.

He knew he could've probably gotten the work they had done by himself in an hour at most with magic, but …

They had spent hours of their day, just to fix up his cottage. Not because they had to, or because he was a witch …

"Here they come!" Sir Lewis waved at the small group of people making their way around the castle. Hannah was carrying what looked like two bulging picnic baskets; Peter carried a stool and plates. Sir Taylor hauled a barrel in his arms, while Sir Andrews lugged bottles of wine and goblets.

Fin continued to gape as they drew nearer.

He glanced back at his side at one of the knights he had despised so fiercely, and he felt a blinding appreciation bloom inside of him.

An hour later, the group sat well-fed and happy, as they then broke out the wine.

"Thank you again, everyone, I … it's the nicest thing anyone has ever done for me." Fin leaned back with his pint of ale, his back to the fire.

"I don't find that surprising, you fussy lout!" Sir Taylor boomed as he drained his tankard. Apparently having been without alcohol for so long had lowered his tolerance greatly.

Fin tensed, and watched Hannah, who remained relaxed and shrugged as she sipped slowly from her cup of wine.

"Shall we play a game?" Peter asked while raising his goblet with a cocked eyebrow.

Fin shot the man a wary glance. It seemed an odd request from the normally silent fellow, but he wondered what was in mind.

"Yeah!" Sir Lewis brandished his tankard jubilantly.

Hannah stood.

"I think I should retire before rumors start spreading about my easy virtue, but you all have fun." She smiled nervously at the knights, warmly at Peter, and brilliantly at Fin before they all waved farewell and she exited.

Fin checked the daylight outside. Despite the storm, the sun had made it through the clouds by the end of the day, and it hadn't yet left the world to the darkness of night, which soothed his worries about Hannah walking back to the castle on her own.

"She'll be fine," Peter said gently. It was easy reading Fin's mind.

"Of course she will! Everyone now knows you don't mess with Hannah," Sir Taylor managed as he poured himself another ale and sat down at the table. "So! What should we play?" he demanded, eyeing the table full of men.

"There is a game going around in Austice called Honesty or Guts, would you like to hear the rules?" Peter's slow smile unnerved Fin.

He had the strange sense that he was about to get very, very inebriated. Kraken sauntered by Fin and gave him a single wide-eyed look before heading toward the bed, completely unconcerned.

He turned back to the table of expectant faces toward himself.

He sighed.

"Fine, what're the rules?"

CHAPTER 20
WHEN WITCHES LOSE
THEIR WITS

Fin acknowledged and understood that this could be very bad for him. He couldn't be all that honest, and he was slightly terrified of whatever nervy feat the knights could dream up on his behalf.

If he opted out of being honest or performing whatever challenge the group dreamt up, he had to drink. Meaning, he was more than likely going to be in a good deal of pain the following day.

"Alright, I will begin, as I thought of the game, and I choose to ask Sir Andrews first. Honesty or Guts?" Peter had an odd glint in his eye that Fin had never seen before, and he wasn't sure what to make of it.

"Er—guts?" The knight looked genuinely afraid.

"Excellent. To prove your guts, you must either fight Finlay, or finish your entire tankard."

Sir Andrews hastily downed the entire beverage in front of him, while refusing to make eye contact with anyone present.

After letting out a loud belch, Sir Andrews rounded on the table of men.

"Lewis, Honesty or Guts?"

The knight thought carefully.

"Honesty."

"Are there any maidens you fancy?" Sir Andrews waggled his eyebrows making both Fin and Peter roll their eyes.

"Well … In a sense, I s'pose. Lost my interest in Hannah for obvious reasons …" Fin's dark expression encouraged the hasty adding on of the sentence. "Lady Jenoure's built for sin, so of course I'd never complain should the lady like to share some time with me, but otherwise … most likely Jade. The newest maid."

"The klutzy one?" Sir Andrews's surprise was clear.

"The very same."

Fin had no idea who they were talking about after Lady Jenoure but decided it didn't really matter. Sir Taylor was laughing heartily at his friends.

"Alright Taylor, Honesty or Guts?"

"Guts!" The man grinned fearlessly, but Sir Lewis's evil smile was not something to be taken lightly.

"If you have guts, you will sing for everyone."

The large man's smile fell from his face.

Fin perked up. This could be golden. He truly expected the man to finish his beverage. Instead, he stood slowly, opened his mouth, and sang.

Fin's jaw dropped.

The man could actually *sing*. When it came to the chorus line of the song, Sirs Andrews and Lewis joined in perfect harmony, and Fin's shock grew.

They were not just good … they were actually great!

Fin sat enraptured by the rich timbre of Sir Taylor's voice, and the uniformed harmonies of the men with him. It was one of the generic sea songs that most people knew, about sailors all in love with a Troivackian woman named Sally Brown.

By the end of the song, Fin felt as though he needed to offer them all some money … until Sir Taylor let out a belch that rattled the dishes on the table, effectively breaking the enchantment.

"I didn't see that coming. Do all the knights sing as well as you lot?" Fin asked, not bothering to mask his impressed tone.

"Some, but none can go as low as Taylor here!" Sir Andrews raised his tankard to the knight, who glowered in response.

"Singin' ain't a knight's job," the man growled.

Fin decided not to antagonize him further.

"So was it Hannah who hung the curtains and got the linens on the bed?" he asked, intending to change the subject.

"She had a spare quilt, and the curtains she, er ... she was half-finished for her dowry chest." Sir Andrews suddenly looked incredibly uncomfortable.

"Andrews ... did you sew my curtains?" Fin queried, not wanting to mock him, but at the same time finding it more than a little funny.

"My mother was a seamstress," he mumbled as he downed half his tankard.

No one dared to torture him further.

"Peter, Honesty or Guts!"

"Guts," he chortled, shaking his head.

"You have guts if you run an entire lap around the castle butt naked," Sir Taylor declared over the table, his eyes already glassy.

All eyes swiveled to Peter, who had been in the middle of raising his wine glass to his lips.

"That seems more than just a small challenge," he stated evenly.

"If you don't, your consequence is to finish that bottle of wine." Sir Taylor gestured to the bottle that was still half-full.

The quiet man drained his goblet and stood. He gave a small shrug, then turned toward the cottage door.

"Peter, you cannot seriously be considering this!" Fin called out, a laugh in his voice of disbelief.

"You're right, Mr. Ashowan. I am not considering it. I've decided."

He stepped outside, and after sharing several different looks, every one of them jumped up, not wanting to miss the show.

Dottie sat in her rocking chair as night settled over the dewy castle grounds. Her son Antonio had already gone to bed, and as she worked on her embroidery, she felt herself stiffen from the slight draft from the still-closed cottage window.

She tugged at the faded, rose-colored shawl around her shoulders a little tighter with her knobby fingers.

That was when she heard it.

Slapslapslapslapslapslap

A sound she had not heard since her dear husband Paulo had been alive. She gazed out the window and stared at the stark white form of a man running past her cottage, his impressive manhood giving her a fond reminder of days past.

She watched his ivory buttocks as they faded into the night, and she smiled.

It had turned into a better evening than she could've ever hoped, as the faint slapping sound grew more and more distant.

Peter sat back at the table, still panting from his lengthy run around the castle, and sipped his wine.

"I must admit, I did not, in a hundred years, think there was any chance of you doing that," Sir Taylor spluttered, the awe in his voice undeniable.

Peter shrugged and placed his goblet down.

"Finlay, Honesty or Guts?"

"You are a hard man to follow, so I will attempt honesty."

"Tell us about the first ten years of your life. No one knows really anything about you."

Fin raised his eyebrows as he thought for a moment. He didn't necessarily need to tell them about magic to encapsulate his childhood, did he?

"I grew up on one of the southern islands. Quildon, to be exact. My mother, as I'm sure you all heard, was a healer. We saw many people from all over the continent, and the world, and they all had special recipes they would miss from home while they were recovering. So I would do my best to recreate them, and I eventually got quite good. I didn't get along with the other children on the island, and so I … was mostly on my own. With my mother."

"Are you a bastard?" Sir Andrews blurted, his incredulous tone making all eyes turn to the knight briefly.

"My parents were married a year before I was born. My father left and never came back when I was eight."

Fin sipped his ale briefly before deciding to redirect the conversation.

"Sir Andrews, Honesty or Guts?"

The knight had been frowning after hearing Fin's history but adjusted his expression hastily.

"Honesty."

"Why were you apologizing to Hannah on your knees a week ago?"

The tension in the room rose so swiftly that it could've choked a weaker being.

"I … I …"

Fin waited, his expression stony.

"I was angry, and I …" The man visibly struggled for the words. "I said unkind things to her and shouldn't have. I didn't want her to tell you, because for some reason you scare Sir Taylor, and that scares me."

Fin stood, and all the men except for Peter winced as he did so.

"Did you hurt her?"

"Not physically, I just … wasn't … I'm sorry," he finished awkwardly.

"Why are you apologizing?" Fin's tone was threatening.

"B-because, I didn't mean to—"

"If any of you are here and acting proud that you're behaving better because you're scared of me? You aren't better. You're the same rotten idiots you were before. If you behave better because you yourselves believe what you did was wrong and want to be better, then, and only then, have you earned some right to be proud." Fin snatched the wine bottle off the table and stormed out of the cottage.

Peter's arms were folded across his chest as he gazed at the knights calmly.

The trio looked a strange mix of sickened, guilty, and angry.

"He's a cook, why does he get to be so high and mighty?" Sir Andrews mumbled.

Sir Taylor stood.

"I don't like him, but … what he says bothers me." The man sounded confused.

"He just takes things too seriously!" Sir Andrews exclaimed clutching his tankard tightly. "After all we did for his house today …"

"I wouldn't like it if someone made Jade cry," Sir Lewis said idly, staring drunkenly at the table.

Peter sighed before draining his goblet.

"Let us leave for the night. You three can have an existential crisis in your own beds."

The group left having learned valuable things that night and having much to think about before their minds would let them rest easily.

Fin relieved himself amongst the trees. He hadn't meant to chase away the knights. He could see that they were improving gradually under Peter and Hannah's command. Nothing huge, but more considerate behavior and a slow but steady increase of manners. However, after Fin's strenuous day and wrought nerves, he was less tolerant. Plus, they really should have learned their lesson, he reasoned in an attempt to try and quench his guilty conscience.

Still … they had worked hard to make his cottage feel welcoming, and had even organized a dinner for him …

He needed to be better.

With a weary sigh, he drank straight from the wine bottle as the sound of nocturnal animals and insects filled his ears, hoping the wine would help his worries to float away.

He leaned drunkenly against the nearest willow tree as he finished his business. He didn't want to throw the knights into his wheel of worries. He had enough with his confrontation with the king, worrying for the queen, the overpowering pull he felt toward Lady Jenoure, and then his duties atop all of it.

He was about to turn back and return to the cottage, when the snapping of twigs and clanking of armor drew his attention to his left, just south of the creek.

In the distance, Fin could see a rather large man making his way through the forest, heading east. On a drunken whim, he decided to follow him and see where he was headed.

He ambled behind the man, not bothering to mask his own sounds, as the wanderer clearly drowned out any sound he made with his armor.

Fin was actually enjoying the leisurely walk, as he continued to drink casually while following the man and remaining on the north side of the stream. Perhaps it was a drunk knight, or perhaps he was an intruder. Fin wasn't certain, but neither option particularly bothered him while the alcohol coursed through him.

He realized that they were nearly at the rose maze, when at long last the man called out softly in the darkness.

"The roses will burn in the summer heat."

A cloaked figure in the distance responded.

"Not unless the soil remains moist."

It seemed to be some kind of code?

"What news have you for me?" the cloaked figure questioned; it was a woman … a familiar voice.

"Not much. Right now, there are fewer Troivackian merchant ships at every Daxarian city, and their goods seem to only consist of trinkets."

A small, aggravated grunt came from the cloaked figure.

"Have you heard about the witches?"

"I've heard their chief of military is quite powerful. I've also heard of at least three other powerful witches there. More than that, I do not know," the man answered.

"Which city will they attack first?"

"Not sure. Perhaps Rollom?"

The figure cursed.

"Doubtful. They are difficult to attack. Anything else?"

"Sorry, 'fraid not." After an aggravated sigh, the figure handed a small pouch that jangled loudly to the man in plated armor.

"That is your three months' pay. I will send for you in another month. Try to discover which city will be attacked first from your former mercenaries."

The man agreed and turned to leave. Fin had been following slightly upward of the man's path, and so when he stalked past the witch, he didn't glimpse him casually leaning against the tree in the shadows with the wine bottle dangling at his side.

Once the clanking faded, Fin took another drink, then felt the tip of a blade in the back of his neck.

"Who sent you?"

The smell of spices filled his nose.

He laughed, and the dagger drew blood. "Lady Jenoure, fancy meeting you here!"

The knife fell away, and Fin turned around to stare into the stricken expression of Annika, clad in britches and a cloak.

"Why are you here?" she demanded, still attempting to recover from the shock of the sight of him once she made out the red hair in the dark.

"Was out for a walk. With wine. Sir Clanks'a'lot seemed interesting, so I followed him." He shrugged and took another mouthful of wine.

"Fin, are you … are you alright? You were with Ain—the queen all night." Annika's tone was tenuous, as though she were caught between wanting to interrogate him, but also wanting to express her worry.

"I only distracted a woman as she potentially bled to death with her child. Why would I be anything but fantastic?" He drank again.

"She's fine. Ainsley has always—"

"You wanna know why I can't be 'round you?" Fin slurred as he relied on the sturdy tree beneath his shoulder to stop him from falling over.

"Well, earlier you said—"

"It's 'cause I like you."

She went still.

"You mean you want to lay with me. It's fine. I know most of—"

"Nah. I mean … Yeah. But … you make me excited. Excited for … you. Life an' you in it." Fin shrugged and drank more again.

"Why have you avoided me, then?" Annika asked, the hesitation obvious in her voice.

"I ... you ... I'm a cook. You're a lady. None of this is good." When he drank again, he drained the bottle.

"... What if I liked you too?" Fin stared at her open expression. She wore a black leather vest over a tan-colored tunic, and dark brown trousers with black boots. Her shoulders were clad in a black cloak.

She had never looked more honest, or beautiful.

"I don't want a fling ... or ... or some other ... lord raising my weird ... child," he managed haltingly.

"So just because we like each other this can only end in a fling or a bastard?" Annika challenged, bitterness lacing her tone.

"What is the most it could be?" Fin demanded sharply. "You hafta get married soon."

Annika said nothing.

"Right. Well. Don't ... worry. I know, you know, I'm a ... yeah. Thanks for Kraken. Truly. He was the best ... gift ever. I won't tell people you ... you're a spy." Fin turned and stumbled, but slowly began picking his way through the forest back toward his cottage, not caring that he hadn't made any sense.

Annika appeared at his side, grabbing his right arm; she draped it over her shoulders, and helped balance out his weight.

"No! Don't ... Please ... no." Fin's pleas faded as he struggled to focus on his footing.

"Fin, I'm just taking you to the cottage, don't worry," Annika assured him as she continued to move forward. "I've carried each of my brothers in similar states, so I know what I'm doing."

"Phillip is a *massive* asshole!"

Annika burst out laughing at the slurred declaration.

"Yes, but please stop saying it."

"But ... but he IS!"

"I'm aware."

"You look better than he does," Fin pointed out matter-of-factly.

"I know, I know ... we can talk more about that later, though."

Fin grunted. "Did he hurt you ... a lot while growing ... growing up?"

"Yes, but it made me stronger, now sort out your left foot or we will be going in circles."

He slowly adjusted the awkward direction of his large left toe and found that their trajectory toward his cottage greatly improved.

In no time at all, the duo found themselves clearing the tree line, and staring at the cheery bright windows, with the faint smell of a good fire still flickering in the hearth in the air.

"Wow, the place has a real touch of magic," Annika exclaimed as she regarded the painted window boxes and door.

"Sir ... Andrews. Mother was a seamstress!" Fin brokenly announced.

Once in front of the freshly painted deep green door, Annika unlatched the handle, and stepped in. The fire had died down to warm embers with a few flames flickering, the table remaining covered with dirty dishes.

"I'm fine, you can ... go back to your chamber in the castle and ... Gods, your reputation! I'm sorry!" Fin exclaimed, pulling away from her and stumbling toward the bedroom.

"Fin, it's fine. I doubt anyone knows it's me when I'm dressed like this."

"Still, just ... don't be near me," he mumbled as he pushed open the bedroom door and stumbled heavily.

Annika stepped forward with a sigh. She closed the door behind herself, then crossed the distance to him before grabbing his right arm, and slowly guiding him to the bed, where Kraken laid curled comfortably. The feline raised his head sleepily to watch the scene unfold, while looking sincerely annoyed at having been disturbed.

Fin sat down heavily on the lovely red and blue quilt and released the empty wine bottle near the side of the bed.

Annika slowly crouched down so that she was between his legs, her hands on his thighs as he swayed where he sat.

"Would you like me to get you some water?" she asked gently.

"Honesty or Guts!" Fin asked loudly while pointing directly into her face.

She laughed softly, shaking her head slightly at the question to the familiar drinking game, making Fin grin stupidly in return.

"Honesty."

"When we first met, you ... you wanted something from me. What was it?"

Annika's smile dimmed slightly.

"I wanted you to let people always come and go in the kitchen without restrictions. It's the best place to hear the servants gossip."

"OOHHHH because you're a spy!" Fin exclaimed nodding his head wisely.

"Yes. Now, we will have to talk about this more when you are less foxed, but ... until then, try not to tell too many people, hm?"

Fin swayed where he sat, but as he stared down at her patient, half-amused face, he gave a half smile, his eyes glassy and lost to reason.

He slowly bent down, closer to the stunning lady who seemed immune to bothersome feelings.

He dropped a gentle kiss against her lips, the softness, warmth, and tinge of electricity gravely intoxicating.

Annika's eyes had closed on reflex, and when they slowly opened, so did Fin's. He gave one last sleepy smile before sitting up and falling back unconsciously on the pillows behind himself.

Lady Jenoure stood up slowly and stared down at the man passed out drunkenly on his bed. She saw in the faint light of the candles from the outer room the graceful slope of his eyes and cheekbones that could have been crafted by a master sculptor, as her heart pounded and she felt a blazing heat in her cheeks that refused to cool.

"Oh no," she whispered, and took a step backward.

Remaining completely ignored, Kraken had sat up straight at the foot of the bed, and as he watched Annika stare down at his witch, began purring contently.

It had begun.

CHAPTER 21
KRAKEN'S DUTIES

Kraken purred and bumped his head against Fin's forehead. His witch had deserved a night of fun, and romance, but it was time to rise. They needed to get to the kitchen. Rodents and bugs needed to be hunted, and while the cottage was lovely for a night of rest and relaxation, there was plenty of work waiting to be done.

Fin groaned, and rolled onto his side, oblivious to the time or world outside of his sleepy state.

Kraken let out an indignant sigh. Stepping over to Fin's pillow, he bent down and began grooming him.

"Alright alright! I'm up!"

Good. It's late as is, and the kitchen is probably cold. I need breakfast, Kraken thought to himself as he patiently waited for Fin to sit up, rub his head, and stand.

"Gods, I had the weirdest dream. I was in the woods, and Lady Jenoure was there … Not sure I recall the rest, though." He shrugged wearily.

YOU DON'T REMEMBER?!

Kraken wished Eric had been present to tell Fin how much of an idiot he was. That child had the most common sense of anyone in the castle! Though he doubted the boy would call anyone an "idiot"—he was far too kind.

Fin yawned, and slowly made his way to the doorway, giving a lazy snap of his fingers at the dirty plates on the table from the previous night. They whizzed out of the window that had magically propped open on its own, then floated down to the nearby river in the woods with a bar of soap. They cleaned themselves off hastily, and once they'd returned, stacked themselves neatly back on one of the spare shelves in the cottage. Fin waited for the task to finish and checked to see if there was any water around. Sadly, there was nothing, and once the dishes had been put away, he set out for his day.

Kraken sauntered beside him as they exited the cottage and headed up the dewy lawn in the blush of dawn. The sun had not yet broken the horizon, but it felt as though it would be another warm day.

The familiar continued mulling over his grave disappointment in his human's loss of memory regarding the progress he'd made with the woman.

Fin needed a mate and human kittens … It was integral to his being—more so than most of his humankind, due to his magic. Kraken could sense it.

For some reason, Fin only had one woman that suited him, and she was a tough one. The woman in question smelled strongly of spices and seemed like a good huntress to Kraken. She had brought him to his witch, which was already a good start, as it showed she had good taste in companions. She was clearly the best potential mate, but why did Fin have to be so selective?! It made things so much more difficult …

The pair entered the kitchen, and sure enough, the fireplace stood cold and empty, but worst of all … the room was a sty.

The maids and stewards that had taken over to cover Fin's duties the previous day had returned the room to its former disastrous glory, making him give out a pained groan while briefly doubling over.

Kraken wasn't a fan of dishware and food floating every which way around the room, so he decided to make himself scarce before it started. It was too early for the small human named Eric to come, anyway, so he decided to head out and look for his gang.

Trotting out the garden door and back across the lawn, Kraken spied some rustling grass in the distance, and immediately slowed.

The hunt required stealth … agility … a sharp mind … and—

MINE!

Kraken shot at the unsuspecting rat and enjoyed his surprise breakfast in no time at all.

~~~~~~~~

At long last, the castle cat entered the perimeter of the city of Austice. Kraken had only visited the nearest six buildings to his home but had found himself a gang that let him know the happenings of the town easily enough (for a cost, of course).

As he rounded the first building, he saw Fat Tony lying on an overturned crate, grooming his paw lazily. The head of the gang was an aptly named ginger cat that Kraken had never seen run or make any sudden movements. However, he was still revered in their circle.

"What's the purr, Tony?"

The leader stopped his work, and glanced down, bored, at the new arrival.

"That depends. Did you bring any more bread?"

A mangy tabby cat suddenly leapt over the wooden gate that blocked off the back of the shops, and landed nimbly behind Fat Tony, making Kraken's fur stand on end and his back arch. He backed away instinctively, which annoyed him greatly once he realized which cat it was interrupting his conversation.

Scrappy Carl always liked to make an entrance.

"My witch just woke up. I'll be back later. I just figured I'd check while I have time."

Scrappy Carl was a tabby with big yellow eyes and a small scar across the bridge of his nose. He had earned the mark from taking a nip at the shopkeeper's wife when the woman had tried to confiscate the fish he had rightfully stolen.

"No information without payment. Which is a shame ... I was plannin' on a nap later," Fat Tony announced as he crossed his paws and trained his gaze on Kraken, who was growing larger and fluffier every day.

"I brought a bread roll the other day, but you didn't have anything to report." Kraken's tail swished as Scrappy Carl sat on the opposite side of the alley from Fat Tony.

Most cats wouldn't ever be able to argue with the leader, but as a witch's familiar, Kraken already got a leg up in feline society.

"Hmm ... You make a good point—though you had taken a couple bites out of it first."

"That was just from when it fell out of my mouth on my way to you," Kraken lied smoothly.

Fat Tony grumbled quietly as golden morning light filled the street behind the familiar.

"*Very well. I will tell you the first part of what I've heard, and you'll get the second part later when you bring me more food.*"

Kraken blinked in understanding.

"*I heard from Jerry, you know Jerry? Cat on one of them foreign boats? Anyway, Jerry says the purr on the docks is that the ships are leavin' with fewer humans than when they came. Meanin' some of 'em are stayin' here, but no one knows where.*"

Kraken's pupils widened. This wasn't good.

"*I also heard one of the passengers had been a witch. That's all I'm tellin' you though, until I get more food.*"

Kraken gave a small bow to Fat Tony, but never took his eyes off of him in thanks and farewell.

Scrappy Carl had a suspicious grin on his face that Kraken didn't like one bit.

The black fluffy cat turned and scampered out from the alley, but as he crossed by the front of the establishment, got distracted by the oh so familiar, and oh so delicious scent of …

"*Sylvia.*"

He turned and saw her sleek gray fur gleam in the morning sun. She was a minx by nature, and Kraken knew he should stay away from her, but she just … smelt so good.

"*Finished talking with my father?*" she purred sweetly.

"*For now. I'll be back later. How've you been?*"

Sylvia slinked down to him, and brushed her long skinny tail under his nose, captivating Kraken's full attention.

"*Bored. Mind if I visit you at the castle sometime?*" She innocently glanced over her slender shoulder with big yellow eyes.

"*Not at all. Though are you sure Tipper won't mind?*"

"*Why does Tipper matter?*" Sylvia turned and rubbed her head under Kraken's chin.

"*If he's no worry to you, then … I suppose it's fine.*"

Sylvia sauntered away, and Kraken let out a breath that he hoped would help calm his heart rate down.

He had bigger fish to eat, but Sylvia was one distraction he decided he could allow himself.

Turning back toward the castle, he set off, hoping that Fin had finished with the cleanup by the time he got back.

~~~~~~~

The kitchen was back in order when Kraken crossed the threshold, though Fin sipped his coffee, looking extraordinarily exhausted and pale.

He appeared to be preparing a simple breakfast for the castle's residents of eggs and fruit. Fortunately, most of the hunting party was taking their time returning, so the work was still manageable, even while hungover.

Kraken didn't see anything worth stealing for Fat Tony yet, so he decided to relax until the small human came.

He jumped into the middle chair, and Fin gave him a small nod of acknowledgment.

"Give me some food. I'm hungry," was what Kraken had said, but it came out as a mew. His alpha meow was coming along, but still not up to par in the cat's mind.

Fin seemed to understand all the same, though, and made a kissing noise while setting some eggs on a small plate.

The sound was annoying, but Kraken knew that it meant food, and so decided not to make a big fuss about it.

The cat was halfway through his breakfast when the door opened and Eric walked in crying.

"My … my dad … wouldn't … let me … see … my mom," the boy sobbed while rubbing his eyes.

This wasn't good.

Kraken bounded over to him and immediately began rubbing his supremely silky fur against the child.

The silk fur rub heals all, Kraken mused wisely.

Eric fell to his knees and wrapped his arms around the cat, sobbing into the black fur. Fin hastily dropped everything he was doing, rounded his table, and knelt down beside the boy and feline to scoop them both into a hug.

"Your father is just scared, Eric. Your mum and sibling are sick, and he is so worried he doesn't know what to do," Fin soothed.

Kraken let out a small snort as his lungs were squashed in the arms of a seven-year-old. It couldn't be helped. He hated getting wet, and hated being squeezed, but the youngling couldn't be left unattended in such a slobbery state.

Even though he was a young cat not fully grown, he had to look out for the more infantile humans—especially the good ones. He could feel how important this belief was to his witch.

When he was eventually released, and the boy had begun speaking normally with Fin, Kraken scampered out of the open door leading to the castle. He had to help solve this new problem, even if it did cut into his naptime. Upset small humans were not a good thing. He needed to fix this.

Several servants gasped and whispered at the sight of the black kitten trotting through the castle, and even a noble or two appeared surprised by his presence, but he didn't let that deter him. He darted through the shadows as nimbly as a spirit, and once he got to the fourth floor, went to the door he had glimpsed in Fin's mind.

His witch had gifted him some very special talents to already add to Kraken's existing incredible skills.

Fin's familiar could convey his general mood and sentiment to his witch (when the man was paying enough attention to him), he could always feel when Fin called or needed him, and on occasion, strange images that had no business being in the cat's head would appear. Kraken had eventually learned that these were places that had become burned in his witch's subconscious, and they would appear to him when the human was worried about someone or something tied to it. He sat in front of the door associated with Fin's worry and pawed at the wood relentlessly.

It was the only way humans that weren't his witch figured out there was an annoying barrier between himself and his destination. Humans weren't very clever, but at least they weren't oblivious all the time.

After a quarter of an hour, a man Kraken recalled seeing with pretty shiny spikes on his head flung the door open angrily.

The cat made a mental note to rightfully snitch the gold trinket later. Perhaps he could get Fin to resize it for him? Then again, it could make him more noticeable while stalking prey, but perhaps he needed a new challenge anyway …

Kraken darted into the room through the king's legs as he thought about the logistics of rightfully taking the spike hat; at the same time, the current owner of the pointy hat quickly realized the visitor to his chamber was shorter than his knees.

"What the— No! No no no no!" The king swung around to watch the swift mass of black fur leap up onto the bed where the queen remained propped up on pillows, her nearly gray complexion appearing waxy in the daylight as her hands rested on her belly. She still hadn't fully recovered from her harrowing evening the previous night.

"Oh! Well … hello!" The queen stared down into Kraken's brilliant green eyes and lifted her hand to allow him to sniff it.

"I will remove him, pardon me, dear." The king lunged for the cat, but Kraken had been prepared for that; he leapt over the queen's body outside of the king's reach, and began rubbing his cheek against the woman, making her chuckle.

"You must be Kraken. I've heard all about you from Eric and Royal Cook Finlay Ashowan."

Of course. I'm the best part of this castle, Kraken purred as the queen reached over and scratched under his chin, her smile softening her tired features.

The king stood frozen, watching his wife visibly relax as she petted the animal.

"That cat must be Finlay's familiar," Norman reasoned aloud. The wariness in his tone made the queen raise her brightening brown eyes.

"I like the cook, Norman, why are you so distrusting of him?" She continued petting Kraken, who nestled down next to her bump, though he was a little skeptical of it—the mound would occasionally shift of its own accord. The kitten in her had to be strong.

"I do ... to an extent. Ainsley, he claims he isn't powerful, but that is contrary to what I've seen from him. However, if he is in fact accurate in his belief, that would mean that there are greater forces in this land that could become a far larger threat than we've ever known," Norman explained, sitting down on the bed beside his wife.

"I understand, but witches have been around for thousands of years, and there has never been such an uprising. There have been the odd cases that have cropped up, but for the most part they have never been a problem."

The king's eyebrows lifted.

He hadn't thought of it that way.

It was true that, in all of history, the cases of violent outbursts from witches were incredibly rare. Perhaps Fin had been right about there being more weak witches, but if he had been right about that ...

He was wrong about his own power, the king surmised to himself.

Kraken watched the king try to reason out his feelings toward the Royal Cook peacefully at the queen's side. He knew humans were sometimes even crueler than cats, and so it could take a long time for them to warm up to one another.

Meanwhile, Ainsley's troubles were gradually fading away, thanks to Kraken's purrs and warmth at her side. She didn't understand why entirely (seeing as her problems still existed), but having the calm, unperturbed animal definitely helped.

"Is that cat *drooling*?" The king's astonished voice broke the temporary silence.

The queen looked down and burst out laughing at the growing puddle on their sheets.

Norman responded by rubbing his face tiredly. There was no end to the insanity anymore.

"Let's talk about something other than the cook. How are the preparations for the festival?" Ainsley asked good-naturedly.

The king leaned his elbows on his knees and gazed out the window tiredly.

"Nearly completed. This is our seventh year doing it, so we know the process a lot better than when we first started. I forget how busy the summers are with the celebrations, festivals, Eric's birthday ... then throw in a war ..."

The queen nodded thoughtfully.

Focus on my cheeks! Why is this conversation more important?! Kraken wondered indignantly as the woman's scratches and strokes grew slower.

"I'm glad you decided to still do it this year. I know we already have a lot going on, but I think the staff and cities need a bit of a morale boost."

"I know, I just wish Hank was here helping. It was his idea, after all, to host an annual 'Royal Employee Appreciation' event." The king briefly closed his eyes at the memory of his old friend and let out a soft, sad sigh.

Kraken felt as though he had lost the thread of the conversation, and so decided that he best not waste time trying to find it again ...

As fun as chasing loose threads was.

Speaking of, perhaps he could find some threads to pursue after lunch? What time was it?

I have too much to do these days ... these silly humans and their issues ... why bother with so much nonsense when you can nap, eat, and hunt?

Kraken jumped over to the night table that held a porcelain basin filled with cool water. He drank from it, making the queen laugh quietly, and the king glare.

When he had had his fill, he jumped down, and headed to the door. He needed to find his witch's future mate and have her slap some sense into him so that they could make kittens and let him get more catnaps.

Kraken sat in front of the closed chamber door, looked back over his shoulder at the king, and mewed.

"I think he wants to go back outside, Norman," the queen observed with a twinkle in her eye.

"Well, he can just deal with it. He spent ages pawing at that door to get in. He can live with his decision, he's just a cat."

Kraken glared, making the king take a step back.

Norman had a brief, insane notion that the cat understood him, but shook his head, dismissing the ludicrous idea swiftly.

Humans had no respect for the supreme schedule of cats.

Well, I guess we have to do this the hard way. I'll remember this, pointy hat man, Kraken thought coolly.

He began pawing the door avidly, making the queen snort again.

"Dear, he could need to relieve his bladder."

The king moved purposefully toward the second-largest nuisance in his life that belonged to the first-largest nuisance in his life. He opened the door abruptly and, after the fluffy black haunches scampered away triumphantly, turned back to Ainsley. The rigidness in his chest softened at the sight that met him; his wife was smiling and looking more like herself than she had in days.

Letting out a defeated sigh, Norman couldn't help but think,

Why is everything to do with that witch both helpful and annoying?

Kraken did his best to find Lady Jenoure that day, but for some strange reason, she was nowhere to be found.

As dinner dishes were delivered to the banquet hall, he returned to the kitchen wearily. He still needed to steal food for Fat Tony, or he wouldn't be able to find out more about the ships …

Upon entering the room, he gazed up at his witch, who didn't look much better than he had that morning.

"I will never again take my mother's healing abilities for granted," Fin mumbled to himself as he drank deeply from a goblet of water.

Kraken eyed the pile of fat near the edge of the table that had been carved off the sirloin being served for dinner that evening.

That was purrfect. Fat Tony would love it.

The feline was beginning to sidle up to the table to retrieve his food, when Fin, in his less-than-ideal state, idly itched the back of his neck, and felt a small scab beneath his fingers.

"What the— When could I have gotten cut on the back of my—" The alarm in his voice, and his abrupt halt in his outer monologue made Kraken freeze, his paw less than an inch from his prize.

Looking up, Kraken saw a pale look of realization dawn on the human.

"Oh no … Oh Gods … oh *no!*" Fin's hand dropped to his side for a split second before he began rubbing his eyes furiously.

Kraken saw his chance, and immediately took the largest piece of fat, though promptly dropped it again when Fin exploded in a shout while doubling over, grasping his still aching head.

"SON OF A MAGE!"

Kraken grabbed the fat off the ground once he had recovered his wits, and he darted out of the kitchen through the open garden door. He was willing to wager one of his nine lives that Fin had finally regained some of his memory from the night before.

More curses erupted from the kitchen into the otherwise quiet evening, as the cat continued dashing across the castle lawn.

Perhaps he would get a better night's rest staying over at Sylvia's …

CHAPTER 22
SHARING SURPRISES

It had been a week since Fin's eventful evening where he had consumed an excess amount of wine and ale, and wound up learning all kinds of noble secrets he had no right to, and that wasn't all …

Peter had run around the castle butt naked.

OH.

He also confessed his feelings for a viscountess and drunkenly kissed her in his cottage.

The memory of the events was ebbing away sleep and peace from his life and mind as he braced himself for the day that he would run into Annika. His saving grace, however, was that she seemed to want to avoid him too.

Which suited him just fine! He could've faced very serious repercussions for his advances on her, but … she had also said she liked him too, hadn't she?

Fin shook his head. Was he a child? Obsessing about a girl liking him back?

She hadn't actually said the words "I like you," even. She had just asked what would happen if she did … she probably found it more amusing than anything. How deluded could he be to even develop such feelings? He barely even knew her!

Pressing his fists into his cooking table, Fin dropped his head.

He let out a weary sigh, when the knights, Hannah, and Peter strolled in through the garden door, all speaking excitedly at the same time.

"Why so down!" Hannah slowly slid into the middle stool, her jubilant tone shifting to concern.

"Yeah, you've been lookin' pretty out of it lately. Stuff on your mind?" Sir Taylor asked, tilting his head as Fin pinched the bridge of his nose, and slowly straightened.

"I know that look," Sir Lewis said suddenly, with an out-of-character wise smile on his face.

Every eye turned to the knight, except for Fin, who instead resumed seasoning a pan of chicken breast coated in white wine, butter, lemon slices (kindly given to him by Kasim), and sliced cloves of garlic. The dried herbs he sprinkled over them were a new mix that, while strange, was definitely enticing. He already had the first two batches in his oven and was in the middle of his third.

Of the group, only Sir Lewis managed to stop drooling at the stomach-rumbling smell in the kitchen and come back to the important matter at hand.

"You did something stupid regarding a woman."

Fin's eyes snapped up.

"OooooOOOOOOHHHHHHH!"

Every. Single. One of them. Made the exclamation as Fin's cheeks burned.

"Someone managed to charm *you*?!" The astonishment in Sir Taylor's voice made him blush even more deeply.

Perhaps he had become too approachable to his team …

"I always thought you liked Hannah." Sir Andrews addressed Fin but looked to his fellow workers.

"Gross." Hannah looked over her shoulder at them. "I think of him more as a grumpy dad."

"I'm only nine years older than you!" Fin exclaimed, mildly insulted despite never once thinking of Hannah in any romantic way.

"Ten years," she corrected, making him roll his eyes

"Close enough."

"I see what you mean, actually. I'd be scared of him ever needing a cane to walk … my shins ache already," Sir Lewis agreed reasonably.

"That's not the point, though. Who's the girl and how'd you mess it up? Did you do that thing you do? Where you talk and annoy people?"

"It's none of your business," Fin snapped, snatching the pan off of the table, and with great force, removed one of the first batches of chicken breasts from the oven and shoved the next one in.

The group remained silent for a moment at the sight of the golden chicken breasts, as though in quiet worship.

"I kind of thought you were gay."

Hannah's words brought everyone back, and all eyes turned to her.

"Are you ..." Sir Taylor cleared his throat awkwardly. "Royal Cook, are you ... a ... aaaaaaah ..." The man struggled deeply.

"What's wrong with being gay?" Peter quipped, suddenly looking incredibly uncomfortable, his cheeks donning a telling blush.

Fin blinked in astonishment.

Huh ... He supposed he shouldn't get upset about people assuming him liking Hannah, when he had wondered the same thing about Peter and been so off the mark.

"Nothin', I s'pose. As long as ... wait a minute, you kissed Andrews!" Sir Taylor rounded on Peter who crossed his arms and glared. Sir Andrews turned white as a sheet as his hand raised and touched his lips at the memory.

Both Hannah and Fin's jaws dropped.

"What ... the ...What by the Gods has been happening out there?!" Fin demanded after there had been a beat or two of shocked silence.

Why was he surprised? Why was he *ever* surprised by anyone in the castle anymore?!

When no one volunteered an answer Fin decided the conversation had spiraled enough.

"Alright, let's deal with the dragons in the room. Peter, is this you defending gay people, or are you informing us all that *you* are gay?"

"It isn't anyone's business," Peter muttered quietly in response.

"Fair enough. End of discussion," Fin dismissed firmly.

Everyone still looked too baffled to function.

"Honestly, Peter." Sir Taylor turned his massive body to his fellow kitchen aide. Everyone tensed, and Fin had vivid visions of having to explain to the king why there was a brawl before lunchtime.

"I don't really care if you're gay. It's in art everywhere. We know you'd never do something to someone against their will. 'Cept for that time with

Andrews, but the boys and I had a chat about that, and we got your point. If anything, learning this just knocks it home."

Fin felt like fainting.

Had Sir Taylor just ... shown ... compassion?!

He glanced at his goblet of water. Had he accidentally been drinking? Had he died?

Peter was frozen. The man didn't so much as twitch.

"I'd like to know how it knocks it home?" Sir Andrews didn't sound angry, so much as close to fainting when he spoke.

"Well ... it's more like how we were to Hannah, right? We like ladies, but that doesn't mean it's good or right to make them feel that way."

Sir Lewis gave the suggestion some thought, then nodded in agreement. Sir Andrews swallowed—still apparently too addled to do much other than stare.

"Sir Taylor?" Peter's quiet voice drew every eye to him. "Thank you, and I ... I've never admired you or respected you more than I do right now." Peter bowed.

"Why ... Why does it not ... matter ... isn't it against ... nature?" Sir Andrews's tone wasn't accusatory or hostile as everyone would have expected; instead, he seemed genuinely baffled.

"Haven't you ever seen the pictures of the Green Man with the other men? If it's good enough for the Gods, good enough for me." Sir Taylor shrugged. "Way I see it, if both agree, no one's getting hurt. Besides, I don't really like kids. Less of them are a good thing in my books. Plus, it's less competition for the women." Sir Taylor grinned, and then the moment got even stranger by Hannah being the first to laugh.

"Wow. This has been ... one of the greatest moments of my life!" she announced. "Though, I still really, really, and I mean *really*, want to know who the girl is that Fin likes and how he messed up."

All eyes turned back to him.

"Not a chance. Back to work, and stay away from the squirrels. You're all nutty enough to warrant a siege attempt from them."

They all laughed at his terrible joke, grabbed the next bundles of vegetables, and headed back outside.

"Oh, and, Sirs Taylor, Andrews, and Lewis?" All three knights turned to the cook.

"I owe you three an apology for the night you were at my cottage. I'm sorry for what I said that night. You three *should* be proud of yourselves.

You have clearly come a long way, and to say I'm impressed would be putting it lightly."

The knights all shifted uncomfortably. "I think at this rate one of us is going to have a stroke from this insanity. Come on everyone, we have to finish before the festival!" Peter herded them out the door, and Fin smiled at their backs as he saw three pairs of ears blush bright red.

He let out a breath once he was certain he was once again alone, and glanced over to Kraken, who had watched the entire exchange through sleepy, half-lidded eyes.

"Gods … I don't know if I can handle any more unexpected news for one day." He sighed, dropping his chin to his chest, and then suddenly something else Peter said made his head snap up again.

"Did Peter say 'festival'?"

"Come on! Let's go!" Fin was being dragged by both Hannah and Peter by both arms to the outdoors.

"I have to prepare dinner, what in the world are you two—"

"What? What do you mean you're preparing dinner? Don't you know what today is?" They stopped their hasty ushering of their superior and turned to stare at him in the late afternoon sun.

Fin raised an eyebrow and glanced back and forth between them.

"It's the Thank You Festival! Or the Royal Employees Appreciation Event! I prefer the first name … bit easier to say, you know?" Hannah was bouncing on the balls of her feet, still clasping Fin's hand.

When Fin's expression didn't change, Peter took over the explanation.

"A few years ago, the king decided to host a festival to thank the castle staff members for their efforts. Rumor has it that it came about after the old Viscount Jenoure saw the effects preparing for Beltane had on old Royal Cook Luca."

Fin made a gesture with his hand to keep the conversation moving.

"Right. The king and nobles fund a big festival that the local taverns provide food and drink for, and let us consume both for free if we show them a wrist tie we pick up on our way there. People from Austice come to celebrate with us, as well as some performers. Usually, charlatans and fortune tellers go to earn the extra coin, but the biggest and best part is the musician competition."

Hannah was jumping up and down again.

"Groups compete to be the Royal Minstrels of the castle, and the ones selected get employed by His Majesty for a year until the next competition. It's always well done, and usually foreign merchants come all the way to sell stuff for it!"

"… The minstrels probably don't think it's so great—there's no job stability," Fin pointed out.

"They don't seem to mind. Minstrels and bards tend to be more nomadic and need to explore other places to keep their material fresh. Some just retire or turn to teaching. Some stay on to work with the new group, while others go travel and perform in different cities and countries. They always have job prospects afterward, though. If they want to stay on, they compete with the rest, and can win again. The current Royal Minstrels—what are they called again?"

"The Daxarian Sirens?" Hannah provided.

"Yeah! They've won two years in a row, but I think I heard them say they doubt they'll make it this year. Apparently, there is a new group that's incredible." Peter finished his explanation and resumed tugging Fin along.

"Do … Do the nobles go to this?" There was an odd look on Fin's face that made Hannah and Peter share a look.

"Usually, they do. Especially given that even the cook gets the time off and needs to eat. Did I mention they even give us tomorrow as a day off as well? The king has local taverns feed everyone instead."

"That is … incredibly generous of him." Fin couldn't help but be awed.

"Well … the staff are happier, and a lot of people come to this. I think the king actually makes money from it." Peter shrugged.

"Hmm … that would work if he gave the foreign merchants a one-time exception to our trade laws where for a set period of time they could sell more than normal to our people. It profits the economy as well with their visit, and—" Fin stopped his outward reasoning when his two aides stared at him in confusion.

"How do you … know about that stuff?" Hannah asked bewildered.

"Eeerr. My mother healed a teacher once and as payment he stayed and taught me for a couple years," he lied.

This was why he could never have real friends.

"Why didn't I hear about this festival sooner?" Fin changed the topic desperately.

"Well, you don't talk to anyone other than us, and even then, it's usually about work—aside from today. Not to mention the event takes place outside of the castle grounds, and we don't have to do any prep for it in the kitchen." Hannah paused. "Though I would've thought Eric would've mentioned it, but then again I guess he's been busy wanting to be with Her Majesty more ... You and the king only ever talked about work ..."

"Well, Lady Jenoure—" Hannah elbowed Peter in the ribs and silenced the man.

Fin glared and put his hands on his hips.

"What was that?"

"Uhh, nothing! Come on!" Hannah was actively pulling Fin again with Peter's help, and he was about to repeat his question about what the jab had meant, when they spotted Ruby up ahead.

"Ruby!" Hannah waved.

"Why hello!" The Head of Housekeeping smiled warmly at Hannah and Peter. Her hair was for once uncovered by a cap, and instead tied in a ponytail that flowed down her back in a thin brown stream. When her eyes rested on Fin, her features tightened, but her smile didn't fade.

"I see the cook is being broken out of his comfort space," she noted delicately before she handed Hannah and Peter braided red bracelets.

"These are the ties for this year. If you lose yours, find Mr. Howard, Lord Martin, or myself. Though I cannot guarantee we won't run out."

Hannah managed to stay still long enough for Ruby to tie the bracelet around her tiny wrist, and then waited while Peter and Fin received theirs. "You two run along, I would like to have a brief word with the cook." Ruby smiled, and watched as the aides shared a look then glanced at Fin.

"It's fine, I'll catch up with you later." He waved them away, then turned to the Head of Housekeeping, who was studying him.

He waited patiently as the woman seemed to be trying to find the words, but he had to admit he was quite curious over what was putting her ill at ease.

"Your ... cat ... is causing trouble." The tightness in her voice made Fin cross his arms across his chest.

"What kind of trouble?"

"He ... pooped in His Majesty's shoes, and while he napped, apparently thought the crown was ... his."

Fin's expression was one of pure mortification, as he opened his mouth, but found himself bereft of words for a moment.

"Oh ... *no.*"

"Oh, yes. If it weren't for the fact the queen was the one to see these things, rest assured that little beast would be the king's newest pair of slippers. Her Majesty … was … *far* more understanding than I, or His Majesty would be in that circumstance."

"Did the queen laugh?" Fin was taking a risky guess, but the fact that Ruby wasn't strangling him was a positive sign.

Ruby's lips pursed.

"She … was in tears from her amusement. Admittedly, I am not in the throes of kicking you both out on your backsides because that little cretin is the only thing keeping Her Majesty's spirits up."

Fin pressed his hands into his pockets.

"Ruby, I am truly sorry. I will … see what I can do. He has never done anything like that with me. Sorry for the mess, and that you had to take care of it."

The Head of Housekeeping looked a little rattled that she had finally won a battle against him, but after a small head shake took it all in stride.

"The shoes were old anyway. Now go enjoy the festival while my good mood lasts."

Fin grinned.

"As an apology and thanks, you will be the first to try my new lemon cookie recipe," he promised.

She laughed cheerily.

"You better, now get going. Have fun for once—I like you better when you're in a good mood."

Fin smiled, then turned toward where Hannah and Peter waited for him in the distance and saw that the knights had joined them as well.

It was strange, but …

Despite knowing that no one in the castle could be his real friend without learning his secret, he was oddly starting to feel like he was beginning to belong somewhere, and that felt pretty damn great.

CHAPTER 23
CONDOLENCES

Fin wandered around the stalls slowly. Hannah had become a human hummingbird the moment she saw the jugglers and fortune tellers. As she flitted to and fro, Peter was somehow being dragged along according to her whims. The knights had run into some of their friends and quickly pretended not to know them, which Fin actually preferred. He didn't need any more metal heads to handle. Though admittedly, his current trio of brutes were turning out to be halfway decent people, if he were honest with himself.

He realized then that Peter and Hannah had disappeared into the amassing crowd, and he found himself on his own as a result. He took the rare free time to absorb the sights and sounds around him, meandering through the event. All around him vendors were shouting their business as they tried to capture the attention of the people flowing by.

"Would you like to hear a message from your lost loved ones? I can speak with those in the afterlife!"

"Place your bets! Who will win the arm wrestle!"

"Spare coin, anyone?"

"Hit the target, dunk the doofus!"

"If she scares your patrons, just cut her off!"

Fin slowed. The last voice he had just heard had been none other than Keith, mage Lee's son.

He saw him leaning against a wooden ale barrel between stalls away from the crowds, talking to a young man who looked worn out. Fin began to walk toward them purposefully.

No one needed to suffer Keith's advice if he had any say in the matter.

"What's happening here?" His voice made both men stand at attention, though neither knew why. This showed on Keith's face as he blinked rapidly in the fading daylight at Fin, and then resumed his lax posture.

"This young man has recently inherited an establishment and is feeling a bit overwhelmed." The pity in Keith's voice made the young man visibly wince as he rounded his shoulders against the words.

"Are you fine with him telling me that?" Fin asked the young man, making sure to keep his tone respectful. He shot a nervous glance at Keith and bowed his head to Fin as he nodded.

The young man couldn't have been older than twenty, and had dark bags under his eyes, a long thin face, and ears that stuck out too far from his head.

"I see. Well, don't listen to this guy. He's never had the prestigious job of running a business. He's a mage," Fin explained patiently while Keith folded his arms across his chest and *tsk*ed.

"You see how some people lash out when they feel inadequate? It is a part of my profession, sadly; with great ability comes great problems. Let us talk more about your own troubles though, hm?" Keith reached out and gently touched the young man's shoulder, subtly blocking Fin from the conversation in doing so.

Fin cast a wary eye at Keith before pointedly ignoring his comments.

"If you just inherited the business, that means you are going through a time of mourning. I'm sorry for your loss, but please don't take his advice. It will not go well." Fin turned and strolled away, hoping that he had made enough of an impression for his words of warning to carry weight.

He looked around the festival located on the lawns behind the businesses of Austice. It was a hot day, and despite the sun not yet setting, many people were already quite inebriated.

Fin saw several maids with their beaus either chatting a little too loudly, or fighting a little too tearfully, or kissing with a little too much reckless abandon.

He had a few coins with him but didn't see anything he really wanted to buy, so he gave up browsing. Instead, he managed to grab a tankard of ale that was handed to him free of charge, thanks to the red tie around his wrist, and found an abandoned bench to sit upon closer to the king's forest.

A large wooden stage had been constructed off to his left, and he could see large swells of people carrying instruments. Commoners from the city were arriving with old blankets to lie on the grass near the stage that backed into the forest, as they buzzed in anticipation.

"Copper for your future?" An elderly woman seated herself on the other end of the bench. Her bright blue eyes studied Fin gaily as her smile revealed a few missing teeth. Though despite the gaps and her hooked nose … there was an aura about her that told him she had once been quite beautiful.

"I'm sure you are very talented at spinning tales; however, I am quite content not knowing a thing. Good evening, madam." Fin toasted her with his ale and sipped, ignoring her prolonged gaze.

"Do not think you are unworthy of greatness."

He pretended not to hear her.

It was an old trick, but a good one. Offer people vague and mysterious statements to hook them in, then withhold more information to make them pay. It was an effective marketing strategy.

"Strange for a witch to be a skeptic of the unknown."

Fin didn't move. Didn't show her his shock. She was baiting him. How could she have known he was a witch? Perhaps she was guessing outrageous things to gage his response to better refine her assessment of him.

"Ah well. Just know: don't turn away from a path simply because you do not think you deserve to tread its ground."

He didn't respond or look, only felt her stand and leave.

After several moments, he finally felt himself relax. He let out a long sigh and glanced around the festival openly with casual interest. The larger-than-life energy was potent, and even Fin couldn't help but feel as though there was a lot of fun to be had that evening.

He was tired, but some small wriggling little voice in him said that there were important things to see or do. He hadn't the faintest idea why he thought this, and after several moments, gave up pondering the matter.

Ah well. I can't see the future, but I can enjoy this peace for the time being.

Fin settled his forearms on his thighs and savored his next mouthful of ale, when he felt the weight of the bench shift again. Not wanting to inadvertently welcome more conversations, he pointedly ignored them.

"Enjoying the ale?"

His head snapped around, and his stomach dropped to the ground when he heard the voice.

"Lady Jenoure! Good evening." Fin bowed hastily in his seat, and unconsciously slid farther away from her. She wore a relatively plain bright red dress, and despite the warmth of summer, had a black cloak wrapped around her shoulders.

Her hair was only part way pulled back, and she wore single pearl studded earrings. She had her legs crossed away from him, but her left forearm rested on her knee to better pivot her torso toward him.

She looked … wonderful.

Lady Jenoure bowed her head in acknowledgment of his greeting, and appeared to be waiting for him to say something …

Right. She had asked him a question.

Pull it together. Just survive some polite conversation with her and go somewhere else.

"Uh, the ale is quite good. Are you having a good evening, viscountess?"

The glint of amusement in her eyes at his stiff awkwardness caused her lips to curl into a teasing smile that made Fin blush.

He busied himself by drinking more ale.

"I only just arrived." Fin nodded and did his best to smile politely at her reply. The expression that came out instead was a pained grimace, which made Annika give an unladylike snort and giggle to herself.

"Relax, Finlay, I won't give you a hard time."

He swallowed with great difficulty. He gave another brief nod as he wrapped his hands around his tankard to stop himself from rubbing the back of his neck.

"I do want your word, however, that there is a …" Annika glanced casually around them, and when she saw that no one was in earshot continued. "An *understanding* that silence earns silence."

He nodded hastily and tried not to fidget.

"Good."

Fin thought that would be the end of the conversation, but she didn't move from her spot at the opposite end of the bench.

He wondered if she would deem him suspicious if he got up and left right then. Glancing over to her, he saw that she appeared to be watching the crowds with mild, but pleasant interest. Fin wondered if she were capable of killing him.

She had already tried to stab him once when she had brought him Kraken. Given the lack of secondary attempts on his life, however, he gathered that perhaps there had been some kind of misunderstanding that night. Regardless, she also knew he was a witch, and she hadn't outed him to anyone as far as he knew. Meaning if she had wanted to do him harm, she would've made a move by now. She had all the weaponry she'd ever need to destroy him.

Fin turned and studied the woman sitting on his left more closely.

Her jawline was quite soft, and the corners of her lips looked as though they wanted to smile but had gotten stuck on the way there. Her head was tilted slightly to the right and a few loose hairs near her face moved gently in the tiniest of breezes. She looked peaceful, and innocent somehow, in that moment, making a small warmth bloom in his chest.

Fin cleared his throat. He knew he was staring and needed to stop.

"It's dangerous. Your … work."

Annika's eyes cut to him swiftly at his words. He saw the warning flash across her face, and gave a single, small shoulder shrug.

Lowering his voice, he continued. "It isn't my business, but be careful."

Her expression was frozen as though she weren't sure if he were about to continue and expose her. Fin realized she was most likely trying to decide whether or not she could kill him in broad daylight.

"Sorry, I will excuse myself now. Thank you for your company, Lady Jenoure." Fin was beginning to stand and exit the horrendously uncomfortable situation, when a man around his age suddenly jogged over to the pair from the crowd.

"Lady Jenoure!" he called out with a broad grin. Annika's expression became shuttered, and for some reason Fin found himself staying put.

"You probably don't remember me! I was here two years ago touring, and I wrote a ballad for you when—"

"I remember the ballad." Annika smiled prettily.

Fin knew that was a bad sign.

"Well, would you like me to sing it for you again tonight? Since that time, I've joined a whole group of minstrels, and I think we have a real shot at earning a place in the castle! We have our songs already picked, but for you, my lady, we could—"

"… Given that the ballad refers to my marriage with the now deceased Viscount Jenoure, I'm not sure that would be well received." She made her smile seem apologetic, but Fin saw the stillness in her that could only come from being all too aware of one's actions. It was a sure sign she was considering doing something she shouldn't …

"Oh! He ... He passed? I uhh, oh. I didn't ... um. I didn't know. My condolences, my lady." The bard gave a sloppy bow and looked as though he wanted the earth to swallow him up whole.

Fin wished it would, for everyone's sakes, but he sadly lacked that skill set.

"Thank you for your condolences. I look forward to hearing your new songs this evening." Annika gave the man a merciful exit.

Gratefully, the minstrel took his leave, and left Fin glued to the bench as Annika drank from her goblet.

"You don't need to stay," she said aloud afterward, despite not glancing at him.

"Was the song ... really that bad?"

She turned to face him then. He saw the dry amusement in her face.

"It was complimentary to a fault. I had only just arrived here from Troivack when he graced the nobility with a tune about my many virtues and beauty."

"That sounds ... embarrassing. Was it hard adjusting to life here at first?"

"It was." She looked a strange mix of wistful and pained, and it was hard to see and not pry further.

Fin knew he needed to leave, even though he didn't want to, if he were being truthful. Their conversing in such a public place was going to draw attention soon, though, if it hadn't already.

"I hope you enjoy the festival. Good evening." He stood and bowed, and she acknowledged his farewell appropriately ... but there was something oddly reticent in her expression.

He couldn't put his finger on it, however, and so he headed out to find Hannah and Peter once more.

One thing that did occur to him as he moved farther from Annika was how she always seemed sad when she showed her true self. Fin didn't like it. Not one bit. He began thinking how much he wanted to help, but knew with a heavy, aching heart, that there was absolutely nothing he could do.

Fin had just spotted his aides chatting with the kitchen knights after searching the entire festival for them. He began heading over to their group when he came across Mage Lee standing before the stage being prepared for the performers. No one dared to go near him, as the man was muttering in his garbage "magic" language.

"… Gods help me," Fin muttered. He didn't *want* to talk to the mage, but … on the other hand … What if the imposter was doing something that could hurt the growing crowd? Like setting fire to the stage?

After glancing around and only seeing a bunch of minstrels tuning their instruments, he approached the man.

"I applaud your career move," Fin announced, standing shoulder to shoulder with the milky-eyed mage.

Mage Lee blinked several times and turned his now clear eyes while keeping his back hunched. When he saw it was Fin speaking to him, however, he immediately straightened and scowled.

"What are you implying?"

"Well, you're auditioning as a court musician, aren't you? I'm proud of you. I know it's hard changing your ways."

Mage Lee looked ready to throttle him, and it took most of Fin's inner strength not to smile.

"Idiot. I'm working on casting an amplifying spell on the front of the stage. Do you see the metal and stone bowls lining the front? Those help the sound to carry so that everyone can hear."

Fin raised his eyebrows.

"Huh. Never heard of that one."

The slow smug smile Lee gave removed any small amount of complimentary thought from Fin's body.

"Really? An air witch never learned this?" Lee scoffed.

"I never said I was an air witch."

Lee couldn't hide his surprise, and Fin was discovering he was quite pleased with the king. He may have told his wife, but he hadn't told Mage Lee anything more.

"Wha— The dishes! I saw them float, don't try to toy with me," Lee grumbled while turning back to the stage.

"Typical." Fin feigned a cough as he said the word, making Lee turn back around while staring daggers at him.

"Pardon me?"

"I coughed. Now if you will excuse me, I believe my aides over there had questions for me." Fin strode away, whistling merrily, leaving Mage Lee to continue muttering angrily to himself.

As Fin strode up to the small group that he saw every day, he overheard some of their conversation.

"… Why not!"

"As I said! It ain't a knight's—"

Hannah was openly pouting as Sir Taylor glanced around nervously. Fin assessed the young woman's state, given that she was not one to whine or be difficult, and guessed she was probably in the upper reaches of tipsy.

"What seems to be the issue?" Fin asked as he finished his ale and joined the circle.

"I had just mentioned to Hannah how great the knights were at singing, and now she insists on hearing them," Peter admonished, shooting the military men an apologetic glance.

The knights collectively looked ready to shove Hannah into a trunk and ship her off to a foreign country, which didn't make the arrival of more knights any better.

"Oyy, Taylor, Lewis, Andrews! Long time no see!" Fin gazed at the new knight arriving, who, for some reason, was still wearing a steel chest plate. He looked to be in his mid-twenties, with curling auburn hair and hazel eyes, and a tankard clasped in his left hand brandished in greeting. Behind him were perhaps four other knights, all drinking, and they too were wearing random pieces of armor as they celebrated the night.

"Sir Harris, how've you been!" Sir Taylor had a desperate look in his eye as he cast a quick glance at Fin, Peter, and Hannah. He *clearly* was nervous about something being said.

"Oh, much better since I don't have to see your ugly face every day! How is it being a kitchen wench?" The men all chortled, but Fin could see the strain on Sir Taylor's face.

"Ahh, what's to say? I get to relax and eat good food. It's like a vacation!" Sir Taylor waved off the comment and took a drink. Something that caught Fin's eye was how the large man turned his body, effectively shielding Hannah from sight.

Oddly enough, Sir Lewis, Peter, and even he himself had somewhat done the same subconsciously.

He felt strangely pleased all of a sudden. "No wonder you're lookin' thick around the middle! So how awful is the new cook bitch of the castle?"

Every back stiffened, as Sir Lewis cleared his throat loudly.

"What? Is he here or somethin'?" one of the other men behind Sir Harris called out, noticing the strange reaction their comrades had.

Fin then realized that not only had the knights blocked Hannah from view, but also himself and Peter. He smiled and failed to notice that the aide beside him was shooting him a nervous glance.

"Errm—" Sir Taylor didn't get the chance to answer for himself.

"Sir Harris, was it?" Fin stepped forward and was pleased to see he was taller than the knight by half a foot.

Sir Harris's smirk dimmed slightly as he stared up into Fin's eyes. After a moment, however, it came back full force and even deepened when Fin held out his hand.

"I am Finlay Ashowan, the Royal Cook."

The knight glanced over both of his shoulders and laughed with his friends without bothering to take his hand.

Oh. I am going to have some fun with you … Fin thought to himself almost gleefully. He'd been feeling a tad unsettled ever since he had spoken with Lady Jenoure earlier, and a knight in clear need of a good lesson would help soothe some of the stress of the day.

He didn't see the expressions his aides made behind him, but the group of knights in front of him were suddenly staring at Sir Taylor again with humorous curiosity.

"Worried for him, Taylor?" one of the knights in the back called out, laughing.

The response was slow to come.

"… Please don't annoy him. I don't wish that upon any of you …."

The group behind Sir Harris quieted somewhat when they realized that Sir Taylor was worried for *them*, and *not* the other way around. It was at that moment when Sir Harris realized Fin was still smiling, and still offering his hand with a strange glimmer in his eyes.

The lines around the knight's eyes tightened slightly. For some reason, he was suddenly beginning to feel as though he had fallen into some kind of trap …

CHAPTER 24
THREE LITTLE DRUNKS

Knight Harris shook Fin's hand slowly, and upon releasing it, eyed the man up and down.

There was something odd about the cook … something strangely authoritative and … untouchable.

"You lot seemed to be arguin' when we stepped up. What was that you were saying Taylor, about 'not being knightly'?" The group behind Sir Harris was back to laughing, and pointedly looking away from Fin, who hadn't shifted his gaze from Sir Harris. He still had a broad smile on his face, though his hands were now on his hips after the firm handshake.

"Nothing! Nothing at all!" There was a great scuffle happening behind Sir Taylor that appeared to require Sir Andrews, Lewis, and Peter to handle.

"You know why you always lost to me in poker, Taylor? You get as stiff as a mage's staff when you're worried." The knight took a step toward the kitchen aides, his feet pointing toward the edge of the group that was still desperately trying to contain something … or someone.

Sir Harris was beginning to frown and smile at the same time, when he found Fin had leaned over so that he was inches from his left ear.

"That's close enough."

"Gods, you girlie-looking freak! Back it up!" Sir Harris jumped, yet despite his bold words appeared unnerved.

When the knight had recovered, he fixed Fin with a glare.

"I was seeing what the fuss was back there. I oughta report you to the captain for bein'—"

"I WANNA HEAR THEM SING!"

Every man present froze as the clear but inebriated voice of Hannah broke the tension.

"What was that?" Sir Harris was rediscovering his sneering smile as Sir Taylor's eyes bulged from his head.

Everyone remained frozen.

It was then that from the fresh shadows of the dusk, a figure in a black cloak stepped forward.

"I believe what Hannah was saying was: she wants to hear Sirs Taylor, Lewis, and Andrews sing." Lady Annika Jenoure lowered her hood, and every knight present either dropped into a bow or straight to their knees.

It took Fin, Peter, and Hannah a few moments of being stunned before they remembered they too needed to show their respects.

"I would also like to hear their songs to see what all the fuss is about. However, I am not the type of lady to force those of a lower status to do her bidding."

"Of course not, my lady!"

"No one would think so, my lady!"

"You're nothin' less than a saint, viscountess!"

Came the many voices of the knights as everyone remained bowed.

"Please rise," she commanded effortlessly.

As everyone straightened, Fin felt something shift inside of himself ... and it wasn't something good.

It was the sinking awareness of how far apart they truly were.

"I think to add honor to the request, we could make this a little more interesting." She addressed them all calmly, her dark brown eyes sweeping over them all without really looking at them.

"W-What did you have in mind, my lady?" Sir Lewis squeaked his brown eyes wide in trepidation.

"A bet."

On the opposite side of the festival, behind the confrontation, the minstrel competition was beginning. As it did so, music washed over all of them, filling their ears with dulcet tones, and yet no one moved.

It was then the viscountess made her declaration. "I bet that I can out-drink three of you knights."

It was a good thing that the majority of those present at the festival had made their way far closer to the stage. It would undoubtedly have been a far larger spectacle if more people had heard what one of the most powerful and wealthy women on the continent was suggesting.

Jaws dropped, eyes bulged, and nervous glances grew in abundance.

"M-My lady, surely you cannot—"

"My lady, we can just sing one song quickly. It isn't worth—" Annika held up her hand, silencing Sir Taylor.

"You haven't heard the terms yet."

Fin's knights all gulped.

"If I can out-drink three of you, and I expect an honest effort, or I will have every knight present transferred to be under Royal Cook Finlay Ashowan's command for a month."

"Hold on, wha—"

Fin began to protest, only to find Peter slapping his hand up over his mouth in an uncharacteristic show of force.

"If your three selected challengers beat me, I will pay for each of you to have a day off of your choosing as long as the captain agrees on the day. If *I* win, however, the knights here," she gestured at Sir Lewis, Andrews, and Taylor, "have to sing on stage tonight in front of everyone."

No one dared defy her. Peter dropped his hand from Fin's mouth.

"My lady, w-we accept these terms, but we want you to have a backup," Sir Taylor managed, though it very clearly pained him.

"Very well. Hannah will be my backup."

Every man present watched, mortified, as the petite blond girl skipped over happily to Annika. No one wanted to point out that a man had been what they meant.

"Sir Taylor, you and your men shouldn't be part of this, as we can't have you on stage stumbling drunk. Why don't you select your three champions?"

The knight turned to look at every pair of eyes on him, and slowly, without moving his gaze, leaned over to Fin.

"Help." His whispered plea sounded as though it was strangled out of him.

Fin sighed.

"Because this is Hannah's fault, I will. I don't think any of your fellow knights will actually aid you."

"They will. Knights always stick together. If someone goes against one of us, it's really all of us."

Fin went quiet and studied each of them. They were strong burly men, why was Sir Taylor quaking in his boots if they were loyal?

"The issue is they're all already drunk and have a lotta pride," Sir Taylor explained when he saw Fin's confusion.

"Pick Harris to start."

Sir Taylor groaned and pinched the bridge of his nose.

"Can't you forgive him just once—"

"What, you think I'm being unfair?" Fin asked innocently.

"I don't trust you."

"He's the most sober of them."

Sirs Andrews and Lewis stepped toward Fin and Taylor and bowed their heads closer to hear the discussion.

"Cook wants Harris to go first."

"… Why do I get the funny feeling that this won't go well for him?" Sir Andrews shot Fin a calculating look, but he maintained his guiltless expression.

"Who'll be the other two?" Sir Lewis asked nervously.

"Myself and Fin," Peter volunteered suddenly. All eyes turned to him. "Get Harris to take the most, I drink daily and am still quite sober, so I can go after. Fin looks like he's still on his first ale, so save him for last to hold out."

Sir Taylor announced their decision, and in no time at all, it began.

A small barrel had been rolled out and two empty goblets set atop its surface. The knights that were intending to be the audience of the competition had made themselves useful as the challengers briefly prepared themselves. Both Peter and Annika had disappeared for a short while but reappeared before someone could be sent looking for them.

The knights had found torches tall enough to provide adequate lighting, as well as a tree stump and stool for the opponents to rest on. The lady would, of course, take the stool. They had chosen a back corner of the festival near some lovely shrubbery for the event, where no one would pay any attention to a group of large men milling about.

As a result, the knights were quite effective as human shields against prying eyes, which was a happy coincidence for Lady Jenoure.

Once the opponents were seated, Annika smiled at Sir Harris, who looked deeply uncomfortable with the situation.

"How about we go back and forth deciding on the drink per person, hm? I will decide what we start with." Annika's musical voice made Sir Harris risk glancing at her face, then over to his left, where Fin stood grinning ear-to-ear. That expression made him somehow even *more* concerned.

"Uh, sure, my lady."

Still smiling, Annika procured a glass bottle that she had had stowed in the inner lining of her cloak.

"I retrieved this from my private stock just for this festival. It is a pleasure to drink it with you, Sir Harris."

The knight blushed and bowed his head, his hands curled into fists pressed atop his thighs.

"Y-You honor me, my lady."

Annika poured each goblet half-full. She raised her cup and locked eyes with Sir Harris.

"To your health and fortune," she toasted serenely. She was an angelic picture of calm and peace.

"And yours," Harris returned, beginning to sweat.

Annika tossed the entire contents of the goblet back and drained it in one go.

This earned several shocked expressions from the knights.

Sir Harris, however, saw this and instead became emboldened.

So he followed her lead.

The knight promptly sprayed the beverage everywhere, coughed, vomited, and then collapsed on the ground.

All eyes rose from the spectacle to Annika, who made no show of being at all perturbed by the disgusting display, or the alcohol she had consumed. She was actually in the middle of picking up the fallen knight's goblet.

She took a gulp and lowered the cup with a dainty shrug.

"Tastes fine to me."

Sir Taylor, Lewis, and Andrews slowly turned to face Fin, who was still smiling down at Sir Harris.

"You're a scary bastard, you know that?" Sir Taylor uttered as he watched the twitching body of his comrade be dragged over to the bushes by his more compassionate colleagues.

"How is it my fault that the lady drinks Troivackian moonshine?" Fin managed a straight face as every man that heard the exchange turned to stare at Annika. She fixed him with a sly subtle smile at his words.

"Peter, I think you're up." Sir Andrews clasped Peter's shoulder, and gently pushed him toward the vacant stump.

He sat down clumsily, looking slightly more serious about the endeavor than he had moments ago.

Peter drew out a strange, green-tinged bottle of his own that he had been keeping under his arm.

Fin watched as Annika's smile became genuine, and instantly paid closer attention.

"What … in the world is that?" Sir Lewis asked, looking around at everyone else, who already seemed to know.

"Absinthe," Peter answered, giving a small bow to Annika. "My family's recipe."

"Gods! Is this a match to the death or something?!" Sir Lewis cried out and tried to step forward, but both Sir Taylor and Fin stopped him.

Peter poured for himself, then for Annika.

They toasted and drank.

The goblets hit the barrel, both empty, and so in went another shot of the green liquor.

Two shots down.

Three shots down.

Four shots down.

Five shots down.

Peter's complexion was nearing the color of the very alcohol he was consuming, and while there was a small sway to Annika, she remained upright and composed.

"I must admit, Peter, I did not expect you to be the greater challenge," she praised.

"St-stop! You'll both die!" Sir Andrews called out in distress.

The sixth shot was poured and swallowed.

Fin leaned back to whisper to Sir Taylor.

"The good news is that Peter weakened Lady Jenoure. The bad news is you may be stuck singing at his funeral."

"Gods help him, cook." Sir Taylor shook his head in awe.

The seventh shot was somberly poured into the goblets, and then down their throats.

Peter stood up abruptly.

The man took four steps, collapsed, and then proceeded to vomit everywhere.

Sir Andrews and Lewis immediately scooped him up and hauled him over to the bushes, where they rested him on his side. They returned, looking far paler than before.

Fin stepped carefully around the vomit and sat down across from Annika. She slowly dabbed the corner of her eye delicately, her hand movements indicating that she was quite inebriated herself.

"I must admit, my lady, you are full of surprises," Fin confessed as Annika drew out the dreaded moonshine once more.

Noting her unsteadiness and lack of coordination, he reached over and gently took the bottle from her. Their fingers touched momentarily, making them both lock eyes for the briefest of moments, before both averting their gazes shyly as Fin poured for the both of them.

"Mmm, well, I was passing by and was oh so curious about the singing," she explained without her usual eloquence.

Fin responded by raising his glass in a salute, which was when Annika held up her hand.

Everyone held their breaths.

"You know … I think you all were right after all. I'm glad I have my backup. Hannah, please tap in for me." Lady Jenoure stood, and gracefully turned toward the young woman.

Fin's face fell.

Hannah stumbled forward, and clumsily seated herself.

Did she … plan this?!

Fin was frozen. What in the world could he do?!

"Son of a mage," he cursed, making all the knights around him glance around in confusion.

Keith was around?

"We forfeit." Sir Taylor stepped forward boldly.

Lady Jenoure folded her arms across her chest. "I believe I said not to go easy on me."

"Hannah is not you, my lady," Fin pointed out, standing with Sir Taylor.

"Oh, very well. As a penalty, Finlay Ashowan must finish his goblet." She sighed, and fixed Sir Taylor with a firm stare. "You better go immediately after to inform Mr. Howard that I have commanded you knights to perform."

Some of the knights that had been watching the entire match in silent amazement stepped forward and clapped the trio on their shoulders in support. Fin raised his goblet to Annika and downed it.

His insides blazed, melted, froze, blazed, and melted again.

If he moved, he would be ill.

They all bowed to Annika as everyone tried to leave quickly to get away from the growing stench of putrid vomit on the grass around them.

Annika smiled graciously as they did so, while Hannah excused herself to go check on Peter. Lady Jenoure and Fin found themselves completely alone.

He held up his index finger once Hannah had disappeared into the bushes, then turned around and vomited. Unlike Sir Harris, however, he stood back up, wiping his mouth with the back of his hand.

"How much of that had you planned ahead?" he asked, blinking away the stars in his eyes, and feeling incredibly grateful that the moonshine wouldn't be staying in his stomach. His throat burned something fierce, but his focus on the woman in front of him helped distract from the fact.

Her smile turned devious.

"Since Sir Harris and the other knights came."

Fin frowned. "Why?"

"They were going to bully your aides mercilessly. If Sir Taylor did sing under their force, he would've lost all dignity. This way, he is the hero making a grave sacrifice." She slurred some of the explanation and shrugged. "It also saved a potential brawl."

He became very aware in that moment how terrifying Annika truly was.

He realized that she could have easily dismissed them using her status and power. However, she was right in her prediction that the knights would've come back another time to harass Sirs Taylor, Lewis, and Andrews. She had manipulated the entire scenario from the beginning with incredible ease.

"Now shall we go hear them sing? After all this trouble, they better be good." Annika swept back a loose strand of her hair, and took a step forward, only to stumble slightly.

Fin quickly caught her and helped her find her feet.

Feeling her in his arms, however, quickly reminded him why he needed to stay away from her. She looked up at him, her eyes slightly unfocused, her lips a deep rosy color and a small blush in her cheeks.

Gods, she felt amazing being so close to him.

Fin's heart was suddenly thundering, and so it was with great difficulty he pulled away from her.

"Perhaps you should return to the castle, my lady."

"I'm seeing those knights sing no matter what you say." She stepped forward stubbornly.

Rubbing the back of his neck and staring at her retreating swaying back, he slowly moved his feet to catch up with her.

"So you knew I wouldn't make Hannah drink that?"

"I knew the second all of you moved to protect her that she was a surefire way to make things go in my favor."

"Where were you watching us from and why?"

"A lady needs her secrets," she answered enigmatically. "So the knights … do they sing dancing music?"

"Maybe. I only heard them sing one song before. Why? Do you really want to dance in your current state?"

"I'm more interested to see you dance, actually," she teased, staring up at him in a way that made him blush and feel pleased all at once.

"I— Uh— I can't dance. Or sing for that matter, so don't get any ideas."

"Don't worry, I already have *plenty* of ideas and plans."

Fin glanced over at her and smiled, shaking his head.

"I doubt any of those ideas are good."

"Depends who you ask," she laughed to herself while staring straight ahead.

People once again surrounded them as they rejoined the festival crowd, and Fin was left trying to dim the smile he wore. He failed to notice that Annika beside him was doing the very same thing, and both of them were wholly unsuccessful.

CHAPTER 25
ENEMY EYES

The Troivackian King Matthias the Sixth watched his men train with his hands clasped behind his back and his feet braced apart. He wore dark brown trousers, a deep burgundy tunic, and a long leather vest. His golden crown glinted in the sun, and the presence of the finery assured his troops that he would not join them for their sparring, much to their relief.

As he watched under the stone archway with his back to the castle wall, he noted a flurry of movement to his left, near one of the stone pillars that held up the stone covering he stood under.

The king's eyebrows twitched in a rare show of emotion.

He waited patiently, knowing what was to come.

"RAAAAAA!" The battle cry of his son rang out as the young boy threw himself into his father's arms. The king caught him, and the corner of his mouth twitched.

He was pleased.

"Papa, did I surprise you?" He stared down into the dark eyes that resembled his own and patted the lad atop his light brown hair. He was careful to ensure his gold rings didn't catch any of the boy's fine hairs.

"Not quite, but your footfalls have become silent. It is good progress."

The six-year-old boy beamed proudly up at him.

"Captain Orion says if I keep practicing my speed, I could maybe join your next hunt!"

"Perhaps. Brendan, where is your brother?"

The little boy made a face. "I don't know. Henry always wants to be with mother. Can't I be with you, Papa?" he asked, staring up at his father imploringly.

The king grew stern, but before he addressed his son, looked to his soldiers. "Walters, widen your stance. If you're knocked on your ass one more time you will be aiding the masons in the construction of the north wall for a month."

There was an emphatic reply, which he barely acknowledged before turning back to his son. "Brendan, your brother needs to learn to be strong. How will he learn if you leave him to hide in his mother's skirts?"

"*You* taught me how to be strong, though! Why should I—"

"Son." The timbre of the ruler's voice changed, and Brendan began to tremble immediately at the shift. "I want you to tell me the name of every man that has been a part of your lessons." He watched his son carefully.

"Th-There's you, Papa, Captain Orion, Lord Miller, stable master Jacob, Sir Roberts—"

"Precisely. You will remember them and their patience with you. It is your duty as a man of Troivack to not only train the weak, but to strengthen them as well."

The ones that want *to improve, that is,* he added silently.

The king couldn't help but pity Lord Miller for his youngest son's indifference regarding his own capability as a nobleman.

Brendan was doing his best not to break eye contact or shed a single tear when listening to his father's lecture. He accomplished this knowing that if he didn't, he would need to stay in his chamber for a week. "Yes, Papa."

"Good. As punishment, you will go to each of the men you listed and apologize for slighting their efforts in your education. After that, you will retrieve your brother and you will help him."

"Yes, Papa." The boy's lip was quivering, and the king decided to show him the smallest ounce of leniency and not scold him for the emotion.

"You are dismissed."

The prince trotted off, his footsteps inaudible, and it pleased the king more than he would ever say.

~~~~~~~~

The queen of Troivack stared down at her son Henry as she tapped her nail on the desk she had been using to review the castle finances. She was biding her time for the child to realize her displeasure was growing.

For when he did, she hoped for his sake he would seek out his brother.

"Mama, what's that?" The child pointed at the magnifying glass she had been using to read some of the messier ledgers.

"A tool for reading small and sloppy writing," she replied tightly.

The boy grinned at her, and her stomach clenched. He was going to be eaten alive at this rate …

"Mother?" The queen felt relief wash over her at the sound of Brendan's voice.

"I am glad you are here, my prince. Please remove your brother from my presence." She bowed her head to her eldest son, who nodded firmly.

Walking around his mother to where his three-year-old brother sat, Brendan scowled.

"Come on. You need to stop being a baby," the eldest prince demanded before roughly grabbing his brother's small chubby hand and trying to tug him to his feet.

The child let out a shriek that made the queen's ears ring. While her jaw clenched at the sound, she turned back to her writing desk and tried to continue her work.

Brendan's cheeks deepened in color at his own frustration. "Stop it!" he shouted back at his brother, which only made the toddler scream louder as tears ran down his cherub face.

Brendan plugged his ears, while the queen fixed her eyes on the wall ahead of her and didn't budge. The chamber door was suddenly thrust open with a bang that rattled the castle floors.

The screaming didn't cease, however, as the king himself strode over to his offspring, glowering darkly down at the boy until the shrieks subsided to small hiccups.

The king turned to the queen. "Did you attempt to soothe him?"

"Of course not, sire."

He turned toward Brendan who met his graze defiantly. "Did you make your apologies?"

"Yes, Papa."

"Very well. Both of you leave the room. I need to have a word with Henry."

The queen rose gracefully and curtsied, then opened the door for Brendan before exiting herself.

Henry began to whimper at seeing his mother leave him, when the king picked him up and held him arm's length away so that they could stare at one another.

The boy went still. Henry peered fearlessly into his father's eyes, his curling black hair and dark eyes dubbing him closest in resemblance to the king out of he and his brother.

For a moment he was glad that the child showed no weakness to him—until he smiled.

"Enough." The disgust dripped from the king's tone, but he felt his insides twist unpleasantly at having to say the word.

He would never admit that he thought his son had the most charming expressions that were dangerously capable of softening the hardiest of men.

He wasn't just any man, however. Matthias was the king.

The child giggled.

"You will not show such weakness on my land." His voice was soft, but cold. The toddler stopped giggling, and instead thrust his thumb into his mouth as he studied his father cheerily.

"Very well. If you cannot conduct yourself properly, you will be left alone until dinner."

The child began to fuss then. The king placed his son on the floor and turned to the door. As he exited, he glanced over his shoulder at the growing concern on Henry's face.

"It's for your own good. No child of mine will be conquered, so you best start learning how to behave."

Tears were rising in Henry's eyes. The king hesitated for only a second as he went to close the door.

That second, however, meant more than anyone in Daxaria could ever imagine.

"Who was it here that insisted the Zinferans were a peaceful people that were unlikely to join Daxaria in their defense in a war?" The king raised a thick black eyebrow as he stared around the table. His chief of military turned to observe the lords with a malicious glint in his eyes.

"When I think about it, I think it was … you, Lord Ball." The king stared right at the man, who was visibly sweating despite his refusal to look away from his ruler. To avoid eye contact was a measure of cowardice in Troivack.

"My lord, it is unusual that they would interfere! Why are we not discussing how the Daxarian idiots even *knew* about our plans?" Lord Ball exclaimed, scowling at the nine other lords present.

"An excellent point. I do find it an odd coincidence that Lord Piereva's sister is reportedly close with the continent's king and queen." Lord Palmer turned on the head of the Piereva family, but the man quickly shrunk away under the dark expression that met him.

"She's a half-sister," Phillip Piereva started fiercely before turning back to the king. "Zinfera's involvement changes our plans to begin the raids through Rollom. We already have men on Austice's shores scouting their troops, but we need someone in the castle to get a better handle of the situation."

The king followed the development of the conversation silently. His dark eyes watched every shifting face carefully. Their reactions told him everything he'd need to know to assess the situation.

It was time to speak. Every eye was on him, silently insisting on his command.

"Isn't your sister supposed to be marrying soon?" The king stared at Lord Piereva, who was still scowling over the mention of his youngest sibling.

"They are trying to align her with Zinfera to solidify their military aid," Lord Piereva replied tersely.

"We have sent one of our own to her as a potential marriage partner. He is a spineless man, but of noble birth from Lord Miller's family. Piereva, if you could command your blood to abide your order, her reaction will be very telling to us."

"Sire?" Lord Ball peered around confused about the king's meaning, his chins jiggling as he spoke.

"Lord Ball, His Majesty is suggesting that we discern whether or not Lord Piereva's sister is a spy or not by seeing if she takes orders from her true home. I recommend the earl's presence in Daxaria to enforce this. Her brother's presence could help alleviate threats that could be forcing her choice in the Daxarian court," the chief of military explained, his intense black eyes smoldering into Lord Ball, who visibly gulped.

"Thank you, Mr. Helmer. It is a relief to finally have someone who catches on when I first explain things. It saves my breath." The king gave a nod to Aidan, which earned the chief of military a glare from Lord Piereva.

"Come to think of it, Your Majesty, I know I told you many interesting things about my time in Daxaria, but—"

"Yes, yes, Piereva, I have given you your praise."

"Pardon me, sire. What I was going to say, was that there was another odd encounter I had dismissed, but now think it might be worth mentioning."

The king turned his full attention to the lord, the weight of his undivided interest enough to make most men choke.

"There was a cook in the castle. He made the best food I've ever eaten in my life, and, well … it was peculiar. He looked a shocking amount like Mr. Helmer here. Red hair. Tall and gangly—though he had sharper features. Bright blue eyes and looked *pretty* for a man." The room burst into titters at the description, but both the king and Lord Piereva were watching the chief of military's response closely.

At first, he said nothing.

Then he leaned back in his chair and began to laugh.

"Mind sharing with us what is so funny?" Lord Piereva's right cheek twitched.

"Oh, Your Majesty … you have no idea what was just revealed," the chief of military guffawed, ignoring Lord Piereva completely.

"I don't suffer those who wish to toy with me." The king's bored voice yet steady stare drew Aidan's black eyes. When the two locked gazes, the temperature in the room rose by several degrees.

"My apologies, sire. Lord Piereva deserves a hearty toast from me." Aidan stood, goblet in hand.

"You, my lord, have found my estranged son, Finlay Helmer."

"How strange, he introduced himself as Finlay Ashowan," Lord Piereva practically spat in reply.

Aidan chuckled. "His mother's last name. Typical. Well, we can use this information to our advantage, Your Majesty."

"How so?" The king was interested, but it showed in neither his face nor his posture.

"My dear long-lost son is a witch as well and happens to be living as a peasant in the castle of the king. I believe that we could acquire more than one spy of our own within its walls."

"You wish to arrange a meeting with your son to convince him to become a traitor?" Lord Piereva scoffed.

"Yes. I will go once Lady Jenoure announces her marriage and see what can be done." Aidan didn't even bat an eye at Lord Piereva's derisive tone.

"What if he does not wish to be of use? He has forgone your name, after all," Lord Palmer demanded, his shoulder-length black hair swinging as he stood.

"Then we tell the Daxarian king that Finlay was a spy, and he will have my son killed. Or we get rid of him ourselves. It is no loss of mine either way." When Aidan seated himself again, the king had a funny glint in his eye as he stared at his chief of military.

"Is he a bastard?"

The room grew quiet, and the chair holding the fire witch creaked as heat ebbed out of him.

"I married his mother before I knew she was weak. He was born a year after. He is as legitimate as anyone here." He cast an appraising gaze around the room, until he locked eyes with the king again.

The inner corners of his eyes twitched. There was something strange about the Troivackian monarch. The man was unreadable and remarkably controlled, which Aidan found more than mildly aggravating and disconcerting.

"I will give you the command when you should go speak with your son. I first want Lord Piereva to journey back to Daxaria and inform his sister that she is to marry the man we've sent. Weak or not, he is a Troivackian and he *will* bend to his king."

The lords listened without interruption.

"We will enter through Rollom as planned, but not as an army. We will invade as we have with Austice, and we will agree on a day where our quiet feet are to become the drums of war."

Fin was stretching and cracking his back on his way back to his cottage as Kraken trotted beside him. He was thinking about how wonderful a good night's rest would be, when he saw Ruby barreling across the lawn heading toward him. She appeared to have come from the east wing exit.

"Kraken, why do I get the sense that I'm about to get in trouble?" Fin stopped and waited before another thought occurred to him. "You didn't poop in anyone's shoes again, did you?"

The feline responded with a mew and fell silent as he too sat and waited for the Head of Housekeeping.

When Ruby finally huffed to a halt in front of Fin, she began trying to speak.

"His ... Majesty ... wants ... you—"

"I know there have been some rumors floating around that I'm gay, but I can assure you I am not," Fin interrupted with a cheeky smile. Ruby shot him an exasperated look.

Once she had finally caught her breath, she tried again.

"His Majesty wants you to order more food from our merchants for next week. We just received word that three suitors are on their way for Lady Jenoure."

Fin's stomach dropped to his feet.

"Oh … I didn't know she would have to choose so quickly."

Ruby gave him a skeptical expression before she continued.

"I believe they are trying to rush her due to the war. It doesn't matter that the king wanted to wait. There are two Zinferans suitors, and one Troivackian, set to arrive shortly along with entourages for all three."

A dark cloud settled over Fin, muddling his mind, and so it took him a moment to process the information.

"If possible, could you please find out more exact numbers? I need to know before I finish the order for tomorrow morning. We have a bit of extra food thanks to the festival earlier this week, which should help, but I prefer to be prepared."

Ruby nodded.

"I will try to get that information from His Majesty before he sleeps this evening. Though he is having to break the news to Lady Jenoure tonight, so it is hard to say if he will have time afterward."

Fin's chest was constricting and beginning to pain him.

Ruby bid him farewell for the night and ran back to the castle to finish informing the rest of the staff.

Fin stood staring after her blindly under the first twinkling stars hanging just over the horizon that still glowed from sunset. After a moment, he shook his head. Fin clenched and unclenched his hands quickly, then looked down at Kraken.

"I guess that's that."

CHAPTER 26
THE WALLS HAVE EARS

The knights were gathered round Fin's table, and they were in the middle of regaling their fellow kitchen staff with more stories about their burgeoning popularity. Thanks to their performance at the festival, they had received numerous compliments and even special attention from the maids. Since the fateful night, while Fin would fill buckets with vegetables to peel, or dirty dishes, the knights would gush about which admirer said what, and which maid tickled their fancy on that particular day. The group sometimes listened over cups of tea to begin their mornings, until he would eventually shoo them out the door.

Sir Lewis was in the middle of a proud description regarding how the new maid Jade he had taken a liking to had shyly approached him to offer her compliments. It was during that tale when Sir Harris sauntered through the garden door.

Everyone fell quiet, and Fin stopped removing the green tops of the strawberries to stare at the visitor.

"Royal Cook Finlay, Sir Harris reporting for duty." The knight gave an exaggerated bow and stood with a mocking smile.

Every eye turned to Fin, who looked as though someone had just defecated over the threshold.

"Sir Harris, I do not believe you are part of my team." Fin's tone was mild as he slowly placed down the small paring knife and berry with his red stained hands.

"Captain ordered me here as punishment for getting sick all over the barracks after the festival." Sir Harris's eyes glinted at Fin in obvious enjoyment.

"The festival was more than a week ago." The strain in Fin's voice was entirely undisguised.

"I only finished cleaning the barracks last night."

Fin turned to the trio of knights, who all gave nods with haunted looks behind their eyes. Their confirmation and obvious traumatic memories over the event did little to appease Fin's displeasure.

"Why is working under me a punishment to you?" he demanded as he placed his hands on his hips.

Sir Harris was still grinning in his annoyingly smug manner, and Fin found himself already beginning to round his cooking table.

"Can't say. Oyy, if you lot are having a brew, I'd love a cup."

Fin didn't reply as he breezed past Sir Harris and swiftly made his way down the garden path.

"Give the captain my regards!" Sir Harris called over his shoulder happily. Turning to his fellow knights, he waved cheerily and approached the cooking table. He reached over to the stone teapot with a wooden handle on the table, plucked up Fin's abandoned teacup, and topped it up.

His eyes rested on Hannah, and immediately gave her a charming smile.

"Well, hello, beautiful."

Sirs Taylor, Lewis, and Andrews collectively growled.

Fin found Captain Antonio speaking to Mage Lee while they stood outside of the empty training ring beside the barracks on the east wing of the castle.

As he approached, the two men ceased their conversation, which appeared to be serious in nature, if their expressions were any indication of their topic.

"Good morning, Mr. Ashowan," Captain Antonio greeted with a small nod as Mage Lee's mood immediately soured.

"Captain," Fin greeted and bowed, then gave the mage a small head bob. The captain noted the slight, but ignored it, as Fin looked troubled.

"Captain, I was wondering why Sir Harris was in my kitchen saying that he is to be in my care?"

"Ah. I heard that the reason my knight was intoxicated to the point of violent illness was thanks to a drinking competition involving yourself, and a few of your other aides."

Fin noticed that Sir Harris had not reported Lady Jenoure's involvement, and his disposition toward the man softened a small fraction.

"I see. I will accept my responsibility in this matter. However, I would like to make a point should other knights displease you in the future, captain?"

The captain jerked his chin down sharply in allowance.

"I am not a nanny for errant men. Please in the future consider alternative means of reform."

"No, you most certainly aren't a nanny," Mage Lee agreed vehemently.

Fin shot the man a long suspicious glance out of the corner of his eye.

"You *are*, however, the perfect pain in the ass," the captain added gruffly, with a rogue smile.

"What do you mean by that?" Fin's tone turned sharp.

"I mean that you, Royal Cook Finlay Ashowan, are an excellent punishment to sound-minded people."

Mage Lee was beside himself in fits of laughter as Fin frowned.

"Mr. Ashowan, you have been somewhat lacking in courtesy and manners. I feel you need to perhaps learn a little humility." The captain's tone was firm, but not entirely unkind.

"I am … aware … of some of my social shortcomings. However—" Fin ground out.

"Social shortcomings? You've the social awareness of a rock!" the mage managed between short bursts of laughter.

"… *However*, I believe a lesson in propriety toward the knights might be a larger concern," Fin managed though his cheeks were red.

The captain's face darkened, and the mage stopped laughing.

"Watch your tongue, Finlay Ashowan. You were only allowed to weigh in regarding Sirs Taylor, Lewis, and Andrews because of their behavior toward a maid under your command—"

"As well as to myself. In fact, I've yet to meet one of your knights that wasn't a bully or disrespectful. I shouldn't have to continually take responsibility for them because of your inability to educate them," Fin added coolly, knowing that he had definitely stepped over a line.

The captain and the witch stared at each other in tense silence for what felt like hours, before the captain seemed to make up his mind.

He pointed toward the ring beside them, his bright blue eye squinting at him.

"We settle differences in one way only in my barracks, cook. If you wish me to let your careless remarks go unreported, you best go pick a weapon."

Fin's eyes widened, but he noticed that there was a strange knowingness in the knight commander's expression. He wasn't sure what to make of that.

He noticed that the knights were beginning to exit their barracks—some barely awake, others stretching in preparation for a day of training. The match would not be without an audience.

He decided to give a single weak attempt to alleviate the situation. "I need to continue preparing for Lady Jenoure's guests, captain."

"All the more reason."

What did that *mean?* Fin wondered to himself, feeling thoroughly disgruntled as he turned to the ring and entered.

Him setting foot on the hard-packed dirt fenced off from the southern side of the western lawn caused a wave of whispers and shouts to erupt amongst the men. Doing his best to ignore them, he walked over to a barrel that held broken spears and the wooden swords the young nobles would use to train. He chose a spear that had its pointed end broken off, and slowly strode toward the center of the ring. The captain stood waiting for him with his hands clasped behind his back.

By then, the ring was fully surrounded with interested spectators. All present were wondering what the cook had done to earn what would be a brutal beat down from their captain.

The captain leaned nearer to Fin so that only he could hear his words. "I have heard interesting things about you murmured amongst the castle occupants."

Fin's expression became guarded as he stared intensely at the captain's glittering blue eye.

"Have you anything to say before we begin?" the captain asked with a raised voice that the others could hear.

"I may want my own children someday. If that could remain a possibility, I would appreciate it greatly."

The captain showed a small smile. "I understand."

Fin then struck his opening stance, which made the captain's eyes twinkle in faint surprise.

With a brief nod, the seasoned warrior gave the word. "Attack."

Fin moved the broken spear with a tight spin to strike at the captain's left knee but missed as the man easily twisted out of reach. The miss didn't stop the movement of the staff as it spun its way around Fin's hand, then neck, to his other hand that grasped it firmly at its middle. He once again struck down toward the back of the captain's knee.

The dull end of the spear was once again met with air, as the captain's open palm collided with Fin's right ear. The hit was hard enough to jar Fin, but not enough that it rendered actual pain. The captain had twisted out of his attack and put himself closer to him.

A small jerk of Fin's wrist brought the side of the broken weapon into the captain's gut. The blow was akin to a slap in that it dealt no damage and was meant more so as a warning hit.

The captain moved to backhand Fin, but he managed to lean back out of the strike, while simultaneously flipping the staff up to knock the hand away.

The punch from the captain's left hand met Fin's gut, catching him off guard, and as he doubled over with a wheeze, an elbow dropped down onto his back, knocking him to the ground.

The knights were all whooping and hollering excitedly, when Fin's leg snapped to the side, and knocked the side of the captain's knee. It brought the man down, giving Fin enough time to pick up the spear and stand while the captain did the same.

The knights were growing quite excited, which was when Fin saw the beaming smile on the captain's face.

It dawned on him that the man wasn't actually trying in the match so much as he was just having fun. Meanwhile, Fin's heart was pounding hard enough to drown out the sound of his own gentle pants.

"You fight like a Zinferan!" the captain boomed in a pleased tone.

Fin didn't bother answering as he repositioned himself.

The knights were going wild.

The captain took a boxer's stance and waited with a blindingly white smile under the hot summer sun. Waves of heat had begun to rise off the dry dirt beneath their feet, but it didn't matter. Both of them were already dripping with sweat, and the cicadas had begun their buzzing from the king's forest, orchestrating the match.

The first to strike was the captain, as a sharp jab made Fin duck to the side to avoid the fist; while doing so, however, he jerked the broken spear diagonally, knocking the captain's inner knee. The captain easily recovered from the attack by taking a quick steadying step away from Fin.

"See here men, this is a good defensive strategy Mr. Ashowan is executing. Each of my upper attacks he uses as an opportunity to use defensive counterattacks. He is focusing on gaining the high ground by knocking me off my balance from below."

Fin tried to strike the outer side of the man's left knee while turning out of the captain's precise left-handed jab.

"You always want to watch where a defensive move takes your opponent, because if they know what they're doing—"

Fin's elbow rose up and struck the back of the captain's head, but the man had clearly been anticipating it, as he dodged enough to minimize the damage.

"… They will flow with the action to use it to their advantage," the captain instructed as he suddenly spun tightly around his opponent's body and clocked an expert punch into Fin's jaw.

His response as pain shot through his head was swift, as he jerked the broken spear in a sharp lengthwise whack that struck the seam of the captain's groin and thigh.

Both men stepped hastily away from each other. Though the captain recovered almost instantly, he still winced.

"I have other duties this morning, as I am sure Mr. Ashowan does as well. Therefore, I will end this quickly."

The captain's stance changed, and Fin's expression of shock was only momentarily visible, as the leader's stance widened and his palms opened.

It was a master Zinferan warrior position.

Fin attacked first. He tossed the broken spear lengthwise toward the captain's face, and as it flew through the air, Fin quickly stepped forward.

He managed to land a single punch by feigning a right hook that the captain knocked out of the way easily with the broken spear he had caught, and instead Fin jabbed with his left into the captain's jaw. The captain responded by ducking, then sweeping his left elbow into Fin's gut, twisting the broken spear inside Fin's stance and knocking him flat on his back.

The roar around the ring only reached Fin when he had regained his breath. The captain offered his hand to his opponent and helped him stand. Once on his feet, the captain leaned down, still clasping Fin's hand, and whispered.

"You aren't the first man I've met that has a beastly father. Mind your anger toward the world, Finlay Ashowan. You cannot control it all."

The color drained from Fin's face as he stepped back and stared at the seasoned veteran, who wore a smile that lifted decades off of his face. The captain clapped Fin's shoulder as they walked toward the exit of the ring, where the kitchen aides and castle knights all stood cheering.

"What are you lot doing here?" Fin demanded, suddenly feeling incredibly self-conscious of his fight.

"We heard the commotion and figured you were involved, considering you had gone to talk to the captain," Peter answered with a teasing smile.

Fin shook his head, and sweat droplets flew off of his forehead. "Let's get back to work."

As he made his way through the crowd, he was mystified by the words of encouragement and delight from the knights he passed.

He decided to ask one of the sirs under his command about the oddity later, when he felt a strange prickling at the back of his neck.

Fin turned and saw Mage Lee eyeing him warily in the crowd, but that wasn't the source of the strange sensation …

Someone else was watching him.

He glanced around and saw no one. Sir Harris appeared at his side then and began to ask several questions, one right after the other, about where he had learned to fight.

Fin was doing his best to answer evasively, while at the same time glancing over his shoulders suspiciously. His team managed to usher him around the corner of the castle toward the kitchens without too much interference, and it was clear their spirits were fully bolstered for their day from the excitement.

No one had been aware that Lady Jenoure stood in the window on the third floor. She'd watched the match with a small smile that her hand-maiden Clara couldn't help but become suspicious of. She glowed with pleasure as she heard the awed comments regarding Fin's skill, and she turned from the window with her eyes cast down but her smile still in place.

Annika turned from the window and raised a graceful hand to the space between her eyebrows, her eyes closed.

I might have a small problem.

Her smile faded, and deep dread filled her.

"Is everything alright, my lady?" Clara asked, her tone conveying her growing concern.

"Yes, it is, Clara. Sorry to trouble you. I just realized I've come down with an affliction, could you please see me to my chambers? I feel I may need a drink."

CHAPTER 27
A REAL DAY DAMPENER

"So how'd you do it?"

"Do what?"

"Earn the captain's 'conflict resolution.'"

Sir Harris had been pestering Fin the entire morning for details following the match. As a result, the original trio of knights, Peter, and Hannah resumed their work without their new team member.

Fin was already feeling sore and stiff from the encounter with the captain. The aches in his arms and legs forced him to silently admit that he was far more out of shape than he had realized. It also meant that he was far more exhausted than normal as he worked on tidying up his table to make way for his dinner preparations.

"Sir Harris, you have dumped your work on the rest of your team. You will stay alone after dinner and do the dishes." Fin didn't look up or bother masking his irritation.

He turned and retrieved a bowl of seasoned bread dough that had been rising.

"I'll make you a deal! If you answer three of my questions, I will do all of the dinner *and* breakfast dishes by myself!"

"You're aware I could just order you to do those things regardless of a deal, right?"

"... You're too fair-minded to do that."

Fin's fists rested on the table as he leaned onto them and wearily bowed his head, sighing heavily. He could easily order the knight away—he didn't owe him any explanation. Then again, if he ever expected Sir Harris to own up to his own shortcomings and errors, he best lead by example.

"Get on with it, then."

Despite Sir Harris being close in age to Fin, he looked as excited as Eric would if Fin gave him a cookie instead of fruit for a snack.

"Alright, what did you do?"

"I spoke disrespectfully to the captain and overstepped my station."

Sir Harris nodded thoughtfully and jutted out his right hip as he listened.

"Yeah? I did something similar when I first got here, and you did a lot better than I did! I'm not just saying this either, you fight better than most of the young knights," Sir Harris complimented with a grin. "It's a good strategy the captain uses when you think about it ... I learned to respect him, and the other knights admired me more for it."

Fin frowned suddenly and straightened.

"Sir Harris, did you have a poor relationship with your father?"

The knight's face fell, and his formerly pleased expression turned angry.

"I'm the one asking the questions."

Fin filed away the reaction in his mind but shrugged casually to encourage the conversation along. Sir Harris shook his head and resumed his questioning, though he was noticeably more subdued.

"Second question: why didn't you say no to the match? You aren't a knight; you probably could've just taken an easier punishment from Ruby."

Fin pinched the bridge of his nose as he forced words from his mouth. He really wasn't one for lengthy discussions regarding his thought process.

"The captain wasn't trying to be an ass. He was right to call me out and I don't fear physical confrontation."

"You just accepted his side? No complaints?"

"I choose my battles. I meant what I had said to him. My argument on the matter I addressed is by no means over. However, I find it best to be mindful of how to get what I want without starting a war."

Sir Harris looked pensive but also respectful toward Fin, as the man slowly raised his heavy gaze to the knight.

"You are out of questions. Be prepared for the cleaning of a lifetime." Fin pointed toward the open garden door, making Sir Harris blustered.

"I meant my third question to be where you learned to fight like a Zinferan," he declared, giving a charming smile that Fin had no doubt made him successful with women.

Fin's wry expression in response made Sir Harris's façade fall, and he grumbled to himself as he exited the kitchen.

The captain made me admirable to the other knights while putting me in my place. Could it be he did so for my words to carry more weight with them?

Fin rubbed his face and began counting down the hours until he could sleep, when the castle door sprung open.

"Hilda's coming!" A maid Fin had never met before appeared. She wore a rose dress with a blue apron, which informed him that she was one of the mid-level maids.

"Am I supposed to know who Hilda is?" he asked as he set the freshly risen dough onto the floured surface of his table.

"The infamous drunkard of Austice?!" the maid replied breathlessly.

"Ah, yes. I have heard of her once or twice from the knights. Does she have specific dietary restrictions?" Fin inquired dully, as the young woman kept glancing over her shoulder as though expecting an attack.

"Other than always needing spirits? No!" she exclaimed while shoving a lock of chestnut brown hair that had become loose behind her ear.

"... Miss, you are not making sense." Fin tilted his head and stared at the woman emotionlessly.

"One of the tavern owners cut her off!"

Fin was doing his best to stay patient, as he attempted to understand the hysteria behind a drunken peasant being forced to become sober for a short time.

"Is there something I need to—"

"The king has summoned you! He is in the counsel room on the second floor—the third door on the right from the servant's stairwell."

Fin's puzzled expression went unnoticed as the young woman scurried away.

Letting out a long sigh and rubbing his face, he felt dread rise in him. He had only fought with the captain that morning and was already out of sorts from the exchange. He hoped it wasn't going to be a stressful encounter with His Majesty.

The first order of business was informing his aides. Fin jogged out to meet them, and found he arrived at the same time as Sir Harris, who had clearly taken a leisurely pace to get there. His new aide's cavalier attitude was an issue Fin would have to deal with later.

Hannah was on her feet immediately when Fin informed them of his instructions for dinner.

"If I am not back in an hour, please put the bread in the oven for less than half an hour."

"Why wouldn't you come back?" The fear and worry in Hannah's voice made a warm sensation in Fin's chest to appear.

"I might be needed for a long time. You all will do just fine. I'll be back as soon as possible."

"Why does the king want to see you? Is it because of your incident with the captain?" Sir Harris's bright eyes gleamed as his love of gossip burst forward.

Rolling his eyes, Fin didn't bother to answer as he turned and headed back to the castle. He hadn't realized the night of the festival that the knight was so energetic. He must have been more inebriated that night than Fin had initially realized.

Not knowing what the commotion was, he strode swiftly all the way up to the room that the maid had directed him toward. He passed by several nobles and footmen that all seemed to be abuzz with worry.

He was beginning to form outlandish speculations over the frenzy, and why it pertained to him, when he thrust open the counsel room door.

Inside were Captain Antonio, Mr. Howard, Mage Lee, Keith, and His Majesty the King.

The royal remained seated as all eyes turned to Fin. The king didn't respond at all to his presence, and instead addressed his captain, who stood frowning at the surprise arrival.

"See that the civilians know to stay in their homes. Send three-quarters of your men to contain the situation and guard the people. None of the knights should wear plate armor in case they need to fish out civilians unable to swim. The rest of the knights shall remain here." The captain bowed and made his exit brushing past Fin, giving him a quick perplexed glance.

"Mr. Howard, you will instruct Ruby to allow the staff to return to their chambers for the time being. Keith, you will guard the queen's chamber."

The two men were dismissed, leaving Fin alone with Mage Lee and the king.

Fin bowed before drawing closer, and once again ignoring the bewildered expressions he received from Mage Lee.

"You summoned me, Your Majesty?"

"Mr. Ashowan, how much experience do you have with water witches?"

Fin took an instinctive step back from the king, and his right hand twitched in surprise at the forthright question.

"Pardon, Your Majesty?"

"Hilda … we were unaware, but she is a water witch." The stress in the king's voice did not go unnoticed by the cook.

"Witches lack proper control and knowledge of their powers to begin with. Hilda was subduing herself with copious amounts of alcohol throughout the years, and no one was the wiser," Mage Lee volunteered, shaking his head sadly.

"She was docile until she was cut off?" Fin supplied as he put the pieces together.

"Precisely." The king agreed with a nod.

Fin folded his arms across his chest. "Why not just offer her a drink?"

"Hilda is … unreasonable at this time. It would seem she is beyond reach with words. She has made the main road running through Austice a powerful river straight down to the Alcide Sea. Should anyone get in her way, she draws the water into her reach and sweeps the individual away. Fortunately, most residents of Austice can swim, but this still poses a problem," the king explained gravely.

"What is it you wish for me to do?" Fin asked, beginning to suspect where the conversation was heading.

"I have sent an emergency message to the Coven of Wittica; however, we need to detain Hilda until they arrive. What can you tell us about water witches?" The king's voice was so forceful it made Fin unconsciously straighten his shoulders.

"They're problematic to fire witches and bonfires." Fin gave a small shrug.

Mage Lee growled at his insolence, while the king's expression darkened.

"Every witch is different. Why is she heading here?" Fin changed the topic. He hadn't meant to be rude; he truly didn't know what kind of answer they wanted. Despite his outwardly calm exterior, he was beginning to panic.

"Something about Keith …" The king turned to Mage Lee with a frown, who shrugged and shook his head in confusion in response.

A snippet of memory snapped into Fin's mind vividly. "Keith told the tavern owner to cut her off," he announced abruptly. "I happened upon the conversation while at the festival."

The king turned to Mage Lee, perplexed.

"I think it is a new owner unaware of the rumors about Hilda. I myself have only heard one or two tidbits of information," Fin continued slowly.

Both Mage Lee and the king looked at Fin, and in unison both said, "You do not let Hilda get sober."

Fin frowned.

"Why is this common knowledge?"

"No one knows where the rule came from, but elders have passed down the warning. Hilda is in her late sixties, nearing seventies, by my estimation. Much about her youth remains a mystery. She has never made it known she wielded such power," Mage Lee explained, his voice taking on a wizened tone.

"I gather we all know the reason to keep her cup full now," Fin pointed out dryly.

He received dirty looks and quickly bowed, immediately offering his apology to the king. Honestly, he didn't mean to aggravate the situation. His growing anxiety was making him feel lightheaded, despite his composure remaining aloof. Other than the unhelpful remarks he kept making, of course …

"What is it you would like me to do, Your Majesty?" Fin addressed the king humbly.

"I am asking you to partner with Mage Lee to neutralize her."

Fin briefly flitted his gaze to Lee before returning it to the king.

The request sounded more like an order.

"She needs to be on castle grounds. Somewhere I've been, if I am to have any kind of help," he began, hoping the panic could not be heard in his voice.

"Have you ever been to the front door?" the king asked seriously.

"No, but if I go now before she arrives it will be fine." Fin answered with a bow.

"Good. Mage Lee, please accompany Mr. Ashowan so that in the event that Hilda arrives too early, he does not get washed out to the Alcide Sea."

Mage Lee gave a short, brisk nod at the king's hard tone, and the two men bowed in unison before turning toward the counsel room door. The pair had begun to move out of the room when Fin suddenly turned back around.

"Your Majesty, please keep as many people from seeing me as possible. I still prefer to not have my abilities known."

There was a tension in the king's forehead as he leaned forward.

"I cannot guarantee anything, Mr. Ashowan. In times of emergency for the greater good, we must make sacrifices. The best I can suggest is to remain under the covered entryway, no one will be able to spot you there."

The reply made Fin's stomach thicken in knots. He wasn't ready to deal with being discovered …

He didn't want to ever hear the horrible names people invented, or to be unable to help those in desperate need that would surely call out for his help.

Lee and Fin exited the chamber without another word and made their way down to the first floor as tensions rose around them.

The memories and worries of his previous experiences when a person learned of what he was, dug deeper and deeper into Fin's mind.

With each step he took, the wriggling maggot of fear gnawed his insides until he was quite certain he would be ill.

"Try not to vomit before we capture the witch," Mage Lee chortled at Fin's pale complexion as they neared the front doors.

"Why can't you handle her alone?" Fin demanded in response without taking his eyes away from the massive, high arching doors that two guards began to open upon their arrival. If the soldiers found it strange that he was accompanying Lee, they did nothing to show it.

"My thoughts exactly. If you wish to stand back and allow me to work, I couldn't care less. The king, I believe, is being overly cautious." The smugness in the mage's tone grated on Fin's nerves, but he was too desperate to retort.

"I will only become involved if you need me to," he responded, somehow managing to keep his voice calm.

Mage Lee turned then and studied Fin closely.

"Is it Hilda or discovery you fear more?"

"Discovery."

Lee frowned.

"You will not be hunted or harmed for being a witch, Mr. Ashowan." he remarked slowly, his voice more patient.

"There are worse things than being hunted." The look on the young man's face forced Lee into silence as he began to ponder what on earth had made Fin so fearful.

The duo exited the front doors and stood on the wide stone landing that spread out before the stairs and overlooked the ring for carriages. In the center circle grew flowers of various blues, whites, and yellows. Rising above the cheery blooms stood a statue of the Goddess and the Green

Man. She was in her virgin form, and he in his prime. Between them stood the first young witch they created as a child. She had long hair, a freckled nose, and an impish grin. Beside her stood her brother, the devil.

"Where is Hilda pulling the water from?" Fin queried as the faint cries of the citizens and rush of water slowly reached their ears.

"Whatever do you mean?" Mage Lee turned, perplexed, as Fin leaned away, shielded his eyes from the sun, and gazed at the sky.

"Hilda is a powerful witch to be drawing enough water to create an entire rushing river down to the sea … Where is she pulling the water from, though? There wouldn't be enough in the city wells alone. If she is pulling water from the air—"

"Pull water from the air?! Are you daft? There is no one with that kind of power! It simply—"

Fin casually waved his hand and drew out a bubble of water from nothing. He drank it straight from the air and turned to stare calmly at Lee, who was rendered speechless.

"It would be harder for her to do that for large quantities. If she pulled it from the clouds, however …" Fin glanced to the sky again and nodded. There were only a few wisps in the blue canvas.

"She will be running out of power soon. Unless, of course, she keeps using her magic to the point that it requires her life energy to sustain."

Lee continued gaping.

"We cannot let her die while maintaining a river in the middle of the city, otherwise it will become permanent."

Finally, Lee found his voice.

"Magic that drains a witch of both magic and life becomes permanent?"

"That is how curses are formed. Yes." Fin nodded as the ground quaked beneath their feet.

"Where was this information when the king was asking about it?!"

Fin gave a small shrug. "I was put on the spot."

He ignored the look of exasperation on Lee's face. Instead, he glanced at the intricate stone carving of trees that cradled the front doors. They mimicked the massive tree shaped pillars holding up the stone ceiling, arching high over the landing beside the stairs.

They were a remarkable show of craftsmanship that made Fin wish he had more time to gawk over them.

"So, we need to delay her enough to make her reasonable without using too much magic. Should we not just leave this matter to the Coven?" Mage Lee's grip on his staff tightened.

"Preferable, but it is doubtful they will get here in time."

"You aren't an air witch." The announcement from Lee made Fin laugh.

"No."

"You are powerful?"

"No."

Mage Lee shook his head. "I think you're a bigger idiot than you realize if you don't believe so," he muttered.

"You studied for at least ten years just to be able to compete with witches. Yet your most significant accomplishment to date was reproducing the biggest idiot on the continent. I'm going to trust what my tutor told me."

Lee turned seriously to Fin.

"That was a grave offense, Mr. Ashowan." His low voice was severe.

Fin closed his eyes.

He knew he had once again let his mouth run off. It was a bad day for it.

His heart was racing, and he was terrified, but he shouldn't lash out. Even if it was just toward Mage Lee.

"Sorry. That was too far, I admit," Fin admonished while rubbing the back of his neck and shifting his gaze downward.

Lee nodded seriously in acceptance and turned his attention back toward the city.

Only, Fin couldn't help but add, "Though your son *is* the one who started all of this by giving bad advice."

Lee glared but decided to change the topic.

"What kind of witch are you, and what in the world did your tutor say?" Lee demanded casting an understanding but also milky eye over Fin.

"Save your magic for Hilda. If you must know, I am a house witch." His eyes remained shut as he tried to calm his emotions.

Mage Lee gave no reaction as he continued to study him using magic—blatantly ignoring Fin's instruction.

"He told me I was born deficient, but that I could be useful to a large household. Doing things like preparing meals and making them comfortable would be the best use of my power. It isn't great, but then again, great witches don't do much with their abilities, so what does it matter?" Fin knew he sounded strained.

It became abundantly clear to Lee then, that Fin's opinion of his own magic was a point of great contention.

"I do not care much for you, Mr. Ashowan. Your manners are atrocious, you're condescending, and you hold unbelievably high expectations of the world." Fin opened his eyes and turned to Lee.

"However, you are honest. I will in turn be honest with you."

Fin folded his arms across his chest, not caring that he could feel a faint mist waft across his face. Hilda was close.

"I've sought to discover your magic twice now. The first time I believed I had not gotten close enough to you to have read it correctly, and therefore dismissed what I saw. This time, however, if I allow myself to believe in the unknown, I believe I have read you correctly all along. You are of all elements, Mr. Ashowan. You are far from weak. I see earth, fire, air, and water in you. More earth and fire, but the others are there all the same. Perhaps they are centered around the home, but I have not met one of your kind before, so I truly do not know."

Fin was shocked. His mouth opened and closed several times as Lee turned away from him, looking all too pleased with himself.

"I can't use my powers outside of my home," he blurted without pausing to think. The stupid mage had knocked him off balance with his declaration.

The Coven had performed similar examinations of his abilities, yet none of them had said anything about his abilities being of all elements. It made sense, though …

Fin was beginning to feel incredibly foolish for letting his weakness slip out, when Mage Lee spoke.

"I saw you quell my mage fire and control items in the air. Perhaps you are only able to use the four elements in your home. It could be nature's way of balancing your magic."

The idea that he had great power to balance great weakness burned through Fin's mind until there wasn't any coherent thought.

When he had finally regained an ounce of his composure, he began to speak.

"You—"

His words were cut off when a sudden spray of water erupted over the ridge of the castle's laneway from the main road leading down to Austice. Riding atop the waves stood a woman with long wavy gray hair, eyes filled with swirling blue, a long dirty peasant dress and hemp cloak fluttering about her in the wind.

Both Fin and Mage Lee walked purposefully toward the edge of the landing.

"Try to finish up quickly, I want to get back to making dinner." Fin sounded bored, and Lee gave him a small bitter smile.

"I'll do what I can, bitch witch."

CHAPTER 28
JUST A DROP

"Bitch witch? Really?" Fin asked exasperatedly, as Lee grinned proudly. "It suits you."

"It's sad that's the best you can come up with," he retorted derisively.

"You think you can do better?"

"Sure. Though there isn't much worse than being called 'mage.'"

Lee's grin turned to a scowl.

The two men then grew quiet as they turned their full attention to the threat before them.

Hilda descended the crest riding atop a waterfall, her power fully directed toward the castle steps as water began seeping up from the ground.

Fin frowned. The higher altitude farther from the sea meant it would be harder for her to pull water from the earth. She would be using far too much power at the rate she was going …

He was in the middle of that thought when Hilda rounded the statue of the Gods.

"WHERE IS THE GUTTERSNIPE THAT HAD ME CUT OFF?!" she bellowed menacingly over the roar of water.

Mage Lee executed his most useful skill in response: acting.

He appeared completely serene.

"This is far enough, Hilda," he called out softly.

"I should've known it'd be one of *your* kind!" She was now at the foot of the stairs. A wall of water rose up behind her, growing higher and higher until it was beginning to touch the roof of the landing.

"Any time now, Lee," Fin remarked, watching the growing wave with his arms crossed over his chest.

Lee chuckled and pounded his staff against the stone landing once, the crystal atop his staff lighting as he uttered the guttural words of magic.

A massive gust of wind propelled forward and forced the wave to bend back on itself. The cheery garden cushioning the statue was consequently flooded, as the water flowed back to the rushing river in the center road of Austice.

Hilda let out a hoarse yelp before throwing her right arm up into the air.

"Oh no." Fin winced. He genuinely began to hope that Lee wasn't all bluster—otherwise his involvement was going to be imminent. He looked to the roof while wondering how many nobles were watching, and felt his heart skip a beat.

He looked back to Hilda anxiously and was just in time to see her gathering more water.

A curling stream rose up from the pounding flood behind her, snaking itself up high into the air. When she waved her arm downwards, the rope-like jet went to curl itself around Lee's staff.

The mage responded with a single nonsensical word that had the water dissipate into steam before being able to touch his person or staff.

Hilda's upper lip curled, which forced the cloud of vapor to rush toward the mage.

Lee shouted another short word, and the steam that would've burned him, blew away.

"The Coven is coming, Hilda. You've gone too far," Lee called as he stepped forward, and once again clunked his staff down. Hilda was suddenly hoisted into the air.

A spiral of water rose with her as she was yanked up. The water seemed to be trying to pull her back down by her feet and was churning ferociously to no avail against Lee's spell.

Another series of Lee's incantations drew a ring of fire that blazed a little more than a foot away from her, making her scream and curse hysterically.

Fin's mind went suddenly blank in response to her cries. The sheer terror in her eyes began to look inhuman, and the sight made Fin feel sick to his stomach.

"NO, MAMA!" Hilda called out nonsensically as she began convulsing with sobs and shrieks.

Her pleas echoed in Fin's mind, alongside his own voice from many years ago. His voice the night he confronted his father ...

No one should feel such horror. It was the only clear thought he had before he stepped forward.

Fin crossed the stone landing and descended the stairs without a single thought of who was going to see him. He would deal with the repercussions later, even if it meant having to flee back to the island of Quildon.

All that mattered was making everyone safe again ...

Including Hilda.

"MR. ASHOWAN, CEASE THIS INSTANT!" Mage Lee roared as swells of water continued splashing upward toward Hilda in an attempt to extinguish the flames surrounding her.

Fin flexed his hands around the pillar of water, closed his eyes, and pulled.

He drew the water and the witch down toward the ground, while ignoring the blistering heat of the ring of fire as it drew closer and closer. Hilda began howling more furiously than before as she stared down at him.

Ducking underneath the perimeter of the angry flames, Fin gave a final tug and stood face-to-face with her. The flames licked his back, and his eyes consisted of nothing but blue lightning, but he couldn't think about anything other than reaching Hilda.

"You're scaring people!" he yelled over the water and flames into her surprised face. "There are children! Don't they matter?!" Fin began channeling water to his back to ease some of the stinging pain from the flames.

"YOU ... YOU'RE A TRAITOR TO YOUR OWN KIND!" she bellowed at him as she suddenly drew the pillar of water up and barricaded herself against him and the flames.

The pillar began to whirl and grow, encasing the ring of flames as it did so and extinguishing it easily. Fin stumbled back, and his eyes returned to normal as he eased his way back up onto the landing away from the water-logged witch.

Once he was back by Lee's side, Hilda returned to the ground and stepped forward, raising her arms and drawing two thin streams of water up as she moved closer toward them. She flipped up two fingers on her right hand, making the one stream whip forward toward Mage Lee's ankles.

He clunked his staff and dissolved the water into steam again but hadn't been quick enough to blow it away. He winced as the vapor bit into his flesh, but he didn't make a sound as he gripped his staff firmly.

"She meant for you to do that," Fin observed.

"I'm aware," Mage Lee barked in response.

Hilda then flicked her fingers toward Fin. Instinctively, he immediately made a curved motion with his hand and guided the water to swirl away from himself, and instead splash on the landing.

She raised her hands into the air with her teeth bared, and her fingers splayed. For each finger, a tentacle of water rose up.

Mage Lee began to slowly spin his staff in his hand, the glowing crystal at its top beginning to hum as he did so. The pitch made both Fin and Hilda wince as the frequency squeezed and rattled a corner of their minds to a point of extreme discomfort.

The wind from the staff grew in power as the water fingers bowed backward away from the castle.

With a shriek, Hilda stomped her foot down and summoned a fresh jet of water to erupt from the flooded front lawn, and catapulted Lee off his feet.

Fin's hands turned to fists, as he felt an unnatural calm settle over himself when he heard Mage Lee cough and splutter behind him.

He descended the stairs once again and walked toward the woman, his lightning touching down around him as she stood waiting for him, sneering.

"A fire witch," she hissed.

All ten tentacles of water dove toward him.

Only they were met with sparks of lightning that climbed up and around to create a ball with Fin as its center.

He stepped forward, his mind blank as he reached through the rapidly shrinking opening of his protective shield and grabbed Hilda by her upper arms. Fin managed to draw her into his perfect sphere of blue electricity without either of them being harmed, right as the shield completed its growth and encased them both entirely.

The ball surrounding them began to whir and spin, snaps of light appearing all around them.

"I'm not a fire witch," he spoke softly to Hilda in the sphere that smelled strongly of the metallic fizzle of electricity. Her long wiry gray hair began to float from the charge of the air around her, making her eyes widen.

"I am a house witch. I protect my home, and right now, *you* are threatening it. I don't like hurting people, but I will not allow you to do more damage."

She wordlessly summoned more and more water toward them, but every droplet that drew near stopped, hovered, and evaporated toward the sky.

In a matter of minutes, the formerly pristine air darkened with thunder clouds as the soggy lawn of the castle dried abnormally fast.

"Please don't make me do worse." The brokenness in Fin's voice made Hilda pause. The mystical swirling blue in her eyes cleared and revealed their true colorless gray as she gradually focused on the man in front of her. She could see his unwillingness to do further harm to her.

"Fool," she rasped as an aching pressure built in her head, warning her that she was beginning to use the energy of her life in her attempts to call her water and override his powers. "To survive you have to give back every evil you receive, to let your enemy know that you will not suffer their wrongdoings."

There was pain in her face when she snarled the words at him, and she didn't seem to realize she had started to weep.

Fin did the unexpected.

He hugged her.

"I'm not strong enough to do that. You'll have to kill me to save me the misery of my impending doom." He could feel the magnitude of magic she was using and its steady drain on her life. The river that had been rushing down the main road of Austice began to slow. It narrowed itself away from the homes and businesses, though it was still a frothing rush that would sweep anyone that set foot in it down to the sea.

"Stupid boy. You're as good as dead already. Deficient witches have no place in the world," she scoffed, unable to resist his embrace as she continued to try manipulating the water around her.

"I know."

"What is worthy in this world anyway?" Her voice had softened, and the waters receded farther down the main street of Austice, away from the castle.

"Good changes have happened in this kingdom in the last fifty years. Having hope that it will continue to improve with our king isn't foolish."

Hilda snorted bitterly, clearly unconvinced.

"I also happen to know of a good bottle of Troivackian moonshine in the castle that you could—"

The water completely drained back into the ground, sky, and sea.

Fin released his embrace, the electricity dissolving around them, though the thunder above them offered a fair warning of a storm.

"Troivackian moonshine, you say? A bottle of that, and I may be willing to forgive the mage that inflicted sobriety on me," she announced, clapping Fin on the shoulder.

He smiled down at Hilda, who he had to admit was most likely completely insane.

Mage Lee stood drenched to the bone, leaning on his staff at the top of the stairs—it was one of the rare times the action did not look rehearsed.

"Mage Lee, Hilda has conceded to be cooperative in exchange for a bottle of Troivackian moonshine. If we could please send for one from Lady Jenoure, I believe we should all have a cup. Or three."

Lee looked incensed beyond reason yet had the good judgment to not to argue the matter.

He turned toward the great front doors, bellowed the orders to the guards on the other side after issuing a sharp knock, and turned back to the witches that had seated themselves on the landing.

"A house witch, hm? Never heard of your type," Hilda managed while tapping her finger against her hand impatiently; her mind was already obsessed over the moonshine.

"Well, you know how most feel about mutated witches. The records of our magic are quite poor," Fin offered as he stared thoughtfully up at the dark sky continuing to rumble above them. He stretched his legs before him in false casualness. He was wet, burned, exhausted, and more than slightly concerned that someone could inflict so much damage over being cut off at a tavern. He knew that he had to remain calm, however, if they were to keep Hilda pliable.

"How'd you wind up here?" she asked, gesturing her thumb toward the doors where Mage Lee stood frowning.

"Bigger home, more power," Fin shrugged simply.

"Ah. Makes sense. I came here for humbler reasons." She nodded toward Austice. "Nicer taverns and ocean views."

Tensing slightly, Fin dared a question that could set her off again, while estimating the length of time it would take the moonshine and the Coven to reach them.

"What happened to you? You're clearly a powerful enough witch to be one of the inner members of the Coven."

Hilda chuckled bitterly for a moment.

"You're too young to know of the days when our kind was hunted."

Fin leaned forward, resting his forearms on his knees as he listened, ignoring the searing pain in his back from the burns.

"Ever since I could remember, I was moved around and hidden with my father and my twin sister. She was an earth witch, and I, a water witch. Our father was a weak earth witch but did all he could to hide us. When my mother found out what we all were, she went into a rage." Hilda lifted a trembling hand to her head and touched a scar that Fin hadn't had a chance to notice before. The mark ran from the beginning of her hairline, well into her thick locks halfway across her scalp.

"She said ..." Hilda licked her lips. "My mother said we had some of the blood of the forgotten and rejected son of the Gods. The blood of Satan, the first witch's twin, the one that was supposed to teach mankind to find balance within themselves. Instead, he chose to use his knowledge for his own gains. According to my mother, we were related to him, and therefore evil. She joined the religion of Acker once she found out."

Fin frowned. He vaguely remembered hearing about the religion from his tutor. However, it had been a long time ago. Hilda must've seen his bewilderment, because she launched into a rant that he didn't want to risk interrupting.

"A woman named Valerie Acker believed witches were too emboldened by their powers, and started the religion that devoutly worshipped the Gods, and demonized their children: the first witch and Satan. Valerie's husband had been a witch, and he had left her for a male lover. As a result, she went mad with heartbreak and grief. She prosecuted him, saying he shouldn't have deigned to behave as a God. The Green Man and Goddess seek both genders only because they are worthy. To crave both genders is a higher calling that neither mankind or witches could understand or deserve."

At this, Hilda laughed bitterly, despite already starting to once again cry.

"Acker was deluded and believed that because Satan and the first witch were twins, they had the same chaotic tendencies."

Fin's memory clicked then.

"Ah yes, the first witch was to commune with nature and aid the people of the world in their connection with the elements. When her brother went to help mankind, however, he became disgusted. He loathed the barbaric emotions and impulses of man. Instead, he wished to expose their vileness to his parents. It is said he scours the world, corrupting anyone he comes across to convince the Gods that mankind should be eradicated," he finished, his gold-flecked blue eyes lost to memory as he recounted the details.

The religion had gained a respectable amount of followers for a century or so, but their numbers had dwindled once the previous King of Daxaria had disbanded the law allowing the hunting of witches.

Fin gazed at the statue in front of them. The Goddess and Green Man had their pupils shaped in perfect circles. Their daughter, the first witch, hadn't any pupils—which was how witches always looked while in full use of their power. Meanwhile, Satan bore menacing slits as pupils, akin to a snake.

It took him several weary minutes to recall all the facts of such an outrageous cult, but once he was certain he had remembered all necessary details, he turned to Hilda beside him.

"What happened?"

The first drops of rain began to fall as Hilda gripped her dirty dress. As if on cue, Lee appeared, holding a clear glass bottle of Troivackian moonshine. Under his left arm were three wooden cups, and once Fin helped him distribute them, he seated himself on the other side of the cook.

Hilda hastily poured for herself, leaving Fin to pour the remaining two cups.

He handed one to Mage Lee and sipped his carefully. It still burned like fire down his throat, but he managed to stop himself from vomiting.

"The members of the religion slaughtered my sister and father after my mother turned to them. Then they set fire to the house. She even watched as they did it." Hilda drained the cup and coughed multiple times. When she had settled back down, she immediately reached for the bottle and poured more into the cup until the liquid nearly reached the rim.

"They thought me dead as well. A tavern owner who came after the carnage kept me alive, and I've been drinking ever since so that I never have to hear their screams again."

"Did the Coven not send you teachers?" Fin asked softly as he took another sip and felt his world begin to spin from the moonshine.

"Teachers have only been sent out to young witches in the past thirty or so years. I am turning seventy this year, boy. I was hunted until the age of twenty. I aged out of their bracket," she spat bitterly.

Fin rested a hand on her back, which she immediately shook off.

"I need no pity."

It was then that three people drifted down in front of the castle steps from the sky. The storm broke the moment their feet touched the ground, releasing sheets of relentless rain that splattered against the ground with enough force to create a mist along the earth.

The trio of newcomers were all cloaked until they each set foot on the stairs. They then all lowered their hoods and stared somberly at the soaked and bedraggled sight of the mage, cook, and drunk before them.

In the middle of the strangers was a woman with auburn hair and wide intense brown eyes who looked to be in her fifties. On her right was a man with snowy white hair and blue eyes so clear, that they almost appeared white. On her left was a woman with copper red hair piled high and eyes the color of honey.

They were all dressed elegantly, and the middle woman was the first to call out to them.

"We were summoned by the King of Daxaria regarding a threat?"

Hilda turned, looking betrayed toward Fin and Mage Lee.

Fin reached his arm out and clasped her shoulders, maintaining the air of calm and casual.

"Speak with them. If you're reasonable, they might respond in kind," Fin whispered, desperately hoping his words to be true.

The water witch held out her wooden cup.

Fin blinked confused, but Mage Lee quickly understood and filled the container hastily.

"Aye, I'm the threat. An idiot mage tried to cut me off, after all," Hilda muttered before taking a deep drink.

"It wasn't me." Mage Lee had overheard and raised his hands up innocently.

"Just your son," Fin retaliated as a sharp clap of thunder echoed above them.

The three witches from the Coven of Wittica moved with an inhuman synchronicity up the stairs toward them and stopped a few steps below so as to be eye level.

"Mr. Finlay Ashowan, are you behind this futile call?" The woman at the center of the witches bore down on Fin, who immediately bowed his head.

"I did not send for Your Excellence," he replied, his shoulders hunching forward reflexively.

The woman stared down her straight nose at him without an ounce of emotion.

"I'm aware. It was your king. What is it you said to him to make him summon us?" Her tone was harsh and accusatory.

Mage Lee began to rise from the stair he was seated upon, when a reply rang out.

"You have been called due to the water witch in front of you threatening my people. Mr. Ashowan was helping to protect the city of Austice, and I will ask you to show him the respect he deserves for his bravery." The King of Daxaria strolled out the castle doors with his head held high, and his hazel eyes sharp.

The head of the Coven of Wittica gave a respectable curtsy to the ruler of the continent.

"I am witch Eloise Morozov of the inner circle of the Coven of Wittica. Earth magic." She introduced herself to the king, pointedly ignoring his earlier chastising.

She swiftly redirected her attention to Hilda. "You will come with us. We can discuss your crimes and why you are not registered with our records back on Wittica."

Hilda turned and gave Fin a slow smile when she sensed him tense. "Do not fear, boy. I've faced worse than the likes of these prisses."

The infamous drunkard stood and allowed the witches that stood on the other side of the woman who had spoken to step forward and clasp her arms. They guided Hilda down the stairs into the rain. The elderly witch cast one last sad smile at the castle, and then was hauled up into the sky with her guards. They quickly disappeared above the thick clouds in a matter of moments, leaving Fin with a gnawing unease regarding their captive.

The remaining Coven witch sighed, ignored Mage Lee, and once again addressed Fin. "I will first ask for my report from you, Finlay Ashowan. You have caused enough of a spectacle with revealing yourself to your king than is necessary. He has already requested your file, and I am sure it was you who made him unduly worried about a water witch." Her bored tone made one of the king's eyebrows lift, forcing him to step forward.

"Mr. Ashowan is not the one who sent for the Coven. Do I need to repeat myself that you are to show him respect for his efforts?" His voice had an edge Fin had never heard before.

The woman narrowed her eyes at the king for the briefest of moments before turning to Fin again. "We appreciate your help in containing the damage to your kingdom," she managed tightly. Fin bobbed his head awkwardly, keeping his eyes fixed on the ground.

"How is it you plan to keep a powerful witch like Hilda contained?" the king questioned as he carefully studied the woman in front of him. He had never thought he would meet a leader of the Coven, but now that he had, decided he wasn't any richer from the experience.

"From what I saw she was of mediocre ability. She will be incarcerated in a cell built for her element and her power level."

"Mediocre ability?! She flooded the main street and nearly drowned the citizens!" Mage Lee burst out angrily.

"Your exaggerations should be saved for works of fiction, mage." The derision dripped from her voice as she ascended the rest of the stairs and openly glared at both Fin and Lee.

"My mage speaks the truth, Ms. Morozov, and you will not address him so rudely. The water witch you just took, named Hilda, has swept several citizens into the sea."

"I will hear your detailed report now, Your Majesty. I also have Mr. Ashowan's official records with me, should you like to review those while I am here." Ms. Morozov patted a small bulge in her cloak. While she did so, she cast a quick dismissive glance at Fin remaining seated on the ground. Fin became incredibly interested in sipping his moonshine.

"Very well. After you, Ms. Morozov." The king gestured to the open door behind himself. She swept past him with a gracious nod of her head, the silk of her skirts rustling audibly above the rush of the storm.

Fin felt his cheeks burn, and his face lowered beyond his shoulders to hide his shame.

Once the door was closed and it was once again only Mage Lee and Fin sitting on the stairs, the elder turned to the cook.

"Good Gods, I didn't realize you were one of the more tolerable witches!" he exclaimed shaking his head in awe.

"Most of our kind aren't—"

"The cat piss of personalities?" Lee supplied, shaking his head and sipping the liquor.

"... I was going to say offensive. She is a fair leader in the Coven, though known for being generally unpleasant."

There were a few more beats of silence as the two sat drinking peacefully while they watched the storm.

"Shouldn't you be making my dinner?" Mage Lee commented as he took another sip of the Troivackian moonshine that had his eyes watering, yet also numbed his body at the same time.

"It won't take me long to spit in a bowl and hand it to you," Fin replied without a moment's hesitation.

"Mr. Ashowan?"

"Yes, Lee?"

"Will our king find anything interesting in your records?"

Fin went still. He had never requested to read his own file and hadn't considered it a major issue until that moment. He hadn't wanted to read what his tutor had said about him, or the Coven's appraisal, for that matter …

It had been a long time ago, after all.

CHAPTER 29
BETTER DAYS WERE HAD

A long time ago, on the southern island of Quildon …

"Ian! Ian, it happened! It *finally* happened!" Fin whooped as his feet stumbled under him. He recovered quickly and continued to rush to reach the boy who was only a year younger.

Ian Morrison stood throwing rocks at a target the two boys had painted only a fortnight ago, but he was soon jumping up and down in excitement.

Ian's bright blue eyes were full of wonder, and the anticipation in the air became overwhelming. "Really?! What is it? What can you do?"

Fin huffed as he skidded to a halt in front of his best friend. "I can make lightning, so I'm probably a fire witch! I blasted my dad off the island!" He beamed proudly as Ian's eyes widened to the size of saucers.

"Really? Wasn't he mad?" Ian asked nervously.

"Don't know! He hasn't come back! Isn't this amazing?" Fin could have cried, he felt so elated.

Gone were the days of cowering in the corner of their cold cottage. He would never fear watching helplessly as his mother was hurt over and over again. He had his magic! So what if it had taken him two weeks to recover from using it?

Then to make matters all the more perfect, his tutor was supposed to arrive sometime that week from the Coven. He would surely grow to be an even more powerful witch!

It was the best time of Fin's life.

"Hm. Strange." Stanley Goss's eyes were milky as he stared down at the lanky, redheaded boy clad in dirty, worn clothes. Fin gazed up at Mr. Goss with burning expectancy.

What a pity, the Coven tutor thought to himself idly, as he felt a pit of dissatisfaction appear in his mind.

"You're a mutated witch. Deficient," he announced, blinking away the milky swirls. He was immediately regretting volunteering to be the boy's instructor. The tutor had truly hoped when he had heard that the boy was the son of Aidan Helmer, that he would have had greater power.

It was a great loss that the fire witch that had once been considered for a position within the Coven of Wittica had fallen into some extremist ideology.

"You will call me Mr. Goss." Turning his back on the boy, who looked a mix of hurt and disappointed, he began to stroll toward the cottage doorway where Fin's mother stood wringing her hands. The little boy remained rooted to the spot while his tutor pointedly ignored the child staring up at his thin black ponytail.

"Mr. Goss?"

He turned and stared down at the boy through his small spectacles, his eerie gray eyes vacant of emotion. His sallow complexion and deep frown lines looked waxy in the damp early April air.

"What is it, Mr. Helmer?" the tutor questioned, shifting his bulging black bag under his arm.

"What is my power?"

The awkward lad was fidgeting with his hands, making Mr. Goss frown.

"I cannot say until we run further tests. Deficient witches aren't as easily categorized. Come along."

Fin felt crestfallen but did his best to cheer himself up. His mother was considered quite valuable even as a deficient witch, so who knew? Perhaps he wasn't completely useless as his father had always said deficient witches were.

~~~~~~

"It is good you have a keen mind in your studies, Mr. Helmer, as I fear you will be quite futile in the area of magic."

Fin stared dejectedly down at the muddy soil beneath his feet. He had once again failed to replicate the shield he had created the night his powers had emerged. They had been trying unsuccessfully for an entire month following Mr. Goss's arrival, and nothing had happened.

Every other aspect of Fin's studies had been going well; math, reading, writing, and science, but magic continued to be problematic.

He would begin his work with Mr. Goss from sunup, and labor well into the night, despite his mother's faint protests. Fin hadn't been able to help at all with keeping the small cottage clean, or even cooking as he normally did. It only added to his guilt of being hopeless and lacking with magic. To make matters even more complicated, his mother had begun healing regular humans again to help them earn money and food. This meant she was often on the mainland for days at a time, and when she would return, she would be left with an absolutely filthy cottage to tend to. Even though she was already exhausted from healing and traveling, she didn't complain once, but Fin knew she needed help.

Mr. Goss, on the other hand, appeared to be indifferent to the mess, as well as to the idea that he should help clean up after himself.

If it weren't for his mother being an eyewitness to the shield he had created, the tutor was inclined to think that Fin had made the entire event up. He had even cast one of the restricted spells that only the close members of the Coven and the esteemed instructors knew. It was a spell that identified the brand that occurred when a witch burned a significant amount of their powers. It was usually a symbol marked on a nearby object, but he found nothing of the sort anywhere in or around the small cottage with its rickety fence.

"We will work on trying to see if you have any other abilities aside from the one you claim. For starters—"

"Mr. Goss!" Katelyn Ashowan was strolling across the soggy lawn toward them, a pinched expression on her face that Fin had never seen before.

As she exited the gate of their property and made her way over to where they stood, Fin could see her fidgeting with her hands. There was something bothering her.

"Perhaps let Fin have some rest. It's possible his mind is overtaxed. You have been working with him far longer and harder than most tutors—"

"Witch Ashowan," Mr. Goss interjected, straightening to his full height. "We have been working to ensure we know what he is capable of, which is a very serious matter indeed. I prefer to rediscover what it is he did before he forgets."

Fin was staring at the ground, his cheeks burning.

He didn't need his mom coming to defend him—she'd only make it worse!

He didn't see the facial expressions that passed between the adults, only heard his tutor sigh exasperatedly.

Dad would've just left me alone, Fin thought glumly.

Even if it meant he'd receive a more private beating, the boy knew he'd never face public humiliation that sullied his father's name …

"Very well. You have thirty minutes until we resume," Mr. Goss conceded with undisguised annoyance.

Fin was still embarrassed, but he held the tiniest bit of optimism that at the very least he could get to see and play with his best friend.

"Show us, witch! C'mon! Ian says you can make lightning," Liam Corway taunted as he kept shoving Fin's best friend down to the ground and laughing. The slightly chubbier boy struggled to stand up over and over again, to no avail.

"I can! Stop it!" Fin kept trying to help his friend, only Liam's fraternal twin brother Wyatt was stopping him, and was pushing him farther away.

The two brothers were amongst the twelve-child brood born between a Troivackian woman and the local Daxarian fisherman that had rescued her. Mrs. Corway had apparently been banished from her kingdom, which involved being thrown overboard into the ocean on the border of Daxaria and Troivack.

It also meant that the mix-blooded children were prone to be larger than their peers. Their dark hair and eyes would watch gleefully over the "weaker" Daxarian kind. Their mother was colorful in her description of her new nationality when their papa was gone on his boat.

"Well, let's see it then! Unless you made it up," Wyatt taunted as Fin tried ramming his shoulder into his opposition's chest without success. It didn't help that they were two years older to begin with.

"I didn't!" Fin's feet had begun slipping in the thick grass. It was then he saw one of the rocks that he and Ian had been using to throw at their target on the ground to his left. Without a second thought, he immediately ducked and picked it up. Wyatt immediately fell over from suddenly pushing against a being that was no longer there.

Fin threw the stone at the back of Liam's head without any thought as to what would come afterward, only knowing he wanted them to go away.

His aim was true, and the boy swung around, looking thoroughly enraged and unaffected by the strike.

"RUN, FIN!" The terror in Ian's voice had the young witch sprinting away as fast as his legs would carry him.

He dashed up the steep hill toward his cottage. He could hear the Corway brothers hot on his heels, but luckily, he had the advantage over the boys, who lived on the lower side of the island. Due to his legs being used to bracing against an incline, he had no trouble setting a respectable pace up the slope. Fin could hear them huffing as he ran higher and higher up toward his home and sent a prayer to the Goddess that his tutor and mother were still standing in the front yard.

As he broke out over the peak of the hill, his heart sank when he saw that Mr. Goss and his mother were nowhere in sight.

With a final burst of speed, Fin barreled through the gate toward the front door of his house as tears began to rise in his eyes. The Corway brothers were catching up to him quickly now that the ground had leveled out.

It wasn't supposed to be like this again …

Unbeknownst to him, Fin's eyes had begun to glow.

"Just 'cause you're home doesn't mean you're safe!" Liam, the bigger of the twins, grabbed Fin's shoulder as he set his foot on the threshold.

As they swung him around, they laughed at the tears running down his face. They taunted him until Fin raised his eyes, and they saw the bright blue lightning that glowed there. The door behind him opened, but he didn't hear it.

"LEAVE ME ALONE!" Fin screamed, and suddenly the two boys saw nothing but a flash of blue light. Next thing they knew, they were winded on their backs beyond the gate of the small cottage.

"Finlay!"

Fin remained stoic yet determined, his fists clenched and shaking at his sides. He slowly turned toward his mother in response to her call. Mr. Goss stood beside her with an unreadable expression.

Fin's eyes had cleared of the lightning, and he suddenly felt quite tired.

"Th-They started it. They kept pushing Ian a-and—"

"I will hear about this later. Go sleep." His mother's strict and firm tone startled him. He hadn't ever seen his mother angry before, and he didn't understand why he needed to sleep in the middle of the day …

He didn't bother to argue, though. Seeing that there wasn't any use in it, he hunched his shoulders and walked to his room.

Katelyn rushed out to the two boys that lay gasping on their backs beyond the gate. She had been the one to deliver them ten years ago, and she did not want to be the one to tell their mother that Fin was the one to kill them.

Both boys seemed fine aside, from having bruised backsides, which she fixed with a small pat of their shoulders.

At the very least that ruddy tutor better stop saying my son is deficient, she thought bitterly to herself.

When Fin awoke, he groggily stepped out into the main room of his cottage to discover that he was in fact alone. The dirty dishes were stacked on the table, the floors covered in dust, the hearth cold.

There were pangs of hunger in his stomach, and no sign of Mr. Goss either.

Slowly, he reached for the broom with bristles held together with red twine. His mother had finished it after his father had disappeared while sitting at her son's bedside.

Fin began sweeping. Once he had deposited the dirt outside, he grabbed the pail used for cleaning dishes, and headed out to the overly full rain barrel.

Once the pail was heavy with water, he returned and faced the catastrophic dishes and table. He lifted a stack of plates, and was about to lower them into the water, when a small instinct told him to stop.

A strange new tiny voice in him, told him to boil the water first.

Glancing at the tiny bit of soap left atop the hearth, Fin tried to ignore the voice, but when he did his stomach tightened into knots.

With a long sigh, he turned to the cold hearth. He couldn't seem to find the flint anywhere.

Glancing around the room, he finally spotted it atop a blanket his mother had been mending on her rocking chair. Fin began to walk toward the chair, his hand reaching for the stone, when it flew into his hand.

He blinked.

Had he imagined it?

Shaking his head and dismissing what he thought he saw, Fin turned to the hearth. He walked over, placed the dry kindling atop the ashes, then one of the last split logs of pine they had. He struck the flint once, only it didn't spark.

He let out a frustrated sigh. He felt achy, chilled, hungry … he just wanted the stupid fire to start!

The log burst into flames.

Leaping back, startled, Fin watched with wide eyes as the fireplace crackled merrily.

Cautiously, he turned to the pail of water and dumped it into the empty cauldron hanging over the flames.

Glancing around the room, his mind was still sluggish from sleep, but a slow, unmistakable feeling was growing within him. Some kind of bond between everything in his home …

Every item seemed to understand and want to please him, even though they were just …. Objects. He could feel their entities shiver as he grew aware of them and their relationship.

This feels weird. But maybe …

Fin pointed at the blanket on the rocking chair.

The heavy cream wool immediately obeyed his silent order, rising into the air and folding itself messily. It landed in its new form on the seat of the chair just as he had willed it to.

Fin was trembling fiercely as he walked over and inspected the blanket. It was folded the exact same way he would've done it.

A small spark of hope rose in him. He had been essentially unconscious the two weeks after his powers came forward. Then his tutor had come, and he hadn't had any time alone, or much time in the cottage at all.

Perhaps he needed to recharge away from people?

He began to fidget as he cast a new eye around his home.

Turning around, Fin's eyes rested on the faded green curtains partially drawn over the window. With a small jerk of his head, they all spread apart and allowed the faint, cloudy light of day pour in.

The boy grinned.

Looking over his shoulder at his open bedroom door, he saw his messy bed. Fin threw up his arm, pointed his finger, and cheered. The blankets sprang into action immediately, tucking and pulling themselves until his bed was perfectly made.

It was then that his tutor walked through the door with his mother, both carrying armloads of firewood.

"I have magic!" Fin was beside himself with excitement as tears of joy threatened to spill over. Mr. Goss began to open his mouth, when the boy cut him off.

"Look!"

Fin pointed at the plates on the table and had one of the piles float over to the cauldron. The dishes carefully eased their way into the slowly warming water one by one until some of the water spilled over into the flames, which hissed in response.

"Mr. Helmer, we—" Mr. Goss began, his tone its usual level of bland. Fin once again cut him off and had the firewood the two adults carried drift out of their arms. The logs levitated over to its designated spot beside the hearth, where they neatly stacked themselves.

When it was finished, Fin turned proudly with his hands on his hips to stare at his audience.

"Well, Mr. Helmer, I think I might have an idea as to what your abilities are." Mr. Goss sighed. "I have only heard about this kind of deficient witchcraft once before. Given what I have just witnessed, however, I think you may be a house witch."

The unenthused response made Fin's smile dim as he looked to his mother who was staring daggers at the tutor.

"W-what … What is a house witch?"

"You are capable of performing magic around the home, and *only* around the home. You are completely useless outside of your property. Given that we have always been outside of the gate when practicing magic, it would explain why you have failed every test."

Fin felt his newfound hope sink through his stomach down through the floor. The fire in the hearth suddenly fizzled out, and he felt his throat constricting as he tried not to cry from disappointment.

"Mr. Goss, there is no need to describe my son as 'useless,' in any circumstance. Even if he isn't able to use his abilities outside of our home, he is still a smart, kind, courageous boy." Kate had her hands on her hips as she tried to hide her shaking over her newfound gumption.

"Forgive me, Mrs. Ashowan, I merely meant on a magical level he is redundant outside of this home. It is dangerous to give him a false sense of confidence in that regard. Should Mr. Helmer attempt to bite off more than he could chew, it could have dangerous consequences. Like today for instance, with those two boys."

The tutor turned to Fin as his mother's cheeks burned.

"I'm sure you will be an upstanding citizen. You could become the Head of Housekeeping for a wealthy lord, or perhaps a wonderful kitchen aide."

Fin didn't want to hear more. He was already wiping away tears when he ran to his room, his bedroom door slamming shut behind him on its own accord.

Suffice it to say, the first year of Mr. Goss's tutelage buried a sharp thorn in Fin's heart. The following ten years weren't much better.

CHAPTER 30
FEEL THE BURN

Fin stood in his eerily silent kitchen. Every staff member and member of regency remained in their personal quarters; the king was in conference with a leader of the Coven. Even the fire had spluttered out during the cook's absence.

It was because of the quiet that Fin finally registered his pounding heart, the anxious flurry in his mind, and then the overwhelming sense of doom.

He didn't know what kind of information the Coven released in his circumstances. He didn't know if they released detailed documentation of his studies, or assessments of his mental well-being, or just the bare minimum information regarding his magic.

Oh Gods … what if the king learns about my father … Fin rubbed his eyes with the heels of his palms, which drew a small yelp from him.

During the adrenaline rush of confronting Hilda, he had failed to register the familiar stinging pain that came with burn marks on his back.

It had been two full decades since he'd felt them, and yet his hands began to shake. Not from the pain, but from the nauseating familiarity of the sensation.

Fin removed his shirt and saw the burn marks along the back of his tunic. He threw the ruined garment into the cold hearth without a second thought. He could see about buying another one in Austice.

Focusing on guessing the approximate height of the straight burn mark across his back, he summoned the jar of burn ointment he kept on hand on the shelf beside the hearth. The mage's fire ring had done more damage than he had initially realized.

Even with magic, Fin would occasionally forget to not grab the hot handle of his cast-iron skillet and would have to slather a cooling salve on a burn. He sincerely hoped that the ointment his mother had sent with him would be effective on larger burns.

He had just unscrewed the cap of the wide brimmed jar, when the castle door suddenly banged open.

Lady Annika Jenoure stood in the doorway, looking a strange combination of angry and terrified.

Fin had the sudden urge to cover himself, but weariness stopped him. It occurred to him then that he had somehow not fallen asleep already at the extensive use of his powers.

If anything, the weariness seemed to stem from more of an emotional and mental strain than from magic.

It has to be due to the larger space and more occupants of my home giving me more power … Fin reasoned to himself.

"Lady Jenoure, I apologize for my indecency. I need to tend to a wound. I will retire to my cottage if you prefer." He bowed but winced at the movement. As a result, he missed the look of pain and tenderness that crossed Annika's face.

"We can stop the nonsense of formality for now, Fin. I saw you get burned earlier, let me help."

He was too tired to put things delicately.

"I can use magic to apply this. I am indecent and you can be placed in a compromising position if you are seen—"

"Son of a mage, just let me help you," she snapped, slamming the door behind her and striding forward. The black-haired beauty snatched the jar from Fin's hand and faced his back confidently.

"This is unnecessary, Lady Jenoure. I—" Fin paused. "Did you just say 'son of a mage'?"

"Yes. I heard you say it before during the drinking competition, and oddly enough it is really catching on—especially amongst the knights.

Though I don't think Keith is helping slow the spread of it. Did you hear yesterday that he advised Ruby on how to fold sheets more efficiently?"

Fin laughed.

"How did that go?"

"A gallon of your 'sedative' tea couldn't stop the unfortunate twitch in the right corner of her mouth. She is now muttering 'son of a mage' all day long."

Both Fin and Lady Jenoure laughed.

Once she had settled back down, Annika dipped her fingers in the strange yellow paste in the jar. Scooping small blobs up, she gently touched the ugly burn that spanned a horizontal line across Fin's back.

"This will scar," she observed far more somberly.

"It can join the others, it's fine."

It was then she noticed what he was referring to.

There was a messy scar the size of a man's palm under his right rotator cuff, and one the size of a thumb near the top of his left shoulder.

"How did you get these?" she asked softly as her hand hovered above the fresh wound.

"No need to worry, my lady. If you are going to be stubborn about assisting me, I'd rather not also have to share personal details."

"You helped save us all, I think this is the least I can do," she muttered as she gently dabbed the wound.

Fin took a sharp intake of breath.

"Gods, were your hands in an ice bath before this?!" he called out.

"No, I-It's the ointment!"

"Like Keith's brain it is!"

Annika burst out laughing and took a few minutes to compose herself. Fin was already grinning to himself. He was grateful she couldn't see how happy he was at hearing her obnoxious laugh—it was far better than her pretty fake one.

"You should be nicer to him. He's just a—"

"Mage?"

"If you weren't injured, I'd slap your back right now," Annika warned, though her tone remained humorous.

"He's just trying to live up to both of his parents. He's been told his entire life what a prodigy he is; no one has told him that while he may be a skilled mage, he has no understanding of real life or people."

Annika resumed dabbing the ointment across his back.

Fin grunted.

"I saw your fight with captain Antonio."

"Oh."

Fin's cheeks burned. He shouldn't have cared that she'd seen … but he did all the same.

"You handled yourself surprisingly well. Where did you learn to fight like that?"

"I … I knew a Zinferan once who instructed me. I've lost a lot of skill from lack of practice, but he taught me about control of movement and breath."

"Did you know Captain Antonio's wife was a Zinferan?"

Fin's eyebrows shot up.

"I didn't! Why haven't I met or heard of her?"

"She died with their son during the birth."

He fell silent. He didn't know what to say regarding such a loss.

"His wife's name was May. Her father was so against the union that he said he would only agree to it if Antonio trained under him for seven years."

"I'm guessing he did?"

"Absolutely. He was already a renowned fighter, but he became extremely deadly under his father-in-law's instruction. As a result, Antonio became an even bigger asset to the kingdom after studying with her father, a master of the Zinferan method. When May died in childbirth only two years after they were married, her father passed three months after from grief. The captain hasn't ever married again."

Fin said nothing for a while as he allowed the ointment to ease some of the pain from the burn, doing everything in his power to not think about Lady Jenoure touching him so intimately.

"I can't imagine losing someone after all of that," he said finally, when he was relatively certain he had gotten his thoughts back under control.

"Huh? Oh. Yes." The lady sounded distracted by something.

"Was that what it was like when you lost your husband?"

She didn't say anything, and Fin was worried he had crossed a line by asking something so personal. He was about to turn around to apologize when Annika finally spoke.

"I loved him, but it was … complicated. He is the one who showed me that there were good people, and that good people could rule a country. I never understood the blind trust in this country until I saw the intense loyalty the Daxarian citizens shared with one another. He was kinder to me than anyone ever had been, even though I didn't deserve it. He became … my closest friend and ally."

Taking Annika's stillness to mean she was finished, Fin turned around to thank her. Only to find that she had been standing close, and she looked as though she were blushing. Instead of stepping away from Fin when he turned, she stayed put. This placed her mere inches from his body.

He stared down at the open expression on Lady Jenoure's face, and immediately felt himself fall even deeper into the dreadfully wonderful space in his heart. The space that had somehow been created for the woman in front of him.

Fin's cheeks turned crimson when he realized her eyes remained fixed on his bare chest. His body was awash with tingling as he gently reached up and grasped her right wrist with barely any thought.

Annika's warm, intense brown eyes flew up to his slightly glossy bright blue ones. It took every remaining functioning cell in Fin's mind to act reasonably in that moment.

He lifted his other hand and summoned a clean dish towel, as well as the pitcher of clean water from the ledge.

Annika was distracted then, as Fin dipped the towel in the water without taking his eyes from the hand he was very nearly holding and began to wipe the ointment off of her fingers.

"Thank you for helping me with my burn." He was doing everything in his power not to pull her into himself. Every inch of him itched to do so …

Itched to hold her and allow everything to turn right in the world.

"Like I said, you're the unsung hero of the day. Mage Lee will probably take all the credit."

"The knights helped the citizens," Fin recalled, feeling the color rise even further in his face.

"True, but they didn't conduct a ball of lightning that propelled enough water to sink the castle."

"You exaggerate and flatter me beyond excess." Fin shook his head, hoping to alleviate some of the pounding blood in his face.

Annika gave a small, exasperated sigh, and met his gaze, smiling.

The look of tender affection she saw in his eyes only made her want to melt into him and forget about every silly thing that she had ever bothered with. She wanted to care for him and hold him and …

"Why have you never asked about my being a witch?" Fin's voice was soft, and it sent a shiver through her.

"I … I knew a witch back in Troivack."

The interest was genuine on Fin's face as he frowned and slowly lowered Annika's wrist, still clasping it softly.

"She didn't like people knowing, or asking about it, and seldom used any magic. She was … one of the few people that was decent to me while I was there." There was a tight strain in her voice, and Fin barely registered that he was rubbing her wrist with his thumb soothingly.

"What happened to her?"

"One day she … used her magic. She did so to help me. I never saw her again when people found out what she was. Some people say she was banished, but in Troivack that means—"

"… Being sailed out to the perimeter of Daxarian and Troivackian borders and tossed overboard?"

"Yes! How did you—"

"A woman on our island named Nora was picked up by one of our fishermen after being banished from Troivack. They had twelve children together. All boys."

"Nora?! When?"

Her shock and disbelief made Fin lean back slightly in surprise.

"Her two eldest boys were twins … they were a year or two older than myself. So … roughly thirty years ago? Why? Is it your former friend?"

"No, not my former governess. I … uh." Annika was clearly flabbergasted by the news. She had revealed the role the witch in her past had played in her life without a second thought.

"I think she may be the former Princess of Troivack. The aunt of the current king."

Fin's jaw dropped.

"Why do you think that?" he managed after a second of incredulity.

"Princess Nora was banished after stating she wanted the throne to herself. Thirty years ago. Most people are simply executed in Troivack, and very few have the privilege of banishment. It offers the barest of possibilities that they could survive."

Fin had only seen the dark-haired, sneering woman of the Corway brothers from afar. He had never wanted to draw closer to her and her permanent hatefulness, but even so it was hard to envision her as a royal.

Annika was clearly having a similar struggle with the new information, which was when Fin decided to try a different question while he had complete privacy with her.

"Do you even want to get married again?"

Annika blinked rapidly, and he could've sworn there was a hint of tears in her eyes before she masked her expression.

"I … If it were to the right person."

"I'm ... sorry. I hope one of the suitors are to your liking." Fin was staring at her, doing his best to remain composed, but didn't realize he had grasped her hand in his own.

Annika moved forward, meaning a slight shift of her weight and she would go crashing into him.

"You should," Fin cleared his throat. "Should go back. Your reputation would be destroyed being here with me like this." The croak in his voice betrayed him.

"Fin, I ... I just ..." Annika tried to speak, then raised her left hand as though she were going to touch his chest. Fin pulled away. Releasing the hand he had clasped unknowingly, he took several steps to the side away from her.

"Lady Jenoure, thank you for your care." He bowed. He barely noticed the pain in his back as he waited to hear her exit.

There were several long moments of pained silence, but sure enough he soon heard the soft sound of the handle unlatch and gently click shut again.

Once he was certain she had left the room, he straightened with a new weight in his chest. He turned to the door to the gardens, not wanting to think more about what had just transpired. Fin was intent on getting a fresh tunic from his cottage when he noticed Kraken pawing the door aggressively.

"What in the world are you doing?" he wondered with a small chuckle.

Upon opening the garden door, he found himself staring down at a small, sleek gray cat with bright yellow eyes. She sat on the garden pathway as though waiting expectantly.

He glanced at Kraken, whose pupils had widened to the size of marbles.

"A friend of yours?" he asked with raised eyebrows.

He didn't get an answer as the two cats dashed off together across the lawn.

Fin sighed.

The day had been far more exciting than he would've liked.

CHAPTER 31
FACING FACTS

Fin had just finished the preparations for a simple dinner the night of Hilda's invasion. He swayed on the spot as he blithely thought how the castle staff and nobility were going to have to deal with having a simple but heavy meal of shepherd's pie—and the equally unfussy dessert of cookies.

He didn't have the energy to care.

Typically Fin tried to avoid weighing down everyone in the summer, and deferred to lighter meals …

By the time his kitchen had cloaked his shoulders in its loving quiet and order, however, he was barely able to mix the batter for the cookies. Kasim had helped Fin develop his lemon cookie recipe by giving him the helpful tip that if he grated the peel of the fruit, it created a zest that was quite flavorful. He hadn't had a chance to offer the fare to the higher nobility—and hoped it would be well received.

Normally he would be beside himself with aggravation at offering what was, in his opinion, a subpar meal. Yet after the day he had just survived, he felt himself wearily concede that it was impressive he had still managed to cook a full dinner.

As his eyes began fluttering, the batter bowl cradled loosely in his left arm, the castle door banged open, and in strolled Eloise Morozov.

The bowl nearly crashed to the floor at his being startled. Fin barely managed to get it back onto his cooking table in time to turn and bow to the woman, who was watching him carefully.

"Mr. Ashowan, my business with the Daxarian king has been completed. I wanted to speak with you before taking my leave. I've received word of some concerning news that will affect you."

Fin's apprehension was written all over his face as he gestured toward one of the chairs in front of his table.

Eloise eyed the seat with narrowed eyes.

The queen of the bloody continent didn't have a problem with it. Get over yourself, Fin found himself grumbling silently. Any other day he probably wouldn't dare think such a thing, but seeing her interact with the king earlier had turned his opinion of her …

Slowly, she lowered herself into the chair after gingerly wiping off imaginary dust with an air of disdain. She then tugged off her black gloves and laid them on his table.

Fin's teeth ground together and a tic in his cheek appeared.

Eloise lifted an eyebrow at seeing this look of obvious stress but continued speaking. "Your king has just reported to me that there is a fire witch in the Troivackian court acting as their chief of military."

Fin froze. *Shit. Shit. Shit. Son of a mage. Shit.*

"The king told me you had no idea who this was," she continued slowly while watching her closely.

Feeling at a complete loss as to what to do, Fin rubbed the back of his neck with one hand and tapped the cooking table with his other. Immediately, the batter began to mix itself, and pans began to float over as he rounded the table to sit in the furthest chair from the Coven witch. Eloise eyed the cookery with vague interest as he did, but she didn't comment on it.

"I understand why you may not want to divulge your relationship with your father to His Majesty. However, Mr. Helmer is aiming to overtake the Coven of Wittica and merge it with the Coven of Aguas."

Fin's eyes widened and his jaw dropped. He knew his father had been ambitious, but to desire to overthrow the Daxarian Coven?!

"He has the support of the Troivackian Coven, the Coven of Aguas, and I believe he is already leading them autocratically. This war is getting incredibly out of hand, so I wonder if it would be possible for you to share with me everything you know or remember about Aidan Helmer. It will help us strategize against him."

Fin knew his mind was sluggish, but the shock of the news was too overwhelming.

"I will do whatever I can to help. My loyalty has never been to him."

Eloise nodded respectfully before he dared to add on to his reply.

"If possible, Ms. Morozov, could you please answer two questions for me?"

She tilted her head and straightened her shoulders but gave the smallest jerk of her chin as consent. Her dark brown eyes were watching him carefully.

"Did you tell the Daxarian king that Mr. Helmer is my father?" Fin's heart was pounding in his chest.

Ms. Morozov's expression was blank when she answered.

"Yes, I did. While I normally would respect your desire for privacy, Mr. Ashowan, this threat affects his kingdom. You could be an incredibly helpful ally for the king, and it could be what makes the difference in this war. You may have the chance to save thousands or millions of lives."

Dread choked Fin. The king knew who his father was. Which meant the king also knew about the abuse he had experienced as a child. Then again, if they weren't aware of why Fin rejected his father, they would want to test his loyalty to them …

"I shared this information in the presence of a select few men that His Majesty deemed necessary to this information and—"

"Why in the world was I not called for?" Fin snapped before he was able to stop himself.

Eloise's eyebrows shot up and her mouth pursed.

"Mr. Ashowan, I—"

"I have a right to be given the chance to explain myself and my personal life. Even in dire circumstances, it would be better coming from me." His cheeks burned in anger, and Eloise opened her mouth to retort, her tongue sharpened and ready. Instead, she clamped her jaw shut, closed her eyes, and gently touched the space between her perfectly shaped eyebrows in an effort to calm herself.

"Mr. Ashowan … All I informed the king and his men of was your blood relationship to the Troivackian chief of military. His Majesty had informed me of his name being Aidan Helmer, and I had naturally assumed they were aware of your familial tie. When it became apparent that they had no idea, I directed them to speak with you further."

Fin grew sheepish.

"I'm sorry for jumping to conclusions." He bowed his head.

"What was your second question, Mr. Ashowan?"

The oven door that had magically opened for the tray of cookie dough snapped shut with a loud bang. It was Eloise Morozov's turn to give a small start at the noise. She tapped a perfectly manicured nail impatiently on his table, her expression conveying her displeasure.

"My second question," Fin's voice was far more respectful for his next inquiry, "is how did my father become a Troivackian noble? What happened to him over the past two decades?"

Eloise let out a small sigh through her nose before continuing.

"There is much speculation on the exact details of the story, but the Coven has been able to garner that after you expelled him from Quildon, he returned to the mainland. With the information your king has just given me, I believe he then gathered his followers, and recruited a few more Daxarian witches before they all went overseas to directly attack the Troivackian Coven of Aguas."

Fin's frown was so deep that it began to give him a headache. Eloise shook her head as she continued her story, while simultaneously folding her arms across her chest.

"Given that the Coven of Aguas cowers under the Troivackian monarchy, it wasn't a difficult undertaking. Once he gained control, he approached King Matthias. Mr. Helmer offered the power of the Aguas Coven witches to the war effort and swore the Coven's fealty. In exchange, the military would help Mr. Helmer conquer our Coven. The Troivackian king agreed to the terms and elected him as an honorary chief of military. Mr. Helmer is not titled at this time, but it is likely that should he succeed in the war and overtake the Coven of Wittica, that would come. As to the number of witches your father wields control over? Your king is awaiting to hear about that information."

Fin's insides were shaking. Hearing anything about his father was overwhelming and gut-wrenching, and yet some dark part of him wanted to know every last detail about the man.

He swallowed with great difficulty and nodded.

It was his turn to answer Ms. Morozov's original question. His eyes were cast down at his beloved cooking table's scratched surface. He gently reached out and touched the wood with his fingertips, silently willing the inanimate object to give him strength to delve into his memories.

After a moment of quiet, he finally spoke.

"My father is a purist. He believes that witches with abilities not centered in the pure elements are broken. The first witch was a child designed by the Gods to fully commune with nature, and be able to maintain balance between humans and earth. Any power that does not serve that purpose, in his eyes, is wrong. He is violent, and he is angry. Nothing is more sacred than his alleged purpose." Fin's hands were slowly curling into fists as vivid flashes of his father's face snapped into his mind. The dark eyes that burned sick fear into him time and time again, still grotesquely alive in his memory …

"A deficient witch should only serve their betters—witches of the original elements, and no one else," he finished his explanation and tried to ignore the white noise blaring in his head.

Eloise Morozov said nothing. Her face remained stony, but her eyes were sharp on his face while no other muscle in her body moved. Nothing needed to be said, the anguish and turmoil was abundantly clear in Fin's eyes.

"I must confess, Mr. Ashowan, I was humbled today."

Fin's gaze snapped up to the Coven witch.

"I did not believe the magnitude of power you faced from Witch Hilda until your king had his captain escort me into the city to show me the damages that were incurred. Our king thinks very highly of you," she informed him casually.

Fin didn't dare to breathe as she then continued.

"Admittedly, the notes your tutor submitted regarding your abilities left the entire Coven of Wittica disillusioned with your magical prowess. From what I have seen today, however, I can say that you are in fact quite powerful. I don't only mean by a deficient witch's standard either—as you know, they tend to be less powerful overall, but I would place you amongst a respectable level even amongst pure elemental witches."

He couldn't believe what he was hearing.

He was too shocked to reply.

"In fairness, it sounds as though you and your tutor did not see eye to eye very often. There was the constant bickering and name calling that began when you were fourteen, then there was that incident when you were sixteen regarding a Zinferan that was staying with you and your mother—"

"Ms. Morozov, thank you for your kind words," Fin blurted out before he could think twice. He didn't want to think about Mr. Goss after hearing praise he never thought he would by one of his own people.

"It is not kindness, Mr. Ashowan. It is a fact." With a gracefulness that was still somehow brisk, the woman stood.

"I am going to formally request the notes you have maintained regarding your powers. If you do not have them on hand or would like to update them before sending them to the Coven, that is fine. However, I would like to compare your findings with the Coven's records regarding the only other house witch we know of in history."

Fin blinked and jumped to his feet with far less elegance than his visitor.

"Our king will be sending for you soon. I suggest you rest before presenting yourself to him." She began to pull on her gloves again in a businesslike manner, clearly uncomfortable with issuing praise.

"I will take my leave, Mr. Ashowan."

Fin straightened and nodded. Ms. Morozov turned to the garden door and strode over, her heels clacking on the stone floor as she went.

"Oh! Wait!"

Whirling around, looking greatly annoyed at being delayed, Eloise froze when she saw that Fin was carefully wrapping up in cheesecloth some of the warm cookies he had summoned out of the oven, and tying it firmly shut with some twine.

He handed the carefully prepared snack to Eloise, who looked a strange mix of embarrassed, pleased, and incredulous.

She turned back to the door, far more hesitantly than before. Fin had just begun to rub the back of his neck again, when she turned and faced him once more.

"You know, Mr. Ashowan ... something you may need to consider, is what your powers mean to you. Some could see them as a military weapon to be used to fight and shield against enemies, but ... that doesn't really seem like the duty of a 'home.' Take time to consider your abilities and what is right for them. It could aid your growth to have a set of ... house rules, if you will."

Fin blinked and bowed again to hide his embarrassment, and by the time he straightened, she was gone.

He stared at the closed door for a long time, completely lost to his own thoughts. It was perhaps only a few minutes before the castle door behind him opened. He turned around and saw the same maid that had retrieved him before Hilda's attack standing present.

"His Majesty, Captain Antonio, Mr. Howard, Mage Lee, and Lord Fuks are waiting for you in the counsel room," she said, her eyes a mix of curiosity and worry.

"Thank you. I will be there shortly," he answered dazedly.

The serving girl began to leave when a thought occurred to Fin.

"Pardon me! Before you return to your duties, do you think you could help me carry some items up to them?"

"Oh, sure. What is it you need to bring?"

Fin smiled as he glanced at the piping hot tray of shepherd's pie and freshly baked cookies. "I'm bringing them dinner."

CHAPTER 32
STATING THE OBVIOUS

After completing his bow to the king, Fin straightened. He felt as though he were about to pass out at any moment. In a single day he had faced off against Captain Antonio, battled a powerful water witch, behaved inappropriately toward Lady Jenoure, been offered sincere praise and advice by a Coven leader, made dinner, and now he was in a counsel room with some of the most politically powerful men of the continent. All of whom wanted to talk about his relationship to his abusive father he hadn't seen in twenty years.

The king, Captain Antonio, Mr. Howard, Lord Fuks, and Mage Lee were staring at him with mixed expressions.

"Mr. Ashowan, thank you for joining us. In light of today's events, we have much to discuss."

Fin nodded and took a steadying breath. A stack of plates had been set beside the shepherd's pie that sat steaming at the center of the long table. Each man had their dishware and cutlery set before them. Bottles of fine red wine Fin had paired with the meal sat with their corks still nestled in their necks, waiting to be opened.

The cookies were stacked masterfully on a wide platter close to Fin's end of the long table. His hands were clasped behind his back as he stared at each man present.

Mage Lee appeared calm, Mr. Howard was frowning, Captain Antonio looked skeptical, Lord Fuks had a mad glint in his eye, and the king remained simply stern.

Eloise Morozov's voice echoed in his mind as he felt the crushing weight of their attention. He took the silence they offered him as an opportunity to sort through his chaotic thoughts and emotions.

What role was a house witch supposed to have?

What suited him and his abilities?

In the somnolent fog of his mind, Fin thought about all the times he had stood while cooking to talk with Prince Eric. He thought about the night that the knights, Peter, and Hannah had shared dinner with a warm fire at their backs. The peace, comfort, and happiness of each time and place given because they knew they were all safe, yes, but after underneath the unspoken knowledge of safety and protection ...

Home was the feeling of care and warmth. When Fin felt the most at ease wasn't when he used his powers to defend his hearth, it was when he used them to make everyone and everything feel good, relaxed, content, and fulfilled.

It was the place where you could rest and be whole. Free of disputes and divides.

Lady Jenoure's face flashed through his mind. In his kitchen, Fin was able to speak to her without restraint or acknowledgment of their class differences.

The king had felt comfortable enough to drink until drunk and confess his worries to the world ...

That was what Fin wanted to use his magic to keep. Even if it was in the castle of the king, he wanted it to not just be a safe place, but a good place.

Fin hadn't had a full plan when he had entered the counsel room, but ... suddenly he knew exactly how he wanted to introduce himself to them as a witch.

Well ... I guess it's now or never.

"Your Majesty, Lord Fuks, Captain Antonio, Mr. Howard, and Mage Lee, will you permit me to dine with you while we discuss what you have summoned me for?" His left hand remained behind his back, while the fingers in his right began to tingle. The perfect execution of the introduction to his powers rested now solely on the king.

Despite the mounting tension, Fin's voice sounded miraculously calm while anxiety still gnawed at him from within.

The king didn't acknowledge any of the other men as he continued watching Fin keenly.

"I will allow it, Mr. Ashowan."

A smile that was a mixture of nerves and devilish mischief lit up Fin's face. He raised his right hand and snapped his fingers.

The dishes all levitated. The serving spatula that had been tucked in Fin's belt rose over to the mouth-watering, seasoned meal, divided the portions evenly on each plate, then slowly distributed them over to each man's place as nearly everyone but the mage and king watched slack-jawed and wide-eyed.

Bottles of red wine slid forward, their corks squeaking as they slowly twisted free of their deep green glass bottles. The wine then drifted around to every empty goblet, pouring their ruby liquid until notes of fullness played from each cup.

The final goblet filled was the one Fin procured from behind his back, while he met the surprised stares of the other dinner guests and raised his drink.

"Thank you for allowing me to dine in your esteemed presences."

The stunned silence lasted a full thirty panic-inducing seconds before Lord Fuks burst out laughing.

"Good Gods lad! No wonder I liked you right away! That explains your strange instincts pertaining to cravings!"

"Lord Fuks, you will notice your goblet is only partially filled. While a bit of red wine is healthy for you, you should still be careful," Fin warned with a strict eyebrow raise.

The Daxarian chief of military's expression immediately soured.

"Royal Cook Ashowan, you control this kind of power? Why hide it?" Captain Antonio wondered, clearly awestricken.

Fin cleared his throat.

"For many reasons I will be happy to discuss at a later date. However, I believe you all have important questions regarding my father." He took that moment to take a long draught from his goblet.

"Yes, Mr. Ashowan. If you could please take a seat, we would all like to hear more about this." The king gestured toward the empty chair beside Captain Antonio.

Fin strode over, hoping he was exuding more confidence than he felt, and seated himself down beside the head of Daxaria's armed forces. A strange sense of pride began to settle in his chest.

"To start, please explain to those present what your abilities are and their weaknesses. While I have more than these four men in my inner counsel, I am trying to limit your exposure to the other nobility." The king raised his goblet and drank.

"Of course." Fin bobbed his head to the ruler in appreciation before addressing the rest of the group.

"I am a house witch. The bigger my home, and more people that share my home, the more powerful I am. I have to visit a place in the house and be in its space for a short amount of time, and afterward I can do all kinds of things. If I am off the grounds of my home, however, I am magically powerless. Though with or without magic, I remain one of the best cooks on the continent."

Fin had no idea where the abundance of mettle he was producing was coming from—he felt borderline giddy! The day must have somehow unraveled his inner self-deprecating voice to the point where all that was left was pure nerve …

Fortunately, everyone chortled in response to his boast, as he sated himself with another healthy gulp of wine. Fin gave a casual wave over his shoulder—an action that magically opened the windows to the counsel room, allowing for a pleasant evening breeze to sweep through.

Captain Antonio had a far-off look in his eyes and a sad smile, as though he were remembering something, while all the other men gave a small start at the sound as the latches brattled open.

"Mr. Ashowan, Ms. Morozov informed us that the Troivackian chief of military is your father. I understand your reasons for not confessing to your relationship when Lord Piereva questioned you publicly. However, why is it you did not come forward privately?"

Fin did his best to reply in a straightforward manner that would end the discussion as hastily as possible. "I have not considered Mr. Helmer my father for more than twenty years. I have known nothing of the man since I … well … since I more or less catapulted him off my home island into the Alcide Sea. I only learned what he was doing when Lord Piereva mentioned him during the Beltane festival."

Mr. Howard choked on the wine he had been gulping.

"Would you mind elaborating on what you meant by, 'catapulted off an island'?" The king's steady and unperturbed tone helped soften the initial reaction amongst his counsel to Fin's explanation. Thankfully, because he had previous awareness of his cook's abilities, he was able to smooth out the conversational wrinkles.

Fin felt his cheeks flush. He took another draught of wine for courage. "In times of great danger, I am capable of releasing enough magic to push someone out of my home's perimeter. Sometimes it is done with great force. However, it costs me greatly to do so."

"Force out a single person, or multiple?" The captain's lone blue eye sparkled when he turned and fully faced Fin. Fin knew exactly what motivated the military leader's question, and he was already uncomfortable.

"At present, I have only ever had to use such a large amount of power in three separate instances. None of those times was for more than one or two people."

"The possibilities of this ability are quite—" The captain's eager tone made Fin's right hand curl slightly against the polished table's surface.

"Captain, I hate to disappoint you, but my skills are centered around nurturing a warm and happy home. Should it be treated as a military weapon or tool, the results could be … unpredictable."

"Unpredictable? How—" The captain's severe expression went unobserved by Fin, who repeated the words Ms. Morozov had issued to him only an hour earlier silently to himself. The words that had filled him and gently soothed the smarting wounds of his pride and dignity that had existed since he had been a child …

"Captain, perhaps we address the questions regarding Troivack's chief of military first. Ms. Morozov was very clear that Mr. Ashowan will need considerable rest after protecting us from Hilda today." The king took control of the conversation then, shooting the captain a look that left no room for argument.

"Thank you for your consideration, Your Majesty. It has indeed been a long day. I understand that much about my kind is still relatively unknown and worrying to the general public, but I would prefer to take time to individually meet and discuss with you all the details of my magic. For tonight, it is most likely best to address the more pressing matter of Mr. Aidan Helmer."

Fin felt as though someone else had said his father's name. He hadn't spoken of the man in years, and now he was saying it to the king of the entire continent …

"Mr. Ashowan, I had noticed this before, but even more so now that we are addressing the serious matter of a kingdom-wide threat. You sound far more educated than a cook—even an accomplished one." Mr. Howard was staring critically at him.

Fin's bright blue eyes slid over slowly to the assistant, who was in the process of swirling the wine in his goblet with a loving twist of his wrist.

"The Coven of Wittica educates all registered witches. They believe that by educating those with power, we will be more controlled and make better decisions."

"What of Hilda today? She—"

"Hilda's youth was during the reign of witch hunters and prosecutors. I will say again; for tonight, could we please address your concerns surrounding my father?" Fin's firm tone made Mr. Howard glower, but he somehow managed to maintain his calm and controlled aura.

"Mr. Ashowan is right, gentlemen. Lady Jenoure's Zinferan and Troivackian suitors are due to arrive any day now, and while we can hasten the marriage to firm up Zinfera's military support, we need every advantage, given Troivack's military strengths."

Captain Antonio gave a small jerk of his chin, then turned back to Fin. Once all the men had quieted, the king once again addressed him.

"Would you say your father tends to be on the offensive or defensive in his strategies, Mr. Ashowan?"

"Offensive."

The immediate reply gave every man pause.

"Are you a spy for your father, Mr. Ashowan?" The soft voice of Mage Lee broke the silence that had momentarily settled in, the sound of which made Fin grit his teeth.

Fin knew he should've felt a kindred bond with the man after the battle from earlier, but it seemed ingrained in himself to want to snap at him.

"No. My father is a cruel man. Were it not for my mother's healing abilities, I would have scars marring me beyond recognition." The room immediately grew somber before he continued.

"It should tell you all something that I have only expelled people from my home with magic three times in my life. The first instance was my father, the second idiot bullies, the third an abusive fiancé that came for a woman my mother was treating. He came after she had fled to us for refuge."

"You are a protector by nature," Captain Antonio observed keenly as he slowly picked up his fork and drove its tines into the soft meaty dish in front of himself.

"Being raised by only my mother and educated on the strength of women witches has made me both sympathetic to the powerless, while also aware of their strengths. A strange notion for your knights." Fin stared directly at the captain accusingly.

The air crackled.

"Mr. Ashowan, we would like to present you with a variety of attack plans that Troivack could use. If you could find one that you believe to be most similar to your father's method of thinking, that in of itself would be of great help." The king swiftly changed the subject, ignoring Fin's obvious jibe—there were more pressing matters for that particular moment.

Fin bowed slightly from his chair to the king.

"I would be happy to try, Your Majesty. Though it is not out of humility that I again say, I truly do not know much about the man. Even prior to his … timely exit, he did not like to be home often."

"Good Gods."

Every head swiveled over to Lord Fuks, who had a mouthful of the shepherd's pie in his mouth.

"Am I cursed when I eat your food?" the elderly man asked while loading another forkful hastily; his investment in the answer was clearly not overly high.

"Not at all. Enjoy, Lord Fuks," Fin replied, already feeling himself begin to smile.

The old man grinned back, despite his mouth being full of food. He then idly added,

"I must say, your father sounds like a real—"

"Dick?"

"Yes, Mr. Ashowan?" Lord Fuks replied before he realized exactly what Fin had said.

Fin stared at him, his eyes dancing with mirth.

The king rolled his eyes to the ceiling, while Mr. Howard pinched the bridge of his nose.

"Mr. Ashowan, I would've thought with your education and awareness of the more cultured side of—" the king began exasperatedly.

"Think nothing of it, sire. Mr. Ashowan is still in the process of working out his juvenile tendencies. Besides, I too am curious about how I will hold up against his parentage as my opponent." Lord Fuks waved his fork in the air in a cavalier manner.

"Your Majesty, I have every confidence that Daxaria's chief of military will stick it to the Troivackian king." Fin sipped his wine, his eyes remaining fixed on the monarch while the captain choked on the food.

"Don't worry, Your Majesty, the Royal Cook has a keen mind! Once he experiences some growth of character, I'm sure he will cease his teasing." Lord Fuks grinned, taking another heaping bite of shepherd's pie. He shot a mischievous wink to Fin.

"You know, Mr. Ashowan, I really am not craving this dish at all." Mr. Howard nearly shouted the words as he continued to openly scowl at Fin. It was as though he was trying to remind Fin of his place, as well as stop the immature jests with the Daxarian chief of military.

"You are craving the entire bottle of red wine. I'm not your mother, you know to eat food with your drink." Fin lifted his fork to his mouth, meeting Mr. Howard's disdainful gaze.

"I feel a tad chilly. Cook, perhaps you could light the hearth?" Mage Lee called over condescendingly. The man was already down to the last three bites of his food.

"If Keith gives Ruby another piece of advice, you won't need me to. She'll spit enough acid to burn the castle down."

Mage Lee had been in the process of raising his wine to his lips, but the cup stilled its journey at the retort. Fin didn't seem to feel like going easy on the old man, so naturally he set to digging his own grave.

"Then again, he nearly made Hilda flood it, so I can understand your concern."

The king watched the Royal Cook let loose his stream of insulting dry responses with growing surprise and incredulousness.

"Why so terse, Mr. Ashowan? Upset that you couldn't get a woman, so you had to settle for a cat?" the mage fired back with a jeer.

"Cats just happen to be less trouble. I have no problem with getting—"

"Your cat has defecated in His Majesty's shoes!" Mr. Howard jumped in angrily.

"The cat did what?" The king's sharp tone was pointedly evaded by Fin, who feigned innocence.

"My opinion still holds," Fin addressed Mr. Howard evenly.

The bickering and trading of barbs went well into the night. Mysteriously, everyone eventually gave up being insulted and retaliating, and somehow …

They ended up having a rousing good time.

A time so good, in fact, that the entire group consisting of a king, a mage, a sassy assistant, a house witch, and a captain, all wound up being told of their embarrassing drunken exploits by a rather gleeful chief of military the next morning.

Though there were quite a few witnesses to some of their more … creative activities that night.

CHAPTER 33
A DIMMED AFTERGLOW

The queen sat patiently beside her husband, who was reeking profusely, and snoring quite loudly, while Kraken lay nestled at her side. The baby in her belly shifted against the soft purrs that rumbled out of the feline and into her womb.

Against all odds, she had grown rounder, and remaining in bed had allowed a healthy glow to return to her face. Every day Ainsley would silently pray that the child in her would continue its regular spins and kicking of her ribs. Secretly she felt that the reason for her improved condition was thanks to Kraken's constant presence. The fast-growing kitten's steady, loving aura and silky soft fluffiness had become her rock for an hour or more of each and every day. Not to mention his antics that never failed to amuse her. He would occasionally appear in her bedchamber with a fresh bread roll with a few bites taken out. Sometimes he would prowl beneath the covers until the queen would wiggle a foot and send him into a panic, making her giggle like a young girl again.

Today was one of the days he was bringing a smile to her face.

The long black tail was swishing over the king's face, dusting him with every snore until a long groan rumbled through the man.

"What the— Oh. It's Kraken." Norman rubbed his face with trembling hands as he slowly peeked up at his wife, who gazed down at him with an arched eyebrow.

"You have some explaining to do, husband." Her soft voice did nothing to stop the piercing pain in Norman's temples.

"I ... er ... I'm sorry? I don't exactly remember what happened ..." He tried to raise himself up, but a wave of nausea sent him over the edge of the bed with a great heave into his chamber pot.

"Oh, don't worry. I gathered a few helpful witnesses to relay to you what all happened." The queen smiled brilliantly when the king had finally righted himself on the bed and accepted the cup of water his wife offered.

"Shall we start with Ruby?" The king slowly drew himself up and opened his dry mouth to protest, when Ainsley called out quite loudly to the hallway.

The Head of Housekeeping entered looking tired, annoyed, but also somehow ... amused. She brought with her a tray filled with toast, bacon, and fresh fruit.

"Good morning, Your Majesty, I hope you feel more like yourself this morning." Ruby laid the tray over the king's lap, then proceeded to curtsy. After she rose, she strode back to the foot of the bed with her hands clasped in front of her.

"Thank you, Ruby. His Majesty is still somewhat sickly, but I'm sure that might be the case for the remainder of the day. Could you please tell your king what transpired during your night?" the queen requested, her radiant expression making the king wince.

"Of course, Your Majesty." Ruby curtsied again before her eyes gained a distant look as she proceeded to share her report. "Last night I was awoken by a series of rambunctious noises that drew me out of bed to investigate. I proceeded to find a trail of oddities all over the castle, though none of which can measure up to what in the world happened to the front and eastern gardens—I have no idea how—"

"Perhaps, Ruby, you could relay to His Majesty what happened when you found Captain Antonio?" the queen cut in smoothly.

Ruby nodded firmly, her lips pursed.

"We found Captain Antonio face down in the center of the banquet hall. We were greatly concerned, particularly given that he was barefoot without a tunic on. I summoned Physician Frederick Durand, and after rousing a couple of the knights we managed to carry him to his cottage. He awoke, sat straight up, looked around and said: 'Good evening, everyone;

please leave me be and bar my mother from the room.' Then he resumed his sleep while sitting up."

The king wanted to laugh, but managed not to as Ruby curtsied once more, took his sullied chamber pot, and excused herself.

"Well, my love, that isn't so bad—" Norman began to say.

"Lord Fuks, could you please come in and give your account of last evening?" Ainsley's angelic demeanor never wavered.

"How many people are outside waiting to act as witnesses?!" The ruler of the country felt his stomach clench painfully.

Lord Fuks entered with a joyful spring in his step. The chief of military wore a black tunic and a red vest freshly pressed. The fine silks of his garment shimmered in the light of the bedchamber.

"Good morning, sire, my oh my do I have some stories. I apologize, my queen; they may make a gentlewoman such as yourself blush."

"I will be alright, but thank you for your concern, Dick."

Lord Fuks turned back to the king, who was already shooting dirty looks at him.

"Last night, after several bottles of wine were consumed, Mr. Howard proceeded to trash the counsel room—"

"He what?! Oh … Oh wait … I do remember that. He was explaining why he loved Daxaria?"

"Precisely! Yes, he was showing every ailment and political flaw of our nearest countries. It was a very heated discussion, albeit a hard one to follow by that point. However, one thing that most certainly happened, was he drafted an official letter to each country explaining why they were … lacking compared to Daxaria."

"Gods, he didn't send hawks with those, did he?!" The king was now wide awake.

"Not for lack of trying. I managed to see each missive into the fire." Lord Fuks's eyes were sparkling as his voice warbled.

"Thank Gods for that …" The king began rubbing his face, feeling immense relief wash over him.

"Sire, that was the beginning of the night."

Norman's head throbbed against his widened eyes, but he couldn't help himself.

"What … else … happened?"

"Did your Head of Housekeeping tell you about your new lawn decorations?"

The king glanced briefly at Ainsley, who smiled even wider.

"Mr. Ashowan goaded Mage Lee to perform a series of … *creative* magical challenges. Your Majesty is now the proud owner of ten new fountains. One of which can be turned into a source of hot bubbling water that refreshes but does not burn, thanks to Mr. Ashowan. We all took a dip, and it was a wonderfully relaxing time. Until, that is, you all grew very hungry."

The king had his mouth firmly covered with his hand, while the queen was working very hard not to laugh in a very unladylike manner.

"The captain consumed half a loaf of bread, then ambled off to put the remains somewhere outside, and when he returned, he was also missing his goblet. He then muttered something about sleeping where he worked to save time and departed. Mr. Howard went and began collecting bottles of wine from the cellars and carrying them around for whatever reason. He would growl like a dog anytime Mr. Ashowan went to take them away. I believe he went outside to get away from our beloved cook, and you can spy him, if you like, out your window still asleep amongst the flower beds."

Mortified, Norman prayed that they had reached the end of the evening's adventures. Lord Fuks knew otherwise.

"Your Majesty then wanted to try flying, and Mr. Ashowan obliged by levitating a sling made out of a tapestry for you, which is also how you managed to get back into your chamber here. He ran out of magic, apparently, just outside the chamber door, and passed out, promptly dropping Your Majesty onto the floor. Ruby, the knights, and myself did our best in returning you to your chamber. Strangely, by the time I had returned with help, Mr. Ashowan had disappeared without a trace. He is now awake and working in the kitchen once more. Though he seems a tad under the weather himself."

Ainsley slowly turned to her husband, who didn't have the stomach to face her.

Lord Fuks bowed and excused himself, declaring he needed to return to his own bed for a well-deserved nap.

"Ainsley, I am so very sorry. I will never—" the king began with notes of deep regret.

"Lady Jenoure, could you please come in?"

"Son of a mage!" Norman snapped as Lady Jenoure strode in, wearing a rich deep purple gown with a jeweled belt settled on her hips, matching the jeweled pendant hanging from her necklace.

"Good afternoon, Your Majesty. My queen has asked me to relay to you my part in the evening. I must say you all made my job both difficult and entertaining to keep some secrets hidden away. For starters, getting Mr. Ashowan down to his kitchen so no one would be the wiser pertaining to his involvement with Your Majesty."

Norman was nodding slowly and trying to stop himself from being sick once again. Ruby should've left the chamber pot.

"Mr. Ashowan was returned safely, and I commandeered your 'Lady Jenoure to-do list' that apparently you had been scribbling for me to review in the morning. I am sorry to say I am not able to relay who my contacts are in Troivack, nor do I know who they are sending over as a potential suitor for me."

When Lady Jenoure saw the look of confusion on the king's face, she clarified.

"These were some of the questions or requests you had scrawled for me. I regret to inform you, sire, that I have no idea what topic number three meant. It was a single word: *costumes*. Though it could have something to do with Mage Lee having two sticks tied around his head, shouting at Mr. Ashowan, 'I'm the Green Man, see?!' but I'm uncertain."

She curtsied apologetically, much to the king's horrified embarrassment.

"Is that … all … ?" he asked weakly.

Annika took her time pondering the question. It really wasn't all that important that the king knew about the random objects they had moved around, or that he had tried to wake his son up to tell him he loved him.

"Yes, Your Majesty." She proceeded to curtsy and excuse herself from the chamber, leaving the king and queen once again alone.

Norman slowly bit into the toast and chewed, even though he had a hunch it would come back up in the near future.

"To be perfectly honest, Norman, if I weren't bedridden and routinely bored, I would be furious. However, this has been the most fun I've had in a long time." Ainsley rubbed her bump slowly with a mischievous grin on her face.

"Who all knows about this?" the king asked, already fearful of the answer.

"Well … Ruby, Lord Fuks, Annika, all of the men that you were 'meeting,' a couple of the knights that had to carry you to bed, and a couple more that had to carry the captain."

"Is that all?"

"Well, anyone who looks at the massive influx of fountains may be perplexed, but we could write them off as gifts for Eric's birthday. Mr. Howard is passed out in the front flower beds surrounding the statue of the Gods, which is harder to explain. Not to mention the statue in the front with a half-eaten loaf of bread shoved under the arm of the first witch, and a goblet precariously placed atop the Green Man's head."

"No one has removed him from the gardens?"

"No one knew where he was until an hour ago. We've already taken care of it."

The king nodded, despite the movement hurting him.

"Sleep, my dear. We will have a lengthier chat once you awaken." The queen gently stroked her husband's back before moving the tray off his lap and over to her side of the bed.

Without another word, the king slunk down into his sheets, grateful to curl up in agony and curse himself out in peace.

Fin vomited for the third time at the end of the garden path and straightened himself unsteadily. Hannah, Peter, and Sirs Harris, Taylor, Lewis, and Andrews all watched from the kitchen doorway, concerned.

"I wouldn't want his flu." Sir Lewis shuddered.

"I have doubts that it's the flu," Sir Harris remarked blithely. "It might have something more to do with Mr. Howard being passed out in the pansies," the new addition to the kitchen knights added with a rueful smile.

They all continued watching as Fin slowly made his way back to the kitchen, his complexion looking only slightly paler than an olive green.

"I'll get the vegetables ready, if you could all …" Fin paused as he leaned on one of the wooden fence posts in the garden. "If you could all please leave the kitchen for a minute."

Everyone exchanged glances and filed out without another word.

By dinnertime, he was feeling marginally better, though the headache portion of his hangover had hit sometime during the soup course of the evening.

He was in the final stages of sending out a dessert of fruit salad drizzled with honey and the juice of freshly squeezed oranges from Kasim's greenhouse, when Hannah burst in through the castle door, bright-eyed and rosy-cheeked.

"Fin, you will not believe what rumors are going around!" She was bouncing up and down and alternating between covering her smiling mouth and biting her lips shut.

Fin took a deep drink from the cup of water he had been nursing for the day and fixed her with his most patient expression. He still looked greatly annoyed, but it was the best he could do.

"Why would I care about the rumors going on? It isn't any of my business." When the final footman had disappeared with the dessert, Hannah stopped bouncing, and began twisting her torso back and forth, making her soft pink skirts swish about her ankles coyly.

"You should care because the rumor is about you and Mr. Howard. Everyone is saying you two are lovers and that you both had a courting date last night!" She succumbed to laughter then and there as Fin felt a tic in his right eye appear.

"Of course, we have all been assuring people that is not the case. It also helped Peter let people know his own preferences, once he saw that no one seemed to have an issue with it. I don't even think anyone here in the castle is a part of the Acker religion, but isn't this hilarious?!" Hannah's chatter rushed out of her mouth in an effort to not interrupt herself with peals of gaiety.

"Why … does everyone care if I am gay or not?" Fin managed slowly as Kraken appeared at his side and gently began pawing his leg in an attempt of gaining some good chin scratches.

"Well, to be honest … a lot of the maids have a crush on you. That being said, a lot of them are also really excited for you and Mr. Howard. They seem to be die-hard supporters of your relationship."

"I don't have a relationship with Mr. Howard, aside from that of cook and pain-in-the-ass king's assistant," Fin drawled while refilling his water cup again.

"We've been telling people that! I mean we all know you like Lady— ladies. You like the ladies." Hannah cleared her throat daintily as the cup that had been at Fin's lips lowered. He looked ready to strangle her.

"What were you going to say just—"

"Oh, would you look at that, I better go and finish my own dinner before someone clears my plate for me. See you tomorrow morning, Fin!" Hannah scurried out of the room quickly.

After staring at the closed kitchen door for several moments of silence, Fin pinched the bridge of his nose and let out a garbled, unintelligible groan of frustration.

Slowly, he bent down and picked up Kraken. He petted the familiar slowly, ignoring the sweltering heat of his hearth at his back.

"I swear to the Gods, I should never drink again," he muttered as Kraken gazed lazily up at his witch. "At the very least, I doubt anyone suspects me of being a spy now."

Kraken said nothing but registered that Fin was feeling all kinds of conflicting emotions. He couldn't waste too much energy worrying about his witch, however. He had his own problems as of late …

CHAPTER 34
TURN AROUND

"And I just think you two will have such a long and happy life together! Mr. Howard loves his wine, and you love food; the match goes hand in hand!" A maid named Madeline had dropped by the kitchen to offer Fin her opinion regarding his torrid love affair with the king's assistant. He found himself wondering if Ruby would finally allow him to install a lock on both doors leading into his kitchen, in light of the new absurdity that flowed through the corridors.

When maid Madeline with her long dark curls had finished her declaration of undying admiration and exuberant cheer for Fin, he at long last paused his work. All throughout the young maid's speech, he had busied himself by rubbing spices into the chicken thighs he was working on preparing for lunch, but once he was quite certain she had finished, he fixed her with his most bored-looking expression.

"I had eaten something that didn't agree with me. There is nothing going on with Mr. Howard and myself. I am not even gay. Now, how is it that this is deemed the 'official kitchen business' that you insisted it was?" he demanded, his gaze unwavering.

Madeline gulped and began rubbing her apron nervously between her fingers. Her naturally tanned complexion paled slightly, and her wide dark eyes flitted about the room nervously.

"I-I'm sorry, Mr. Ashowan, I didn't mean to interrupt you, I just wanted t-to tell you how brave and—"

"Again, I am not gay." Fin's lazy tone was no less disconcerting to the maid.

The poor girl stammered a few more incoherent sentences before he finally decided she had suffered enough.

"I'm sure you are busy and need to return to your duties, but thank you for your encouragement—even if it was a misguided belief. Perhaps you should let Mr. Howard know that, with or without a partner, he shouldn't be too sad about not finding someone special."

Grateful for the excuse to leave, Madeline nodded hurriedly and then dashed out of the room without another word.

Fin began to smile to himself when he considered how Mr. Howard would feel about the news that he was dallying with a male cook.

"Mr. Ashowan." The unmistakable voice of Ruby broke the newfound silence that he had only just begun to once again partake in.

"Ruby, I hope you're having a good morning so far," he greeted her without hesitating in his work.

"Oh, just dandy, the suitors have all arrived at the same time! The Troivackian was supposed to arrive first, but I suppose Lord Piereva caught up with their ship and slowed them down." Sarcasm dripped throughout her flustered speech.

Fin's hands stopped on their own accord and his heart skipped a beat.

Once he became conscious of this obvious reaction, he resumed working and hoped the Head of Housekeeping hadn't noticed his hesitation.

"I will prepare the additional meals necessary. I will also have refreshments sent up to their quarters for the guests and their entourages." His clipped tone made Ruby frown slightly. Fin had been becoming gradually more palatable over time, so it was peculiar that he suddenly resumed his former snarky notes.

"Everything alright, Mr. Ashowan?" Ruby queried, folding her hands patiently against her apron.

"Why have you stopped calling me Fin?" He turned the question and dodged having to answer.

"Well, I keep hearing His Majesty and other nobility call you Mr. Ashowan, and next thing I found myself doing the same. Would you prefer me to resume calling you by your first name?"

"Whichever you are comfortable with." He didn't raise his gaze as he proceeded to mix warmed butter over the chicken thighs.

Ruby continued to study the man for another beat of quiet before shaking her head and turning back to the castle door. As she stepped through the doorway, a young maid with white-blond hair and sunken eyes began to try to wedge herself into the kitchen around the Head of Housekeeping's girth.

"Reagan, what in the world are you doing here?" Ruby demanded severely.

"I—er—I-I'm here to—"

"Oh, for the love of the Gods," Fin muttered before swinging around. "Go help tend to the newcomers," he snapped.

Ruby seemed to gain a spark of understanding, because she suddenly grabbed the young woman's slender upper arm and began dragging her away while lecturing her in hushed tones.

Once he was alone again, Fin pressed the tops of his fists into his cooking table and closed his eyes with a long sigh.

He knew it had just been a matter of time before Lady Jenoure was going to be plagued with nobility vying for her attention, and eventually, her hand.

It didn't make it any easier now that the time had finally come.

Fin had pointedly ignored thinking about the inevitability of Lady Jenoure's marriage, and now that he did so, immediately began working to convince himself that it would never have worked anyway. Besides, there were plenty of other women in the world.

Men too, apparently … not that that particularly meant much personally to Fin.

After he tightened his fists briefly against the table's surface, he braced himself and pushed off. He had the tray of chicken magically fly into the oven before he summoned a large glass jar of homemade cool tea from the cooling hole. It had peaches, lavender, and mint.

It was made by boiling water and letting peppermint tea steep between ten to twenty minutes before removing the tea ball, while leaving the other ingredients to soak in the water in the cooling hole for a full day.

It was a splendid summer drink, one he was sending in a decanter to each suitor's chamber.

Except for Lord Piereva.

For the earl, he sent regular hot tea with a very special root Kasim had shown him … Along with some very tasty but dry muffins.

Once he had the trays assembled, he called for the footmen, who arrived promptly and whisked the teatime meals away.

Seeing Lord Piereva's tray disappear through the doorway brought a smile to Fin's face, and it was around that time that his aides traipsed through the garden door.

"Fin, Captain Antonio wants to see you when you have some spare time." Peter announced as the group brought in the peeled vegetables for the evening salads.

"It might be a while; the suitors for Lady Jenoure have just arrived. I'm sorry to say I will have to send you out to peel more vegetables before lunchtime." Fin's bland tone was painfully obvious as his facial expression matched his voice.

Hannah and Peter shared a meaningful glance, one that had Fin frowning in an instant. The knights became taken aback by his shift in expression, having missed Hannah and Peter's wordless communication.

"How many people will be staying here and how long?" Sir Harris drawled in a near whine, appearing oblivious and or uncaring of the tension in the room.

Fin's sharp gaze cut to the knight, who nearly winced under the piercing stare of the cook.

"I was informed that one of the Zinferan suitors recently inherited his title from his deceased uncle and that he travels with an entourage of ten people, while the other Zinferan travels with fourteen. The Troivackian noble brings a modest five, while Lord Piereva has returned as well with his usual twelve. Approximately forty-four people in total."

Every aide's face paled, but no one dared to groan aloud.

"I've done some preparations for this; however, the vegetables will be the toughest, as we cannot prep them too far in advance. I recommend you all get started." Fin turned back to the next two trays of chicken thighs and waited for his colleagues to leave.

After a good deal of shuffling, he was certain they'd all picked up the extra vegetables on the ledge and departed, when the softest swish of skirts drew his eyes back upward. There must have been some level of ferocity in their gold-flecked depths, for Hannah took a sharp inhale of breath when he rested his gaze upon her.

"Yes?"

Hannah took a deep breath in, clearly fortifying her strength before speaking. "Are you alright?" she blurted out a little too loudly.

Fin's eyes narrowed for a brief moment before he continued his work on the food. "Perfectly fine. Why do you ask?" Suspicion laced his words as he began to wonder what Hannah was getting at. He sincerely hoped she wasn't going to offer her opinion on his relationship with Mr. Howard.

"Are you upset because of the suitors for Lady Jenoure?" Hannah asked softly, her cheeks burning.

Fin raised his head and lifted an eyebrow, otherwise going perfectly still. "What makes you ask that?"

"We ... Well ... I ... You two are always bickering, but you talk to each other more than anyone else." Hannah looked anxious but clenched her hands into fists at her sides in steely resolution.

Fin dropped his stare down to the table in front of him for a brief moment before slowly drawing himself up. "Lady Jenoure and I share camaraderie due to my education level. I am not what you would call ... 'normal' in that regard." When his aide responded with a small frown, he sighed and added, "Hannah, I ... I've been educated as well as most lower-level nobles."

She nodded, her frown clearing at once. It didn't come as a surprise to her. "Were you the bastard of a lord?" she whispered conspiratorially.

"No." Fin snorted somewhat bitterly and rested his hands on his hips. "I am perfectly legitimate; I've just had an unusual upbringing. Now, please don't think again about something so untoward. Such rumors could ruin Lady Jenoure and that would be greatly unjust."

Hannah looked like she wanted to say more, but she was cut off when the castle door opened once more, revealing none other than Mage Lee and Keith.

Fin wanted to throw a chicken thigh at them but managed not to.

"Mr. Ashowan, we were wondering if you happened to know where the tenth fountain that was sent for the prince's birthday wound up. We have relocated most of the ... wondrous gifts." Mage Lee cleared his throat while Fin smiled cheekily at him. Keith stared back and forth between them, perfectly perplexed.

"However, we cannot seem to ... find the last one. We wondered if you or your aides had seen or heard where it had wound up." Lee eyed Hannah warily as he carefully crafted the question.

"Can't say I have, but come find me after dinner and I would be happy to lend you a hand."

Keith's puzzled expression cleared as swiftly as the knights' barracks when Sir Taylor broke wind, and instead he beamed.

"Father, isn't that wonderful? I can stay and offer my skills to the new guests while he helps you this evening. I cannot believe you said he was a good-for-nothing know-it-all with a stick up his—"

"Come along, Keith," Mage Lee barked as he grabbed his son by the back of his collar and dragged him away.

Hannah covered her mouth as she and Fin stared at one another. Both immediately burst out laughing.

"Keith really has no filter or self-awareness, does he?" Hannah managed, wiping errant tears from her cheeks.

"He must get it from his father." Fin rubbed the back of his neck, still smiling.

"Oh! Before I forget ..." Hannah strode over to a small burlap satchel she had placed on the window ledge earlier that morning.

From it, she drew out a black apron that she handed to Fin.

"What's this?" he asked dumbly as he looked at the expert stitching along its ties.

"I made one for all of us kitchen staff! I noticed how easily your white apron becomes stained and thought a darker color might be better. I even added a pocket! A secret one on the inside." Fin felt his cheeks grow red and words died in his throat. He then noticed in the bottom left corner a small skillet sewn in with gray thread. Its handle was crossing a familiar broom with red twine holding its bristles together.

"Hannah, this is ... amazing. You did this yourself?" He immediately removed his stained white apron from around his hips, and tied on the new black one that he could tell was made with stronger material.

"I did! I have to go give the rest of the aides theirs now." She glowed with pleasure at Fin's praise.

"Did you embroider all of them?" he wondered, smiling warmly down at her, his former foul mood dissipating quickly.

"I did! You'll have to wait for them to show you, though. No peeking," Hannah winked, her cheeks remaining rosy.

Fin held up both his hands in surrender. "I understand. Get going then, I can't wait to see how they look."

Hannah had one foot outside of the garden door, the hot summer sun pouring in, when Fin called out. "Thank you. I ... feel a lot better."

She cast a smile over her shoulder that would've made lesser men weak at the knees before she bounded outside happily.

Once again in solitude, Fin looked down at his present, his heart full to the point of bursting.

When he glanced back up at the now empty doorway, he couldn't help but feel a deep gratitude bloom in his chest.

Everything is going to be alright ... one way or another.

He thought peacefully to himself, right as the fattest ginger cat he had ever seen strolled across the end of the garden path. Taken aback, he peered around the room for Kraken and found the fluffy black feline peeking out around the doorway and then looking back to his witch.

"You sure seem to be popular lately."

The kitten let out a broken mew before slowly trudging out toward the new visitor, his tail drooping ever so slightly as he went.

Annika fingered the corner of the coded message in her hand with a tremor of agitation. The suitors had just arrived, so it would be hard to meet with her informant—but he claimed it was urgent.

While she didn't like arranging a meeting during the daytime, she acknowledged she had no choice but to go as soon as possible. Everyone would be keeping a sharp eye on her, particularly in the evening. With three prospective marriage partners sharing a roof with her, it was to be expected.

"Lady Jenoure?" Annika's handmaiden Clara called softly to her mistress, who had already thrown the missive into the flames of the hearth that blazed despite the heat of summer.

"Is it lunchtime already?"

"Yes, my lady." The maid was perhaps in her early thirties, with quiet, deep blue eyes and a complexion as pale as the moon. She had been with her mistress since her very first day in Daxaria.

Annika sighed and looked at the afternoon garb she had laid out for her first meeting with the suitors.

She had chosen her most unflattering dress. It was a plain, navy-blue sheath with a conservative neckline, and long loose sleeves with long holes connecting from the shoulder down to the cuff of the dress.

She donned the fresh attire, and added simple gold studs befitting her station, and a gold ring to her middle finger.

Once she had finished with that ordeal, she bound her hair back in a simple knot at the base of her neck. After a brief glimpse of the looking glass, she deemed herself ready.

Simple. Elegant. Dull.

Adopting the slowest pace possible, Annika made her way down to the banquet hall that already sounded chaotic. She closed her eyes, briefly preparing her most vacant expression as the sounds of clattering dishware and loud, obnoxious laughter filled the air.

She heard the doors open, and she stepped into the stifling, hot sun-filled banquet hall. The nobility seated at their tables along the wall, and the knights at their center tables, all quieted as she strode smoothly down the wide aisle that led to the throne where the king sat staring at three men.

"Ah, Lady Jenoure. Thank you for coming so promptly." There wasn't any note of irony in the king's voice, but Annika knew he was aware of her dawdling.

"May I present, Lord Geun Nam. A lord from the Southern region of Zinfera." The first Zinferan man turned around, his high cheekbones and dark slanted eyes regarding her with a haughty raised eyebrow. He wore bright red loose pants, and a white coat embroidered with gold flower designs. His hairless chest was exposed, and a red sash that matched his pants was tied around his hips. His long black hair was partially pulled back in a bun, and he wore a small gold cuff earring in his upper right ear.

After giving Annika a critical once-over, he bowed with a flourish.

"Pleasure to make your acquaintance." His voice was as smooth as chocolate.

Annika kept her expression as vacuous as Keith's brain when she curtsied back.

"Beside Lord Nam is Lord Milo Miller. He is set to inherit a title, as he has inherited one of his father's many estates in the West of Troivack."

The man towered over nearly everyone in the room. His shoulders were broad, and his stance was strong, as was customary of Troivackian men. The thick black waves of his hair were cropped short, and as he turned, Annika found herself momentarily stunned by his blue eyes. Troivackians were known to be dark, but periodically one was born with blue eyes or paler skin due to mixed marriages with Daxarian women. The evidence of such a pairing in his family history was clear on Lord Miller's face. His clear blue eyes were intense and at first off-putting, until he smiled at her genially and bowed.

"A pleasure to see you again, Lady Jenoure. We met briefly at one of the Troivackian court balls many years ago." When he straightened, his pleasant expression remained perfectly intact.

"I do not recall meeting you prior, as it has been a long time since I've been in Troivack." She curtsied, feeling more than a little rattled at his show of friendliness despite being of Troivackian nobility.

No wonder they labeled him as weak back home, she thought to herself.

"Last, but certainly not least, I believe you will recall Jiho? He acted as a Zinferan diplomat for our Beltane festival. Since then, he recently inherited his uncle's title and lands. He is now Lord Jiho Ryu. He was regaling us all with the incredible story of his life—you should really hear how he went from being a dockworker to a lord." The king's obvious admiration marked the man as his preferred suitor for Annika, and so when she locked gazes with the new noble, she was prepared to hate him.

Except, in his dark eyes was surprising depth and peace. There wasn't lust or judgment like the first Zinferan. In fact, just as Lord Miller had, this man smiled in a warm manner and bowed. His hair was cropped unusually short for a Zinferan, and swept to the side with some kind of pomade that smelled exotic and enticing. He wore a crisp, silk white tunic covered by a long periwinkle silk coat and tan pants. He had done a beautiful job of melding the two different cultures together in one.

Annika curtsied again, almost forgetting to keep her outward facial expression that of a simpleton.

"Shall we eat?" The king's pleasant tone permeated the hall, and as if on cue, each man bowed and offered their hands to Annika.

She didn't have to feign being struck dumb right then.

She looked to the king for help but froze when she registered another set of eyes on her that had been hidden behind the suitors.

Her brother stood, scrutinizing her every move as he always did.

She then knew exactly how to handle the awkward situation.

With another deep curtsy, she rose.

"My lords, you all flatter me with your kindness and consideration. However, I do believe as an unmarried woman it would be most appropriate for my brother to escort me to my place."

There was a glint in her brother's eye that made her want to punch him in the face. She knew what that particular look meant.

It meant he was going to toy with her, and unless she wanted to raise suspicion, she was going to have to let him.

CHAPTER 35
FINISHING TOUCHES

Fin was whisking the meringue with an added vigor as he tried to keep his thoughts regarding Lady Jenoure's suitors at bay. The pesky images of her sharing her real laugh with some other man, or them bantering together, or showing her vulnerable expression, had plagued him all night.

Somehow, the more he tried not to think about it, the more the thoughts bombarded him.

Thunder rumbled in the darkened skies outside the kitchen's garden door. Its growing fury ratcheted from far above with low booms and sharp cracks, but he barely registered the commotion as he continued trying to focus on anything but Annika.

Just as he had worked the ingredients in his bowl into frothy peaks, Sir Taylor strode in alone, shaking his head.

Fin watched the kitchen knight proceed to remove the white apron Hannah had made for him and hang it on the garden door handle.

Fin was becoming more and more intrigued, as arguably one of the largest knights in the castle turned and walked over to his side, still not having said a word. Sir Taylor proceeded to crouch down and begin rummaging around the smaller table Fin had tucked under his larger cooking table. The new addition held his extra knives and plateware that he needed while the suitors were visiting.

He opened his mouth to ask what in the name of the Green Man's antlers was he doing, when Sir Harris jogged up the path.

"Hannah! Hannah, you don't need to tell the cook! Seriously, I didn't mean—" Sir Taylor straightened, a new paring knife in his hand.

"Do I look like Hannah to you?" he growled, rounding the table, crossing the room, snatching his apron off of the door handle, and stomping past his startled fellow knight.

"Depends on the angles," Sir Harris countered over his shoulder as Sir Taylor strode back down the garden path and out of sight.

When Sir Harris turned back to the kitchen, he found himself staring at Fin, who was pointing at him and beckoning him forward. His gaze was filled with murderous intent.

"What did you do?" Fin's tone couldn't have been any more threatening.

"Nothing! She's overreacting!"

"What did you do, and this time unless you want to lose some fingers you will tell me." Picking up his favorite knife and tossing it once in the air, Fin maintained eye contact with the knight.

Sir Harris instinctively curled his fingers into fists and stepped back.

"Gods—it truly was nothing! Peter hasn't shown up today, probably having to deal with all the maids telling him to ask Mr. Howard out on a date. So without him there, I took it upon myself to point out to Hannah that she shouldn't only spend time with Peter if she's looking for a husband. At this point, she should marry one of us knights because she isn't getting any younger."

The look of startled incredulity on Fin's face as Sir Harris recounted the event made the knight feel all the more defensive, so he tried to finish the story.

"She then went berserk and threw her paring knife in my general direction before storming off."

The silence that followed could've rivaled that of a funeral.

Fin put the knife back down, picked up the meringue bowl, and returned his attention back to the teatime snacks. He then said, "Good luck."

Sir Harris was in the process of throwing up his arms in exasperation when the woman herself careened into their midst. Tears streamed down her face and her cheeks were red, but her eyes … Fin knew she could kill someone.

"Hannah, perhaps before you explain to Sir Harris why he shouldn't say—" he began quietly, hoping to calm the obvious chaos in her.

"Fin, one of the knights beat up Peter. Someone named Sir Thoel." Hannah's fists were curled in rage, and every piece of her trembled for revenge. "They broke two ribs and pummeled his face. Physician Durand is tending to him, I just found out because of one of the maids. Apparently, there was a follower of Acker amongst the knights who goaded his friends into help— What're you doing?"

Fin's face had drained of color as he rounded the table and picked up his broom. He gripped its wooden handle firmly, his expression unreadable aside from the cold deadly intent in his eyes.

"I'm going for a walk." The ferocity in his tone was obvious despite its flatness.

"What are you going to do to him?" Hannah asked, her voice hoarse with raw fury.

"If I'm lucky, something permanent."

Fin stalked out of the kitchen, down the garden path, past Sir Taylor who had just returned to his fellow knights, and around the western corner of the castle toward the barracks.

"What is he doing?" Sir Andrews asked, staring after Fin with a raised eyebrow.

"Someone named Sir Thoel beat Peter. He's bedridden." Hannah had been forced to jog to stay in Fin's wake, and she had paused by the group to explain while she caught her breath, her ire palpable.

The knights shared only a moment of silent glances before Sir Taylor announced, "I feel like stretching my legs for a walk."

Hannah watched as the men stood and moved militaristically, their intention abundantly clear as they quickly marched toward the barracks that Fin was already nearing.

Hannah watched them all go, her heart thundering in her chest.

She did not like being powerless when her best friend lay injured in his bed over something so ridiculous.

She bolted back to the kitchen. Kraken scampered out of her way, panicked as she skidded to a halt in front of Fin's table, mere inches from the chair the poor feline had been resting on. Hannah then spotted the particular tool she had been looking for and smiled with a crazed glint in her teary eyes.

Fin stood in the middle of the training ring, his hands folded over the hilt of his broom in feigned casualness.

The captain appeared near the gate to the training ring with a frown. Fin's eyes moved unnaturally when they shifted to the man. Without any other part of his body acknowledging he saw Antonio, he shouted out.

"One of the knights, a follower of the religion of Acker, assaulted one of my aides. The man is now bedridden. I seek his due on his behalf." Fin's voice unnaturally boomed over the men that had gradually come to see what was happening.

The rest of the kitchen knights had just arrived, and they leapt over the training ring fence and positioned themselves in a flanked formation behind him. Each of them wore the aprons Hannah had made, which very clearly divided them from the rest of the knights that had gathered wearing muddied, grungy tunics and trousers, some even wearing pieces of their plate armor.

The captain straightened to his full height. He turned toward the crowd of his men, and they in turn all stepped away to reveal the only one of them that followed the religion.

"Sir Thoel, did you act alone?" The captain's growl made many of the knights shift away from the knight who had been standing at the back. He was tall, with sandy brown hair and blue eyes with occasional dark streaks. He was lean, but the five knights that stood behind him appeared bulkier, though shorter.

Fin stared at the man, his brow lowered.

There was something shifty in Sir Thoel's eyes that immediately sent warning signals to his mind.

"We were there, captain," one of the lackeys voiced, though he sounded far more hesitant.

"I see." The captain strode up to the leader of the men, his blue eye glinting as thunder rumbled above them. "This goes beyond a mere dispute. What you did, Thoel, was assault a civilian. Mr. Ashowan, I will have this man and any of his participants flogged should you deem that the best punishment."

"No, captain. Sir Thoel needs to know what I will personally do to anyone if they think they can harm one of my aides." The obvious slight of neglecting to call the man by his knightly title made Thoel sneer.

"Fine by me," the man announced without waiting for the captain's input. "Defenders of a sinner should be held just as accountable. Five against one is a little unfair, though. I will bring those who were with me when I distributed justice on behalf of our Gods." Sir Thoel strode forward. The five men behind him looked significantly less confident as they neared the group of kitchen staff.

When Sir Thoel stood three feet away from Fin, his jeer turned into a twisted smile revealing a stained front tooth. The sight would've been more than a little chilling if he didn't know the man would be lucky to be alive by the time they were through with him.

"You made a mistake thinking the Gods are on your side, cook. You should've just let the captain flog us."

"What's wrong, sweet buns? Worried we're going to show you what we do to bad biscuits?" Sir Andrews called out with a smirk of his own.

"Worried we're going to *batter* you up?" Sir Harris called out with a small snort.

"You're all idiots." Sir Thoel tried to sound derisive, but his cheeks had flushed in anger the moment Sir Andrews had called him "sweet buns."

"Would you look at that? Thoel is scared we'll leave his meat tender!" Sir Harris called back.

Fin's intense glower slowly melted into a cold smile as he watched the man facing him grow more and more uncomfortable.

Thoel was now a shade of crimson red.

"You'll burn in the fiery pits of—"

"Our cook can whip more than just cream, you ass," Sir Lewis shouted out, making the knights around the ring burst out laughing as they began to catch on to what the kitchen aides were doing.

"Are you going to stand there taunting us, or are we going to fight?" Thoel seethed.

"Oh, we're getting to that," Sir Taylor rumbled.

Sir Thoel roared, his hands curling into fists as he addressed Fin again.

"Why'd you bring the broom, cook? Need a weapon to go against just me?"

"Hardly. I was going to sweep you off your feet and show you a good time." Fin's chilling smile as he delivered the statement, followed by his slow wink, made Thoel snap. He launched himself toward Fin, who swiftly stepped to the side and tripped him.

Thoel stumbled forward into Sir Andrews's fist, the blow landing firmly in the man's gut.

"What's wrong, Thoel? Can't take a *yolk*?" Sir Harris dropped his elbow sharply into the man's back, knocking him to the ground.

Fin stared at the remaining four men, who all hesitated when he squared off with them again. His confidence that his kitchen knights would handle Thoel was abundantly clear.

The first of Thoel's men to step toward Fin was one of the bulkier albeit shorter knights, his dirty blond hair nearly touching his shoulders. He casually tossed his broom at the man. The movement was so sudden that the knight caught the broom without thinking, which occupied his hands and mind. This meant the roundhouse kick Fin executed crashed into the side of his head, knocking him out without any defensive action. The remaining three knights in front of Fin paled. He then felt two of the kitchen knights return to his side. Thoel must have been dealt with.

The remaining three lackeys decided to move as one this time. The man in the center of the trio, a scar running through his right eyebrow, swung an uppercut at Fin. He blocked the attack, and immediately stopped the following jab from the knight's other hand. Fin then gave the man a sharp kick with his heel into his groin. The two kitchen knights at his side had apparently been Sir Lewis and Sir Andrews, and they had handled their own opponents just as efficiently.

The captain strode toward them.

"Sir Harris, you once again have shown the men the importance of mentally distracting one's opponent. These men don't usually go down so easily." Antonio then turned to Fin, whose expression had become unreadable.

"We will need to discuss more serious consequences for Sir Thoel. I will place him in the castle dungeon for tonight while we decide his fate. The king will be consulted. Will tonight after dinner work for you, Mr. Ashowan?"

"I was going to keep helping Mage Lee find the ... the tenth fountain." His voice had dropped so low that only the captain and himself could hear. "But this takes precedence," Fin added quickly.

"Ah." The captain straightened and glanced back toward the barracks. "I happen to know ... where that fountain went."

Fin was about to ask another question when a sudden shriek followed by a bang and distinct crack, sounded behind them. Both he and the captain spun around already in combat mode, then froze at the sight before them.

Hannah was standing over a bloody and barely conscious lump that must have been Sir Thoel, wielding Fin's iron skillet.

The knights surrounding the ring were all shouting at the same time, and it took a few moments for both the captain and cook to figure out what exactly had happened.

Apparently, the kitchen knights had been turned around, trying to listen to the captain, when Thoel had pulled a knife from his boot behind their backs.

Little had Thoel known, one hundred and fifteen pounds of blond rage was watching with a skillet.

Both the captain and Fin stalked over and regarded Thoel's new injury …

Injuries.

"Broken jaw and … a lot of teeth lost." The captain stood and accepted a tea towel Sir Taylor offered to wipe his hands. The fabric, stained with Thoel's blood, was dropped atop the man.

"She could've killed him, he got off lightly," Fin observed gravely as he reached over and grabbed the pan from Hannah without sparing her a glance.

She wasn't finished, apparently, as she then snatched the pan back from Fin, and turned back to the crowd of knights that were watching, completely enthralled with the events.

"IF ANY ONE OF YOU TRIES THIS *SHIT* AGAIN WITH PETER, OR HARRASS ANY OF MY FRIENDS THAT ARE MAIDS, THERE IS NOWHERE IN THIS GODSFORSAKEN KINGDOM YOU WILL BE SAFE FROM ME. I KNOW WHERE YOU ALL SLEEP, I COOK YOUR FOOD, I KNOW WHO WASHES YOUR CLOTHES AND BEDDING, AND IF I HAVE TO CHASE YOU INTO A SIX-FOOT-DEEP HOLE, I WILL. *GOT IT?*" The furious roar from Hannah made a few knights go pale, and if any of them thought that they should poke fun at her, the kitchen knights that all stood behind her glaring at them kept their mouths shut.

She whirled around and brandished the pan in Sir Harris's face. Fin stepped forward to intervene when she spoke.

"YOU! I will marry when I am *damn* well ready and to whomever I damn well want! So you can—"

The expletives that left her mouth made Sir Harris's jaw drop.

Some of the knights even learned a few new curse words, and others merely developed a healthy respect for the little maid.

Fin took back his pan once he had recovered from his own shock. Hannah turned around wrathfully, exited the ring, and walked through the crowd that parted to make a clear path for her.

When she had cleared each layer of knights, applause, cheers and whistles erupted behind her.

She turned back around, her eyes flashing, but they continued their loud roars of approval all the same. With a final huff, she resumed her trek back to the kitchen.

"Where are you running to?" Lord Piereva snapped as he winced against the pain in his gut that had been churning since late the previous night.

Three of his men were whispering with some of the Daxarian guards, and they all began rushing from his quarters toward the door.

"There's a huge brawl going on down in the training ring!" his squire explained, the desire to witness a good fight bright in his dark eyes.

"I see. I've been meaning to go down to the ring to see if the Daxarians measure up to our standards in Troivack." Lord Piereva stood and immediately twitched while hunching his shoulders over his middle.

"All of you leave," he barked without further explanation. His men were used to such sudden shifts in their master's mood and knew that it was best to obey without further question.

The Daxarian knights, however, had the audacity to shoot him dubious expressions and exit his chamber at a far more leisurely pace.

Lord Piereva made a mental note to teach them manners.

… Later.

He dove for the chamber pot and dropped his trousers.

"I'm sorry to hear your brother is unwell." Lord Jiho Ryu bowed slightly, offering his concerns to Lady Jenoure while she ate. She nodded with an air of disinterest.

"Yes, not sure what it was that could have made him so violently ill. Lord Miller ate and drank everything he did—it truly is a mystery."

When she was certain no one was looking, Annika risked the tiniest of smiles, as she began to suspect who might have been responsible for her brother becoming indisposed.

Little did she know, the Zinferan on her right was having a very similar thought—only he didn't know why his friend the cook would do something like that to the earl.

… At least not yet.

CHAPTER 36
TRIAL AND ERROR

"Gods, did you ever stop to consider that I wouldn't have wanted you to seek justice for me?" Peter was propped up in his small single bed, his ribs bandaged and his face swollen.

Fin perched beside him on a small three-legged stool, having brought the man his lunch early, knowing that he wouldn't have time to later. He really could only stay for a brief visit to let his aide know of the morning's events.

"There was no calming Hannah down. Not to mention her … colorful speech at the end that may make the knights start to behave a little differently toward the maids," Fin explained with a grin.

"I'm surprised the knights didn't revolt against her."

"On the contrary, she had two formal requests for a courting date from two of them in the hour following. I think, for some strange reason, it made her very popular and desirable to them. Even Sir Harris is ready to drop down on one knee."

Peter shook his head mystified.

"I'm a man myself, but sometimes, my own kind behaves in a way beyond my comprehension."

Fin laughed and slowly stood with a stretch.

"I better get back. Until we find another aide to temporarily cover for you, we're going to be horribly busy. Get better quickly." As he headed toward the door of the cramped but well-kept chamber, Peter called out.

"How are you doing with Lady Jenoure's suitors being here?"

Fin slowly turned back around.

"Did Hannah say something to you?" he asked suspiciously.

"No. We've just caught you two having enough moments together that we figured it out." Peter's eyes twinkled.

"What moments?"

Peter began to look incredibly uncomfortable as he shifted his body against his pillows with a wince.

Unable to inflict further suffering on the man, Fin dropped his head to his chest, and with a sigh, waved his hand.

"Don't worry about it for now. I'll get it out of you when I feel it's a fair fight."

Peter tried to smile, but this evidently caused him even more pain, and so he settled for a bemused grimace.

"Take care of yourself," Fin added softly with a kind smile as he turned and closed the door behind himself.

Peter's chambers were in the glamorous east wing servant's quarters, on the second floor, and so Fin decided to take the exit by the rose maze on his journey back to the kitchen for a change of scenery.

As he strode down the winding stone steps, he passed by two maids heading in the same direction, whispering behind their hands to each other when they saw who was nearby. He unconsciously hunched his shoulders against their attention. Shoving his hands in his pockets, Fin rounded the servant stairwell exit, and turned immediately right to go outdoors. The gossipy women turned left, much to his relief.

The rain hadn't yet broken out, despite the ominous thundering from earlier, and there were even rays of sunlight beginning to beam down in cracks of the gray day.

As he walked, his eyes cast to the ground, he thought about whether or not to prepare a fluffy vanilla cake with strawberries and cream for dessert, or if that was too simplistic. He almost failed to hear the pounding footfalls approaching him as he mulled over the dilemma.

Fin stopped in his tracks as he watched Mr. Howard barrel toward him from the direction of his kitchen. An errant dirty blond curl sprung up from the humidity, while the assistant wore entirely black save for a long silk vest of icy blue.

"Mr. Ashowan, have you and Mage Lee still not found the tenth fountain?" he demanded angrily, without any other form of greeting.

"No, but—"

"What? What is it with witches and mages, hm? Do you just enjoy messing around with—" Fin hastily slapped a hand on Mr. Howard's mouth, silencing the man instantly.

He shot the outraged assistant a bored expression with a single raised eyebrow.

"What does the word 'secret' mean in your vocabulary?" he whispered.

Fin lowered his hand, but not before he noticed the maids from earlier watching them from the nearby castle windows behind Mr. Howard's back.

He knew what he was thinking of doing was going to land him in some degree of trouble, but … he'd had a stressful morning. Having a bit of fun would help.

"Mr. Ashowan, I ask that you restrain yourself from touching me. Apparently, there are enough rumors circulating about your preferences." Mr. Howard straightened himself with great dignity and tugged gently on the lapel of his vest importantly.

"Mine? Last I heard, they are all rooting for my aide Peter and yourself." Fin made sure to keep his voice barely above a whisper, as he shot the man a cheeky half-smile.

"Myself and … and an aide?" Kevin Howard shook his head and slapped his right hand to his face before dragging it down slowly, stretching his features comically.

"Peter is a wonderful man, I'm sure you'd both share a love of the finer things. Perhaps stop by while he's recovering from the beating to offer your support." Fin's serious expression and addition of the information on the aide's current state of health, worked in effectively distracting Mr. Howard. He had also said the last sentence a little louder for the eager ears nearby.

"Yes, I was hearing about that from the captain. I heard your kitchen knights handled the situation? I've informed the king that a disciplinary meeting will be held this evening for a short while post-dinner. I will send someone to retrieve you."

"Actually, the entire kitchen staff handled the situation." Fin crossed his arms while speaking lightly, keeping his eyes on Mr. Howard and not on the growing audience from within the castle that the assistant hadn't noticed.

Mr. Howard visibly balked while blinking rapidly. He fixed Fin with an expression of dramatic confusion.

"Wait— Did you use— Don't you have a female maid under your command?!" The broken sentence made Fin grin.

"I didn't use magic, and you should know that Hannah was the one to break Sir Thoel's jaw and knock out some teeth."

Mr. Howard's jaw dropped.

Fin laughed and clapped him on the shoulder. He then leaned in so that he was a tiny inch from the man's ear.

"You'll hear all about it after dinner."

He resumed his trek back to the kitchen with his hands in his pockets, and didn't turn back around, even when Mr. Howard hammered the last nail into his coffin by shouting at his back.

"You better give me the full story this evening!"

The hearty laughter that came from Fin puzzled Mr. Howard, until he turned toward the eastern doors to the castle and noticed a cluster of young maids scampering away the moment he saw them.

"I'm going to kill him," Mr. Howard seethed as he stalked into the castle and tried not to curse too loudly.

Annika sat in the center of the rose maze, completely unaware that a steamy dramatic love affair was being imagined by the maids of the castle, while she bided her time in the presence of Lord Miller.

She had successfully dismantled any conversation from progressing, and to her satisfaction, the man was fidgeting with the flouncy tea set she had personally chosen to use for her first chaperoned outing with him.

"You look—er, lovely." He smiled, albeit strained, making Annika give a bored, single shoulder shrug. She continued to stare around the garden indolently.

"Thank you, my lord." She reached for her teacup, which she had generously doused with moonshine prior to his arrival in the garden, and gulped from it gratefully.

"It's always strange in these situations, I'm told. Do you miss Troivack at all?" The poor man was grasping for straws.

"No."

He could grasp until his fingers fell off; she was not going to give him an inch.

"Oh? What do you like so much about Daxaria?" The lord's eagerness at having a new potentially interesting topic almost made Annika pity him.

"The food is good," she answered shortly as she picked up the straw-berry rhubarb tart on her plate, and bit into it gingerly before taking another sip from her teacup.

"Ah, that it is! Everyone who recently came here from Troivack has admitted that much about the castle's latest chef. He must have studied for many years to be so talented. To have such flavors …" Lord Miller reached out and plucked up a blueberry square with crumbled brown sugar and baked oats atop.

"I suppose." Annika placed her empty cup back on the saucer and waited as one of the footmen rushed forward and refilled her cup. Silently wishing she had the opportunity to add some more Troivackian moonshine, she crossed her legs and leaned back in her chair.

Lord Miller took another sip from his own cup and let out a long sigh.

"Pardon me, my lady, I must break Daxarian customs." The man withdrew a plain silver flask from his black coat's breast pocket and topped the brew with the clear liquor that Annika immediately recognized.

He must have noticed her stare, because he broke into a warm smile.

"Would you like a taste of home, my lady? I know you must remember how strong it is, but perhaps a little nip?"

Annika couldn't resist.

She proffered her cup wordlessly, and when he really did only splash in a tiny amount, she grew impatient.

"I've not forgotten the moonshine, go ahead," she ordered firmly.

"My lady, I'd rather you not become so indisposed in the middle of the day on our first—"

"I'll be fine. Have you ever drunk with Lord Piereva?" she drawled.

The aggravating man shook his head and twisted the cap back onto the flask.

"You've been away for a few years now and—"

Annika sighed and withdrew her own, ornately designed flask, unscrewed its cap, and filled her cup to the brim. She gave up trying to be tactful about it. Besides, perhaps it would add to her undesirable personality.

When she had finished putting the flask back in the discreet pocket in her skirts, she locked gazes with Lord Miller, who had watched, speechless.

She waited for his judgment, his barrage of lectures on the proper etiquette of a Troivackian woman. She took a gulp from her tea without looking away from him once. When she didn't cough, vomit, or faint, but instead continued looking thoroughly bored, he surprised her for the second time that day.

He began to laugh.

It was a hearty, booming sound that sounded as though it lived in the cave of his chest at the ready at all times.

He really was a black sheep of Troivack. A one of a million type that only came about every few decades, and usually didn't last long …

Annika found herself fighting off a smile, despite knowing that his chances of survival were despairingly low.

"Well, my lady, a toast to the superior liquor of our country?"

She raised her teacup and gently chinked the porcelain without another word.

For her second "meeting" of the day, Lady Jenoure was supposed to have a late and leisurely lunch with the Zinferan Lord Ryu. The date was set up in the courtyard garden, and everyone but absolutely necessary personnel had been sent away. The clouds seemed stubborn in sharing the torrential downpour they had threatened earlier in the day, and so the garden had been lit using tall torches planted in the ground around the couple.

Annika was already tired and annoyed at having to maintain a constant façade. She blithely admitted to herself she had grown lazy since her time in Troivack, back when she was constantly behaving as another person, and manipulating everyone and everything.

"The greenhouse is quite an impressive structure. I have never seen anything like it," Lord Ryu observed calmly. He hadn't forced any conversation on her after she had given him one-word answers to his opening greetings.

However, it was becoming a problem, as he seemed to thoroughly enjoy the silence.

Annika was in the process of gearing up to be the chattiest noble alive, when the man continued.

"We have a greenhouse in every lord's household to provide fresh fruits and vegetables in the chillier months, though we hardly get the same amount of snow where I am from. In fact, your Daxarian winters nearly killed me back when I first arrived here. I had to stay for nearly two years under the care of a kind family on the Isle of Quildon." Lord Ryu raised his goblet of water to his lips and sipped thoughtfully, clearly comfortable with performing a monologue to his lunch company.

"Who did you stay with?" Annika blurted the question before she could stop herself.

Lord Ryu turned his eyes to her and smiled fondly.

"A single mother who was a gifted healer and her son. He's actually the cook here in the castle now. I had nothing to do with that promotion, however," he added with a good-natured smile.

"He is a talented cook," Annika managed as she delicately speared the pasta that had been prepared by the very man they spoke of. It was a refreshing dish, prepared with tomatoes, basil, Troivackian feta cheese, and Troivackian black olives. It was a light, delicious meal that somehow comforted her worries as images of a certain redhead came to her mind's eye.

"I'm surprised you aren't asking me more questions about my new ascension into being a lord. Everyone else has nearly questioned me to death. I am grateful for the reprieve." Lord Ryu raised his goblet in thanks, then returned to looking around the garden, remaining perfectly still.

Annika couldn't put her finger on what felt so wise and old in the young man. He couldn't have even been a decade older than herself, and yet he felt even older than Lord Fuks or Mage Lee.

There was a grounded strength that had a calming, yet authoritative aura. He would be an excellent lord, that much she could tell.

She continued watching him closely without saying a word, trying to figure out the strange man.

"You are opposed to marriage amongst us three, aren't you?" The lord suddenly turned with a kind smile on his face. He stared at her compassionately, gently folding his hands.

"I am happy to help my country, why would you say such a thing?" It would take a lot more than an abrupt accusation to throw Annika off her game.

"I was here for Beltane, remember? You were incredibly clever and witty back then. While you still kept to yourself, you aren't nearly the dullard you're trying to convince us that you are." His tone wasn't accusatory so much as amused and praising.

"The festivities had a lot of libations. I may have been more forthcoming." She shrugged enigmatically as she took another sip from her cup.

"Is it that you do not want to marry again? Or is it perhaps that you care for another?" Lord Ryu asked gently, dropping his voice so that only she could hear. His tone was a pleasant combination of soothing and understanding.

"Nothing of the sort. I am sorry I am displeasing you," Annika replied, meekly dropping her eyes in feigned hurt.

Once again, her performance didn't warrant the reaction she had been anticipating.

Lord Ryu burst out laughing, his brilliant smile catching her off guard as she hastily sipped her goblet to hide her flummoxed thoughts.

"Oh, you're good, my lady. However, I didn't get where I am today by being a foolish man." He smiled fondly at her and sipped his goblet again.

The rest of the luncheon passed in thoughtful quiet between the two of them.

Though Annika had to thoughtfully admit she was beginning to worry ...

It was a final tea date in the mid-afternoon between Lord Nam and Lady Jenoure where she finally caught a break.

Plush red lounge couches that the lord had brought from his home had been set out in the gardens, a canopy erected, and a table covered in platters of fruit, bread, and cheese between them. Two decanters of wine sat out ready behind two awaiting ornate goblets that had been polished to a gleam. Annika didn't have time to admire the artistic layout, however, as she was in the throes of trying to arrange herself gracefully on the chaise with little success.

The cloudy day had continued on, yet despite this, the lord still had one of his servants fanning him.

His bare chest was exposed once more in an ensemble of a gold silk coat and white linen pants, but it didn't bother him to be disrobed in front of her. Instead, he eyed Annika with a quick, bored glance.

"Welcome, Lady Jenoure. I know you must be quite weary from having to meet with so many of us in a day," he drawled, closing his eyes.

"Not at all, my lord."

Lord Nam opened his eyes, a coy smile on his face. "Is it common for you to find yourself in the company of multiple men?"

"Of course not, my lord. I simply meant you all have been kind."

The amusement on the lord's face melted away, and he gave a small snort.

"How dull." His eyelids fluttered closed.

After a few awkward moments of silence, he opened his eyes again, and with a sudden burst of energy, swung his legs over the edge of his couch.

"What kind of man is it that you like?" he demanded with an openly suggestive smile that almost made Annika laugh.

"Frugal," she replied, delighted in watching the look of disgust flash briefly across his face.

"Frugal in his generosity, you mean?" he demanded, clearly trying not to openly scorn her.

"No, as in he knows how to find contentment with what he has. Perhaps someone who enjoys a bit of banter, deeply cares for others, and is stronger than he realizes." She couldn't stop the smile from spreading on her face then, and even Lord Nam was momentarily stunned by it, despite her controversial words. A small blush had crept up in her cheeks as her gaze fixated on the ground.

"I see. You are far more innocent than I would've imagined for a woman of your age." He let out another longsuffering sigh before continuing.

"Such a man lacks ambition, or the ability to relax and enjoy life. It sounds like a laborious existence." Lord Nam waved his hand lazily.

"I prefer to think of it as responsible and purposeful," Annika countered evenly, not taking kindly to the jibe at her age. She wasn't even in her thirtieth year!

"How disappointing. You really should learn to embrace a better reality." Lord Nam reached out his hand without glancing her way, and Annika watched gleefully as a servant rushed forward and filled a goblet for their master and handed it to him.

"Careful. If you splatter even a drop, I will have you scrubbing my chamber pot for a year." He didn't even bother sparing his trembling aide a glance.

Annika nearly whooped in joy.

You're absolutely perfect, she thought to herself delightedly.

Annika felt a million worries begin to melt away inside her chest and mind.

She had found the perfect answer to almost all of her problems …

She just had to toy with Lord Nam a tiny bit more and hope her bet would pay off.

CHAPTER 37
THE GOOD, THE BAD, THE FLUFFY

Kraken sat on the dock at the bottom of the steep hill that Austice had built itself into, and gazed out at the docks before him, remaining perfectly still—not even a whisker twitched. Scrappy Carl yowled obscenities at him from the stern of the Zinferan merchant ship on its way back to its homeland.

That's one problem taken care of, Kraken thought to himself blithely, as he watched the ship grow smaller in the distance. Once he was certain the boat was well and truly underway, he turned around and saw Fat Tony, sitting side-by-side with Sylvia, watching him.

"Well played, kit. Scrappy was gettin' pretty puffed lately. Caught him the other night swappin' paws with Popkins Perkins, and I'm not interested in starting a turf war just yet." Tony lumbered his way toward the black kitten that was already the same height as Tony, though nowhere near the same girth.

"You're growin' pretty quick. That have somethin' to do with bein' a familiah or are you just gonna be one of them big cats?" Fat Tony demanded appraisingly.

"*I think I'm just a big cat. My dad said he was part wildcat? At least I think he did. I was too young to be pulled from the litter, so my memories are hazy.*"

"Why were you pulled early?" Sylvia purred with genuine interest.

"*Tavern keeper found us in his alley and drowned everyone but my brother and myself—my mum had hid us real good. Random man found us and gave me to a woman who gave me to my witch.*"

"*Damn pity when that happens.*" Fat Tony let out a small snort. "*So listen, kit, if you want to be my new runner, you gotta train with Paws first.*"

Fat Tony turned and began to amble back up the dock toward land, weaving in and out of the regular dock traffic with ease despite being the approximate shape and weight of a pumpkin.

"*I don't know of Paws. What will he teach me?*" Kraken asked as Sylvia shot him a flirtatious blink on his right.

"*Paws is the master of stealth, subtlety, scrapping, and even human seduction.*"

Kraken's quick steps faltered as he stared in alarm at the orange tabby, who had stopped to catch his breath gratefully on the cobblestones of Austice's main road.

"*Human seduction?!*" Kraken could not hide his disgust.

"*Keep your scruff on, kit. He just teaches how to make any human like you.*"

Kraken let out a yawn, and sat down, feeling significantly more at ease.

"*Oh, that's easy. Endear yourself to the human females and their kittens. The males unconsciously wish to protect their females and offspring, and don't like tearing a companion from them,*" Kraken explained, casually glancing around at the many dirty trousers and skirts that swept by the trio of cats.

"*That don't always work, kit. Take it from a seasoned vet,*" Tony cautioned casually.

Having regained his wind, Tony began trotting farther west down the road along the Alcide Sea, making Kraken glance around all the more skittishly as he noticed the human folk growing dirtier and stranger. Some babbled to themselves, some shouted obscenities, some were half-exposed on the streets.

Fat Tony made a turn, and suddenly the three cats were moving back uphill. Though the narrow alley did eventually widen, and the homes gradually became nicer, Kraken still found his ears twitching at any small sound.

Eventually they found themselves outside a home connected in a row with others, a faded, chipped green sign hanging above its door, made illegible by the ravages of time.

"When someone asks why you're there, just say Tony sent you. If Paws wants payment, tell him I got the fish for Tuesday."

To say Kraken was apprehensive would've been an understatement.

He could feel every one of his long, silky hairs wanting to stand on end, but he fought it off. He had earned his promotion. He had to see it through.

It wasn't every cat that sought out a gang, but he knew his witch better than the human knew himself. Fin was more involved in politics than he realized, and Kraken was not going to let the fluff-head fail. He wanted his own cats to command, to find those enemy humans that were hiding in the city, and to alert his witch to their presence as quickly as possible.

Kraken pawed only once at the chipped and worn door that had probably, at one point, been painted the same green as the decrepit sign, and mewed. He waited, then repeated the action, until he found himself doing it over and over in rapid succession.

At long last the door swung open, and an elderly woman who very clearly was lacking in her vision leaned out of a shadowed house and peered around blindly.

Darting between her legs into the musky dankness of her home without a second thought, Kraken tried to put his apprehension behind. However, when the smells hit his silky black nose, he could tell there were fifteen cats just on the main floor of the house.

Some were trying to make kittens, some were grooming, some were sleeping, but none were Paws.

How he knew this, Kraken had no idea. Slowly, he made his way over to a narrow set of stairs that led up to the second floor. He had to mind his paws on dusty, sticky steps, as they creaked under his soft footfalls and threatened to cave at any moment. As he climbed, he passed many questionable scenes and smells that he didn't wish to commit to memory. The small, cramped house had stained wooden floors and furniture. Shredded curtains, the smell of burnt food ...

Kraken felt sorry for the human that lived there.

None of the other cats seemed to care that they were making the being that provided them food and shelter live in absolute squalor. He was already not thinking highly of Paws as he reached the top of the stairs.

For some reason, his instincts told him to head to the room at the end of the narrow hallway to the left.

He was almost in front of the scratched-up door when three cats burst out of the room, hissing and growling at each other.

The two that came out last seemed to be fighting as a team. One had funny black spots on his gray fur, while the other was a snowy white, fluffy male.

The one they ushered out was a snarling female calico.

"*LET ME TALK TO HIM! STOP THAT—I WILL FUR YOU UP IF YOU DO NOT RELEASE ME! LET ME IN!*" she screamed, outraged, as the two cats forced her out of the room.

When the fine-aged female noticed Kraken watching her unseemly behavior, she gave a courtesy hiss before darting down the stairs swearing her revenge, urine leaking from her as she went.

The two thugs turned to Kraken, their backs already beginning to arch.

"*Fat Tony sent me. I'm here for training.*"

The duo stared at each other briefly before turning with low growls back toward the room.

Whatever Kraken had been expecting after witnessing the sty from downstairs, it wasn't this.

The room had wooden crates stacked to create a ledge around the entire room, with a thick carpet underneath his paws. Bowls sat atop the bar, filled with mysterious liquids. Some had strange leaves floating in their depths, others a fish eyeball.

There were a series of candles lit around the room casting hazy illumination, and as Kraken regarded the scenery, he couldn't help but notice the purrs and chirps die down to complete quiet as they all rested their gleaming eyes and whiskers on him.

"*What can I get for you?*" A tabby cat missing his left eye sat behind the crate. Kraken quickly realized that he was the only one that would be allowed on that side. It was similar to what the humans called a "bartender." Stepping closer cautiously, while also painfully aware that he was still being watched, he leaned closer to the tabby.

"*I'm here to see Paws. Fat Tony sent me,*" Kraken chirped quietly, growing tired of repeating himself.

Before the tabby could answer, a low purr rumbled through the crowd.

"*A new runner for the gang?*"

Kraken's head pivoted and his eyes locked on a cat that was black from his shoulders down to his tail, but had a snowy white face save for two strange triangles and a dot by his throat.

"*I am. I'm Scrappy Carl's replacement,*" Kraken announced, hoping that this would help the news spread.

"*I see. Well come here, let's have a purr, hm?*" the mysterious cat called in pleasant, rumbling tones.

By the time Kraken reached the side of Paws, everyone had resumed what they'd been doing before.

"*I'm Kraken,*" he greeted briefly.

Paws nodded slightly as he used his tail to gently swirl the bowl in front of him, which had a particularly delicious-looking fish eye.

"*Paws. James Paws. Though it would seem you've already heard of me.*" He gently lapped up his drink, all the while keeping his bright green eyes locked on the kit beside him.

"*I only just heard about you this morning.*"

"*I see. Well, do you think you got the claws to train with me then?*"

There was a rumble of amusement in the cat's eye that made Kraken suddenly second-guess himself. He couldn't understand what exactly about James Paws had made him aware of an underlying danger, but he found himself dwelling over it with trepidation. He knew, though, that regardless of what was before him, he would do anything to ensure his effectiveness for when his witch eventually needed him.

"*I do.*"

"*Very well then.*" Paws straightened from his bowl and the tabby from earlier limped over.

"*Would you care for some treats, Paws?*"

"*Why not. Shaken before poured, if you wouldn't mind, Brolly.*"

The tabby bowed his head behind the crates and produced a small burlap sack of dried meat, which he shook, making every cat's head in the vicinity swivel over once again.

With surprising agility, Brolly managed to send a few of the treats skittering out onto the crate that Paws sat upon. The cat deftly snapped up the treats so quickly that Kraken almost thought that they had fallen through the slats to the floor.

His nose told him otherwise.

"*Shall we begin?*" Paws gave him a half smirk at the young kit's astonished face, but Kraken blinked, and nodded.

Paws was going to be an interesting teacher, he could tell.

Fin stood with his hands on his hips, staring at the barracks, refusing to be the one to break the silence. After a very stressful meeting regarding Sir Thoel's fate, he had needed this.

"Captain, could you please repeat that?" Mage Lee was still confused at what Antonio had been insinuating. Fin had guessed all too easily, having recalled certain details of the night that was to never be discussed in public.

"The tenth fountain … my men found it in the barracks." The captain cleared his throat while glancing around nervously to ensure none of the knights had left dinner early.

"That makes no sense! How could a fountain possibly—"

"Mage Lee … do you remember what happened when I challenged you to make that tenth fountain while we were all lounging in the ninth fountain?" Fin asked, pinching the bridge of his nose and trying desperately not to burst out laughing.

"I told you." Mage Lee cleared his throat uncomfortably as he started. "I told you I was the Green Man, so of course I could make a tiny fountain, then I said I needed to relieve myself and the captain said the barracks were nearest if I needed to use the facilities—"

Lee's eyes suddenly grew round as the full extent of his memory flexed. His mouth hung agape, and Fin couldn't hold himself back any longer. He roared in laughter, not caring who heard him.

"My men are quite fond of the new fountain in the … garderobe. No need to move it." The captain was looking to the rosy horizon in the distance as he tried not to display any emotion.

Fin was in the process of wiping his eyes when he straightened and turned to face Lee, who had turned a beautiful shade of vermillion.

"I'll give you this: you mages sure can make things fun."

Still chuckling to himself, Fin thrust his hands into his pockets and began striding back toward his kitchen, shaking his head.

Dusk was embracing the warmed earth, with a blush along the horizon and bright stars beginning to awaken above.

As he walked in the silence, his smile slowly faded from his face, and Annika once again appeared in his mind. He hadn't had to think about her for a few hours, but it made her reappearance all the more forceful as he looked toward his night with resigned dread.

He had the feeling that sleep was once again not going to be forthcoming.

~~~~~~

Fin was in the process of pounding the dough on his table, the sky outside still threatening but not delivering rain, when Ruby entered the kitchen.

She took one look at Fin's pale yet determined face, then at the dough on the table he was brutalizing, and guessed that he was not in a fit mood to begin with.

"Mr. Ashowan, with the absence of Peter you will be needing another aide. I have selected one of the maids who, as your preferences dictate, has clean hands and nails. She has already been sent to your aides outside, though I must ask what you intend to do when it rains?" She had meant to keep the greeting short, but as it often did, it got ahead of her.

Fin stopped his merciless thrusts against the dough but didn't turn around.

"Very well. I will introduce myself when they come in. Should it rain, I will either erect a tent for them or allow them in here, depending on how the lunch preparations come along." He resumed his work, but Ruby couldn't withhold her astonishment and annoyance.

"Honestly! What in the world is so bad about them working in here with you? I daresay this room is—"

Fin turned around, and fixed his weary, flat gaze on her. Ruby then saw the dark circles under his eyes and stopped herself. "A discussion for another day," she ground out irritably, as she turned and slammed the door behind her.

Pounding his hand on the dough one final time, Fin magicked the bread into the nearby oiled bowl, and the tea towel to lay over top. He then opened and slammed his oven door shut with great gusto. He had pulled out a roast with vegetables and apples simmering in its juices with enough force to make the dish slosh on his arm and burn him. He cursed tightly, clenched his fists, then took a steadying breath.

Nothing had happened between himself and Annika. All there was was a strong pull. Why was he being such an ass? Everyone around him were just doing their jobs, they didn't deserve his agitated responses …

Setting his jaw firmly in place, he released his burned hand and briefly closed his eyes.

She is not mine, and she never will be. I need to get over it.

Opening his eyes again, Fin had just picked up his knife when he felt it. Terror. Pain. Danger.

Adrenaline surged through him.

Someone was in trouble, and they weren't far away.

CHAPTER 38
THORNS AND ROSES

Someone was in trouble.

Gods, was it the queen and the baby again? Hannah? Eric?

Fin tried to force his thoughts away from the splitting pain in his left side.

He clutched his forehead in agony as his thoughts raged hard against the static burning in his mind.

"Where should I go?! What should I ..." Fin forced the images of every place he had been in the castle through his head to see if any of them jumped out to him. He tried to hold the faces of those he cared for, when all of a sudden, he knew.

Annika.

She was heading toward the rose maze from the forest.

Fin shoved the carving knife into its sheath at his side and took off at a sprint.

Miraculously, as he ran no one saw him, but as he neared the halfway point to the entrance of the maze, he looked over his shoulder instinctively. Fin could see a small, hooded figure he knew had to be Lady Jenoure approaching the exit of the maze in the distance. She was stumbling, and periodically doubling over as she hastened toward her destination. As he squinted, he could see some kind of flurry behind her in the trees. As she neared the thorny hedge, he reached his hand out, lightning springing from his fingers as he cut a small clearing for himself to dart through. He could hear the faint panting of Lady Jenoure coming from another hedge a few turns away from him, as he sought to reach the center to intercept her. He immediately ran forward upon hearing her, only to hit a dead end. He could no longer hear her.

He cursed softly as he then heard the footfalls of Annika's pursuers in the distance.

He darted back the way he came, took a left instead of a right, and once again could hear Annika's rasps. He looked at the thorny hedge in front of him, and in a moment of desperation, mentally screamed at the hedge to unfurl for him. He didn't want to burn it and show her attackers where she was.

To his surprise, the hedge obeyed right as her black cloak fluttered into view. Without another thought, Fin wrapped his arms around her and spun her back through the hedge swiftly before she could react, the thorny leaves already beginning to furl closed. The roses were unhappy that he had forced his will upon their thorns—but he didn't have time to feel shock over sensing them.

Fin's hand already covered Annika's mouth when he felt her stiffen, his body shielding her smaller form with his own. They could hear her pursuers stomp past where she had been moments before.

"She can't have gone far. Not with that wound in her side. Let's split up." The man's voice was gruff and breathy as he addressed his followers.

Meanwhile, Fin was doing his best to keep his own quick breaths quiet. When he gazed down into Annika's pale upturned face, her dark eyes were wide as she registered who had grabbed her.

They shared a moment of silence as they heard the feet of the men grow momentarily distant.

"Can you get to the kitchen?" Fin whispered, his voice slightly hoarse.

Annika's eyes flitted to the dead end of the hedge, then to the turn where one of her pursuers were bound to appear at any moment.

"I don't know that I can carry you, but lean on me best you can," he instructed softly.

Despite not hearing an answer, he led Annika toward the burned opening in the hedge. Holding on to her hand, Fin managed to guide her through, and set them off at a brisk walk with him supporting her weight.

Rain began to spittle down on them, but as they reached the corner of the castle, the deluge that had threatened to come for days finally broke upon them. They were only a few steps from their destination but were both soaked in a matter of seconds before they could enter the castle through the garden door.

Once in the warm confines of the kitchen, Fin immediately enchanted both of the doors locked, and double-checked that his spell to stop onlookers peering in through the window was intact. He felt momentarily bad about his aides being stuck in the downpour, but then again, he was quite certain that Annika was in no shape to lie to them about her astonishing apparel and state of well-being.

He managed to seat her on the ledge by the window, where he would get the best light to check the wound.

Stepping back with his hands on her shoulders and concerned by her lack of expression, he was only mildly surprised to find Annika studying him as well while looking more than a little stunned.

"I heard them mention an injury, where—"

"It's nothing! I can go to my room and—" Annika twisted toward the kitchen door to the castle but gave a small yelp. The pain made her clamp her mouth shut and visibly wince as Fin slowly but firmly kept her seated.

"Where?" Fin asked again, but more gently.

"Left side. The ass got me while I was fending off the other three." She grimaced as Fin gently removed her cloak. He quickly noticed the blood dribbling around her fingers as she clutched her side. His panic, rage, and worry exploded in his chest. His face must've morphed into a troubling visage, because with her other hand—also caked in blood—she gently touched his cheek.

"It's okay. It won't kill me," she whispered softly while hoping to soothe some of his apparent anguish.

Fin ignored her and lifted her hand from the wound to inspect its depth.

After kneeling on the ground and gently swiping away some of the blood that had already slowed its flow, Fin could see that she had been right. The wound was not life-threatening, but she still needed to be stitched.

"I need you to lie down on my cooking table so that I can sew you up," he explained, raising his gaze to hers.

"You know how to do that?" Annika whispered, a faint smile tugging at the corner of her mouth.

"My mother is a healer, I've helped her in the past," he explained shortly, helping her to her feet and guiding her over to the table that still had the lunch preparations sitting out.

Fin's eyes fluttered, and the table stacked beneath the cooking table levitated out and cleared itself. The meal and all the prep drifted over to its surface, and a wet soapy cloth from a nearby bucket wiped it down in a matter of minutes. All the while Fin did nothing but support Annika and will it to happen.

He then gently pressed his fingertips to the table's surface, and Annika watched amazed as the dampness left over from the cleaning immediately evaporated.

"Handy skills you have," she murmured with a small grunt, as Fin helped her up before turning back to his kitchen.

He found the needle he used for stitching up the roasts and some threads that would have to do.

It wasn't until he turned to her after sterilizing the needle, that he realized he would need her to lift her tunic to accomplish his task.

She must've figured out what had him frozen, because she smiled ruthlessly.

"Never seen a woman's side before?" she teased, staring at the stone ceiling of the kitchen.

"I … I'm sorry. I have to lift your top partially to mend you." He was the color of tomatoes.

Annika laughed, but winced slightly, snapping Fin out of his stupor. Without thinking, his hand shot out and gently rested atop her silky black hair, tied back in a sleek ponytail. Fin gently rubbed his thumb over her forehead and hairline.

"Do you want something to bite down on while I do this?" he asked apologetically.

"Fear not. I'm always prepared." When he realized then that he was touching her, he dropped his hand to the table. He still didn't let it fully fall back to his side, however …

With a fleeting look of disappointment that Fin was relatively certain he had imagined, Annika procured her flask from the pocket of her trousers. After she took several gulps of the Troivackian moonshine, she nodded at him to signal her readiness, her composure never wavering.

"You look more troubled about this than I am. Trust me, I've been in worse scrapes than this," she said jovially.

"Who did this to you?" Fin's question came out quietly as he studied Lady Jenoure's good-natured façade.

Her expression immediately sobered.

"Troivackians that came with my brother. I don't know how many of my informants he may have found, but my brother apparently doesn't know it's me yet. He has his suspicions, is my guess, but the men didn't see my face. Three of them are dead in the woods. I'll have to hunt down the last two once you finish up with me here. So could we please get this started?" she added impatiently as her mind fixated on the unpleasant task ahead of her.

"You're going to … there are three bodies in the woods?!" Fin's shock snapped her eyes to him. She studied him with an unreadable expression, her face immediately masked.

"It was them or me. Is that a problem?" Her tone was cool, and her eyes took on a deadened shade of dark brown that made Fin stare down at her with faint remorse and disgust.

Annika felt her stomach churn sickeningly at witnessing his reaction to who she truly was.

She turned, her face composed, her nerves fortified. She refused to let him see how disappointed she was. "Who is it that made you become this?"

Annika's head snapped back. But she lost her composure when she saw that Fin's expression hadn't changed. She had misunderstood his reaction to her words. He was disgusted that her past had required her to have to resort to such callous methods.

"Troivack is a brutal place. Especially for women. However, my grandfather recognized I was the only one of my father's children with a knack for deception, and he took me under his wing, albeit reluctantly. He was one of the most skilled spies of the kingdom," she explained, trying desperately to school her features once again.

Fin slowly began to roll up her tunic. His hands were hesitant as he did so, but he figured it would be better to start sewing Annika's wound closed while she was distracted.

The plan backfired quickly when he failed to continue asking questions. Instead, he fixated as inch by inch, Annika's smooth, naturally tanned skin appeared under his hands. He pretended not to notice the goosebumps rising on her skin, and genuinely failed to notice the blush on her face when he finally came to the wound.

It spanned perhaps four inches, and upon further inspection, Fin was relieved to see it didn't look to be deep enough to have hit any of her organs.

"See? Not that bad," Annika declared as Fin gingerly pierced her skin with the needle. He could tell she was trying to get him talking again to distract herself from the pain. Her entire body had turned rigid, and he instantly became worried that he would have to tie her down to finish the job.

"It would seem, Lady Jenoure, that you and I have become each other's nursemaids these days," he said slowly, not moving the needle until her body had relaxed into faint trembling.

"That a problem?" Annika demanded, a little too breathily.

"Well, I suppose I prefer you than Mr. Howard."

"I heard that rumor about him and Peter—I must confess, quite a few of the noble ladies here in the castle are quite taken with the notion."

Fin resumed his work then, lacing two stitches before pausing to give Annika a rest. She was already sweating profusely.

"The ladies?!" Fin paused his work to laugh. "I thought it was solely the maids. Gods, he is going to murder me."

"You started it?!" Annika laughed, then gasped in pain at having done so, which instantly ceased all of Fin's humor for several long breaths.

"Well, it was originally about me and Mr. Howard, but I may have ... redirected it a bit," he admitted with a hesitant smile, after Annika's breathing gradually deepened once more.

He could tell she was physically fighting the urge to laugh as he hastily tried to finish another two stitches.

"I'm surprised you—" Annika took in a sharp breath and Fin once again found his body responding on its own accord, as his right hand snatched her own. He let her squeeze his bones until they neared their breaking point. "I'm surprised you knew I was in trouble."

Fin released her hand after a moment to resume his work.

"I can sense when someone in my home is in extreme pain, terror, or danger," he explained as he worked his way toward the end of her wound, unaware of the sweat coating his brow.

"Why didn't you go to save Peter, then?" There was a strange note of uncertainty in Annika's voice that Fin found himself quick to address.

"Peter was attacked on his way back up to the castle after visiting the village one evening."

"You two aren't ... I mean, are you ..." Fin completed two more stitches, and noticed that adrenaline or shock must have kicked in, because Annika had stopped seizing up.

He failed to notice the apprehensiveness in her voice as she hinted at his sexuality.

"I am definitely not gay," he answered, refusing to look at her.

Which is why you should be a little more self-conscious of allowing me to socially see anymore of you than is appropriate. Fin thought to himself as he knotted off the last stitch and immediately straightened.

When he gazed down into Annika's face, she remained unreadable to him, which somehow made him smile.

"You must be a fantastic spy; I can't glean anything from you and I just sewed you up." Fin slid his hand gently under her back and slowly helped her to sit up without agitating the stitches. She stayed seated on his table, allowing herself a moment to adjust.

"Oh I am. I can be the seductress." Her expression morphed into one of sultry teasing. "Or the timid, dutiful woman." Her eyes dropped, and she curved her shoulders ever so slightly, her mouth drawn down almost in a look of pained shyness. "Or the dullard." Her face became vacant as her mouth hung open somewhat and her eyes went out of focus.

Fin let out a small chuckle before he gently tugged at the collar of her tunic, bringing her true self back to her beautiful features.

"In my kitchen, I want only your honest expression." He smiled warmly down at her.

Annika's eyes snapped to his, her mouth closed, and she swallowed. She was staring at him, her face a mixture of nervous anticipation.

"Who are you trying to be now?" Fin teased, his eyes glowing as he gazed down into her suddenly shining brown eyes.

She still looked pale after having been stitched up, but some color was beginning to rush to her cheeks.

"I—I-I'm ..." Annika's expression was searching his, when something in her gave way. She moved too quickly for him to do anything to stop her.

She grabbed the front of his tunic and pulled him to her.

Then, she kissed him.

CHAPTER 39
BATTER UP

The second her lips rested on his, fire burned through Fin. There was nothing else in the world, only the feeling that everything was finally right. Everything was incredible. No thoughts could exist.

For Annika, tingling exploded in her belly. She leaned closer to him, feeling his warmth, and knowing that she belonged in its enticing reach.

She didn't know how long it had been in the silence with her mouth on his, but when she pulled away and saw the slight reddening in his cheeks and his look of breathless confusion, she felt her stomach flip.

"I-I'm so sorry. Please don't feel like just because I-I'm a lady you can't say no. I know I shouldn't have—"

Fin's hands were around the back of her head, his thumbs pressed gently against her jaw and cheeks when he kissed her again.

This time it was more desperate, yet somehow still tender, as he loosed his pent-up passion for the noble he had no right to share a meal with, let alone kiss.

His body rocked forward, drawn to every inch of her, wanting to touch every part of her being. Fin felt as though he couldn't ever stop as everything from the soles of his feet to his tallest hair finally felt like he was doing what he had been Godsdamn meant to do.

Annika gripped his tunic, still pulling him to her, wishing she could forever live in that moment where she was so happy that she could cry.

Fin felt himself wanting more, needing more, and as he gently pressed even closer, Annika began leaning backward, pulling him down toward the table with her. Fin's right hand moved from her face to her back. Her tunic still remained rolled up, but when he felt her exposed back, it was as though a jolt shot through him and snapped him back to his senses.

He immediately released her and braced his hands on either side of her on the table. He took shallow gasps to recover more fully from the surrender of fervor that had inebriated him, and he didn't dare look at her as he did so.

Annika couldn't mask her disappointment fully as she stared dejectedly at him. She knew what he was going to say the minute he stopped. She watched the way he was regaining control with every breath and felt her hopes sinking down through the floor.

He pushed back from the table and stepped away from her. Annika's hands trembled ever so slightly as she unfurled her tunic back down, and for a brief moment, rubbed the fabric between her fingers hesitantly.

"My, lady, I—" Fin's voice was hoarse as he stared at the ground, trying to settle his pounding heart.

"Don't you dare."

Fin's eyes snapped up to see Annika glaring at him, the hurt and frustration obvious on her face. "What do you—"

"Godsdamnit, Fin, this is ridiculous!" she snapped as she stepped down onto the ground, straightening her shoulders and squaring herself to him. She resisted the urge to wince at the pain that came from the movement.

"It isn't ridiculous. You know we can't, you know—" Fin started desperately, his gut clenching and his heart already aching.

"What do you want from me?" The coldness in her tone made Fin slowly turn his gaze back to her.

"Please don't ask me that." His voice was quiet, but no less harsh.

"Do you just want to bed me? A quick roll in the sheets? Is that why it isn't worth pursuing? A meaningless fornication isn't worth risking your neck; *that* I can completely understand. Tell me that's the reason, and I'll accept it with no hard feelings."

Fin's jaw clenched and his eyes shifted to a spot on the window behind Annika. The rain pounded it relentlessly, the tattering the only sound in the room as she stared furiously up at him. After a few moments, she spoke again.

"Just admit that's it. I'm taking a great risk too, you know. You'd be fired, sure, but I'd be scorned and outcast. I'd never marry again. Hell, I could even end up causing Daxaria to be slaughtered in a war over it." The bitter loathing in her tone failed to make him look at her again.

"This wouldn't go anywhere past a few trysts." Fin's voice was tight, his face still. "You deserve better than a few reckless meetings that could cost you—"

"I'm the one who will decide what I want to risk. Not you. Right now, I just want you to tell me what it is you want. Honestly, I'm starting to think you like toying with me. Making me want you more and more, then being cold and distant to make me feel alone in my feelings for you. Making me chase you to confirm it. Well, I'm not going to make a fool of myself for you," she snapped acidly, stepping nearer to him.

"If all this is is a physical need to scratch an itch, why don't we just bang it out now and leave it at that, hm? I promise I won't do anything stupid like renounce my fortune and title for you over one coupling." Her words dripped with anger and challenge.

Fin's eyes finally fell to hers, and that was when she saw how incensed he was. He stared down at her icily, and stepped nearer while staring down at her, immediately reawakening the infuriating pull toward him she couldn't dream of denying.

"You want me to tell you why I won't say anything? Why I won't just take you on my kitchen table?"

Annika didn't scare easily, but he was making her feel … aggressively worried. She didn't let him see that, though. She steeled herself and scowled up at him.

"Desperately. Enlighten me."

"Because if I do that, I won't ever let you go. I want every part of you, and I'll take it, and then? You'll hate me. You'll hate what being with me will cost. You'll lose not just your fortune or favor in court. The war aside? You will lose the right to be close to the queen, who you love. You won't be able to make a difference in this kingdom if you can't be a spy, and that's who you are. I am not worth you giving up everything. You barely know me."

Fin's words had an odd effect on her.

Her ire and hatred melted on her face, and instead she suddenly looked distressed and as though she could weep.

"Then let's find a way! We can try to find how it could be acceptable. You already are growing closer with some of the most influential men on the continent—y-you've saved the queen and her child, you saved all of us from Hilda! You—"

Fin cupped her face again, and for a heart stopping moment, Annika thought he was going to kiss her again, which silenced her words at once.

Instead, he pressed his forehead to hers, and stared into her eyes with open anguish.

"I'm sorry. I'm so sorry—"

"Stop it," Annika bit out, her voice cracking.

"We can't." The words choked Fin, but he still said them, his hands dropping to his sides as he once again stepped away from her.

For a minute, Annika genuinely appeared to be on the brink of tears. She stared at his face pleadingly, but when she saw his resolute stubbornness, her iron core sucked back her emotions. Her face went perfectly blank.

She looked him in the eyes without a whisper of emotion.

"Coward."

Turning on her heel, Annika stalked over to the garden door, her hand on the handle as behind her Fin stared defeated at the floor, rubbing the back of his neck. He couldn't watch her go. The urge to have her back in his arms was too strong.

"Oh, Mr. Ashowan?"

The singsong voice Annika used made Fin's insides twist painfully.

Using every ounce of self-control he possessed, he masked his face and looked at her, only to regret it instantly.

She beamed a flawless smile at him.

Her fakest one yet.

"No hard feelings, you're right. I barely know you." She left then, without a second of hesitation to delve back into the pouring rain outside.

Leaving Fin rubbing his face and finding himself in desperate need of shouting.

When the aides returned after the lunch flurry was over, they could all see something had him well and truly distraught. There were the restrained movements, the lack of verbal response—oh, and the kitchen knife that floated behind him of its own accord.

The newest kitchen aide, Heather, and the rest of the kitchen knights gaped openly on the garden path, while Hannah slapped her hands on her eyes and wordlessly herded the group back from where they came before he noticed his audience. She then bullied all of them around the edge of the gardens so that Fin would neither see nor hear them.

When she was certain they were outside of earshot, Hannah nodded to signify they could begin to speak.

"What the hell was that?!" Sir Harris exploded his eyes wide with panic.

"Are there ghosts in the kitchen?" Sir Taylor wondered, his blue eyes round.

"Is Mr. Ashowan a mage?!" Heather squeaked before she hastily covered her mouth again.

Hannah held up her hand and once again silenced them.

"He really is terrible at hiding his nonsense," she muttered with a sigh before speaking up. "No. Fin is a witch. If he were a mage, he would have one of the crystals the mage academies give out to their graduates, remember?"

The aides all had their jaws dropped.

"Is that why we had to work in his cottage instead of the kitchens when it rained?" Sir Andrews asked faintly.

"Yes. I have no idea why he hides it, but I don't want to bother him by letting him know his secret's out with his staff," Hannah explained patiently.

"W-When did you find out?" Heather's voice came out as a whisper.

"Peter and I found out shortly after Fin got the new window replaced by Lord Fuks. I guess he forgot for a day or two that he didn't charm it because I could see and hear inside, and I saw him using his magic as he cooked." Hannah paused, shaking her head before continuing. "He charms the window to show himself cooking away, but none of the floating cutlery—enough of that, though. We have a bigger issue," she began importantly.

"What could be bigger than finding out our cook is a ... a ..." Sir Andrews faltered on the words, still trying to wrap his head around it.

"A witch. Yes, yes. You'll see because it ties together with that." The kitchen staff were too befuddled to argue with her.

"Fin and Lady Jenoure are in love, and I'm certain that it is why he is losing control of his magic," Hannah declared, meeting each and every eye upon her.

Sirs Lewis, Harris, and Andrews shared nervous chuckles as they glanced at each other.

Sir Taylor was the only one still struggling to emote; yet he was the first to speak.

"Well, he certainly aims high enough," he remarked glibly, nodding at Hannah.

"Yes, he does. Then again, Lady Jenoure has been a little obvious herself over him."

The blank, blinking stares Hannah faced over her last statement lasted for a few moments before they all broke out laughing.

"L-Lady Jenoure?! The infamous *viscountess* known as one of the most beautiful women on the continent? The woman with songs written about her, wealthy and powerful men after her—and you think she wants the cook?!" Sir Harris had tears streaming down his face as he doubled over gasping. The only one of them not in full commotion was Heather.

"I get it," the maid said with an attempt at appearing nonchalant.

The knights gradually quieted down, and Sir Andrews was the first to address the new kitchen aide.

"What do you mean you 'get it'?"

Heather briefly glanced at Hannah, who pursed her lips, rolled her eyes, and nodded in affirmation to the girl.

"You know Mr. Ashowan is really attractive, right? He makes amazing food, and even though he's not a knight, he can fight—everyone knows that. He defended Hannah, and now he also has magic powers? He is very desirable. I just thought he was gay until the last few minutes." She shrugged.

All the knights grew concerned by the seriousness with which the girl spoke.

"Fin is desirable to women?" Sir Harris ventured slowly, his voice filled with awe.

"The majority of the women in this castle feel that way, yes," Hannah affirmed patiently.

Sir Harris turned his hazel eyes to her deep blue ones imploringly.

"Do … do you like him?"

"Not even slightly in that way. We had this discussion a long time ago, but I suppose that was before you joined us. I see him more as a constantly tired and irritable father. I'd say he's like an older brother, but I see him yelling at me to get off his flower beds better than I do him having a bunch of boyish revelry with friends or pulling pigtails."

For the first time in the discussion, everyone was in agreement.

"Alright, so Lady Jenoure and our cook are a thing—isn't she in the middle of picking a new husband?" Sir Lewis observed quietly.

"She is. Which is why we need to light a fire under his ass. He is trying to contain everything but failing *horribly*. Hence the knife show." Hannah waved over her shoulder in the direction of the kitchen.

"He could more than likely earn quite a bit of wealth and status if he relied on his powers or actually tried—he's just being an idiot. The king has sought his company more times than I wish to count." Hannah shook her head with a sigh. "So, we need to help him along at every turn," she ordered imperiously.

The knights glanced at each other, and she was worried she had lost her audience, when Sir Taylor stepped forward.

"What would you have us do?"

Hannah grinned her demonic smile.

The smile that was starting to become quite frequent …

Much to Sir Harris's delight.

Fin was in the middle of a deep stress the morning following his encounter with Lady Jenoure, and everyone was pretending not to notice. Except for the young prince sitting at his table.

While the aides had a more gentle, nuanced approach to dealing with the disgruntled cook, the precocious seven—soon to be eight—year-old had his own methods.

"Why are you being weird?" he asked after watching Fin slap down the head of lettuce with enough vigor to rattle the knives on the table.

Fin's eyes snapped up to the young boy, and he immediately sought control of his features.

"Just a lot on my mind. So your father changed the day of your masquerade?" Fin asked, trying his best to turn his mind away from Lady Jenoure.

"Yeah! I mean … I don't mind 'cause I'm not great at dancing." Eric leaned his cheek into his right hand, looking weary beyond his young years. Fin nearly laughed aloud.

"If it makes you feel any better, I can't dance a single step. On Quildon, there weren't even town dances. Everyone generally kept to themselves there," he explained, managing a small grin at the boy. Eric listened, sipping his milk, unable to feign interest in the Fin's dull history.

He suddenly perked up, unaware that he now sported a dapper milk mustache.

"Hey! What if you learned with me? Then, I wouldn't be the worst and, and you could come to my party. My dad changed the theme too … it's now a costume party, but I kind of like that better. I want to be a kraken! Or maybe a dragon!" Eric rushed out excitedly, his voice unknowingly increased in volume.

The kitten sharing the name of the sea creature was on his way out the garden door, along with the aides, but at hearing his name he turned and let out a small mew. Fin didn't understand why the rest of them all turned around slowly with conspiratorial smiles as well.

"That's right, Fin! You should learn to dance with him!" Hannah rushed out gleefully while taking several steps back into the kitchen.

He shot her a withering stare that she promptly ignored and continued beaming.

"Yeah! I'm tired of Morgan making fun of me. I could ask Lady Laurent to teach me here instead! Mother won't mind, and I could get my snack sooner," Eric announced, looking entirely too pleased with his idea.

Fin could feel his cheeks growing hot as everyone around him shared animated looks.

"What about all of you? You all can dance?" he asked, with the faint hope that they would provide him an escape.

"We're knights. Of course we can." Sir Lewis blinked, astounded that Fin was forgetting their elevated status. He then frowned down at his apron, and his shoulders slumped for a brief moment before straightening.

Fin's gaze darted to Hannah.

"Even I know the country dances." She shrugged.

He was still skeptical over the mischievous glint in Hannah's eye, but turned his attention back to Eric, who was already giving him wide, pleading eyes.

That is not even fair, he thought grumpily.

"Alright. Fine. I'll participate in your dance lessons, but we're pretty busy these days, Eric. So we will most likely have to start these instructions veeeery early in the morning. Are you sure that's what you want to do?" Fin was expecting the child to hesitate at the very least, but he underestimated the prince's commitment to his idea.

He was nodding so enthusiastically that there wasn't any wiggle room for Fin to argue the point further.

"I'll go to the dance lessons, Eric, but I don't think your parents would like a lowly cook at the ball. It isn't proper," Fin pointed out reasonably, not noticing Hannah's look of determination and the knights sharing secretive smiles.

Eric looked thoroughly annoyed.

"All day I have to learn about proper things. How to walk, bow, talk ... I hate it. Why can't I be friends with who I like and have them around?" Eric looked visibly upset, so Fin decided not to bring up their class divide and instead comfort the boy.

"There are a lot of things that are tough in the world, but just remember one thing ..." Fin smiled, and despite Eric wanting to wallow in his predicament, Fin could see he was eager to hear his advice.

"In my kitchen, it isn't like out there. In my kitchen, we can all eat, talk, and laugh as much as we want. It doesn't matter if your dad's here or the local vendor, my kitchen is safe. So if you want a break from all of that, come see me, okay?"

Eric beamed up at Fin, and the knights grinned as they all turned and left the room to return to work.

Eric dug back into his afternoon snack of jam slathered on gooey cheese and bread, and Hannah spun around enthusiastically and skipped outside.

Fin shook his head, but he did feel marginally better after having helped someone else with their own issues. If only his were so easily fixed.

CHAPTER 40
STEWING STORMS

Annika's afternoon following the kiss …

Annika stood on the other side of the garden door for a moment, trying to make sense of the jumble of emotions inside herself and gain better control of her face.

Anger, Annika was familiar with. Anger could fuel her task at hand in the downpour …

But there was another … an ache in her chest, an almost painful rasp that clawed its way up to her throat …

Sadness and grief.

Abso-bloody-not! Annika's hands curled into fists as she mentally cursed herself and began to step down the garden path. *Some man is going to turn me into a simpering idiot? I'd rather tie myself to a Troivackian ship and be dragged back than become something so pitiful.*

As she stomped her way toward the forest, thoroughly furious and refusing to be "heartbroken," she was able to ignore the pain in her side. Her resolve was teeming with the indignation that she could ever be broken up over a bloody cook who was weak, stubborn, insufferable, a good kisser—

Godsdamnit, Annika couldn't help but think to herself as she reached the perimeter of the woods and listened intently. Nothing but the sound of pounding rain and thunder reached her ears, and so she ventured into its shadowy depths carefully.

I just had to kiss him. Just haaaaad to go being all … vulnerable and gross. Godsdamnit, Hank, I blame this on you thoroughly! she snapped out toward her deceased husband.

Before you, I never would've succumbed to such vomit-worthy scenes or emotions. Hell, I never would've been interested in him!

The memory of Fin's caring protectiveness when Hannah stood up to the king flashed through her mind's eye.

His facing off against Captain Antonio, when he had that look of calm, steely resolve that hinted at control over a great power …

His drunken kiss sending every piece of her humming with electricity and life.

GODSDAMNIT!

Without even having to think about what she was doing, Annika immediately moved between thick trees stealthily and silently. She had been forced from her horse during the attack, and so guessed that her attackers would more than likely return to the scene, trying to surprise her as she retrieved her steed.

Slowly, as she pushed through soggy ferns and brush, she heard the voices of two men in discussion.

"… can't be in the maze, we would've found her."

Annika could spy the Troivackian duo from her current location. She stilled immediately; the maple tree under her hands was easily wide enough to hide her figure.

"Do you think she had help?" The shorter of the men had his back to her and was speaking while clutching her horse's reins in his hand. Fortunately, both of them had failed to notice the horse's ears twitching in her direction.

"It's possible. I still cannot believe that the 'Dragon,' was actually a woman. No wonder Daxaria is proving to be so easy to conquer." The taller of the men looked well groomed but was very clearly a Troivackian peasant—though if he were here with Annika's brother, he had to at least be in the military. He had a short black beard and a receding hairline, but perfectly white teeth. His clothes were tough to distinguish in the rain, but there wasn't any sign of finery on him.

"She *did* take out Zern, Nathan, and Davies though." The shorter man Annika couldn't see, but his odd accent when he spoke indicated he was of the peasantry class.

"Aye, well ... didn't know she had a second knife with her." He shrugged.

Annika turned her attention to her horse and eyed the compact crossbow strapped on the beast's left side.

Too risky.

Annika knew that while she was a keen shot with a bow, and a good arm with a knife, she only had one knife left.

Then again, she also had enough rage to throttle fifty men as the feeling of Fin's lips remained imprinted on her mouth.

Not to mention his piss-poor excuse to not even try to find a way for their relationship to be accepted in some measure by the king.

Their relationship ...

There wasn't even a relationship to speak of!

Annika could feel her ire growing the more she thought of Fin's rejection.

Well, I guess he just means more to me than I to him. Enough of this, this doesn't change my plan. I will not be made to be an idiot by him again, she announced in her mind darkly.

Regardless of Fin's dismissal of her, she still wasn't going to marry any of the suitors. She didn't need to be shackled to some husband. It would make her political tendencies annoying to hide. Though Lord Ryu seemed far more aware of her true nature than she was exactly comfortable with.

He was definitely a clever man ...

The king was quite astute for having selected the newly ennobled Zinferan for her. If she *had* to choose between the three of them, he would definitely be the most likely one.

Fin's face appeared in her mind again, and she suddenly saw red creeping into her vision.

"... We'll join the others after Lord Piereva speaks to the men that have already come ashore."

Annika's attention snapped back sharply to the two Troivackians then. She hadn't been able to hear what they had been saying before, but what "men" had already come to shore?

"Aye, I imagine we could actually take over the country with just the soldiers we have now, to be perfectly honest. These idiots are so blindly trusting, I could be dripping in the blood of their children and they'd still offer me food." The two laughed heartily.

"I'd wager you a gold coin that if one man held a knife to the queen's throat the king would hand over the entire kingdom without a battle."

"That wouldn't be any fun, though."

Even though red was filling her vision, Annika felt herself smile crazily. She was entirely unaware that she looked thoroughly terrifying.

Without thinking anything else, Annika stepped out from behind the tree and threw the knife with precise aim at the taller of the two men. It struck him between the eyes, freezing his cruel smile in place forever.

The shorter one swung around, but Annika was already behind him. She shoved her heel into his groin, and as he doubled over, uppercut him in the throat.

"I wager you a gold coin you didn't know how badly I needed to hit someone today," she hoarsely informed her opponent over the clamor of the storm around them.

Despite his weakened state, the shorter man managed to land a weak blow against Annika's side—the side that had been freshly stitched.

She gasped, but not before she once again shoved her heel into his groin. As he doubled over with a sharp cry, she grabbed his own dagger from his belt.

"You fight like a dirty Troivackian." Annika smiled with a deranged glint in her eyes from beneath her hood. "I love it."

The soldier peeked up at her, anger, pain, and the tiniest hint of fear flashing in his eyes.

"Who the hell are you?" he croaked as Annika flipped the blade in her hand.

"A Daxarian who has had a bad day," she ground out before giving her final blow.

"None of them returned?" Lord Piereva's eyes flashed dangerously down at his squire. The man's spine was rigid; he was too frightened to even tremble as he gave his report on his knees.

"No, my lord. We intercepted the message the mercenary known as Corey was attempting to send as you instructed. We then sent five men out to discover the spy in the castle at the rendezvous point, but there hasn't been any trace of anyone. I gathered more men and went to the meeting spot before dinner this evening; we found some traces of blood and evidence of a fight, but nothing else." The squire paused for a short breath before adding, "The rains have washed away most of the trail and proof."

Lord Piereva fixed his murderous gaze to his chamber window on his left, his dark eyes staring boldly into a place no one else could see.

"The spy must have figured out it was a trap and came with back up. I will be honest, Kelsey, I did not anticipate there being someone in Daxaria capable of having such foresight." The squire knew better than to trust the restraint Lord Piereva was exuding as he slowly turned back to stare at the top of the young man's head.

"I will have you seek my sister now and bring her to me. I have not yet given her the orders from our king, and it has been days since we arrived." The squire leapt up eagerly to his feet. Without paying any heed to his bruised knees, he flew out of the room, grateful to have escaped a physical retribution for the bad news he had delivered.

In the silence, the earl began thinking of the possible Daxarians that had an ounce of acumen and could've outwitted him. The list was quite short, but frustrating nonetheless.

The mage would make the most sense, as he could surely take on five men and dispose of them easily while remaining unscathed.

Lord Piereva would have to seek out information on where the Royal Mage named Lee had been that day.

Another option was Captain Antonio. Though the man seemed too direct to be secretive. He also would have a harder time sneaking away from his men—unless, of course, his knights had been the ones to help dispose of the bodies. Still … the captain was too forthright to be a proper spy.

Lord Fuks was too insane to be nuanced. The chief of military's son Les Fuks was too spineless to ever endeavor spying on Troivack.

Lord Piereva hesitated then.

Son of the chief of military …

Aidan Helmer's son … a weak cook. However, he shared blood with a powerful fire witch. That could not be overlooked …

It was a conundrum to be certain, but Lord Piereva knew he'd get to the bottom of it. After he spoke to his sister, he would go seek out the mercenary named Corey and force answers from him. It was his own foolishness that he hadn't had the informant followed after intercepting his means of communicating with someone named the "Dragon."

He was deep in thought when he heard the gentle knock on his door.

Lord Piereva barked admittance and turned to stare at his sister, who was looking strangely pale.

"What's wrong with you?" he demanded, his eyes narrowing.

"I fear I may have caught whatever malady you were suffering from upon your arrival," she answered weakly.

At first Lord Piereva was suspicious, but she really didn't look well—she was even hunching over her middle subtly. He remembered the pain of his own mysterious sickness well and deemed her words to be truthful.

"Well, this news should make you feel better. Your true king has ordered you to choose Lord Miller to marry." He watched her carefully then, even though he knew his irritating brat of a sibling would bend to his will.

"It is time for you to return to Troivack, you fortunate runt."

Annika blinked slowly.

Lord Piereva glared.

"Very well. However, I must wait until after the prince's ball, otherwise the Daxarian king will become suspicious and could hold us prisoner."

He snorted condescendingly.

"That pathetic soft sack? Unlikely."

Annika's face remained perfectly still when she replied meekly, yet somehow ... firmly.

"With the added pressure of the Zinferans being here, he may become desperate."

Lord Piereva cast an appraising eye over his sister. She might not have been as dim as he had remembered her being back in Troivack. Perhaps being surrounded by fools had forced her to start using her head.

"Very well. You have until after the ball. I heard the event was moved due to the suitors arriving early."

"Yes," she answered shortly, her face beginning to turn gray as she stared vacantly over his shoulder.

"Be gone. I don't want your sick in my chamber." Phillip dismissed her with a wave, and even magnanimously overlooked her lack of curtsy when she rushed from the room.

At least that was one annoyance dealt with properly. His sister had agreed to her true king's order, ensuring she had no business being a spy. Not that he had ever thought that tall tale to be likely.

After the ball, he would take her home to be wedded and bedded to the weak son of Lord Miller. Hopefully whatever brats she bore would inherit the Piereva strength.

After that, Lord Piereva didn't pay his sister another thought, as his concerns turned to his need to check on the troops that had successfully snuck into Austice.

How the hell did this happen? Fin and Annika were unaware that they were thinking the exact same thing at the exact same time.

Fin kept his eyes fixed on the glass tower instead of anywhere near the table where Lord Miller and Lady Jenoure sat dining right in front of him. He feigned indifference to the Troivackian praising his skills in the kitchen and tried to look at ease.

"Mr. Ashowan, did you hear me?" Fin slowly turned his head and locked his calm icy stare with Lord Miller.

"Thank you, my lord." Fin bowed. He couldn't look at Annika.

"What business did you have in the greenhouse? I hear the keeper is quite mysterious." The honest, eager interest in the lord's voice made Fin's left eye twitch, and the noble visibly leaned back in response.

Fin had been called over by Lord Miller after he had finished his work with Kasim for the day, and he was seen leaving with a sack of exotic fruits. He had almost been able to pretend he hadn't heard, but one of the footmen standing guard of the entrances had stopped him.

"Kasim is a private man. He provides the kitchen with fresh fruit and vegetables year-round, and even grows some that aren't native to Daxaria," Fin explained, his eyes once again fixating on the distance.

"I see, what a wonderful way to ensure a variety of food! I'm afraid our current Troivackian government is quite indifferent to such marvelous ideas. Whatever is sustainable and consumable is good enough. Except for our wine and liquor, which we are quite famous for."

Fin gave a short nod but said nothing else.

Despite his outward apathy, he had been worried sick about Annika ever since she had left the kitchen. He didn't know if she was going to be killed by her remaining assailants, or if her wound had become infected …

He didn't have a right to express his worries to her, however.

Lady Jenoure drank deeply from a teacup filled with moonshine and a splash of tea, as she tried to ignore the pain in her side from her wound, and her churning stomach at Fin's proximity.

"I'm something of a self-proclaimed academic, so I find this quite interesting. I want to travel the world and learn about different cultures and record them for everyone to learn about. In fact, if Lady Jenoure graces me with her hand in marriage, I would insist she join me on these ventures." The man was smiling in a friendly manner, and there was a merry twinkle in his eye. He seemed warm, kind, interesting …

Fin hated him.

"I wish you the best in your travels. I must return to the kitchens." He bowed and exited the courtyard as hastily as possible, his fist clenching and unclenching at his side while the other carried the sack slung over his shoulder.

After his departure, Annika fixed the lord with a slightly unfocused stare.

"You don't want to return to Troivackian court?" she asked, her mind fuzzy from all the moonshine she had been forced to consume to hide her excruciating physical pain.

"I suppose I really should try and keep that on the down low. My father expects me to return, and if I am to secure our marriage, he is going to give me a piece of land for me to rule and profit from on my own. However … I want to know all about the world. I have no interest in politics. I want to travel and see everything before assuming my responsibility. Once I return, I'll enforce the best methods to be a profitable and good lord to my plebes." The excited flush in the man's face was unprecedented, and Annika found herself stunned into speechlessness.

"I know I'm not like most Troivackians, but then … neither are you." The emphatic statement made Annika close her mouth and wait for an opening in the conversation to excuse herself. She couldn't mentally handle the Troivackian anomaly sitting across from her, not with Fin's faint smell of freshly baked bread lingering around the table.

In truth, Annika felt so irritated and restless that the urge to flee and disappear from the entire castle was growing. The fact that that impulse was exactly what the man across from her was suggesting was dangerously appealing.

Raising her teacup to her lips, Annika's foggy mind began to consider her future a little more bleakly.

She'd ensure that Daxaria would win the war at any cost.

After that, though … could things really go back to any semblance of normal?

CHAPTER 41
GROWING PAINS

Kasim stared blankly at the charred rose hedge in front of him, then turned to look at Fin. He stared with an unreadable expression at him for a few wordless seconds, before once again returning his attention to the shrub.

The head of the castle greenhouse and all the plants within, a skilled and powerful earth witch, wore a rich maroon linen coat with the sleeves rolled up, but his chest remained bare. He wore matching pants and had half of his locs tied in a knot behind his head as he continued staring at the damage of the maze, while Fin grew more and more tense.

"So ... can you fix it?"

"Mr. Ashowan ... why is your first response to things to call down lightning?" Kasim's tone was innocently curious as he stared expectantly at Fin.

Fin felt his cheeks tinge red.

"I don't always call down lightn—"

"First day we met."

"That was because I saw vines moving on their own and could *feel* the strength of your power," he explained defensively with a wince.

Kasim sighed, shaking his head. He then clucked his tongue and shot Fin one final disapproving glance before reaching out a long-fingered, ebony hand toward the shrub.

Fin watched as fresh growth burst forward from the healthy stubs of the brambles and leaves spiraled out of the new magical growth. As the hole resealed itself, a perfect, single, pale pink rose peeled back its petals into a magnificent bloom like a bow atop a perfectly wrapped gift.

Kasim gently plucked the flower and turned to Fin. He held it out to him, but when the man tried to take it, Kasim quickly lifted it out of his grasp and gently bopped him on the head with it.

"Be more careful, hm?"

Fin gave a half smile as he took the rose from his friend, and the two turned in unison to stride back to the castle, where the occupants were more than likely finishing up their lunch.

"I won't bother asking you why you set fire to a hedge—I know you better than to try finding out," Kasim noted with his hands clasped behind his back.

"Which is one of the many reasons I like you so much," Fin responded, grinning more easily before adding on: "I don't always use lightning, you know. The second time I needed to go through the bush, it … it moved for me. Which was strange. I've never really influenced plants to move unnaturally before. I can make things grow a little bit better than the average person—"

"My eggplants beg to differ," Kasim interrupted disapprovingly, but his tone was jesting.

"I didn't know the beetles would be so tenacious!" Fin explained, his tone jumping higher as he once again sought to prove his innocence and skill.

"Back to what you were just saying, plants are more aware than you think, Mr. Ashowan," Kasim began to explain as they neared the castle doors. "They sense things in the earth and the creatures they privilege with their support. While you may ask favors of plants and the earth, they may choose not to listen, or just as easily decide to obey you."

They stopped a few feet from the doorway, far enough that anyone on the inside of the castle wouldn't be able to hear them.

"They always obey the earth witches, though," Fin pointed out with a frown.

"We earth witches tend to be recognized as part plant—and charming ones at that." Kasim's brilliant white teeth flashed, and Fin found himself already grinning.

"So you're saying they might not listen to me next time?"

"That hedge is pretty pissed off with you, my friend. They only listened because they like your hair and you caught them off guard by speaking to them. I don't know that they will be as … receptive next time," Kasim explained, still smiling.

"They like my hair?" Fin repeated, raising an eyebrow in disbelief.

"Roses are quite fussy. I cannot always understand why either."

"I didn't realize I could be aware of the earth. Objects I can sense, and in dangerous circumstances people in my home, but plants? That surprises me." Fin glanced back at the rose maze and felt a pang in his chest as he remembered the night that he and Lady Jenoure had strolled through the colorful blooms.

"Being aware of something forms a connection, which then solidifies it in your world of awareness," Kasim expounded as he turned back toward the castle, his feet remaining completely bare despite leaving the greenhouse.

"I don't know that I want to know how much the cabbages like manure though …" Fin jested with Kasim, who laughed warmly as they mounted the steps together.

"Well, Mr. Ashowan, I will see you next Sunday." Kasim gave a small nod of his head before he turned and strode smoothly into the castle. His feet never made a sound as he disappeared down the corridor and around the corner.

Fin began walking in the opposite direction back toward the kitchen, when Mr. Howard appeared from around the corner, clutching two scrolls to his chest.

"Good afternoon!" Fin called, waving the rose he still had in his hand at Mr. Howard, who immediately stopped in his tracks and glared.

"What is that?" he demanded tightly.

Fin had actually forgotten about the radiant bloom in his hand, but at seeing Mr. Howard's expression to it, couldn't help but smirk.

"This is a flower. Why? Does this scare you?" Fin's borderline evil smile melted into a bright grin as he tilted the rose down toward Mr. Howard's face. The man glared daggers in response.

"Because of your 'prank,' I have received an inconceivable number of maids declaring their support of my love for Peter. The other half of the staff support my torrid relationship with your own person," Mr. Howard snapped angrily, a small blush rising to his cheeks.

"Well, aren't you popular! Doesn't it make you feel good that so many care about your happiness and well-being? I bet you've never spoken to seventy-five percent of the people in this castle before my well-intentioned meddling."

"You're a pain in the ass that I wouldn't hesitate to shove down a flight of stairs."

"I am grateful, then, that the kitchen is on the ground floor."

Kevin Howard scowled in silence at Fin for several long moments.

"Well fine, if you don't want the rose, I will find someone who does." Fin's air of indignation only succeeded in making Mr. Howard's cheek twitch.

As he started strolling past him, he paused and turned his chin over his shoulder.

"You need to accept the love offered to you in this life."

"I'd sooner accept the pox than anything you offer," Kevin Howard barked as Fin waved the rose over his shoulder, heading back to his kitchens.

When Fin entered the room where his magic had continued his work for him in his absence, he took a quick appreciative sniff of the rose in his hand and felt a small piece of his heart lighten at the soft fragrance.

He set the bloom down on the far right of his worktable, away from the mess, and turned his attention to the tasks at hand.

He took his magically imbued knife gently in his hand, stopping its own magical work, and took over dicing a ripe ruby tomato for the dinner that evening.

He worked with an outward calm that was as forced as the blank static in his mind. Annika was alive, so he shouldn't be so worried. However, the wound in her side could easily become infected. Not to mention sitting, standing, curtsying, could all be very painful …

Fin's heart twisted. Without seeing a physician, she wouldn't be given the herbs necessary for managing the pain. Then again, she could have had her own private stock …

Even so, if the wound became infected, she would need a physician …

Fin had nearly convinced himself several times over that sneaking away to see her was merely what a decent person should do. However, the small hissing voice in his head had reminded him that a decent person wouldn't jeopardize her reputation by acting familiar toward her.

Sighing, he slid the diced ingredient into a wooden bowl atop the counter.

He was about to lose himself to another tornado of thoughts surrounding Lady Jenoure, when his ears picked up unfamiliar voices on the other side of the shut garden door.

When he had been handling the rose bush conundrum, Fin had closed and sealed all the doors for anyone but himself. Given the summer heat, he doubted anyone would seek out the kitchen, with its high fires and enclosed space.

Setting the knife firmly on the table, Fin made his way to the garden door and opened it wide. He saw a group of Troivackian knights standing in the garden, talking and laughing amongst themselves, their plate armor glinting in the summer sun.

"If you don't mind, please get off the turnips." Fin's icy voice reached the men easily as they all cast uniformed looks of annoyance and boredom in his direction.

"We were told we could relax here until Lord Piereva has finished testing the troops," one of the men called, his face somewhat slimmer than his two bulky companions.

"You were not instructed properly. Get off the gardens." Fin could already feel the need to teach a good, *permanent* lesson to those knights well up in his belly and chest, which in turn made his fists clench hard enough to nearly shatter bones in his palm.

"So you'll get us some chairs to sit an' drink then?" One of the Troivackian men had spoken up. The man had a neck as thick as the entire width of his shaved head.

"I am busy preparing food. If you all could please go off and—"

"Oyy, we obey our master Lord Piereva. He would skin you alive if he heard you were contradicting his order," one of the men sneered cloyingly.

"He is not the master of my kitchen. Now leave on your own feet or by spontaneous exertion that lands you on your back," Fin demanded, forcing a falsely lazy gait as he strolled out onto the garden path. He only stopped when he was a few feet from the men. He eyed their boots, which crushed the vibrant green plants beneath their feet, with a brief flit of his eyes, and felt his gaze turn steely.

The men chuckled darkly as they all slowly straightened to their full heights, though much to their displeasure, he was still an inch or two above nearly all of them.

"You think we're scared of a *Daxarian* cook just because—"

Fin hit the man in two places with the heel of his palm and watched satisfied as the soldier fell to his knees before his face rushed the ground.

The Troivackians that remained standing all drew daggers, though they had swords at their sides as well.

"I won't ask again. Get off my turnips." Fin's deadened expression failed to convey his murderous intent, as the men all snickered, though with slightly more concern as they eyed their fallen comrade who was still sleeping like a newborn babe.

"Gentlemen, I fear you are needed back in the training ring. Lord Piereva has summoned you." Lord Jiho Ryu appeared behind the beefy men soundlessly, making them all jump and whirl around panicked.

Jiho eyed their drawn weapons with a single narrowed stare, making them all hastily sheath their weapons and bow. Though they looked thoroughly sour as they did so.

Lord Ryu stood with his hands clasped behind his back, and watched them haul up their unconscious friend, all while casting murderous leers toward Fin.

Once the troupe had disappeared around the castle corner, Jiho turned to Fin with a cocked eyebrow.

"It isn't like you to pick fights," he observed as Fin picked up a rake leaning against the fence post and began loosening the packed dirt from where the Troivackian soldiers had been standing moments ago.

"I feel very protective of my turnips," Fin explained mildly, not wanting to meet his friend's eye. He didn't want to think about Jiho with Annika … it was doing things to his breathing.

I could've also given and taken a good beating to feel moderately better, he couldn't help but think to himself.

Jiho strode over, placed himself directly in front of Fin on the pathway, and waited for him to finish his task.

Jiho watched his friend closely as he worked, then saw how Fin turned away from him to place the rake back where he had first picked it up, without looking at him or saying anything.

"Have I done something to upset you, Fin?" Jiho asked, tilting his head ever so slightly as he watched Fin shove his hands in his pockets and hunch his shoulders ever so slightly.

"Not at all. Congratulations on becoming a noble, I'm sure your sister is thrilled." Fin finally locked gazes with Jiho but had to immediately fight off a flinch at the directness. He managed a smile at his friend, and genuinely meant his warm wishes as he thrust every other emotion from his mind.

"Fin, I lived with you for years, I know something's bothering you. Something with me, apparently." Fin strode past him, heading back to the kitchens and completely ignoring the man's observation.

"Everything is as it should be, you should get back before they notice you're missing," Fin called out, forcing his tone to be more jovial. Jiho frowned at the peculiar wording, and so trekked behind his footsteps.

Once back inside his kitchen, he realized Jiho had followed him.

He always was silent as a cat, he thought dryly.

"Did you want a drink before you went back?" Fin asked as he picked up his knife and resumed working.

Jiho didn't answer, but instead continued studying Fin in his unsettling way, until his eyes dropped to the rose on the table and then jumped back up to him with sudden clarity.

"Oh, good Gods, a viscountess?!"

Fin dropped his knife in shock. His eyes snapped up, as Jiho stared at him in awe.

"What are you talking about?" he snapped. While his voice was convincing, his face had paled ever so slightly.

"It's because of you, isn't it?" Jiho was suddenly smiling as all the pieces of the puzzle fell into place before him.

"Have the Troivackians made you drink their moonshine? You're not making any sense." Fin steadied himself as he shook his head and forced a smile despite his insides beginning to twist.

"It's because of you Lady Jenoure doesn't want to get married. Gods, the two of you are in love with each other, aren't you?"

Fin reviled the words and shook his head.

"I'm not—"

"Why are you treating me so coldly then?"

Fin's mouth snapped shut and he fixed Jiho with a confident level gaze.

"I'm not treating you coldly, I just have a lot on my mind because of all the extra mouths to feed and—"

"We're better friends than that. I wondered why you hadn't come to greet me yet! It couldn't have been because of my ennobling—that wouldn't really affect you at all. Besides, when you saw my elevated position last time you had no qualms whatsoever. I haven't seen you since then, so it was nothing I've done. Which means something else is making you uncomfortable. Lady Jenoure has been acting as though she is the slack-jawed village idiot, but I know she is far more intelligent than that. It's therefore obvious she doesn't want to marry. Not to mention the only time she ever snapped out of her façade for even a moment was when it had something to do with you, or the food," Jiho concluded, smiling proudly while Fin stared aghast at him.

"You got all that from me behaving strangely?"

"The rose. Something about it inspired me and my instincts are rarely wrong." Jiho smiled brilliantly.

"For the love of—"

"I understand you can't admit anything or else face grave consequences. I'll be seeing you later, Fin, I think we should have a little chat over drinks."

Jiho turned and waved over his shoulder without turning back around. He strode purposefully back out into the sweltering summer day, leaving Fin standing alone in his kitchen, too stunned to move.

"How in the hell did he do that?!" Fin then proceeded to mutter every curse he knew over and over. When he ran out of them, he restarted.

He glanced at the rose on his table after he had time to settle his thoughts and then thought about Annika once more. Her teasing tone, her flask glinting as she topped up any beverage she had in front of her, the sad gaze she had given him in the maze …

Godsdamnit. Snatching the rose from the table, Fin turned to the castle door and stalked out of the room.

CHAPTER 42
STROLLING THROUGH STRIFE

The king peered down at the Troivackian knights training in the ring in the early reaches of dawn with an unreadable expression on his face. He had positioned himself in the window on the second floor to watch them, standing far enough back that he wouldn't be seen.

The soldiers fought relying on their brute strength more than nuanced movements, an accurate report from Captain Antonio. Norman continued watching them bash each other mercilessly. There wasn't an ounce of humor in their faces, and none of them spoke as they exchanged blows. Lord Piereva seemed to have fully recovered from his illness, as he set to hammering down anyone that crossed blades with him.

Direct. Ruthless. No hesitations.

Norman turned from the window to see Annika standing pressed against the corridor wall, looking particularly pale.

"Shall we?" He offered his arm to her, as she straightened with a perfectly blank expression and took his arm gratefully.

Even through his sleeve, Norman could feel the heat rolling off of her in waves.

"Is your wound infected?" he demanded in low tones.

"It is indeed. Do not worry, I've poured moonshine over the affliction and drained it this morning. Clara has already stitched me again."

The king cast a worried glance down at the top of her silky black hair. "You had to have it stitched again?"

"Lord Ryu wanted to go riding last evening for our courting time."

The king let out a small breath of displeasure as the pair made their way to the war council room in the north end of the castle.

He went considerably slower than his usual brisk pace, out of consideration for Lady Jenoure's condition, and began contemplating the list of questions he had thought of the previous night for their meeting.

At long last they made it to their destination, where Annika hastily crossed the room to the nearest chair and half collapsed into its waiting seat.

"Please forgive my lack of curtsy, Your Majesty." She leaned her head back against the chair's high back and listened as the king slowly seated himself closer to her than his usual spot would have him.

"It is I who should ask your forgiveness, Annika. You are shouldering no small feat from me, and I ask you to do so with nothing but a smile." Norman shook his head sadly as he grimaced. "I'm afraid I once again must ask your duty and inform me if you've learned anything."

"The last two of the men I dispatched …" She took a deep breath before continuing as a sweat broke out over her brow. "They mentioned that there were other Troivackians in Austice. I don't think we know of any men other than the ones under the castle roof … my gut tells me something is wrong." She managed to crack open her glassy eyes and stare into Norman's piercing hazel ones.

The king leaned back in his chair, and gently stroked his pointed beard thoughtfully.

"I'll send a couple of my more discreet men to investigate the lower end of Austice and see if there is potentially any word of abandoned buildings becoming occupied more recently," he reasoned aloud.

"I have to …" Annika rested her forearms on the table in front of her and pressed on them heavily in a very unladylike manner.

Norman's worry for her tripled.

"I have to go to my holding on the waterfront before the prince's ball anyway, so I will investigate myself." She leveled the king with an uncharacteristically direct stare.

"Is there anything else you need to tell me?" Norman asked gently, clearly hoping that he could allow the poor woman back to her chamber.

"I had to send Corey away after he buried the bodies. They clearly worked out that he was one of my informants, so it wouldn't be safe to keep him nearby," she managed to say, slowly pushing herself back to her feet. The king swiftly rose to his feet and reached for her forearm.

"I figured as much. Now if there isn't anything else, go rest. I am ordering you to stay in bed for the remainder of the day." Norman gently laid her hand on his arm and turned her toward the closed counsel room door.

"No hurry. It is more relaxing here than my chamber," she informed him with a small, pained chuckle.

"Would that have anything to do with that dour woman your brother 'gifted' you as a new maid who is undoubtedly a spy?"

"The one and only," she grunted as they neared her chamber.

"How is it you managed to evade her to meet me this morning?"

When they reached her chamber, the king unlatched the door for her and gestured inside for her. Clara, who had been stitching on a chair by the fireplace, immediately rose to her feet. The dutiful lady's maid was at Annika's side instantly.

"Clara sent her to go beat the dust from the tapestries in my room," Annika managed to reply as she gracefully shifted her reliance on the king's guidance to the maid's.

"At first light?" the king asked, clearly amused at her antics.

"With my illness I'm having trouble sleeping, so I am up at all hours. My new 'gift' has been wonderfully helpful to me in those times." Annika managed a weak smile as she slowly made her way toward her bed and seated herself atop the deep burgundy coverlet.

"Very well, I shall leave you for some semblance of peace." The king headed back out the way he had come, but suddenly turned back around.

"Why is it you need to go to your estate in Austice before the ball, by the way?"

Annika's eyelids fluttered as she began to sway gently where she sat. "Hm?"

Norman shook his head over his own callousness; he had already pushed her enough for the day.

"Never mind. I will ask again at a later time."

Once he closed the door, Annika eased her way back to rest against her snowy white pillows and let out a shallow breath as Clara hovered nearby, pouring her mistress a cool cup of water.

"I don't like you deceiving the king," the maid announced disapprovingly.

"He'll thank me for it later. Can you honestly see me going back to being a good wife to someone?" Annika accepted the cup offered to her and drained it gratefully.

"You were a good wife?" Clara's soft voice didn't fail to convey her note of sarcasm.

"Toward the end, I was the picture-perfect wife, and you know it. So what if I had a rough start?"

"You set fire to Lord Jenoure's banquet hall."

"I set *one* fire and you've never let it go," Annika muttered, closing her eyes against the pounding headache in her temples.

"What about when you removed the painting of his mother and replaced it with a depiction of a naked, muscled, well-endowed Troivackian man?" Mirth danced in Clara's deep blue eyes. Her milky white skin remained unblemished, as was her usual, from emotion.

"Hank had that one coming. He insisted I wasn't making myself at home and badgered me about it for the first three months of our marriage. Besides, at least the subject of my painting trimmed his mustache. Unlike Hank's mother."

"What about the time with Lord Jenoure's flock of sheep when you—"

"Clara, yes I rebelled at first—especially because I was insanely bored in his country estate—but could we please revisit the glory days when it doesn't feel as though I'm roasting in hell?"

Back when Annika had first married Hank, she hadn't been able to continue her espionage profession. The boredom and frustration had led to her acting out in anger over her unsettling helplessness of being forced to marry and live in a foreign land. The result had been several juvenile acts of personal revenge. Why had an old man wanted to marry her anyway?

Hank had always responded with good humor and kindness, forcing her to repent and become ladened with guilt. The results were her maturing at a rapid rate, a gift from the man she did not deserve.

Clara gave the smallest of smiles down at Annika's pained and sweaty face. If her mistress was still able to be snarky, her fever was not going to be the death of her.

"Very well. Sleep now, and is there anything you would like me to give to Zuma when she returns from her task?"

"Have her run into town and buy Eric a birthday present," Annika managed as she felt her body grow heavy with the need to sleep.

At least all of this is helping me not think about a certain idiot …

At long last, oblivion rose up to meet her as she drifted off into a dreamless slumber. Clara stood over her mistress, thoughtfully watching the beautiful woman's chest gently rise and fall.

"You do need another husband. I just hope whichever suitor you pick knows what they're in for." Without another word, she exited the chamber, closing the door carefully behind her.

Annika opened her eyes thanks to the sound of someone entering her chamber and could immediately tell her fever had broken. She could also tell that she was as weak as a newborn, thanks to the fight her body must've given to regain its health.

"Are you feeling better, my lady?"

Annika's teeth were on edge as she slowly sat up and masked her face with her "dullard" persona.

"Yes, Zuma. Did you get Eric's birthday present?"

The maid's beautiful slim face turned toward a wrapped package on one of the chests in Annika's room.

"Yes. I bought him a mahogany sword."

Annika didn't even have to pretend she was displeased in order to banish the woman from her sights.

"What's the point? The wood is exquisite, but he's a child still in training. Will he hang it on his chamber wall?" Her tone was rife with sarcasm.

Zuma's face tightened, and Annika took great pleasure in seeing the woman's apparent dislike of her.

"Please return to town and return it before the shops close. Perhaps instead we can get him some proper child-sized chainmail. *That*, he could actually use." Annika waved Zuma from the room.

As she watched Zuma pick up the parcel and make her exit, Annika noted without an ounce of surprise she was clearly headed toward Lord Piereva's chambers, in the opposite direction of the castle exit.

Slowly easing herself off the bed, it was then Annika noticed a single rose on her bedside.

She picked up the bloom and gently touched her nose to the velvety petals, giving it a tentative sniff. Smiling slightly at the faint scent, she continued staring down into its perfect beauty as she wrapped her hand around the post of her bed and drew herself up carefully.

Clara walked in then, and the corner of her mouth twitched at the sight of her mistress on her feet looking at a flower.

"This bloom is incredible, I thought the roses were finished for the year," Annika explained, lifting her happy expression to her maid.

"They should've been. That appeared on your bedside during the lunch hour when Zuma and I were away. Your suitors are very considerate."

Annika's pleasant expression fell at Clara's words.

"What do you mean this just appeared? Who the hell was in my chamber?"

"I don't know, my lady ..." Clara thought to herself for a moment. Her lack of shock or concern would've been disturbing to anyone but Annika. "It isn't like you to sleep through the door opening and closing."

Annika felt her heart skip a beat. Who could have entered her chamber without disturbing her?

Fever or not, she couldn't become sloppy!

Especially not with my brother on the same bloody continent, Annika reminded herself silently, her trepidation growing in leaps and bounds.

"Find out as discreetly as possible who wasn't present at lunch," she demanded urgently as she sat down on her bed and tossed the rose back onto the night table.

Clara wordlessly curtsied and exited the chamber with a small swish of her skirts.

Annika stood back up, her ire fueling her weakened body.

She couldn't let this strange occurrence get in the way. She would take a bath, then she would prepare for the next stage of her plan.

As she looked at the perfect flower once again, her mind racing with possibilities, her stomach hit the floor when she realized the obvious answer.

The rose was a message from her brother. Thanks to Zuma, he knew where her chamber was, and if she dared to misbehave, he'd come to her in her sleep.

That has to be it, right? Lord Miller is too wrapped up in learning things to come up with anything romantic. Lord Nam is more likely to gift me gold or jewelry, and Lord Ryu ... He seems too sensible. She shook her head, trying to clear it. Her mind was still sluggish from sleep and sickness.

I mean, it's not like it'd be Fin ... right? Annika laughed aloud.

Kraken was more likely than Fin to bring her a rose at this point.

He had made himself perfectly clear, after all.

Lord Piereva leaned back on his horse as he listened to his squire inform him of the maid Zuma's findings, as well as the reports from his men. He rode into Austice with only two other Troivackian knights.

"… the cook knocked out Sir Evans."

His head snapped to his left side, making the squire involuntarily wince. Lord Piereva backhanded him at the sight of his reaction before speaking.

"A Troivackian never shows fear," he growled. He waited a few moments before asking what he had initially wanted to know.

"How did the Royal Cook knock out Sir Evans?" he demanded, as his squire wiped the blood from his split lip and the Daxarians that walked the streets watched them with mixed expressions of horror and curiosity.

"The men say he tapped him twice and he fell over. Sir Evans swears the man had a weapon," the squire recited, unconsciously setting his horse slightly farther from his master.

"I see. What was the alleged reason for such an attack?" Lord Piereva followed his squire and sidled up just as close as before the young man had redirected his steed.

"The other knights said something about turnips, while Sir Evans said he was whining like a bitch about nothing."

Lord Piereva grunted and shook his head disapprovingly. As he did so, he suddenly noticed a cat with a snowy white face and chest with triangles of black fur sitting on the sidewalk in front of them. Two smaller cats that were obviously females flanked him. The squire immediately reset his horse's course around the feline.

"See that cat there?" Lord Piereva jerked his chin in the cat's direction. The animal hadn't moved an inch as he watched the men pass.

"Y-Yes?" the squire returned, uncertainly.

"Despite all this traffic in this street, he moves for no one. Sir Evans could use half that cat's mettle and would already have been promoted several times over."

The squire didn't know how to respond, so he adjusted his sweaty grip on his reins and said nothing. He hoped it was the right decision.

When no further physical retaliation befell him, he relaxed the tiniest bit as they began to see more impoverished plebes pass them the closer they came to the docks.

"Where are we to meet Reynolds?" the squire asked after a safe amount of time had passed.

"In the basement of a tavern around here …"

As Lord Piereva proceeded to give directions, his mind turned over the news of the cook knocking out one of his men. His eyes squinted, and his jaw set itself unconsciously.

Perhaps I should start investigating Helmer's runt after all.

CHAPTER 43
A FRIENDLY FACE

Lord Piereva strode through the garden door to the kitchen, waving over his shoulder for the knights to remain outside in the blistering sun and whirring insects.

Fin looked up only briefly from the cake that he was pouring an opaque glaze over to see who was paying him a visit.

"Lord Piereva, to what do I owe the pleasure?"

"One of your aides outside dares to threaten me. I will have your word that you will see her punished."

Fin straightened and fixed the man with a blank expression.

Are there poisonous fumes in this kitchen? Are the kitchen staff brain damaged?! Lord Piereva growled in his mind as he wondered why none of the people he had met showed any ounce of fear.

"What did Hannah threaten you with and why?" He almost sounded bored.

Lord Piereva grit his teeth.

"You even know exactly the aide I'm speaking of! I suppose your lack of disciplining the wench is—"

"Did you behave inappropriately toward Hannah?" Despite the light tone Fin used, he drew out his cooking knife and began slowly polishing it with the tea towel he had tucked in the front of his apron.

"I was questioning the group of knights regarding you, a mere cook, being in charge of their duties. She was disrespectful when she told me to go talk to you." The growl in Lord Piereva's voice only made Fin glare. He watched the unmoving cook gripping his knife warily.

"I am in charge of those knights because of their sexual harassment toward Hannah. Meaning there is zero tolerance for that kind of behavior toward my staff. Are you saying there is nothing you said to Hannah that would've warranted her telling you to come see me?" There was something about the intense stare Fin was giving him that made his temper darken.

"You dare question me on behalf of a mere maid?"

"Maid or queen, man or child, harassment is not tolerated by anyone in my kitchen or toward my staff." Fin's voice was quiet, and he remained completely unaffected by the murderous glare from the man in front of him.

"I will bring this up with your king to see if he feels the same," Lord Piereva hissed.

"Please do. Until then, I ask that you refrain from talking to my staff. Is there anything else I can get for you, my lord?" Fin asked, his emotionless voice grating on Lord Piereva even more.

"Why yes, there is. I happened to speak with the Troivackian chief of military about you. It would seem you lied about your relationship to him," Lord Piereva snarled, ignoring his orders to not reference the discovery before Aidan Helmer himself descended upon his offspring.

Fin stilled and straightened.

There was a strange, unnatural glow in his eyes that had Lord Piereva taking a step back.

"I did not lie. I have no father in the Troivackian court. I was raised by my mother alone," he explained quietly.

"You expect me to believe your mother had a virgin birth?" Lord Piereva scoffed before continuing, enjoying the sight of Fin's hand clutching the knife hard enough to turn his knuckles white.

"Or are you saying you're a bastard?" The last word dripped with scorn and condescension.

Fin continued staring at Lord Piereva in silence, calculating the noble's odds of death should he be "accidentally" clubbed with an iron pan.

No ... I can't do anything that could end up harming Annika ...

Then again ... I can always do what I do best.

Fin almost chuckled aloud, but kept it firmly locked in his chest.

He tilted his head suddenly and peered with a small frown at Lord Piereva.

"Do all Troivackians have to shave their earlobes?"

Whatever Lord Piereva had been expecting in response to his taunts, it hadn't been that.

"You impertinent little sh—"

"You dared to insult my mother with your casual assumptions. Now, be on your way, I have work to do." Fin waved airily, indicating that Lord Piereva was to exit, before he began slicing the cake so deftly and precisely that the noble was momentarily mesmerized.

"You think you can dismiss me? You are worth less than the dirt beneath my boot."

"Unless you plan on eating aforementioned dirt for the rest of your time here in Daxaria, I recommend you remove yourself from my kitchen."

Never in his life had Lord Piereva been treated thusly. There wasn't an ounce of fear in the cook, and what was more, he appeared some-how … amused.

It was then a small voice of reason weakly spoke in Lord Piereva's head, not used to being heeded.

For him to be so confident … it means he has magic.

Lord Piereva smiled slowly.

"I think we should have another talk soon, Mr. Ashowan. I'll be keeping a *very* close eye on you." There was a strange glint in his eyes as he stared at Fin. The cook, however, continued ignoring him and turned his attention to a batch of cookies that were cooling.

With a swish of his ebony cape, Lord Piereva left the kitchen, making Fin's instincts prickle as he did so.

Something wasn't right.

That tyrant would never give up so easily. Fin began pondering carefully what had changed Lord Piereva's ambitions, but he couldn't figure it out. Whatever it was, it was making him feel incredibly uneasy.

When he couldn't ignore the loud warning signs in his gut, he sum-moned the serving staff to deliver the teatime snacks. Once that task had been completed, he took a moment of rest, crossing his arms and leaning his shoulder against the side of his hearth. He stared blindly at the table as server after server came and cleared the plates.

He brought up my father … so he must've wanted to get a reaction from me, but why? Was he trying to see if I would use my magic? Does my father even know what my abilities are, exactly?

Sighing, Fin shook his head and headed out to the garden pathway as the last footman disappeared with a tiered plate dish ladened with cakes, cookies, and small sandwiches.

He stared at the tidy rows of herbs that flourished under the meticulous care of the Royal Gardener, and slowly crouched down.

He had been putting off trying out this new branch of his abilities but decided he could use the distraction.

Closing his eyes, Fin attempted to reach out his magic toward the herbs. Not to request anything, but to see what he could sense about them. He still found it hard to believe.

Tickles!

Tickles!

Danger?

Danger?

Friend?

Fin's eyes fluttered open, surprised.

The basil leaves had begun curling in on themselves, while the dill fluttered despite there being no breeze. The pepper plants gently lifted their ripening vegetables toward him as though eager to meet him.

Not all the plants had responded, but Fin was surprised that he could sense anything at all. The peace the delicate greens felt was unlike anything he had sensed before.

They all seemed completely content and at one …

He could also tell that they would not obey him nearly as easily as they would an earth witch, but that he could sense their well-being was more than he had been anticipating!

It wasn't at all like when he commanded objects in his kitchen.

"Mr. Ashowan?" Fin straightened immediately and turned to see Peter standing beside Hannah with an unreadable smile on his face.

"Well now there's a sight for sore eyes." Fin offered his hand and Peter shook it, grinning.

"Physician Durand says I am fit to return to peeling and prepping vegetables so long as I don't do any heavy lifting. Ruby says Heather can stay on to help—at least until the suitors leave."

Fin nodded with a small grin.

"Very well, I'll grab you a paring knife and get you working. You might regret getting out of bed so soon."

Peter chuckled. "Not a chance. I was going mad with boredom. Though there was a bit of excitement yesterday afternoon."

Fin nodded idly as he turned to the kitchen. He failed to notice the devious smile Hannah shot Peter, who in turn had to take real pains not to laugh.

"I happened to be taking a lap around the second floor of the castle to work up my endurance, when I heard Lady Jenoure's maid Clara inquiring about a rose that appeared in her bed chamber. She was talking with some of the entourage for both Zinferans, but no one knew anything about it."

Fin gave no indication that the news affected him as he rounded his cooking table, other than his face becoming devoid of any emotion as he reached underneath the table and procured a knife for Peter.

He handed the small blade to him and began wiping down the cooking table to begin preparing for dinner.

"Apparently Lady Jenoure is a little upset, if what I was given to understand was correct ..."

Still, Fin remained stoically unreadable.

"I hope everything is put to rights for the viscountess, then. You two better get to work. Tonight, we are serving duck. We will serve it with a beet salad and mashed potatoes with caramelized onions. So lots of peeling to get done."

The look of disappointment on both of the aides' faces made Fin narrow his gaze.

As the two turned and slowly trudged to the garden door, Hannah suddenly perked up and swung around.

"How was your first dance lesson this morning?" she asked excitedly.

Fin continued staring at her skeptically, and after a moment of saying nothing, she had the decency to blush.

"It would seem I am as unskilled as the prince. Now get back to work."

Fin watched them go and didn't move a muscle until they were out of eyeline.

They better not be doing what I think they're doing ... he thought to himself slowly before turning to the task at hand of preparing dinner.

Fin strode through the castle door and across the corridor to the larder door, where he began collecting ingredients for dinner.

As he did so, his mind turned to the news that Annika was upset by the rose he had left on her bedside ...

It had been a stupid impulse on his end.

She had been flushed with fever and fast asleep when he had knocked and opened the door a crack to drop off the bloom, and against his better judgment, he had still entered her vacant chamber.

He had left it there for her to see, hoping that at the very least, perhaps it'd brighten her day.

He didn't know it'd lead to such a fuss ...

Why is anything to do with that woman complicated?!

Shaking his head, Fin proceeded with starting to pull out the ingredients he would need to prepare the dinner. He was in the middle of the chore, when a series of giggles drew his attention down the corridor.

He had to blink several times over to make sure he wasn't hallucinating at the sight of a blond woman clad in bright yellow silk, flanked by a brunette wearing pale green and another woman in pale purple, strolling down past the servants dining hall.

Fin hurried back into his kitchen. Something about their presence didn't bode well with his already overworked instincts.

He thought he was out of the woods after a few moments when he heard neither a knock or a titter, but the Gods liked to have a laugh on occasion at his expense. The unmistakable sound of raised whispering voices suddenly broke out outside the castle door.

Gods, what now?

To Fin's slow horror, the door opened and in walked the ladies. Each of them lifted their skirts even higher off the ground to avoid getting them dirty. They peered around the room in awe and wonder, as though they had never before seen a kitchen. Then they all shot Fin sidelong glances and whispered behind their hands.

"I beg your pardon, ladies, but is there a purpose to this most unexpected visit?" Fin hoped the pained note in his voice went unnoticed by them.

"Mr. Ashowan, I am Baroness Emily Gauva, this here is Lady Aurora Danen." The blond woman in the center gestured to the brunette with straight hair in pale purple, who had wide blue eyes.

"And this here is Lady Everly Lamont." The other brunette had a face full of freckles and somber hazel eyes.

Fin gave the shallowest of bows and hoped they grew annoyed and left.

"We came down to this er ... room." Lady Gauva cast a disparaging glance around the kitchen as the women behind her giggled.

None of them noticed the broom behind them that levitated in the air indignantly and shook itself angrily at their backs. Fin could feel the tic under his left eye begin anew. He forced the broom to go back to its corner and remain motionless.

"I see that you have come to my kitchen. However, I am very busy preparing for dinner this evening, so if there is nothing more, please have a lovely day." Fin bowed, dismissing them as he then chose the most un-savory task of his cooking to begin with in hopes of scaring them off.

He opened the bottom of a beheaded and plucked duck and began pulling out its entrails.

Fin didn't look but heard all humor in the women drop away, and instead a small squeak drew his attention upward. He tried not to smile in triumph at the matching expressions the three women wore as they stared sickened at the mess on the table.

"W-We came down because," Lady Gauva swallowed with great diffi-culty and began to turn a delicate shade of green.

"M-my maid, Valerie, sh-she heard that y-you tried to give a rose to M-Mr. Howard," Lady Lamont jumped in, sounding quite faint when she spoke, but what she said had Fin fighting off the urge to laugh hysterically with everything he had.

"I see, and … where is it your maid heard such a thing?" Fin sounded as though he were being choked, and to both his utter horror and delight, the women all suddenly looked at him sympathetically.

Lady Gauva rested her lily-white hand on her chest as she stepped forward and her tone took on one of a "wise matron."

"Mr. Howard was muttering about, and I am sorry to have to repeat these words to you Mr. Ashowan, but he said, 'That idiot cook trying to give me a flower—I know his game.' That is all Lady Lamont's maid was able to hear, and we just wanted to come offer our condolences for your rejection."

Fin was terrified to speak. He was going to laugh until he was crying if he tried.

Fortunately, the women believed his silence and small blush were from shame.

"No use in dwelling on it. Mr. Howard has chosen your aide Peter—a slap in the face, I'm certain, since Peter is under your care, after all. However, try to rise above the inclination to take out any hurt feelings on the man. You shouldn't stand in the way of love."

Fin risked a small nod.

He was slowly getting himself back under control when he man-aged to speak.

"Th-Thank you. For your kind words."

Lady Gauva nodded, looking entirely too pleased with herself.

"Perhaps you can go tell Mr. Howard my congratulations, and to be a little kinder to me … I … I don't think I can manage it on my own." Fin's lips twitched; he wasn't certain what was lending him strength enough to keep a straight face through it.

The ladies all sighed clutching their chests as they shared determined glances to their new cause.

"Of course. Mr. Howard has always been a bitter brute, but we will not let him abuse your gentle nature any longer." The ladies began to chatter over how insensitive the king's assistant was, and Fin was relatively sure he'd be laughing until nighttime. It was around that time when they were interrupted, however.

"What is it you've done to earn the presence of these glorious ladies, Mr. Cook?" A smooth male voice that, though quiet, was easily heard, made the three nobles twirl around with a mass rustling of silk.

Leaning against the doorframe of the garden exit stood a man of average height, sandy brown hair, and deep green eyes. He was lean with a clear complexion and, all in all, quite pleasing to look at. Or so Fin guessed, given the excited breathiness in Lady Gauva's voice when she spoke.

"Oh my—Reese Flint!"

Fin caught the profile of the ladies and saw their pinkened cheeks. He immediately became intrigued and studied the man in the doorway more closely.

Who was he?

"If you fine flowers wouldn't mind letting me have a word with the cook here, that would be greatly appreciated. Besides, you all should be enjoying the sunshine on such a gorgeous day and going for carriage rides down by the water." He smiled brilliantly at them, and the women seemed to all forget how to speak for a moment.

"O-Of course! Come, ladies, we will let Mr. Flint speak with our beloved cook."

The three noblewomen filed out of Fin's kitchen all wearing dazed, excited expressions.

Fin turned to look at the man he had never met before, who strolled in with an easy grace and peered around the room with casual interest.

"Do I know you?" Fin asked after a moment of awkward silence.

"Not yet." The man turned a warm smile on Fin, one that made him both equal parts curious and wary.

"I am Reese Flint, the newest bard and minstrel for the Royal Court of Daxaria, and I am just *dying* to get to know you."

CHAPTER 44
MAN OF MYSTERY

Fin stared at the man in front of him blankly, something he expected the newcomer to bristle about given his far warmer reception from the ennobled ladies.

To his surprise, however, Reese Flint didn't seem to mind at all.

Reese pulled up a chair and seated himself in front of Fin, ignoring the mess of innards on the table, and turned his gaze expectantly toward him.

"What is it you're here for?" Fin was more confused than annoyed at that point, but then again it never took him long to make the journey to the other emotion.

"Stories, Mr. Ashowan. A good bard and minstrel endears himself to the community to learn their stories. Their passions, their sorrows, their … lives. We then try to encapsulate it through the most noblest of art forms: music." Reese placed his hand on his chest and gave a small bow from his seat, accompanied by a flourished wrist motion.

"You come here … when I am trying to cook for hundreds of people … to ask me to tell you … stories?" Fin's expression was unreadable, but the young man didn't seem to be phased in the least.

"Of course! You can cook and talk, can you not? I see you are an independent fellow who likes his quiet—I noticed all your aides work outdoors. I've found, though, that the quiet ones can be the most interesting at times! I once was bedding a lovely tavern owner who hadn't spoken more than five syllables the entire evening, and wouldn't you know it? As soon as I start kissing their—"

Fin cleared his throat loudly as he continued staring in shock at the man before him.

"Right. Not everyone likes the details. Anyway, it turns out this tavern owner used to own and run a brothel, but when the girls got too old, this kind person opened a tavern for the girls to work in instead!"

Reese finished, looking entirely convinced in his reasoning. As he stared at Fin's stricken expression, he decided to continue his persuasive antics to entice Fin to share his inner thoughts.

"Take this gossip about a love triangle between yourself, the king's assistant, and the aide who works under you, for example! That alone is enough fodder for an entire ballad or two. Though, I must tell you, it isn't nearly as awkward as bedding a witch and a mage at the same time and them only discovering the fact while in the middle of the act. Did you know a witch and a mage are two very different things?! I'll tell you now in case you ever are in such a situation yourself: they become *very* violent when you tell them of being ignorant of such a thing."

Fin debated punting the man out of his kitchen then and there.

"Let me tell you, if you ever get a chance to bed a fire witch? The sayings are true. Fire witch on the streets, brings heat in the sheets." Reese fanned himself slightly as his eyes grew distant with memory.

Fin blinked. He had never in life ever heard a man be so abundantly open about being a whore. Not while sober, anyway …

What's more, Reese took obvious delight in the entirety of seducing, sleeping with, and talking about it with the world.

As amusing as the bard was, however, Fin had work to do, and he opened his mouth to tell his guest. Reese, on the other hand, felt there'd been too many seconds of silence, and so plundered on with his usual reckless abandon.

How was anyone supposed to interject a sentence if all he did was talk?!

"I once had a particularly exciting evening with a Troivackian, and let me tell you, that entire populace in my experience cries more in the throes of passion than a newborn babe."

Fin's jaw dropped. He both wanted to hear more and not at the same time. While he was attempting to make up his mind, Reese predictably continued talking.

"I see now that my chatter has encroached on time spent better on getting to know *you!* So tell me, you tall drink of water, what's your story?" Reese Flint winked and beamed his most enticing smile yet.

In the seconds that ensued Reese's lengthy introduction, Fin finally found himself slowly snapping out of his stupor. Freed from the strange hold Reese had had on his ability to function, he slowly resumed his preparation of the duck on his table.

"I'm a private person who doesn't like random people crowding my kitchen."

While the words were curt, the tone in which they were spoken was hesitant and faint.

"Fair enough! I'll come back again tomorrow. Don't you worry, Finlay Ashowan, you and I will be thick as thieves in no time. By the way, I loved your sausage," he said, standing swiftly.

"I beg your pardon?" Fin's mind went blank.

"You made sausage last night for dinner, and it was perfection. Just like you." The man gently wiped his thumb across his lower lip, a movement that Fin wasn't sure why, but drew his attention immediately.

"Just a thought for you, though, have you ever slapped a couple buns over the meat? Pile some good sauce in there and I think you'd have a messy but fulfilling time."

Fin's jaw dropped for what felt like the hundredth time that day. His face was frozen between a smile of amusement and shock.

"You're the professional, though, so ignore me if that isn't how you'd like it." Reese then proceeded to all but skip out of the kitchen, leaving in his wake a seriously perturbed cook.

Fin looked down at the floor, where Kraken sleepily cracked open a bright green eye.

"He's going to come back every day until I talk more with him, isn't he?"

Unless it isn't really talking he's interested in … Fin thought to himself briefly before shaking his head and the thought free of the confines of his skull.

Kraken gave a large yawn and resumed his slumber, leaving Fin sighing and continuing his preparation for dinner alone. Never in his life had he been so at a loss for words for such a prolonged period of time, but then again, he'd never met a man like Reese Flint before.

After receiving a discreet message from Mr. Howard, Fin stood awkwardly in his cottage in the presence of the king and Annika. The shutters were closed, the fire dwindled down to embers as the summer heat weighed down every breath, but he had lit enough candles that the room was cast in a bright glow.

Annika stood to his left, her hands clasped in front of her, and the subtlest of frowns on her face as the king stared levelly at the both of them from his seated position at the table. Annika was clad in a plain black dress and had worn black leather gloves for the clandestine meeting. With their cloaks on during the cloudy night, the noble duo was nearly fully invisible.

Fin hadn't a clue as to why he was there, and sincerely hoped no one had caught wind of their kiss earlier that week.

"Thank you for allowing us in your home, Mr. Ashowan. It would've been too obvious if I had summoned you to the council room, and it would've placed Lady Jenoure in an even more awkward position with the suitors present in the castle."

Fin gave a brief nod as he tried to ignore the aggressive tingling in his body at Annika's close proximity.

"Forgive me, the two of you have met, yes?" the king began sternly.

Fin tried his hardest not to let out an audible sigh of relief mixed with a laugh.

It was then he made the mistake of looking at Annika to share in the glad tidings of not being discovered. She had in fact looked to him as well, and the moment their gazes locked, it was as though every drop of blood in Fin was pulled to her.

"Yes, Your Majesty. We have met," Annika replied, swiftly returning her cool gaze to the king.

"Excellent. I have summoned you both here in light of a few pressing issues as of late." The king stood, his hands clasped behind his back as he strolled in front of the two in front of him.

"It has come to my attention that Lord Piereva is suspicious of you, Mr. Ashowan. He has assigned a man to patrol by your kitchen every hour and report what he sees. Is there a reason for this?"

Fin felt his spine stiffen, and while he sensed out of the corner of his eye a shift in Annika's stance to peer at him, he didn't dare look at her again.

"I believe for some reason Lord Piereva learned that my father is the current chief of military for Troivack," Fin explained, bracing himself for the questions that would undoubtedly follow.

To his immense surprise, none took place.

The king frowned deeply as he nodded to himself, continuing to study Fin closely.

"I see. That is problematic indeed … they will most likely assume you are a spy. Or at the very least try to recruit you," he reasoned, leaning against the table behind him and crossing one leg over the other.

"Your Majesty, why is it you have called for my presence?" Lady Jenoure bowed her head demurely and almost made Fin roll his eyes at the sight.

"Annika, you have a unique advantage in that you have a maid who is under the employ of your brother reporting to him. A maid that could report … false information, should you allow it," the king began slowly.

"Yes, Your Majesty?" Annika asked after sending a darting glance at Fin. It was odd that the king was bringing up her espionage activities when he claimed to have no knowledge of the depth of relationship between herself and Fin.

"I want you to continue feeding your brother's belief that Fin is the spy. It will occupy his time, and he will not be able to take action against Mr. Ashowan while under the castle roof," the king explained, watching the two people in front of him carefully.

"Sire, you would like me to be a decoy?" Fin realized, surprised.

"Yes. I understand this puts you in some peril. For that I am sorry, and I can assure you we will do everything we can to keep you safe. However, there are concerning reports we've received that we need a little more breathing room to examine," the king explained vaguely, though he did appear apologetic while looking to Fin.

"It should be fine with me. I'm not that interesting of a person anyway." Fin shrugged.

Both Annika and the king snorted.

When they realized that they both had had the same reaction, the two nobles stared suspiciously at each other.

"Lady Jenoure, is there a reason why, when you do not know Mr. Ashowan well, that you found what he said funny?"

Fin knew better than to doubt her ability to lie.

"I know what I've heard around the castle. For someone who is allegedly 'uninteresting,' he has an impressive variety of opinions about him. Some admire him, others hold him in respectful regard, a select few are wary of him. It takes a complicated man to warrant a complicated reputation," Annika explained wisely, while shooting Fin a look so dirty that he felt he needed to bathe immediately after the meeting.

"... Or it takes a private man with an imaginative staff," Fin grumbled, quietly.

"A good observation." The king gave a single slow nod to Annika, pointedly ignoring Fin's remark. He still appeared slightly uneasy, but the explanation had sound reasoning behind it.

"Mr. Ashowan, I want you to write down nonsense with random numbers, and hand them to anyone of import that strolls through your kitchen. An example would be if you wrote, *The Dragon has found six eggs, prepare a basket.*"

Fin nodded. Simple enough. He could write several in advance to save time.

"I will tell the nobles you are practicing your ability to write and that they are to give their appraisal of your penmanship. It sounds ludicrous enough to draw a great deal of attention to you from Lord Piereva, so be prepared. The noblewomen of the castle are quite curious about you, so they may not think too much on the odd situation."

Fin had to fight off the urge to cringe at the idea of having to see and deal with multiple nobles in a day.

"I'm sure Mr. Ashowan would relish the opportunity to meet more of our esteemed, titled peers." Annika sounded genuinely sincere in her comment, and it was Fin's turn to shoot her a withering look that she ignored wholly.

"Excellent. Annika, I want you to direct the maids' attention to the strange goings on—as well as address your notes on Mr. Ashowan's reputation."

Lady Jenoure nodded dutifully without a word and at last satisfied, the king straightened, and fixed his gaze on Fin once again.

"Should you feel you are in danger at any time, please let me know by issuing a code to Mr. Howard. Let's say ... 'The roasts have gone bad.'"

Fin nodded once more, and the king then turned to Annika.

"We will take our leave this evening."

Gracefully, she strode over to the hook where they had both hung up their black cloaks. She shook her cloak slightly before sweeping it over her shoulders, keeping her gaze downcast the entire time.

Fin struggled to keep his eyes off of her and failed horribly. Fortunately, the king was too preoccupied in donning his own cloak and failed to observe this obvious show of emotion.

"Have a good evening, Mr. Ashowan." The leader of the country gave a single solemn nod before opening the door and stepping out into the night.

"You as well, Your Majesty, and Lady Jenoure." Fin bowed low; it was the only way he could stop himself from staring at her.

Once the door had closed, he stood erect and rubbed the back of his neck, staring at the door. *If anything, that visit just confirms how ill-matched we'd be. This cottage is all I could offer her.* Fin peered down as Kraken suddenly brushed against his leg. It was when he looked down to the small animal that he noticed that he had inadvertently been clenching his fists.

Fin managed a tight smile down at Kraken, whose pupils were the size of marbles. Black tail swishing, the feline then sauntered over to a small black pile on the floor in front of the door.

Fin frowned as he stepped forward and bent down.

His heart skipped a beat when he recognized what he was looking at then. It was Annika's gloves. A rush of happiness, worry, fear, and excitement burst through him. She'd dropped them on purpose. She was going to come back to see him and … and … *Then what?*

CHAPTER 45
EVERYTHING AND NOTHING

Fin stared dumbly at the closed door, caught in the unpleasant whirl-wind of his chaotic emotions. Lady Jenoure was coming back to see him. Why, though?

He picked up the black gloves on the ground and slowly turned back to his small cottage. He carefully placed the soft, shining leather on his worn kitchen table … He almost laughed at the absurdity of seeing gloves that were probably worth more than half his belongings resting so inno-cently in his home.

Fin slowly lowered himself into a chair as he continued studying the leather material, lost in thought. Even from where he was sitting, there was the spicy smell of Annika tinting the air, making his heart do an impressive series of somersaults. Gods, he wanted to be with her …

We truly know nothing of one another. It isn't worth the risk to her. Fin began his usual litany of reasons why he couldn't ever pursue Lady Jenoure. The same tired list he had been reciting at least ten times a day since their kiss …

She and I could end up hating each other, and then she would have risked and gambled it all on me. I'd never forgive myself for letting her take such a ridiculous path just to find out if we might work. He slowly felt his heart slowing down as the sobering logic of reality trickled down his back.

Even if I were to gain some small amount of wealth, I am untitled, and a marriage between us would be deeply frowned upon ... she would be forced out of the castle. Our children would be outcasts ... Fin imagined Annika dressed in peasant clothes, forced into hours of hard labor in order to get food on the table. He knew weaker women than Lady Jenoure had done it, but that wasn't the point ...

She'd been raised in great wealth and luxury her entire life, would she really be satisfied with such a bleak future? She'd never be able to see the queen again, and would have to quit espionage, or become a mercenary, which was far more dangerous ...

There really was no way they could make it work. It wasn't like he could prance up to the king and say, *"Your Majesty, I've saved your wife's life and your unborn child's, not to mention hundreds of lives in the castle from Hilda. I'm helping you evaluate battle plans and assessing whether or not my father will attack in a predictable way. I'm now a decoy spy. Give me a title and a raise or I'll let the entire country burn!"*

"Speaking of letting the country burn ..." Fin muttered to himself and began rubbing his face tiredly.

Annika is supposed to marry in order to gain military support from Zinfera. She can't let Daxaria fall to ruins just because she doesn't want to— Wait a moment. Why is she telling me we can be together? She wouldn't lose the Zinferan support just to run off with a cook. What is she planning? His mind began whirring to life. There were pieces missing from the story ... Annika was doing something ... but what?

Well, unless she tells me, I have no business knowing, Fin finally acquiesced to himself, after moments of wracking his brain trying to see what she could be plotting.

I'll be firm. I will apologize to her again about the kiss the other day, explain about the rose as a calm adult, and everything will be fine.

The brattle of the latch lifting in his front door had Fin's heart tripling in speed immediately. His mind went blank as the familiar cloaked figure slipped into the cottage, and gently closed the door behind them.

He was only just remembering to breathe as he stood up when, with a slight billowing from her cloak, Annika was beside him, standing on her tiptoes. Her lips brushed near his earlobe, sending electric tingles throughout his entire body. Every hair on his arms was raised and his skin became covered in goosebumps.

"There is a Troivackian knight patrolling around your cottage—he's most likely one of my brother's men. Is the cottage still soundproof?" she whispered, her bare left hand resting on Fin's forearm, and he could feel his previous resolve deteriorating all too quickly.

After blinking several times and swallowing with great difficulty, he replied in a surprisingly normal volume.

"Yes, it is. No one can hear or see in." He snapped his fingers, and all the shutters and the front door creaked slightly. "Now no one can get in."

Annika was still touching his arm when he glanced back down at her. The expression on her face humbled him as an array of emotions crossed through her warm brown eyes. Brown eyes that he knew could turn sharp and deadly, eyes that shone when he made her laugh …

"Excellent." Annika slowly pulled her hand away, though she remained glued to his side.

Fin refused to admit that he felt the loss of her touch more keenly than he had been prepared for.

"I left my gloves here so that we could have a few minutes to chat. Though the king is waiting for me, so I won't be long." The stiff formality in her voice made his stomach twist unpleasantly.

"How is your wound? I know you were—" Fin started immediately, the notion of him behaving with any measure of composure a forgotten memory.

"Mr. Ashowan, you've made your position clear. Please do not be heartless and behave so dotingly." Her clipped tone cut through him, and Fin found himself slowly straightening his shoulders. He had unconsciously been leaning closer, trying to be nearer to her being.

"My apologies." He fought the urge to rub the back of his neck as Annika swept by him and plucked up her gloves from his table.

"I came back here because what I have to say would alert the king to our being more closely acquainted than he knows," she began in a businesslike manner.

All Fin could do was swallow—albeit with great difficulty—and nod.

"His Majesty is unaware of how much you know about my espionage work. The rest of our … encounters will obviously never come to light. I returned in order to give you some tips and insight for your duties."

Annika didn't bother removing her cloak as she clasped her hands gently in front of herself, her face a cool mask of poise and grace. At that moment, she was a viscountess. A member of higher nobility bestowing Fin her expertise so that he wouldn't make the whole scenario a blundering failure.

"Code words to use that will provoke my brother the most; His Majesty mentioned one of them before: Dragon. That is my code name, and so if you use this, he will definitely grow more interested and suspicious."

While Fin was able to calm his features into one of serenity, his eyes still blazed as they continued meeting Annika's.

"Another few words would be: Spice boats, rose dusk, and Troivack ale."

Fin's eyebrows twitched.

"I don't suppose you'd be interested in telling me what those words meant when you did use them. For the sake of keeping things convincing," he pried slightly.

"Sadly, I cannot. That is a matter of great secrecy; not even the king knows all of it." Her reply was brisk, and Fin was relatively certain he could see the tension in her shoulders.

"Are there any other helpful tips my lady might suggest?" Fin couldn't help the slightly dry tone of voice as he tried to remember how they were being so rigid toward each other was thanks to *his* decision, and he needed to live with that.

"Yes. Stop doing things for free. You're worth more than this." She gestured vaguely around the cramped space. "I am not saying that for any other reason than as someone who knows about political advancement," Annika explained when Fin's expression turned wary.

"Villagers who volunteer to fight in a war and serve their country don't expect anything more than a small pay," he pointed out tightly. He was already feeling himself grow deeply uncomfortable.

"A village soldier who saves hundreds of people, including the king's wife and unborn, receives financial rewards *and* at the very least a promotion in the military," Annika pointed out flatly.

"If you'd had an ounce of political acumen, you'd be already in a far more esteemed position. You probably would've already been knighted if you had played your cards right. Not to mention being a witch? You could even seek to become a diplomat between the Coven and His Majesty." Her gaze was fierce as she leveled Fin with a no-nonsense look.

It took him a minute to gather his thoughts and burning pride to reply.

"There have not been enough incidents with witches in the kingdom to warrant a diplomat between the Coven and the castle. As for being knighted and promoted … I don't want to be a knight. I don't want to be a warrior. I'm a cook. I love cooking, creating recipes, taking care of people in my own way from afar. Sometimes a good bowl of soup or a buttered piece of fresh bread can make a terrible day feel better. I love what I do. I don't do it because I need money, or I want power … I do it because it's how I make the world better." Fin no longer could meet her eyes. He had never once in his life felt ashamed for his profession. Had never felt guilty for not wanting to be more … At least until the past few weeks.

"The only reason I would ever want more is to …" Fin trailed off and felt his right hand clench into a fist. No. He couldn't say it.

"For me?" Annika's voice was soft.

He couldn't look at her. Couldn't take whatever he'd find in her face. Pity? Disappointment?

"I'll admit, I don't want to be seen or treated as weak or deficient like when I was growing up, but …"

"… You like being a cook," she finished for him quietly.

Steeling himself, Fin looked at Annika. He was attempting to brace himself for whatever soul-crushing reaction he'd find in her beautiful face.

What he saw, however, was a look of such clear, abundant …

No. Don't think it. Please, no, Fin begged himself.

She wasn't upset or angry with him.

She was something much, much worse.

"Why do you keep everyone far from you if you like what you do?" Annika asked gently. The warmth in her voice could've brought a cold-hearted killer to his knees.

"Not everyone feels as accepting of witches. Not to mention a lot of people think we can just magic away their issues or predict their futures. You can be friends with someone who says they understand, but if they're ever in trouble and you can't help them, things aren't ever the same." A haunted look crossed Fin's face, and even though Annika wanted to ask questions, she held her tongue.

"I think the people in your kitchen are more accepting than you realize. You've taught them well." Even though there was a soft teasing note to Annika's words, Fin couldn't help but fight a cold sweat.

"I don't really want to find out again," he replied, his voice rasping.

Giving his head a shake, he rubbed the back of his neck and let out a long breath.

"I really am sorry. I honestly have no idea why for you it's … me, of all people." Fin suddenly felt incredibly weary, as he once again met Annika's eyes and noted the gentle pursing of her mouth.

"For many reasons. But if Hank taught me anything," Annika took a shaky, steadying breath, "love is one of those damnable parts of life we can't always fully understand."

Fin felt doused in warm glowing magic.

She'd said it.

He couldn't dismiss what he thought he saw in her gaze from before anymore.

She loved him.

At that moment, nothing else existed.

Time could've stopped, for all he knew.

There was a force greater than he could fathom filling the air, and he didn't know what to do about it.

"If you could trust me, Fin—take a leap of faith?—I think I could make it possible for us." She whispered the words, and he felt emotion grip his throat closed.

"I just need to know you are in this with me as much as I am. I won't lie and say there isn't a risk, but I'm willing to try if you are." Despite her face being composed and controlled, Fin saw her grip her gloves.

His heart screamed to accept.

Yet the image of Annika toiling away the rest of her life as a peasant leapt into his mind's eye and stopped him.

How those warm loving eyes could change and regard him with cold hatred. How she would place her trust in him, but he would fail her one day. Then all he would be able to do would be to watch the chasm between them grow and grow helplessly, while they remained imprisoned together by their youthful transgressions.

Petrified by indecision and the shadows that lurked in his mind, Fin said nothing. He continued wrestling with himself, trying to win … win against the voices of his father, his tutor, the villagers, his former best friend Ian …

Even the voice of reason!

Annika shifted.

"I won't make this offer again, Fin. Believe it or not, I do have a little bit of pride left. If you're worried about having to see me upon rejecting me … truthfully, while I soon won't be required to marry one of the Zinferans or the Troivackian … I might consider doing so regardless. It seems my time in the castle after the war may be better explored elsewhere," she said with a sad smile, as she swallowed back a lump in her throat she wanted to hate.

She wanted to be angry with him, wanted to rage at him, but there wasn't anything in her to ignite with fury. Annika hated it, but he was being honest with her. He was showing her exactly who he was, and that in itself was a far larger risk than he normally took.

It wouldn't be enough, though.

How could she draw out a man who had been beaten into submission for nearly thirty years?

Because that much was obvious whenever she saw him.

While he was beginning to find his place in the world, he might not be ready to take risks for a while yet, and she wasn't really the kind of lady who liked to wait about.

Her words about potentially marrying again made Fin go visibly pale, but she turned to the door to leave all the same.

"I'm sorry about the rose," Fin blurted out, his voice coming out a croak.

Annika whirled around, an incredulous look on her face.

"That was you?!"

"I-I-I meant to give it as a 'get well soon' gift. You were sleeping, though, I shouldn't have entered your chamber, I know I—"

Annika crossed the room in three steps and kissed him.

It was breathtakingly perfect, and yet just as perfectly heartbreaking when she pulled away from him.

Fin stared down into Annika's openly broken expression.

"Think of it as a goodbye kiss. Take care, Fin, and be safe."

Without another word or a second glance back, Lady Jenoure had whisked herself into the shadows of the night.

Then all too quickly, the silence swallowed Fin whole, leaving him standing alone and defeated.

CHAPTER 46
OLD BUT GOLD

E ric stared.
    He stared back.
Eric sighed and slowly narrowed his tired hazel eyes into a glare.

"Your face will freeze like that at this rate."

The prince continued to glare as the man dipped his cookie into the goblet of milk and took a satisfying bite out of the dessert.

"Your Highness, it really isn't necessary for you to eat the entire plate of cookies. It is good for you to share."

Eric slowly turned to Fin, who was in the process of watching the exchange between Reese Flint and the prince with growing humor.

"Fin, why is *he* here?" Eric asked directly, ignoring the bard, who was seated in Eric's usual chair mowing down on Eric's morning snack with reckless abandon.

"Sorry, he is trying to make me tell him a story by refusing to leave my kitchen," Fin explained as he sipped from his coffee cup and rubbed his left eye wearily.

He hadn't gotten much sleep the previous night.

"Make him leave. You're really good at making people leave," Eric demanded, ignoring the garbled disagreement from Reese, whose mouth was full of cookie.

"I'm a little too good at it now that you mention it," Fin muttered as he took another mouthful of coffee.

"What was that, cook?" Reese Flint had swallowed the cookie in such great haste that his eyes watered from the sheer volume pressing down his throat.

"Nothing. Reese, do you really want to peeve off the seven-year-old who is going to be running the kingdom in another twenty years or so?" Fin wondered while setting his cup down on the table.

"Seven-year-olds remember nothing. Their minds are like ... what's that thing ... you'd know ..."

"A sieve?"

Reese snapped his fingers several times and pointed at Fin.

"Exactly. He'll forget all about me by then, and if he sees me again when he is all set to rule, I intend to be a handsome silver fox. I'll have transformed from my present glowing youthful self, and I will be quite unrecognizable." Reese then took the opportunity to reach for another cookie, only to see that Eric had slid the plate to his other side out of reach from the man.

"I'll remember you just fine, and I'll make sure you never get to eat another cookie again." Eric glowered threateningly.

Reese placed his hand on his chest. "My dear prince! Are you to grow up to be a tyrant?"

Fin would've laughed had he the heart or the energy.

"Alright, bard. Shove off—I got work and no time or patience for you today. Eric, you can finish the cookies, but then you better get to your studies."

Reese studied Fin closely then, an oddly mature and serious look overtaking his handsome features. "Why so tired, Fin? Got a lot on your mind?"

It was Fin's turn to glare at him. "I said shove off." He then picked up his cleaver, grabbed a watermelon from the basket to his right, and in one swift loud bang, cleaved the melon into two halves.

"Your knife show is impressive, but it'll take more than that to—"

Eric turned to Reese, stared him square in the turned cheek and said, "If you don't leave, I'll tell all the noble ladies that you took cookies from me, and I'll even pretend to cry while I do."

Reese was out of his chair and out the door without another word.

Eric turned to Fin and let out a wizened sigh that Fin had come to know meant the child was about to say something beyond his years.

"Is this about that girl you like?"

Fin was surprised the boy remembered. "Don't worry about it, Eric, I've just got a lot on my mind."

"Did you …" Eric leaned in, held his hand up to cup around his mouth, and dropped his voice to a whisper. "Did you kiss her? Is it cooties?"

Fin managed to smile slightly at that. He was about to answer him, when the door to the kitchen burst open.

"Mr. Ashowan! Someone is here for you! She came with Mage Lee's wife and is waiting at the front doors! She has an official letter from the king and wants to speak with you as well." The young maid was one Fin recalled seeing offering her support of his romance with Mr. Howard. She was very excited to see what new drama was spilling out around him, as her freckles practically glowed pink in delight.

He looked at Eric, sporting his usual magnanimous milk mustache, who gave him a small shrug of his tiny shoulders.

Sighing, Fin put the cleaver down, and trudged out the kitchen door, leaving the prince to finish his snack on his own.

His mind tried to conjure up whom he knew that could carry the king's letter and ask to see him.

A woman, if the message was correct …

His experience with women had been: those on the island, the patients he had helped his mother with, and now the women in the castle.

Perhaps it was someone from the Coven? Then again, he had already sent off his documentation of his abilities, what reason could they have for coming unless there was something wrong with what he sent?

After passing another set of maids whispering and glancing at him with obvious interest, Fin took the east wing exit near the rose maze to go around from the outside.

There would be fewer prying eyes … aside from the Troivackian man that had been trailing him the moment he left his kitchen.

The knight was having a hard time remaining inconspicuous outside, however, so despite his better judgment, Fin glanced over his shoulder and gave the man a small smile and wave.

To his immense satisfaction, the knight scowled, turned around, and walked away.

Fin continued his journey around to the front of the castle, and as he strolled closer to the massive stone steps, he hadn't set foot on since the day he faced Hilda, he could hear an authoritative woman's voice coming from the massive stone landing.

"... Preposterous! My husband is the Royal Mage to His Majesty. I will not be forced to wait outside like some mere—"

Fin resisted the urge to twitch when he realized who was shouting at the guard at the front door.

Another mage.

He was about to turn around and head back to the kitchen, not caring that he was going to ignore whoever had had the misfortune of traveling with Mrs. Lee, when his gaze crested over the landing. In the distance, he spotted a slender woman standing slightly behind the infuriated mage, clutching her hands patiently in front of her worn skirts.

She had a few gray strands floating around her wavy, shoulder-length light brown hair, and her pale face was strained with a forced blankness that he knew all too well.

Mrs. Lee was hitting some of the high notes in her litany, when the familiar face of Fin's mother turned and locked eyes on her son.

Kate let out a loud shriek and, without a second glance at her traveling companion, ran straight toward her son.

She threw her arms around him, laughing joyously, and squeezed him with all her might. Fin towered over her, yet her arms still felt comforting as he hugged her thin body back. He breathed in the familiar scent of his mother: lavender and sage. His old home.

"Oh, my boy! Let me look at you!" Kate released her son from their embrace, but still reached up to grip his upper arms as she studied him with tears in her eyes.

"Somehow I forgot how handsome you are." She moved her cool, soothing palm to his cheek as she studied him more closely.

She then noticed the dark smudges under his eyes, and the fine lines that had appeared at their corners at some point during the four months since he had left home.

"I see we need to have a talk." She gently brushed her thumb against Fin's high cheekbone and slowly turned back around.

Both Fin and his mother then noticed that they had a rapt audience back by the doors. Mage Lee's wife, two of the Royal Guards, and apparently Mr. Howard had appeared and were watching the reunion with mixed reactions.

"Mr. Ashowan?" Mr. Howard called over to them, the tightness around his eyes and his wary tone making Fin's mother cast a humorous glance at her son.

"That man looks important," she whispered to him through her teeth as she feigned a smile and took his arm to guide her as they walked back toward the doors.

"He's the king's assistant," Fin explained in hushed tones.

"Why does the king's assistant look like he knows you and doesn't like you?" Fin's mother had purposefully slowed her pace.

"I'll tell you later."

Once they were back in front of the group that had gathered, Mr. Howard waved a scroll with the king's seal on it.

"Mr. Ashowan, your mother traveled to us bearing this. Do you have any inclination what this is about?"

"Pardon me … mister?" Kate asked politely, gesturing toward the man who was glaring daggers at her son.

"Mr. Howard. I am His Majesty's assistant," the man explained while only sparing the woman a brief glance before turning his annoyed gaze back to Finlay.

"Mr. Howard, I would be happy to discuss the contents of the scroll; however, it did carry very specific instructions that I was to address the matter with His Majesty only." Kate's docile and gentle appearance must've softened Mr. Howard somewhat, because his taut expression faded slightly. With a sigh, he turned to the castle doors and disappeared back inside without a second glance at Mrs. Lee.

"You're a peasant who can read? How extraordinary. You must tell me about the brutal hardships you've overcome to have reached a rudimentary understanding of our literary language." Mrs. Lee was tall for a woman— taller than some men, in fact, as she stood at an imposing five-foot-ten inches. She easily dwarfed Fin's mother, both in size and volume; however, Katelyn Ashowan had long since grown out of the woman who cowered from her husband.

She stared coolly up at the mage with long white streaked hair, royal blue robes, and a mage crystal hanging around her neck.

"I would be happy to. Perhaps we can swap stories about your struggles to understand rudimentary manners."

One of the guards burst out laughing but was quickly silenced by Mrs. Lee's acid glare.

Fin gripped his mother by the shoulders and began to steer her away from the group, as Mrs. Lee's jaw dropped and her imperious voice shouted at them in outrage while the guards fought to regain control.

"Please tell Mr. Howard my mother will be waiting in my kitchen—"

"No need, Mr. Ashowan." The king himself stepped through the doorway, wearing a deep frown. Everyone dipped into a bow or curtsy immediately.

"If you two could please follow me."

Fin and his mother shared a brief glance before they straightened and strode past the bowed heads of the guards and Mrs. Lee.

His head and heart were racing with possibilities. He had only just seen the king the previous night, why hadn't anything been mentioned? What was going on?!

The king said nothing until they were safely closed up in the counsel room, which had very obviously been cleared of its occupants in a great haste. Maps and books were left strewn across the entire twelve-foot table, and every chair sat crookedly.

"Mrs. Ashowan, I am pleased to make your acquaintance," Norman greeted warmly.

Fin's mother blushed but gave another curtsy.

"Th-Thank you, Your Majesty." Her voice came out a whisper.

"I see here that I sent for you nearly two weeks ago by a special falcon carrier, and you have ridden hard relying on the seal to gain you military aid in your travels."

"Yes, Your Majesty. In the city of Rollom I went to the magistrate and showed him the seal. He then summoned an escort party for me—they were all very kind!" she added hastily, before nervously wringing her hands in front of herself.

Fin saw the small glimmer of friendliness in the king's eyes and knew that the man found his mother endearing. Most people did.

"Yes, they did well. How is it you came to become travel companions with Mrs. Lee?" he asked gently.

At that, Norman saw the first familial resemblance between Finlay and his mother. The woman developed a small tic in her left cheek before she answered.

"Mrs. Lee was traveling under the invitation of her husband. We crossed paths and I ... invited her along."

Fin knew by the enunciation of his mother's words that the one and only Mrs. Lee had invited herself along.

"I see." Norman nodded. If he had gleaned the same information Fin had, he didn't show it.

"Mrs. Ashowan, would you—"

"Kate."

"I beg your pardon?" Norman's tone was gentle, which was more than likely why Fin's mother felt comfortable speaking again. A gesture that made Fin appreciate his king all the more.

"Please feel comfortable to call me Kate if you prefer! Though Mrs. Ashowan is fine as well …"

Despite the woman nearing fifty, there was a youthful exuberance around her that made her hard to dislike.

"Very well, Mrs. Ashowan, would you mind kindly just waiting outside the door for a moment. I would like to have a word with your son." Kate smiled beautifully and could've been mistaken for a woman ten years younger in that moment, as she curtsied once again and rose.

"Of course!" She turned, and as she walked by her son gave his side a small pinch.

"Don't do that thing you do," she hissed worriedly before continuing out the door as if nothing had happened.

Fin kept his eyes on the king throughout the whole exchange, and once the door was firmly shut, a slow, wry smile spread across Norman's face.

"What's 'that thing you do,' Fin?" The humor in the king's voice and face made Fin break out into a juvenile grin.

"I tend to aggravate people in a very efficient manner."

"That you do. Were I not on that receiving end on occasion, I'd admire it," the king mused, only partly jesting.

Fin laughed slightly, then watched as the smile on the king's face dimmed and he exhaled tiredly. It was then Fin could see the stress and paleness on his face. The king had been carrying on as usual, exuding the aura of a calm wise leader, but in that moment his weariness broke through.

"Why was my mother summoned here with a scroll bearing your seal?" Fin dropped his voice and kept it non-accusatory.

"Remember … the night … with the fountains … and the wine …"

"Yes? Why— Oh no." Fin's jaw dropped. "How?!"

"I recall you … telling me about her healing abilities, and I was saying how I wished she could help with my wife and then—".

"Ohhh … noooo!" Fin had zero memories of the occurrence but knew exactly what must have happened. He rubbed his face furiously as though trying to work some sense into his head.

"The handwriting is mine without a doubt, albeit messier than my usual. I summoned her to help birth my second-born. I suppose Lord Fuks didn't stop all the falcons that night." The king sighed. As the two men finished processing the new consequence that their night of revelry had brought, they lifted their faces to each other.

When they locked eyes, there was a shared beat of silence, and then they both burst out laughing.

"Gods, we have to tell the other men about this!" the king roared, doubled over with tears streaming down his face.

Fin was unable to speak as he found himself void of any breath that wasn't used howling in hilarity.

His poor mother on the other side of the door, however, was more than a little perplexed on what in the name of the Gods was going on in the chamber. After all, how was it even possible for her son to be familiar with the ruler of the continent?!

Eventually when the king and Fin had both calmed down, they agreed to keep the details on Katelyn Ashowan's invitation to the castle a secret from her. Though the rest of the participants of their drunken escapades would hear all about it before evening fell.

CHAPTER 47
MOTHER DEAREST

The queen watched fascinated as the slight woman at her bedside rested gentle hands atop her rising belly, a strange warm glow appearing over her unborn. The witch who was mother to the Royal Cook was known as Katelyn Ashowan, a mutated healing witch.

As she continued staring in silence at the queen's womb, her eyes had sparks of gold in them.

The king was less calm than his wife, as he stood off to the side, torn between inactivity and wanting to demand what kind of magic Kate Ashowan was using on his wife, and why?

Ainsley must've sensed her husband was debating interrupting the process, because she shot him a warning look that kept him glued to his spot.

After another tense moment, Fin's mother straightened with a beautiful smile on her face.

"You've done well, Your Majesty. The babe is happy and healthy, though …" Kate glanced nervously at the king, a small knot of worry appearing between her thin eyebrows.

"What is it?" Ainsley asked gently, though she had already paled in fright.

"I worry you will deliver early. It was wise of your physician to place you on bed rest. Your body is unable to continue its balanced growth for much longer past another …" She pursed her mouth in deep thought as she tried to calculate when they would expect the delivery to be. "Shortly after the second moon from now, if I help you along," Kate concluded, though she sounded hesitant to say so.

"The babe isn't supposed to come for another three months!" the king exclaimed as his voice wavered against his will.

"I know, Your Majesty, and I am sorry. If it is any consolation, I have delivered a babe a fortnight even earlier than what I see for your own, and he lived on to be a strapping young man! He was a little smaller than the rest of his peers but took over his father's farm well enough."

The story did bolster the queen's spirits for a moment, until she reluctantly asked, "Is that the only tale of success you have?"

"I've had other babes around your time, some survived, some didn't. I am sorry that I cannot promise you more than that, Your Majesty." Kate curtsied with her head bowed solemnly.

Ainsley and Norman shared a look of such pain and grief in that time before Kate straightened, that even when she did rise and look at the couple, she could feel their agonizing despair.

"Do not give up all hope just yet. Sometimes that is what makes all the difference in the outcome, you know!" she cheered, trying to sound as stern with the monarchs as she did her other patients.

Ainsley smiled sadly while she continued gazing into her husband's eyes.

"Your son said that very same thing to me." Ainsley continued rubbing her stomach and tried to ignore her aching throat and the tears that wanted to fall.

"He learned it from me, of course, but I taught it because it is true. Now, would you two like to know the gender of your little warrior?" Kate kept her tone light and pleasant in hopes of drawing the distraught couple out of their dismal thoughts while also wondering just how close was her son with the royal couple for the queen to have been comforted by him?

Both the king and queen's heads snapped to her, their eyes rounded in wonder.

"Y-Your magic can tell us that?!" Ainsley was breathless when she asked.

"It can indeed. Not all parents wish to know—though that is because they think it a bad omen to know before the birth. I can promise you that that is not the case." Kate hurried to add on the last reassurance, as she could see that there was a sliver of hopefulness in both their eyes that they both desperately needed.

Ainsley looked at Norman while trying to maintain her composure. "I-I would like to know."

Norman smiled lovingly down at his wife, the faintest sheen of tears in his eyes. "Anything for you, love."

Kate blushed at such open affection between the most powerful people on the continent, but she couldn't help but smile. She could tell their marriage was something incredibly special.

"Well, Your Majesties, you are going to have your hands full with a little princess soon."

Ainsley burst out in a joyous nervous laugh, as the tears escaped her eyes without any further fight.

Norman looked dazed for a moment, then a dreamy smile spread across his face.

"Eric is going to have a sister." The king suddenly lunged for his wife, kissing and embracing her as she laughed and cried simultaneously.

Kate, feeling like an unnecessary witness to the emotional moment, excused herself quietly and left the couple alone.

She stepped outside of the chamber and closed the door softly behind herself. As soon as she released the handle, she let out a long sigh before smiling so widely that her cheeks ached.

Kate knew she would do anything and everything possible to see that babe into the world safe and sound, and she would do everything possible to see that the lass would grow into a woman as wonderful as her parents.

"Is everything alright with Her Majesty?"

Kate jumped. She hadn't heard the dark-haired beauty on her right approach, as she had been too absorbed in her own thoughts.

"The queen's health is a matter of confidentiality. If she chooses to share that information, that is up to her." Kate gave a small apologetic smile before she turned and leaned back against the wall beside the door, her hands folded tidily in front of herself.

She had anticipated the dark-haired woman to continue on her way and leave her be, only the lady seemed to be studying her closely instead.

"Can I help you, dear?" Kate asked, tilting her head quizzically to the side as she studied the woman in turn.

"You just don't look much like Fin."

Kate's eyes widened and blinked several times as she studied the stranger in front of her with renewed interest.

She was clearly a member of nobility, given the rich purple gown she wore with simple yet expensive jewelry. A long silver necklace with a glittering black diamond pendant hung around her neck, nestled in a circle of diamonds. The necklace matched her bejeweled earrings and hair ornaments that had her hair partially swept back. Yes. She was obviously a wealthy woman.

Kate looked at the woman's hands and noted that there wasn't a wedding ring.

"Fin looks a lot like his father; the only thing he got from me, unfortunately, was my heart. He did get the gold flecks in his eyes from me and the bright blue from my father, though that is harder to notice at first glance." Kate shook her head while smiling to herself fondly. "He also inherited my bumpy feet, sadly."

A corner of the noblewoman's mouth twitched, and Kate immediately grew suspicious.

It was strange how so many members of nobility seemed familiar on an intimate level with her son.

"Given your first name basis with my son, I take it you two have met?" Kate asked politely, not anticipating the sheer volume of emotions that would play through the strange woman's eyes before they resumed a pleasant blankness.

Fin, my love, what have you gotten yourself into? Kate suddenly felt overwhelming fear about what was wearing lines into the corners of her son's eyes.

"We have met on a couple of occasions, Mrs. Ashowan. He is somewhat of an enigma in the castle—he has been a part of a number of odd occurrences."

Kate sighed, and in a gesture of surprisingly easy familiarity, she stepped forward and hooked her arm through the noblewoman's arm and gently tugged her into a stroll.

"Fin likes his privacy, there's no doubt about that, though you must understand my worry as his mother about why in the world so many powerful people seem to have a close relationship with him." Kate shook her head, her gaze cast at the ground ahead in deep thought.

"He is a brilliant cook who has been incredibly vocal about his beliefs, regardless of who is challenging him," the lady ventured carefully.

"Oh Gods." Kate's free hand went to her mouth as she shook her head and terror swelled in her eyes. "He'll get himself killed here," she whispered fearfully.

"On the contrary, he seems to somehow make friends as he does these things. The king and his closest advisors are good people," Annika soothed with a caring glance. "Fin explains his points well, and so they listen—if anything, you should be worried that your son isn't assertive enough," she admitted, before realizing she had just indicated, in no uncertain terms, the exact level of knowledge she had about him.

If Kate thought this odd or peculiar, she did nothing to show it.

"Oh, he's plenty assertive if it's for someone else, but for himself? To Fin, feeling safe, warm, and able to cook good food is enough. It doesn't take him much to carve out a niche for himself—even if for others it'd be a little lonely." Kate looked slightly downcast as she voiced this, clearly lost in her own thoughts on the matter.

"You don't think he's lonely?"

"I think he prefers loneliness to the potential pain of hurting someone he cares about—or losing them. Ah, why am I filling your head with thoughts about my son? He's the cook here, and I'm not going to lie and say he isn't the best there is, but you are a lady! You're very kind for indulging my thoughtless rambling. You must have your own exciting life!"

Kate stopped and smiled warmly up at the noblewoman, though she didn't understand the sudden stricken look on the woman's face.

He has your smile too. Annika felt her stomach clench painfully.

"I actually am leaving to attend my waterfront estate this morning and shall stay for a few days. I have some household matters to attend to," Annika explained vaguely, once she regained her composure.

The duo rounded the southwest corner of the castle and began heading back up toward the northeast corner, which was closer to Annika's chamber.

"I'm surprised you live in the castle with an estate here in Austice."

"Yes, well, court is so thrilling I'd hate to miss a minute of it." Annika's distant tone earned an interested glance from Kate.

"You sound tired, dear."

Lady Jenoure cast an amused glance at Kate, who, even though she was only a couple of inches shorter than herself, felt somehow significantly smaller. Which probably made the witch seem non-threatening and easy to share the very private information of Annika's schedule.

"I have two more courting times before I can go check on my estate."

"Oh, how wonderful! Are the men handsome?" Kate queried, her excitement oddly intoxicating.

"They are," Annika admitted, but despite her efforts, she failed at blocking the glumness from her tone.

"If you'll forgive my saying, I know political marriages aren't always joyous unions. Are you doing alright?" The gentleness with which the question was asked evaporated the heavy air around Annika quicker than she knew to be possible.

She tried to smile and feign her way through her answer, and yet when she stared into the earnest eyes of Katelyn Ashowan, she somehow didn't have the energy to pretend. The woman was so obviously kind, honest, and good, it was hard to tarnish the interaction with a lie.

"I'll be fine."

The short reply was all Lady Jenoure could manage, and she smiled as serenely as possible, even though she could feel the pain she exuded in the corner of her lips.

"I see." Kate frowned, her face full of sorrow as she paused right at the corner of the north west junction of the castle. They were a mere few feet from Lady Jenoure's chamber door—not that she was aware of it.

Grasping the lady's hand in her own, she stepped in front of the dark-haired beauty.

"Do not settle, but do not let the idea of passion stop you from making a wise decision either. I did so once, and not only did I pay for it dearly, but so did my boy."

Annika flinched unconsciously, and once again Kate failed to see the exact emotional reaction her words caused.

"Sometimes the pain of bearing through no decision is better than a wrong one," she concluded with a firm nod.

Annika did manage to smile more genuinely then, when Kate suddenly frowned.

"Why is there a wound in your side?"

Annika's jaw dropped.

Fin stood at his table, wiping down the remnants of the dinner dishes, when he heard a soft knock at the garden door.

He peered up to see Jiho Ryu step over the threshold, wearing a deep blue tunic rolled up to his elbows at the sleeves, brown trousers, lustrous tall brown boots, and a long black vest.

"I thought it'd be a good time for a chat." Jiho grinned at Fin as easily as he had during the two years he had spent living with him. Though something had changed in Jiho's eyes. Something about him was more reserved. Fin recognized the shift from his time interacting with the nobility he had met since joining the castle staff. There was a moment when a wall of social divide erected itself in their mind, and it showed in their gazes, whether they knew it or not. There inevitably always came the moment where Fin was looked upon as the lower end of "those to be commanded."

He sighed, dropping his gaze. When he looked back up at his friend, however, there was only a look of pure mischief. Jiho's refined expression immediately faltered. As soon as the noble mask had disappeared, Jiho once again resembled the troublemaking dockworker from years prior.

"Oh Jiho … you aren't going to know what hit you."

Jiho began to open his mouth, when Katelyn Ashowan launched herself on the man from her hidden position behind the garden door—she had been grabbing a tankard of ale when her former patient had appeared.

Her arms were wrapped around him, and she was laughing musically.

Fin delighted in watching Jiho's stricken expression at being embraced so suddenly, but just like Fin, he recognized the familiar scent of lavender mixed with sage, and an astonished smile lit his face. He then wasted no time in wrapping his arms around the small woman clinging to him.

"Kate Ashowan! What in the world are you doing here?!" Jiho managed after the shock had worn off.

She released him and gazed happily up into his face.

"I might ask you the same thing! Look at you all decked out in finery. How is your ailment? You're eating right?"

"Yes, of course." Jiho was holding the soothing familiar hands of Fin's mother in his own and looking every bit like the chastened youth he had once been while under her watchful eye.

"I'm glad to hear it. Shall we all have a drink? I must hear about what happened to you once you went back to Zinfera! Your letters were always so vague, and while I do enjoy hearing about the spectacular trees in your country, I'd much rather hear about *you*. Tell me, are you married? Do you have any children?"

At the mention of matrimony, Jiho's levity dimmed greatly, and he flicked a sharp glance to Fin, who appeared expressionless aside from his piercing stare.

Fin gave a look filled with a heavy-handed warning.

Jiho looked back at Kate, who was watching puzzled at the two men's exchange, waiting for a reply.

"How about we all have a drink?" Jiho invited, masking his face once again and gesturing toward the cooking table with a sweeping arm.

Fin gave a tight smile and retrieved two more tankards to be filled.

His gut was double knotted in apprehension, the first knot being the haunting image of Annika Jenoure's face as she left his cottage the night before.

He got the sense that the night ahead of him was going to be another difficult one. Even though it had all the ingredients of a wonderful time with his friend and mother seated at his table with ale, there was the weighted burden of dread over whatever Jiho had actually come to say that evening.

CHAPTER 48
THE KAMIKAZE COOK

"And she didn't think to curb her tongue even after all of that?!" Kate gasped in laughter as Jiho finished his story of becoming an official noble.

"She was a proud woman and didn't like to admit defeat. Often, most nobles damn themselves by refusing to be anything less than absolutely right all the time." Jiho chuckled as he finished his third tankard of ale that evening.

Kate hiccupped and Fin rounded the table slowly.

"How about I help you to bed, mum?" he offered while gently clasping his mother's upper arms.

"Ohhh I'll be fine!" She attempted to step up out of the chair and would have fallen to the floor faster than a bag of potatoes were it not for Fin holding her up.

"It's fine, I needed a breath of fresh air anyway," he remarked with a small chuckle.

"G'night Jiho!" Kate cheered with a half wave as she allowed her son to escort her from the kitchen.

The mother and son stumbled along the waxing moonlit path to his cottage in amicable silence, when Kate suddenly threw out both her arms and turned her face up to the moon with a beaming smile.

"Oh, I haven't felt *this* divine since before you left! You know, it is terribly lonely without you there. I know I was away too often, tending to people in Rollom, and for that I'm sorry." She whirled around in the moonlight, and Fin managed to smile slightly as she fixed him with a most complex expression of regret and love.

"I'm sorry I wasn't enough to make up for your father's awfulness, and I'm sorry I didn't throw him out sooner. I won't regret marrying him, though—because it brought me you, and you are the best thing to ever happen to me. Why you seem to know so many powerful people ... to say I'm impressed and surprised is an underst-statement!" she explained sincerely, slurring as she stumbled along the path ahead.

"Glad I've exceeded your expectations, mum," Fin replied, his hands deep in his pockets and his tired mind still working desperately not to think of a particular Troivackian woman.

"Oh, love, that isn't what I meant, and you know it. You know I had a long talk with a lovely woman today. She was hovering outside the queen's chamber—had a devil of a wound in her side I helped heal, but—"

"Annika?! I mean ... Lady Jenoure, you saw Lady Jenoure?" Fin burst out, too stunned and his mind too dulled by ale to mind his tongue any better.

"... Yes! Annika Jenoure! Lovely woman." Apparently, the ale had dulled his own mother's perceptions, for she had missed her son's sudden attentiveness as she skipped along the path.

"She and I had a lovely chat about how you aren't assertive enough. I believe that you are too vocal as is, while she believes you aren't vocal enough for your own purposes. She truly is a brilliant woman—why, if it were up to her, I have no doubts she'd have you ruling the country by the sounds of it!" Kate trilled happily as they approached Fin's cottage door.

He kept a wary eye out for any Troivackian knights that might be following and noticed a shape or two shift in the distance, but they thankfully were too far away to overhear the conversation.

"I'm sure the viscountess was merely being charitable, as she enjoys my cooking," Fin reasoned aloud as he opened the door for his mother, and she stepped over the threshold with only a slight trip in her step.

"I know you know the king, the queen, Lady Jenoure, Mr. Howard—even Jiho is incredibly important now! How did this all happen?" she wondered aloud as she stumbled her way toward Fin's bedroom.

"Coincidences," Fin supplied with a small shrug of his shoulders as his mother pulled off her shoes and stockings and clambered into his bed.

"Oh son, the Goddess had a plan for you and she's seeing to it! Don't be so naïve. You must have great importance to have crossed so many wide paths. Why are you not forging your own?" she asked as she settled her head on the pillow with a contented smile on her face.

"Probably thanks to the following repetitive phrases while growing up: 'You think you're special and you're not.' 'Don't burn more than you have, you'll die out quicker.' 'Find work you enjoy and don't demand more.' 'Save others from themselves whenever you can,'" Fin muttered to himself idly while rubbing his eyes distractedly.

"My dearest, why would you listen to anyone but yourself? The Goddess talks to you about what you alone can do." Kate sighed happily as her eyes fluttered closed.

Fin smiled to himself at his mother's flushed, happy face.

He stepped into the small room and drew the quilt up over her shoulders, magically adding a log to the hearth and stoking the flames slightly higher.

As he began to turn to leave the bedroom, his mother's soft hand darted out and gently clasped his own.

"We didn't get to have a proper chat yet, but tomorrow we will, yes?" she asked softly in the darkness.

"Of course, mum," Fin assured, giving her hand a small squeeze before resting it back on the bed.

He had just set foot in the doorway to the room, when on impulse, he turned back around and asked a question that had drifted through his mind idly for years.

"Why did you marry my father?"

For a moment, he was certain that his mother had already fallen into a deep sleep, and so began to resume his exit.

"You've never asked about him since he left. Aside from wondering if he'd ever return ..." Kate's voice was quiet, and Fin could hear the exhaustion thickening her words. "Well, my love, you aren't so darn handsome for no reason. Your father was the same back then, and when I saw him, it was like I'd been struck by a vision from the Goddess. He was so passionate, and in the beginning so ... vibrant. His ideas back then weren't as radical as when you were a child ..." Fin could hear sleep claiming his mother, but she managed one final phrase.

"To be honest, I barely knew him. That's love though, you pick someone you like and play the hand that your choice deals you."

Fin's spine went rigid.

He walked out of his cottage on stiff legs and headed back to his kitchen. His mother's words were deeply troubling for some reason …

He'd sleep in front of the fire and possibly do more prep for the next day's meal. He sincerely doubted he'd get any better sleep than the night before.

The castle lawn was already dewy, and the temperature had cooled to far more comfortable temperatures, making Fin eager to feel the warm embrace of his kitchen.

Upon pushing open the garden door, however, he found that Jiho still sat at the table, his hands folded on its surface as he stared blindly into the low flames of the hearth.

"I'm surprised you aren't in bed yet," Fin observed, unable to fully disguise his bleak tone.

Jiho turned around and smiled, but it wasn't the bright, shining one he had worn while visiting with Katelyn Ashowan. It was a sad one. His eyes had drawn up their new cloak of nobility, and Fin felt his stomach churn.

This *definitely* was not going to be an easy conversation.

"We really do need to talk, Fin," Jiho stated calmly. Fin summoned his tankard and filled it with ale.

"So talk." Fin strolled around to stand behind his table as he began summoning beans from around the room. Unable to stay still, however, he then busied himself by walking over to the water pump along the wall and filling shallow basins.

"Would you sit down? You make things more awkward when you avoid me like that."

"I'm not avoiding you, I just have more than two hundred mouths to feed, three times a day, every day," Fin snapped with a dark glance over his shoulder.

Jiho's face turned stony. "Sit down. We can't keep avoiding this."

The dark look on Fin's face indicated to Jiho that the order was not well received.

Despite releasing the pump, the iron handle continued working on its own to fill the basins, as Fin rounded his table, snatched up his tankard, and stared dangerously at Jiho, who met his gaze without flinching.

"What do you want to discuss?" Fin demanded in a low tone, after sending a single pulse of magic out to ensure the room was locked and soundproofed.

"So you and the viscountess … you know that if you want to become ennobled you would have to—"

"I'm not getting ennobled. I like being a cook, and Lady Jenoure and I have no relationship to speak of." Fin's curt tone and tense expression made Jiho sit up straighter.

"So it's a one-sided love affair? Her loving *you*? Or vice versa?"

"Not your business. All that *is* your business is that there is no relationship. There is no scandal or shame attached to Lady Jenoure." The jarring, forceful response was followed by a hasty draining of the tankard recently filled in Fin's hand.

"On the contrary, I'd rather know ahead of time if my bride is in love with another man."

While his expression didn't change, Fin's grip on the handle of the tankard tightened.

"You're already calling her your bride. I take it she has agreed to be your wife?"

"She has an agreement with your king not to declare her intentions until after the costume ball being held for the prince's birthday. However, King Norman has made it clear I am his first choice," Jiho explained evenly, watching Fin carefully.

"I was unaware the king was selecting a mistress," Fin replied wryly, sending his tankard back to the barrel to top up his drink.

"Fin … you know how this works. Gods … I remember your study notes for your politics lessons. I came here because you're my friend, and I'm sorry, but unless you are going to try and become ennobled, Annika will marry. Better myself than one of the other two here."

"Oh, you think so, do you? That Troivackian wants to travel the world to learn how to be a better lord and provider to his tenants. He isn't bad looking, and they have a shared respect for Troivackian moonshine. You're a little too confident, I think." Fin shrugged, pretending that his insides weren't raging in fury and pain.

"Annika is a skilled political player; she loves the thrill of it—that much is obvious. Lord Miller is a lump of fanciful Troivackian mush that she'll dominate and be left thoroughly unsatisfied with. She adapted incredibly well to an entirely new continent before, she'll do well in Zinfera. I can imagine that she'll bring several of the more unruly harem women of our emperor to heel," Jiho mused with a slight smile as his eyes drifted to the worn surface of the table.

There were no words in Fin's mind, only an all-consuming roar that bore his will to decimate his surroundings and the Zinferan in front of him.

"Annika has friends here."

"She is close with the queen alone. She will still return to visit on occasion. Fin, I know I seem like I'm being cruel, but you need to be rational. If you aren't with her or seeking a way to marry her and not ostracize her, should she spend her life withering away?" Jiho pointed out evenly, his keen brown eyes watching Fin in a most disconcerting manner.

"You're not being cruel. You're being an ass. I know what I cannot have, and I have made the right decisions to protect someone I care about, and yet you seem to think it a kindness to rub my face in what I've sacrificed. Get out of my kitchen."

"Sorry, Fin." Jiho stood, giving him a pitying shake of his head. Fin had never considered hurting a friend before that moment.

"I know you've had life kick the shit out of you more than a couple of times, I don't mean to add another blow. Just know, I promise I'll take care of her."

"... What kind of two-faced tadger are you?" Fin's voice sounded ragged with restraint.

"Fin, I—"

"Gods, Jiho, you started as a dockworker shit on by everyone, when did you getting a lucky break mean you got to take your turn dousing us peasants with your nonsense? Especially those of us who were there for you when you were on death's bloody doorstep?" Fin only took a single breath before continuing. He knew the ale had loosened his tongue and deadened his mind, but he couldn't hold back any longer.

"You've become a pretentious fuck. I don't want to be a noble and I've accepted that that means I have to take some thicker lumps at times, but why do you get to look down on me for choosing a profession I like? I can't be with someone I ... I ... For the love of— Jiho, I am trying to be a decent person here. Yet you're using the knowledge that that's exactly who I am to kick me while I'm down. What the hell? We were *friends*!"

The fire behind Fin roared to life, surging up and over the stone's mantle in a fury.

"For the love of Gods, man, do you know how lucky you are to even have a *chance* to be ennobled? To climb the ranks? Men have slaughtered for a lot less than your opportunities. You're behaving a juvenile fool."

"Because I don't want to become a pompous ass?"

"*Because you could make a Godsdamn difference. You know what it is like to be kicked around, you could help change that! But you don't want to!*" Jiho's volume had risen exponentially as he stood slowly and glowered at Fin.

"Don't shove your own damn, self-imposed ambitions on me. It's my own damn life and just because I'm a peasant doesn't mean I'm worth less than you."

"*I KNOW!*" Jiho took a deep, steadying breath, centering himself again and briefly closing his eyes. When he once again met Fin's cutting gaze, he was back in control.

"Fin, I'm trying to make you aware of the consequences of your choice. If you aren't happy with the destination after the toll you paid to get there, you might have chosen the wrong path."

"No, that isn't what you are trying to do at all. I've made a horribly difficult decision I believe to be right, and you are only making it harder because it isn't what *you* would've done."

"Fin, come on—"

"Gods no. You don't get to talk to me like that anymore. Even the Godsdamn king of this continent calls me Mr. Ashowan. So that's what you should call me from now on. You'll speak to me like a noble speaks to a respected servant. A noble that has no Godsdamn business commenting on the servant's private affairs when it has *deliberately* not interfered with your own."

Dishes began rattling around the room, and a look of pale, astonished fear filled Jiho's features. Lightning sizzled and crackled around the room.

"You're going to start a fire!"

The room settled slightly, but Jiho could still smell the metallic note of lightning in the air. Fin's eyes were shining in an unnatural way that Jiho had only ever seen once before, and at that time he had not been the cause of the swell of power.

"Fin, if you're in love with Annika and want her, then for the love of Gods do something about it before you blow the castle up," Jiho remarked, despite every hair on his arm rising up and pulling his flesh upward as though begging him to flee.

"Oh sure. I'll have her denounce her title and have her wealth be taxed until it dwindles next to nothing as punishment for her disobedience against the king. I'll stop her committing to the necessary political marriage that would save the country. She'll be alienated from the only true friends she has ever had, all to toil her days away bearing my children and cleaning our cottage."

"Right. Then what is it you want? Do you want Annika to end up with the Troivackian? Because that means the country still falls to war where Daxaria loses. If she marries Lord Nam, she will most likely smother him in his sleep on their wedding night. I'm her best political match. I'm sorry, but I am. This is the reality. You always said you'd count yourself lucky if you found yourself a quiet woman who would be happy to garden, knit, help your mother, and visit with the locals so you'd never have to. To be honest, that would suit you best. You always said your personality matches your powers, and that kind of woman certainly suits your abilities," Jiho pointed out logically.

Fin didn't like the logic, though. He had no words to explain what precisely was the matter with it, but any thought of a woman not Annika being meant for him caused violent urges.

Then there was the idea of Jiho being her husband.

"I promise I won't marry her here in the castle. After she agrees to have me, you'll never have to see us again. Just try and keep a bit of dignity and self-control until then."

Fin's eyes met with Jiho's calm, distant brown eyes that had the impenetrable barrier of nobility shining through.

Everything in him snapped all at once.

Jiho was launched from the kitchen and through the forest beyond the castle lawn by an explosion of invisible magic that could only be felt by him, and only heard from the door bursting open.

Fin didn't know where the man landed, but the hinges on the garden door would need to be replaced in the morning.

He spent what felt like an hour regaining control of his breath and settling his magic down. Once he did, he conceded he needed to sleep.

Grumbling to himself, Fin set out his mat in front of the fire and laid down with his tankard still in hand. The ale dulled his awareness of the repercussions of his actions completely, and all he could think of was how peaceful everything finally was. Unable to sleep, he magically continued sending his tankard to the ale barrel and summoning it back only to be drained shortly after again.

He had never been drunk and angry before …

That didn't register to Fin's addled mind, however.

What he lacked in sleep, he made up for in exuberant drinking until the pink fingers of dawn splayed over the horizon.

Fin stood, swaying noticeably, but instead of attempting to sleep more or drinking water, he sent his tankard over to the barrel of ale and topped himself up yet again. He had long lost count of the number of drinks he'd consumed.

The only coherent thought he managed through the pleasant haze was: *Might as well get fired if I'm so set on burning bridges.*

CHAPTER 49
CHAOS IN THE KITCHEN

"Repeat that again, Dawson." Lord Piereva's eyes were wide.

"The door was blown off its hinges and *something* was shot deep into the woods. We haven't a clue what it was," Sir Dawson recounted, still bowed before the earl.

"Why hasn't anyone investigated this?!"

"The kitchens are isolated in the southeast corner, my lord. There is only an old servant's quarter above the kitchens, but it has been vacant in recent months. Down the hall is the dining area for the servants, and the larder. Beyond that are more servant's quarters that would've remained empty during the explosion on the first floor, and no one on the second floor may have heard the bang."

Piereva's mouth was clamped firmly shut as his mind flitted through several thoughts and conclusions.

"Who is watching the kitchens right now?"

"Sir Wickfield is currently watching the kitchens. Though no other activity was seen for the rest of my time during the watch."

"I see. For now, you are dismissed. Tell no one else about this," Lord Piereva snapped out as he began rubbing his beard thoughtfully.

Sounds to me like magic. A smile that was more of a jeer twisted the corners of his lips. *I think it's time I start putting a little weight on that cook.*

~~~~~~~

As Hannah skipped down to the kitchens, she couldn't help but battle a yawn. It had been another long night of work, but she knew her efforts would pay off soon.

Without a doubt, Fin was starting to face his fears, she was sure of it!

Why, she would even bet—

Hannah froze. Lady Laurent and the prince were walking away from the kitchens, speaking quietly amongst themselves. "Good morning," she said with a deep curtsy, but the royal pair only spared her a brief glance as they continued along.

Thinking better of it, apparently, Lady Laurent turned back around to face the young kitchen aide.

"Pardon me, but is there a reason why the kitchen is locked up today? Mr. Ashowan and Prince Eric are to have their lessons at this time."

Hannah gripped her skirts tightly.

What the hell? Fin is always up at the crack of dawn!

"I suppose our cook has just slept in today, sorry for the inconvenience, my lady." As she dipped another apologetic curtsy, unease settled in Hannah's gut.

The nobles didn't bother saying anything more, as they swept back up the hall, leaving Hannah to straighten and immediately bolt the rest of the way to the kitchen door.

She pounded on its worn surface several times, attempting to push the door open by force.

"FIN? FIN?! YOU *HAVE* TO BE IN THERE!" There was an all-consuming panic and rage coursing through Hannah.

I'll check his cottage! she desperately thought to herself as she fled back down the servant's corridor. About to barrel up the small stone steps that would lead her to the main castle corridor, Hannah ran straight into none other than Peter.

"Woah there, what's wrong?" he chuckled with a wince of pain as his ribs protested fiercely.

"Fin isn't in the kitchen! He didn't show up to his dance lesson with the prince, and I just … I have a bad feeling. Come on!" Hannah took off at a sprint, leaving her friend to join her at his own far slower pace.

She didn't bother looking over her shoulder, as Peter followed her down to the west passage, where they could exit closer to the cottage.

Hannah was already halfway across the lawn before Peter had fully descended the steps, when she saw the small figure of Katelyn Ashowan in the distance. She picked up speed immediately.

"Mrs. Ashowan!" Hannah hollered out, her heart straining as it thundered in her chest. Kate turned and smiled brightly at the young woman rushing her way at an impressive pace. "Is Fin still in his cottage?" Hannah managed in a gasp once in front of her. Hannah doubled over and nearly choked on her dry throat immediately after asking the question.

"Hm? No no, I'm sure he's already hard at work—my, you sure are energetic in the mornings!" Kate admired while waiting for the girl to catch her breath. "I'm actually in search of the barracks; His Majesty requested I aid some of the knights with some long-term injuries while I'm here. Would you happen to be able to point me in the right direction?" she asked, scanning the castle and its lush, rolling lawns with an invigorated smile on her face.

Hannah made a wild gesture over her shoulder before she charged off toward the garden door.

Katelyn Ashowan watched, perplexed, with a furrowed brow as Peter slowly strode up to her.

"Pardon me, did you tell Hannah that Fin is in the kitchen?" he queried with a pale, pained smile.

"Why … yes, I did, but young man, are you alright?"

Before Peter—a man in his early forties—could reply, Katelyn Ashowan reached up and gently touched his cheek.

A golden glow that blended with the warm hue of dawn emitted from his cheek as she gazed up at him with a furrowed brow.

"Oh, you poor dear! Here, come with me to Fin's cottage and I can heal those ribs up for you straight away!"

Peter balked then.

"How did you—" he swiftly remembered just whose mother he was talking to and instead asked, "Y-You can heal me that quickly?"

"Of course! I … er, I have a good touch. I can't mend bones *magically*, but I can relieve all your discomfort!" She laughed nervously. "I am a licensed physician, after all. Come with me, I'll have you good as new in a few minutes!" Kate blushed at her lie, after remembering Fin's strict order that she was to tell people that she was an esteemed physician rather than a witch to the general castle staff. Though she doubted that she'd be able to keep up the pretense for long if she admitted she could heal broken bones in minutes.

The two strolled back to the cottage, with Peter too distracted with the prospect of being healthy once again to recall that there was a small matter of a missing cook.

~~~~~~~~

When Hannah finally rounded the garden path, the knights were all standing in front of the door, discussing something with puzzled expressions and scratching their heads.

"… appears to be off its hinges," Sir Harris was finishing saying when Hannah finished her approach.

"Why won't it open, though?" Sir Taylor wondered aloud, sounding abundantly exasperated—he had become a little reliant on Fin's "coffee" beverage over the few weeks he had joined the kitchen staff.

"This door won't open either?" Hannah gasped, before choking yet again—she really needed some water.

"Gods, woman, were you doing laps from Austice to the castle?!" Sir Harris demanded as he pounded her on the back—an action which only made the coughing gasp worse.

"Fin … missed—" Hannah resumed struggling to breathe or swallow for another full minute before finding any success.

"He missed his dance lesson with the prince! I pounded on the castle door and there wasn't any reply. I just … saw Mrs Ashowan, and … Fin wasn't in the cottage either." Hannah was still working on her occluded airway and wiping away errant tears, but she saw the look of confusion on the men's faces.

Sir Taylor turned back to the door and began pounding on its surface with more purpose.

"Oyy! Ashowan! We need the fruit for breakfast!"

Not a peep from within was heard.

Sir Andrews rapped at the door next.

"Cook! Breakfast will be late!" he hollered casually, though his expression showed his more serious concern.

They waited a beat before Sir Lewis stepped forward.

"Mr. Ashowan! We need to grab our stuff and then we'll leave you be!"

Sir Harris let out a lengthy sigh.

"Amateurs. Come on, when has our cook ever been *truly* motivated?"

The three remaining knights shared puzzled glances.

"When he has to have another knight work for him?" Sir Taylor speculated with a raised bushy black eyebrow.

"When Hannah has been in trouble?" Sir Andrews offered, casting a small shrug at the girl in question, who gave a single shoulder lift and a nod in agreement.

"When Lady Jenoure prances in to annoy him?" Sir Lewis pointed out innocently.

"Yes to all three. So, let's try all of them, shall we?"

Hannah gave Sir Harris a flat look of unimpressed irritation.

She stepped forward and pounded on the door.

"Fin! So help me—I will get your mother over here!" she called angrily, continuously pounding on the door.

But still ....

Nothing happened.

Looking a little too smug, Sir Harris stepped forward and gave a single sharp resounding rap on the heavy wood.

"Fin! The captain sent a new knight to join us and he's harassing Hannah! Lady Jenoure is trying to calm everyone down, but it's getting a bit violen—"

The door didn't swing open so much as fall open. The heavy oak door keeled over with a bang onto the stone floor to reveal a kitchen that was ...

A disaster.

Half-peeled fruit sat piled on various plates on the floor and the side shelves. Beans were soaking in tubs all over the room, and the cook himself stood throwing slices of bacon haphazardly into his skillet, using the stone hearth to hold himself up.

The aides wrinkled their noses.

Despite the food and sizzling bacon, the stench of ale was strong.

"Eyy! Wass this about? ... Hannah— Hey there's Hannah! How's it ... How's it goin', Hannah?" Fin called, smiling happily.

"Fin ..." Hannah began, her expression growing into full-blown horror at a controlled, yet brisk rate.

"Ashowan, where the hell is your tunic?" Sir Taylor barked as they stared at the pale yet toned chest of the cook.

"Oh s-ssspilled stuff on it, it happens y'know. So it'sss dryin' over there." When Fin gestured toward his ale-stained tunic drying by the window, he inadvertently caused a pile of fruit to topple over magically.

"Oh Gods." Hannah slapped her hand to her forehead.

"Ashowan, what the hell happened to you?" Sir Taylor demanded, carefully side-stepping a precariously stacked plate of cantaloupe wedges that for some reason was on the floor.

"Nothin's wrong. Jusst bein' free. You know? I mean ... I can do this, thiss stuff. Easy." Fin's bare arms shot straight out, and all of a sudden, every single piece of fruit rose into the air, along with half a dozen paring knives that immediately began peeling the rest of the fruit in the room so energetically that the peels went flying all over the place—including onto the heads and faces of the kitchen aides.

"Agh!"

"Gods—Fin, stop!"

"What the—"

"FINLAY!" Hannah shouted impatiently.

"Ahh … right … shit … son of a mage. I … Can explain!" he stammered, stumbling as he attempted to stand on his own without the hearth holding him up. The fruit returned to their designated plates around the room.

"Hannah, you were right. He's awful at hiding this nonsense," Sir Taylor growled, flicking an errant apple peel from his face.

"What the hell do we do?! I always thought it was insane we cooked for hundreds of people with only a few of us— Where are Heather and Peter?" Sir Lewis demanded looking around the room panicked.

"Peter should be here soon, and Heather is experiencing a bad cycle right now … she will try to join us later," Hannah explained offhandedly, scanning the room and gnawing her lower lip.

"Cycle? What cycle?" Sir Lewis wondered as he brushed a glob of pear from his arm.

"A woman's cycle, Sir Lewis." Hannah was too distracted to be bashful over the topic.

"A woman's what?"

"Sirs and lady, this is a very una*peeling* topic," Sir Harris announced, shaking his auburn curls to loosen the errant watermelon seeds from his tresses.

"Gods, what the hell are we going to do?" Sir Andrews rubbed his eyes as the fruits began to restack themselves magically.

"We need to get breakfast ready for hundreds of people with our cook being drunk off his ass?" Sir Taylor asked with a dazed expression on his face.

"… So it would seem. We can deal with whatever made him like this later. For now, we need food for the servants immediately. Meat. We need— Gods, get that bacon out of the pan before it burns." Hannah winced as Sir Harris ran over to the cast iron pan and grasped its handle, without realizing how hot it would be, and snatching his singed palm back with a hiss.

"Son of a mage …" Sir Taylor's look of dawning dread expressed the general mood of the group as Fin sent a tankard over to the ale barrel and had it fill itself and return to him, spilling over the sides.

A pounding on the castle door interrupted the chaotic situation, making all heads turn, and an unnatural silence settled over the group.

"Mr. Ashowan? Is the servants' breakfast coming soon?"

Ruby's voice sounded from the corridor, and each aide glanced at each other anxiously.

Fin replied before any of them could stop him.

"Sssure thiiing, Ruby! Fruit salad an' *bacon*!"

Everyone held their breaths, hoping the Head of Housekeeping wouldn't attempt to investigate further.

"Very well, just be quick about it!" The sound of her footfalls faded, and the group breathed easier once again.

Hannah strode over to Fin and grabbed his bare shoulders.

"Alright, I don't know what in the world happened to make you act like a drunk bard, but can you get breakfast for everyone out? We will try to handle the rest." Hannah released him as he swayed merrily.

Fin responded by doing a tight spin on the spot and snapping both of his fingers.

All the fruit flew back into the air and began spinning and tilting in sync with one another, while also color coordinating themselves and heading toward the kitchen door. In other words, the fruits were dancing ... and were oddly coordinated, despite their inebriated master.

"... We're so screwed." Sir Andrews slapped both palms to his face.

"Fin!" Hannah grabbed him by his shoulders once again.

"Please, please try to remember people don't know you're a witch. Please. What is the simplest breakfast you can get out that door without magic in the next five minutes?" she demanded desperately.

Fin snapped his fingers and continued dancing to silent music in his head. He then began to sing slightly out of tune.

Come in, my friend, sit doooooown,
And have y'self a pint.
The dice are fair, so grab a chair
And join us for the niiiiiiight ... !

Fin looked at the knights expectantly. "S'nooo cookin's gettin' done without some singin'!"

The knights all shared a look and sighed as they joined in the familiar tavern song.

Come on, my friend, deal in,
And bet yer coin away
No use for gold when you get old
So have fun while you may

Come now, my friend, perk up,
And set yer drink aside
Yer lookin' pale, put down the ale
At least ye've kept yer pride

Come back, my friend, t'morrow
And hope yer luck is better
No man is poor who has his friends
But no one likes a debtor!

They finished the song, maintaining their usual tight harmony despite Fin's less than perfect efforts. As they had sung, the food had slowed its previously frantic dancing and sorted itself onto well-organized platters of the nearly burnt bacon and … ham. Apparently, Fin had also roasted a ham prior to their arrival.

Once the dishes were organized, Sir Taylor opened the door after an affirmative nod from Hannah, and the servants filed in, giving the crowded and oddly messy kitchen skeptical looks.

Both Sirs Andrews and Lewis stood shoulder-to-shoulder, blocking the half-dressed drunk cook from sight as he chugged down another tankard and leaned against the ale barrel.

After nearly twenty minutes of toe-curling tension, the final plates were carried out. It wouldn't be for another two or three hours that the nobles sought their own morning meal.

However, they still had teatime, lunch, dinner after that … and Fin didn't look like he'd be in his right mind until the following morning.

"I don't know about the rest of you, but I'm shitting enough bricks to build a house." Sir Andrews turned and stared at the red-cheeked cook, who was already sending his tankard back to the ale barrel.

"Who here knows how to cook?" Sir Harris demanded, his expression for once serious.

"I can cook a good hearty stew," Sir Taylor volunteered, stepping forward.

"Perfect! I think we can make sandwiches for lunch if we can coax Fin to prepare a few more hams. What about teatime?" Hannah looked around frantically at the men.

"I …" Sir Andrews stepped forward, looking thoroughly uncomfortable as he cleared his throat. "I can make a chocolate cake and oatmeal cookies. My mother had a special ingredient for the cookies that—"

"Good! Let's get to it! Who is on breakfast for the nobles?" Hannah demanded desperately.

"I can do eggs and meat—I've not a clue how to bake bread though," Sir Lewis piped up nervously.

Hannah clapped her hands together.

"We'll make the drunk in the corner add fruit to compensate."

"Eyyyyyyy," Fin called out in reply with a bleary smile stretched across his face.

"Gods," Hannah muttered before they all sprang into action. "How could this day get any worse?"

CHAPTER 50
CHARRING CHATS

The kitchen aides had just begun lunch preparations after sending out their haphazard breakfast offerings but didn't waste a moment of time before they scrambled to begin preparing for the day without their cook's assistance. Peter had joined them and was equally as mortified by the situation as his fellow workers—though in considerably sunnier spirits than the rest of the aides with his healed ribs.

Fin was passed out on the floor behind the door, and the best solution the group had come up with to hide him was to stack potato bags around his unconscious body. While they worked, each one of the aides braced themselves for the chaos that would dictate the day—they all wondered how in the world they were going to pull it all off.

Ruby was the first threat to their tenuous grasp of the situation.

Upon witnessing the sight of the disastrous kitchen and the aides frantically working, the Head of Housekeeping raised a skeptical eyebrow at the ragtag team that were all desperate to not appear suspicious.

"Where is Mr. Ashowan?" she asked, loudly enough to make all heads turn to her. The knights shared uncertain glances.

Ruby narrowed her small eyes at the knights, who all visibly paled, when Hannah stepped forward.

"Fin seems to have come down with the flu and is resting. He says he'll try to be back in time to prepare supper." Hannah's face was emotionless, but her big blue eyes were fixed on Ruby, her tone perfectly insouciant.

"I see. I thought he sounded strange this morning. Perhaps I should send his mother over to see him, she has a way with healing I've never seen. Why, it's almost as though she's magic, the way she has healed some of those knights."

The aides all shared strained innocent expressions.

"Oh, we couldn't possibly ask her to see to Fin. He'll be fine, she needs to focus on the knights, I mean, after all, they're the ones preparing for a war," Peter jumped in swiftly as he strode forward to stand beside Hannah.

Ruby glanced back and forth between the two dubiously but nodded slowly after a moment.

"I'll leave you all to it. Make sure you clean up this mess before Mr. Ashowan sees it, you know how particular he is." Then with one last sweeping glance, she cleared out of the room, leaving the group to let out their held breaths.

"Fin owes us big for this," Hannah grumbled angrily as she turned back to her task of slicing tomatoes for the luncheon sandwiches.

There was a muttered agreement amongst the aides as they became engrossed in their objectives, and the thoughts regarding Fin's debt to them stayed on their minds through every fumbled cut and burn they received.

While they succumbed to the general panic of their day, and attempted to complete their designated tasks, the group failed to hear the faint litany of curses drifting closer to the kitchen as a certain Zinferan stomped up the garden path.

"Where the hell is that bastard?"

Lord Jiho Ryu appeared in the kitchen door, looking as though he had been through a losing battle with a muddy hill for most of the night.

Dark bags smudged under his eyes, no less than three errant twigs were entangled in his mussed black hair, and dirt was splattered all over his once fine clothes. The Lord's previous composure and aloof air was long gone; his gaze instead was deadly, and his ire was visibly growing hotter as it remained coiled in his chest.

The aides all looked up and immediately became weary. A new obstacle had appeared all too quickly.

"Mr. Ashowan is ill, perhaps tomorrow he will be better and—" Peter started slowly as Lord Ryu openly glared around the room.

"His cottage is that way?" he asked, pointing in the direction of Fin's home.

"Err ... we think so," Sir Lewis answered vaguely. The group was a little uneasy about lying too extensively to a member of the nobility.

Spinning around on his heel, Lord Ryu stormed off.

"He's going to come back here, isn't he?" Sir Andrews sounded resigned, but the dread was apparent in his eyes as he removed a skillet from the heat of the hearth.

"Probably," Sir Harris admitted, still exuding his normal aura of carelessness.

"Is Lord Ryu capable of punishing us as a foreign noble?" Hannah asked with a slight note of worry in her normally confident tone.

"Us knights not as easily, you and Peter are a little different," Sir Andrews explained, his tone apologetic while his eyes remained trained on the door.

"Well ... can't do anything but keep cooking. Maybe throw Fin his tunic," Peter suggested, after a brief glance at Hannah, who was beginning to gnaw on her lower lip.

The group had resumed their harried new duties, when they heard the much louder unmistakable cursing of the Zinferan Lord. As they all stared out the open door, they could see in the growing daylight Lord Ryu exhuming the occasional plume of dust as he stormed back up the garden path.

"I swear to the Gods none of you will be punished—unless you fail to tell me *where the emotionally stunted giant redhead is.*"

"Someone woke up on the wrong side of the bread," Sir Harris said carefully as he poured a cup of water from a pitcher on the cook's table.

"It's *bed* not *bread*," Lord Ryu snapped as he continued glaring at the entire staff.

"Oh no. In your case it's bread. You are crusty in more ways than one this morning, my lord." Sir Harris offered Lord Ryu the cup of water with a cheeky smile.

Jiho stared at the grinning knight stonily for a moment.

He then slapped the cup of water from his hand while maintaining eye contact.

"Well. You certainly know how to make a splash when meeting new people." Sir Harris feigned a hurt expression.

Sir Taylor behind him slapped his forehead, Sir Lewis's jaw had dropped but was unable to look away, and Sir Andrews was visibly fighting against laughing.

Hannah opened her mouth after another beat of silence, when there was a low moan from under the potato bags.

Slowly, pulling his tunic over his head and sending several potatoes cascading free from their sacks, Fin sat up.

He rubbed his eyes and stared drunkenly up at the people in his kitchen.

It had only been an hour since he had fallen unconscious, and he was still magnificently inebriated.

He began to stand when Jiho rounded on him and punched him hard across his left cheekbone before grabbing hold of him by the front of his tunic.

Yanking Fin, who was several inches taller than him, over the barrier of potato bags, Jiho then hauled him outside the garden door.

"*You sent me* leagues *into the forest, you idiot!*" Jiho seethed before his nose suddenly wrinkled. "Gods, you reek. Have you just been drinking endlessly while your staff scrambles to cover for you?!"

"It's fine. Jus'll get fired. It's fine," Fin slurred with a half-grin, his half-open eyes deadened.

"You're going to throw away the job that you *claim* is more important than the woman you're in love with?!"

"I'ss can cook anywheres." Fin fought to straighten himself against the wooden fence of the gardens, only to have Jiho give a sharp upper-cut to his gut.

He immediately doubled over and vomited.

When he finished and stood unsteadily, wiping his mouth with the back of his hand, Jiho once again grabbed the front of Fin's tunic.

"You have a team of people that are risking getting flogged and demoted *for you*, without knowing a single reason as to why! A team who has to know you're a bloody witch because there is no way that they prepared an entire breakfast without any help from you. You're going to screw over these good people, destroy your reputation as a cook, *and* our friendship because you won't go after *her*?"

"We're getting flogged?!" Sir Harris's incredulous voice burst out of the kitchen, making Jiho's eyelid start fluttering ever so slightly, as though he were actively trying not to roll his eyes.

Fin didn't say anything for a moment, his drunken features stilling as he stared at his friend. Then, for the first time since he'd come to be aware of his pull toward Lady Jenoure, he showed his true emotions.

His defeat, weariness, and hopelessness were so potent that Jiho released him without thinking.

"Fin … come on. Why won't you try? This is insane and doesn't make any sense."

"I 'lready told you."

Jiho's face hardened, and his gaze sharpened. "Do I need to hit you again?"

Fin's shoulders sagged and he gave a hollow smile. "Go 'head."

Jiho was about to do just that, when it just so happened that the only force in the world that could ever command full obedience of him made their presence known.

"Jiho. Lord or not, you will cease this instant and tell me what you think you two are doing."

Katelyn Ashowan was striding up the garden path, and while she wasn't hurrying, she was moving like a captain moving to command his troops.

Jiho turned, his mouth opening and closing several times as he tried to find some way of explaining what was happening.

"Fin, are you sick? A woman calling herself the Head of Housekeeping said you came down with the flu." Once she was standing in front of the two men, they both shrank under her level stare as though they were once again rambunctious youths.

"No, I'm not," Fin muttered as he raised a shaking hand to rub his eyes.

"Are you drunk?!" Kate demanded as she noted the unsteadiness.

Before Fin could lie, she snatched at his hand, though she immediately let it go with a hiss as a fire blazed in her eyes.

"Is this what you've been doing since you've gotten here? Working drunk? You take this opportunity—this job—so lightly?" She bore down on him in such a way that the slight healer seemed more like a giant towering over him. At least that was how it seemed to Jiho and the aides, who watched transfixed.

"He's never done this before," Sir Taylor interjected from the over-crowded doorway.

Katelyn Ashowan turned her irate gaze to the bear of a man, and he visibly winced.

"Pardon the interruption, ma'am," he added hastily.

"I see. So what is so damn special about today, hm? The two of you getting into trouble again?"

"I have nothing to do with—" Jiho started defensively, but one threatening look from Katelyn had him firmly closing his mouth.

"Is it because you think I will let you drink as much as you like and I'll make you as good as new whenever you please? Because I said it to you before when you tried your first drink and I'll say it again now; if you choose to be an idiot, you will suffer like an idiot!" Fin said nothing in defense, only nodded quietly while slowly rubbing his face.

"Wait! You can sober him up?!" Hannah had launched herself from the doorway before a second thought could stop her.

Kate glared at the new interruption, and while Hannah did take a step back, she braved speaking again.

"Ma'am, I understand that our cook is behaving badly … but … we really need him back to normal. We're barely managing to keep up." Hannah pleaded, folding her hands demurely in front of her skirts. "Could you please help him, if only for our sakes?"

Katelyn's jaw set as she turned with flashing eyes to her son.

"I have never been disappointed in you before today. I cannot believe you are *my* son. That you would abandon your staff like this …" she trailed off angrily, and Fin's cheeks flamed red as he fixed his eyes on the ground.

Everyone present shifted uncomfortably in the silence after her ringing reprimand.

"All of you get back inside. Your cook will be with you shortly. None of you will want to see this," she announced, placing her hands on her hips as she continued glowering at Fin.

One by one the aides and Jiho filed back into the kitchen. Once they were all back inside, Sir Taylor hoisted the door off the floor and set it against the door frame to give Fin and his mother privacy.

Once that was concluded, it began.

The sound of retching carried on for several minutes.

It was then followed by a long period of silence, followed by even more unpleasant sounds.

After nearly an hour, Fin returned.

His face was tinged with green, and he appeared to be a bit wobbly on his feet, but it was clear he had sobered significantly.

When he strode into the room with his mother behind him, he didn't meet anyone's gaze. He turned to the door and with a snap of his fingers, the hinges in the wall began to reattach themselves. The door was mended within a minute.

Once that task had been completed, Fin turned to the expectant faces regarding him, all of them varied in their emotions.

The knights all bore sympathetic expressions, Hannah looked hesitant, Peter looked serious and intent, Jiho looked annoyed, and his mother continued bearing a dark cloud that could crack at any moment.

"I want answers, *now*," Katelyn Ashowan demanded tightly.

Fin let out a slow breath.

"Before I do, I would like to apologize to all of you. It had not been my goal to be unable to perform my duties and leave you all stranded. I made the mistake of thinking I could handle myself, and I am very sorry for my misjudgment. I will never place any of you in that position again. Thank you for your consideration and for covering for me when I did not deserve it." Fin gave a small bow to his staff, which effectively made them all grow incredibly uncomfortable.

Their cook wasn't one for long speeches, or for vulnerability. To see him in such a state was more than a little unnerving.

"Good. Now, what in the world has gotten into you?" Katelyn's firm tone wasn't less angry, but it was quieter than it had been previously.

Fin stared at Jiho directly.

"He and I had a fight regarding a matter that is affecting me more than I thought it would," Fin explained vaguely.

Hannah rolled her eyes to the ceiling, muttered an expletive, then turned to Katelyn.

"Mr. Ashowan is in love with Lady Jenoure—you've probably seen her by now if you've been to see the queen. Black hair, curves that make most men forget they have tongues?"

"I have … met …" Kate began slowly as she turned with a new shocked expression on her face, to look at Fin, who was staring at Hannah in frozen horror.

"You … knew … everything?" His voice was ragged.

Peter stepped forward, looking slightly less intense than before, though no less somber.

"Yes. You forgot to charm the window Lord Fuks gave you for the first two days and we saw your magic. We also happened to overhear a few conversations between you and Lady Jenoure … it wasn't hard to figure out what was happening between you two."

Fin raised both hands to his face and rubbed aggressively.

"You've always been terrible about hiding your nonsense," Jiho muttered to himself.

"That's exactly what I've been saying!" Hannah chimed in, shaking her head and crossing her arms over her chest. "We have no idea why you want to hide the fact that you're a witch, or why you won't pursue Lady Je—"

"Young lady, I'm going to have to stop you right there." Katelyn Ashowan rounded on the group, her face a mix of several strong emotions. There were still traces of her anger, but there was also now sadness and anxiousness.

"You do not know what witches face. There is still a large group of people that have hung on to anger and hate for our kind out of fear. Fin once saved his best friend from drowning, but because he didn't use his magic to do so, everyone scorned him. They assumed Fin thought he was better than them and wouldn't waste magic on a normal human. They stoned my boy, and called him horrible names for years, and he has been alone—"

"That's enough." Fin cut his mother off stepping forward and shooting her firm glance.

"Very well. However, pursuing a noble is out of the question. That lady will only be damned if she happens to return your feelings." Katelyn shook her head morosely as she stared at her son with understanding and severity.

Fin avoided staring directly into his mother's face. It was clear he was ignoring her pity and addressed the group in front of him again.

"I'm sorry to have worried you all. I will try to keep a better lid on my juvenile impulses and—"

"Oh, good Gods!" Jiho snapped as he stepped forward and fixed the two Ashowans with a look of exasperated anger.

"*I* managed to become ennobled, Fin, you can too! Besides, the lady herself is quite intelligent. I have no doubt that she'll have some kind of plan if she truly wants to be with you—if you would just take a damn chance!"

Hannah stepped forward next, glaring at Fin with her arms still firmly crossed. "We don't expect you to use magic for anything other than what you've already agreed to. Like starting lunch, for example."

Fin straightened at the thinly veiled reminder and gave a quick nod over his shoulder that summoned several ingredients over to his table from around the room. The various food items immediately began preparing themselves.

"Wonderful, now that that's dealt with." Sir Harris stepped forward and placed a hand on Hannah's shoulder—only to have her slap it off her immediately.

"Look, it seems kind of crazy to all of us that you have all of this magic and have already been helping the king only to—"

"Helping the king?!" Katelyn exclaimed, turning wide-eyed to Fin.

"Err ... yes. How does it make sense that it's impossible for you and Lady Jenoure to be together when the impossible has already happened more times than anyone can count?" Sir Harris tried to awkwardly ignore Fin's pained expression as his mother began staring intensely at him once again.

"We've all been rooting for you," Hannah added with a firm nod.

"Yeah. Honestly, cook, even as knights, I can say that it seems like there has to be some way it can happen." Sir Taylor moved forward again, Sir Lewis and Andrews nodding behind him.

Fin felt his throat constrict when he saw all of their earnest faces offering support and encouragement. His gaze fell to Jiho then, who, at long last, no longer looked ready to throttle him.

"You're not alone anymore, Fin, you have an honest to Gods shot. With all of us and Lady Jenoure herself already thinking it's a possibility? I'm serious. You aren't wrong for wanting more for yourself or wanting to try and change what it means for you to be happy." Jiho then addressed Kate. "When has Fin ever tried to be closer to someone? When has being alone ever bothered him before? You always say the Goddess has a plan, isn't it worth taking a chance to see if this is it?"

Fin's right hand twitched and a muscle in his jaw worked resiliently to fight back the overwhelming surge of gratitude he was feeling.

"You're limited on your own, we can all see that now—you seem to have the emotional maturity of a chicken," Jiho started glibly. "But you're a good person. You deserve this. So what if your path isn't straightforward? When has anything in your life been obvious? You're usually pretty good at turning a bad situation around, and now when it seems like there isn't any other way, all of a sudden you have all of us here wanting to help. Seems a bit too much of a coincidence, don't you think? Why not go where the water's pulling you?" A corner of Jiho's mouth lifted and his brilliant white teeth flashed.

Fin still wasn't able to talk; he didn't know what to say.

Kate's cool hand slipped into his own and drew his suspiciously shining eyes downwards.

"I ... I don't know exactly what you've been doing here since arriving, but ... if loving this woman brought you all of these people? Then maybe ..." She whispered the words. "Fin, I think you need to play your hand now. I trust that they will make it possible. I'll do anything I can to help you as well." She nodded to the group of friendly people staring at her son with collective determination and care.

Fin swallowed with great difficulty and raised his gaze to the expectant faces around the room.

"She—" The word came out choked. He cleared his throat and tried again. "She said goodbye already. She won't offer a chance to me again." He licked his suddenly dry lips.

Hannah snorted. "Please. Women say that knowing men's propensity to be slow as snails. We have a separate deadline than the one we say. Whether we realize it or not."

"The costume ball!" Peter jumped in, smiling brightly as he looked pleased to have reached the answer so quickly.

Hannah nodded.

"That's probably it," Jiho agreed intently. "So, Fin, what are you going to do?"

The smile grew slowly, but by the time it had finished spreading, it was blinding. Fin felt his heart skip several beats as he gazed around the room, for a moment unable to process the overwhelming support. He felt the freedom and terror of leaping into an unknown future, but as he stared at each face before him, he knew his determination and courage had hardened.

"I think I'm going to start taking my dance lessons a bit more seriously."

CHAPTER 51
POKING THE WRONG BEAR

It was the morning of the ball, and Fin had gotten little to no sleep the previous night. He had tossed and turned, trying to find the right words to say to Annika, and it was proving to be more than a little difficult. He kept imagining the various responses she could give to each well-crafted speech he would make, and the amount of possible replies was making his heart beat faster than his whisk as he worked on the morning omelets. Lady Jenoure could respond with disgust, disappointment, or even ignore him entirely ... but there was also the chance that she could smile.

She could smile, embrace him, and tell him all of her foolproof devious plans. Then they would never have to agonize over touching each other. Never have to say goodbye in all of the worst ways.

It was when Fin envisioned that particular outcome that he would smile, despite his anxious uncertainty. Giving his head a shake, he tried to block his thoughts regarding the ball and focus on preparing the extensive meals for the day. He would need every ounce of attention and care when it came to Eric's birthday cake, as the confectionery was designed to act as Fin's gift to the young prince. He had begun creating a cake in the shape of a dragon, experimenting with various alcohols to somehow make it appear as though it were breathing fire. A feature Fin had no doubt would bring the boy some excitement.

After a few moments of working in the growing heat of the kitchen, he went and opened the garden door to let in some fresh air, despite it being a downpour outdoors. He pushed the squeaking door into the rain, and was turning back to the glowing kitchen, when he noticed the dark figure standing at the end of the garden path …

Whoever it was, they stood leaning against the fence at the end of the path, with a black hood drawn over their face.

Fin's gaze sharpened.

He reached out to the garden plants in his mind and asked how long the man had been standing there.

There when you came.

Here with others.

Friends?

Tickles!

Trouble?

The soft small voices that drifted through Fin's mind made the hair on the back of his neck stand erect. They were equally wary about the stranger, and so he replied, *Bad stranger.*

The plants shifted away from the hooded figure, but he didn't seem to notice—his eyes were trained on Fin alone. Not that his eyes were visible, but Fin could feel their intensity on him.

As he stared motionlessly at the stranger, he studied their build and height, and after a few moments, he was relatively certain that it was none other than Lord Piereva standing there.

Fin left the door open, his stomach riddled with knots as he strolled back to his table, picked up his knife, and began cutting up the fruit he had already set down.

Slowly, the lord strode up the path and through the door. He lowered his hood to reveal his glinting eyes, a cold smile lighting his face.

"Good morning, earl," Fin greeted softly, his eyes studying the oddly cruel expression on the Troivackian's face.

"You're a busy man," Lord Piereva began as he continued watching Fin. A puddle of rainwater around him continued to grow, though he predictably failed to apologize.

"I prepare food for hundreds of people several times a day. It makes sense that I'd be busy," Fin explained as he continued cutting fruit without looking at his hands.

Lord Piereva's icy smile grew.

"Most impressive. Especially when you are taking the time to learn to read and write," he continued, his eyes glinting.

Fin was surprised at how quickly the lord had come to him regarding his "secret" note passing in the castle, and so he made a point of hesitating before answering to further the suspicion the man clearly had.

"It's important to learn new things," Fin ventured while making his tone hesitant but keeping his face still.

"It is indeed, it is indeed … Would you mind terribly showing me how your writing is coming along?" The lord's head weaved side to side as he asked the question. At that point, Fin wouldn't have been surprised if a forked tongue flit out of the man's mouth.

"I would be happy to, my lord; however, I have two breakfasts to prepare and there isn't any paper or ink here today." Fin walked over to the ledge of the room and picked up two bags of apples and hauled them effortlessly to the table.

"How unfortunate."

Slithering forward at an unnatural speed, Lord Piereva was suddenly in front of him. He snatched the front of Fin's tunic and twisted it in his fist before jerking him close enough to be nose-to-nose.

Fin didn't bat an eye, despite his heart lurching at the surprise.

"I know you're a little witch, just like your devil of a father." The earl's eyes were slightly crazed, and Fin could feel something evil brewing in the air. "However, your father doesn't care if you live or die. So whatever offer you may or may not get in the future, I advise staying on his good side. Explosions or not, I doubt you know what the Troivackian chief of military is capable of." A trickle of cold laughter stained the earl's voice.

Lord Piereva had anticipated a flicker of emotion, a whiff of magic.

He got neither.

Instead, Fin regarded him carefully before speaking. He didn't appear bothered in the least that he was being held in a very threatening way.

"I don't have a father, Lord Piereva. So whether or not a stranger cares about my livelihood, or lack thereof, matters little to me. Though I must confess, I am quite curious what kind of deal you think I should be agreeing to. Particularly with a man who sounds about as trustworthy as your even-tempered moments."

Rage and hate deeper than most were capable of feeling appeared in Lord Piereva's eyes. Fin hadn't seen anything like it since Aidan Helmer himself …

"Lord Piereva, I suggest you release me."

The earl sneered for a moment before dropping the cook's tunic. Fin continued meeting his gaze until he had reached the doorway of the garden.

"I'll always be watching you, Mr. Helmer. I suggest you act cautiously." The smug smile Lord Piereva bore after calling Fin by Aidan's last name almost made Fin blow him farther into the forest than he had Jiho.

"Ah—I understand you've been travelling a great deal this year, and that taxes the mind, but my last name is Ashowan. I can write it down for you if you'd like to bring me some parchment and ink."

Lord Piereva's gleeful expression dimmed as he then stormed into the rainy morning without sparing another glance back.

Fin's hands were on his hips as he watched the lord disappear, his improved mood in threat of decline. Giving his head a shake, he instead chose to focus on his work. He was beginning to cut up the rest of the fruit when a quiet knock from the castle door broke the tempestuous silence.

"What is it?" Fin called briskly as he kept his eyes on the oranges he was in the process of peeling. He was too absorbed with thoughts of Lord Piereva's crazed look to think more about who could be visiting him at that particular ungodly hour of the morning.

Jiho stepped through the doorway looking tired and wary at the same time. He wore a deep blue silk vest that extended past his slim waist, tan trousers, and a snowy white tunic underneath. His hair was half tied back, though the small bun at the back of his head was less than immaculate.

Fin stopped his work after the two men locked gazes, then strolled over to his garden door and closed it firmly. He didn't need any spectators for what was sure to be a less than comfortable conversation.

"Coffee?" Fin asked simply as he strode back to his table purposefully.

"Gods, yes," Jiho replied desperately as he stepped farther into the room with his hands clasped firmly behind his back.

"What brings you to my kitchen before the sun is fully risen?" Fin set the clay mug down in front of the chair on the far left and waited as Jiho slowly seated himself.

"We hadn't really spoken since you launched me into the woods," Jiho explained shortly.

Fin pressed his lips together as he tried not to laugh at the flat tone Jiho had used.

"That is true. Though after getting a couple good shots in, I thought we had resolved the matter," he reminded dryly, smiling. He picked up his own coffee cup and took a drink as the fruit and knives began to magically take over his previous task.

"We dealt with how you were being an ass, yes. Though if I'm being honest, your resolve seemed quite deep not to go after Lady Jenoure. I'm surprised it only took a room full of people lecturing you." Jiho's eyes were watching Fin carefully as he sipped from his mug.

Fin smiled down at the table as he thought back to that fateful day.

Aside from his mother, he'd never had people rooting for him. Never before had a group of people come together to support and accept him, especially when he was being a dunce. If that could happen ... why couldn't even crazier things come about?

"I know the odds are in my favor when Hannah gets fired up," he confessed, grinning and setting his cup back down. The day began to lighten outside the large round window and the rain continued its rhythmic pattering on the glass in the background of the conversation.

"Your blond aide? I've been hearing the strangest stories about her from the knights here at the castle," Jiho speculated with a small frown.

"You two should chat more. She nearly killed a man with my frying pan, you'd like her." Fin's mild tone did little to fix Jiho's alarm.

"She what?!"

"It's fine, he was going to try and stab someone."

Jiho closed his eyes for a moment and took a deep breath.

"Why is everyone around you insane?"

Fin laughed and turned around to grab the very pan he had just referenced.

"Maybe it's the water?"

Jiho snorted and set down his cup.

"By the way, how was it that you were conscious when I came back? Normally after blasting someone, you sleep like the dead for nearly a day," Jiho realized suddenly.

"Ever since coming here I think I've grown more powerful. Bigger house, more people to take care of ... I think my abilities grew to accommodate me."

Jiho leaned back in his chair thoughtfully.

"Ever think about what that could mean if, oh I don't know, a war broke out?" At Fin's alarmed look, Jiho continued. "Do you think you'd be able to protect the entire castle if it became threatened?"

"That is a big uncertainty. I wouldn't want the king to rely on that, only for me to pass out or worse after prolonged use."

Jiho didn't argue but there was a curious glint in his eye that Fin didn't like one bit. Fortunately for them, however, they were interrupted when Hannah, Heather, and Peter strolled through the castle door, followed by four drenched knights entering through the garden door.

"Right, well, I better leave you all to it." Jiho stood and strode over to the door before casting a mischievous look over his shoulder. "Tonight's the ball, Fin, think you're ready?"

Glancing at the faces of his aides, Fin saw their hopeful, firm, and trusting smiles.

"Not at all, but I'm going to try. I'm pretty sure you lot would kill me if I didn't."

"You're not wrong." Hannah's deadly expression didn't show any hint that she was joking.

Jiho looked at her with sudden interest.

"I don't think we've been properly introduced. I am Lord Jiho Ryu."

Sitting on a worn chair under the eaves of Fin's cottage, Katelyn Ashowan had just polished off a sandwich for her lunch. She was just beginning to resume her work on sewing Fin's clothing for the ball, when a shadow crept up over her hands. She peered up into the cool gaze of the black-haired, dark-eyed man who was obviously a noble, and immediately her stomach twinged. There was a coldness in his eyes she had not seen since her husband staring at her as though she were prey, and it made her nauseous.

"Good day, my lord." Katelyn bowed from her seat and hoped against all hopes he had no business with her.

"That there in your hands. The material looks finer than what a peasant should own." The lord cast an appraising gaze at the cream-colored tunic she had in her hands.

"Ah well, I hold out hope that my son will be married one day. It'd be wonderful if he'd look as fine as his father did on our wedding day." Kate pretended to smile innocently, but her uneasiness around the noble was growing far too rapidly.

"His father, you say?" The lord's eyes shone, and Kate immediately regretted whatever it was she'd said to make him look like that.

"Yes. He's no longer with us, of course, but he was something fierce on our wedding day." Kate could feel panic rising in her throat. What was this man on about?

"Odd that your boy doesn't use his father's name." The lord's lips were curling at their corners and Kate thought she'd retch.

"You seem to have taken a keen interest in Finlay, my lord," she observed, forcing an idleness in her voice that she did not relate to in reality at all.

"He is an interesting person. I hear he felled one of my knights in two blows and has beaten other knights of Daxaria, yet he has never faced any consequences. Odd that he doesn't acknowledge he has ever had a father and prefers taking a woman's last name."

Kate could feel herself growing pale. She wanted to be away from the man as quickly as possible.

"As a mother, I find my son to be a wonderful sort, as all mothers see their children. I must confess, my lord, I am still quite tired from my journey here, I believe I will retire for a nap. Good day." Kate rose to her feet and dipped into a respectful curtsy.

She had only just risen when the garment in her hands was snatched from her.

"I would like to ask around the castle to confirm this wasn't pilfered from anyone. If you've done nothing wrong, I will have it returned to you." Then the lord turned on his heel and strode away with his shoulders straight and his head held high.

As he retreated toward the castle with his black cape fluttering in the daylight, Kate's hands tightened into fists.

"If the Goddess has any sense, that man will be punished for every misdeed in this life and the next," she cursed angrily before storming into the cottage.

She couldn't imagine what they were going to do for Fin's clothing for the ball, but as she closed her eyes and took a steadying breath, she envisioned the crowd of faces all eagerly wanting to help her son.

She knew in her heart everything would be fine, and so her thoughts turned back to the lord that had blackened her morning.

Katelyn Ashowan had grown out of leaving retribution to the fates every time someone deserved a good comeuppance, and so she began crafting her own plan of how to bestow vengeance on the earl and remain unscathed.

CHAPTER 52
A LITTLE HELP

The aides were in full motion the day of the prince's ball as they peeled and even helped with some of the dicing and chopping of vegetables under Fin's watchful eye. The rain let up by late morning, and so they took some of their work outside, if only to relieve themselves of the excruciating heat of the kitchen. That being said, they no longer had to be beyond the view of the room, as now they all had admitted to their intimate knowledge that Fin was a witch.

None of them asked questions, and after the first hour of fruit and knives whizzing around the room, they no longer flinched in surprise or concern.

The staff was in the middle of carrying in some of the food after they'd peeled them at the end of the garden path, when all items working magically laid down suddenly, and ceased their work.

As the aides looked around themselves in confusion, Fin didn't have time to explain before Reese Flint threw open the castle door. The bard leaned against the door frame with an arm above his head, crossed ankles, and his eyes covered by strange dark glasses that none of them had ever seen before.

"Well well well! The aides are working *in* the kitchen? It would seem like there's been some development here." Reese sauntered the rest of the way into the room and seated himself at the table with a roguish smile directed at Fin. "Good morning, gorgeous."

"Reese, today is not a good day for this and— Can you even see out of those?" Fin frowned as he tried to judge where the man's eyes were fixed.

"I can! This handy little number I found lying around while I was paying a visit to the man named Kasim. You know, the one who guards the greenhouse tower." Reese tapped the side of the glasses once before trying to pick up a sliced strawberry, only to have Hannah slap it out of his hand.

"Kasim is in charge of the greenhouse, he isn't the guard."

"Oh sure, and you're a 'normal' cook." Reese waggled his eyebrows playfully.

Fin snatched the glasses off the man's face and hastily stored them in his pocket.

"I don't know why you are fixated on me, but you need to leave. Otherwise, we won't have enough food to feed everyone." Fin folded his arms and stared disapprovingly down at the bard.

"Don't mind me, I can just watch!"

Hannah slapped her hand down on the table's surface, making Reese turn to stare at her. Her cheeks were red from the heat of the room, and her hair had grown quite frizzy despite being braided from the harried work.

"Look here, if you want to be a pain in the ass, that's your business, but when you get in the way of us working that's mine. Get. Out."

Reese's face lit up as he grinned at Hannah, completely unperturbed by her threatening stance.

"Oh, now *you* saucy little lady I have been hearing about left, right, and center around the barracks. The men of this castle are quite taken with you and your feisty ways."

There was a beat of silence while Fin's eyebrows were raised nearly until his hairline. Crossing his arms, he watched and waited to see what Reese was about to suffer at the hands of Hannah, who looked as though she were envisioning a bloody effigy.

"Fin?" Hannah's gaze never left Reese's.

"Yes?"

"Can I hit him?"

"That depends. First, you have to tell him to stop making you uncomfortable, then if he persists, I will take care of him myself."

Reese straightened in his chair and all levity left his face as he regarded Hannah more seriously.

"My lady, I promise you I did not mean any harm. I will cease this instant if my words make you displeased."

Hannah looked at Fin helplessly.

"They don't normally learn that quickly."

It almost sounded like a complaint coming from her.

"I think you're becoming a little bloodthirsty these days," Sir Taylor called over warily. "Might want to keep an eye on that."

Hannah scowled and turned away from Reese, who turned to Fin with a pleasant smile on his face.

"I never mean harm. All I do is for the sole purpose of music and mutual fun." He winked charmingly.

Fin shook his head at the man. Reese really wasn't like anyone he had ever met. It seemed he was in perfect control of himself and really was just a hedonistic thrill seeker who didn't let his preferences come at the cost of others.

"Listen, we really are busy, Reese. As fun as it is insulting you while you shamelessly flirt with anything human, we have a long day ahead of us."

Sighing, Reese stood up and strode back to the door.

"Very well, I suppose I will go and try once again to get to know the stunning Lady Jenoure. She's finally returned from her estate and apparently even brought a guest that she's hiding in her quarters." Reese sauntered back to the door, unaware of the eight pair of eyes boring into his back.

"I was unaware Lady Jenoure had gone somewhere," Fin started carefully.

"Well, why would you be? She's a viscount— Ohhhh!" Reese turned around with his eyes sparkling.

"No. No no no no," Fin snapped desperately, waving his hand furiously to try and ward Reese off.

It was no use. Reese was a dog who had found his bone and he was not going to give it up for anything.

"My dear, sweet, limber cook, do you have a little crush on the famed beauty of Daxaria?" Reese was practically vibrating in his fervor. "Did she smile at you and give you purpose? Did she tell you to be kinder to your aides and no one had *dared* speak to you like that before?"

Fin was saved having to reply by Sir Taylor, who stepped forward, picked Reese up by the shoulders, and tossed him into the corridor before slamming the door shut.

He turned back to the room, shaking his head and sighing.

"Cook, you need to be a much better liar if you want to keep any secrets."

Everyone in the room burst out laughing, and slowly resumed their duties as the anticipation for the ball rose with each passing moment.

The final course of the banquet was served, and the last servant carried out the last platter of dessert. Night had already fallen around the castle, but the darkness did little to dampen everyone's bright mood and spirits. There was a hum in the air, the stars were twinkling brightly, and there was even a cool pleasant breeze rustling the forest in the distance. The time had come. Fin only had a few hours before he would be required to send out a final wave of food late in the night for the wine- and ale-soaked nobility, but he had until then to talk to Lady Jenoure.

The aides turned their expectant faces to him once the door was closed, and in the silence burgeoning with anticipation, Fin felt his heart begin to race.

"Well, I guess I better try and disguise myself now."

The knights glanced at one another and shared a quick nod before they stepped forward.

"You see, cook, we uh … we kinda guessed a while ago you'd want to go to the ball, so we've been … preparing things for you," Sir Taylor began slowly.

Fin was rendered momentarily speechless. Once he recovered, however, his cheeks had brightened up like one of his delicious cherry tarts.

"Err, that's okay, but thank you. My mother and I have sewn together something that could pass for—"

Words died in Fin's throat as Hannah reached into a basket hidden behind a crate of onions and drew out a fine black linen tunic, coat, and trousers. The coat was embroidered with gold thread and looked fit for a member of nobility.

"How did you …" Fin's words trailed off as he fought back the wave of warm gratitude in his chest. The aides beamed proudly.

"Well, I'm the only one as tall as you, so we tailored one of my coats. Was a little too lean in the shoulders for me anyway," Sir Taylor explained while giving a single shrug of his tree trunk-sized arm.

"It's a costume ball, so I made you a mask, a cloth to tie around your hair, and a hat." Hannah nodded to Peter, who had gone to another shelf in the kitchen, and drew out a black cloth, a sea captain's hat, and a black mask.

"I was unaware sea captains wore masks," Fin managed to jest weakly, even though he was feeling anything but cavalier about the gifts his friends were bestowing upon him.

"Fine, just say you're a leprous sea captain." Sir Harris shrugged with his arms firmly crossed over his chest.

"That doesn't make any sense—" Sir Andrews began indignantly.

"For the love of— Everyone up there is drunk! I doubt anyone is going to quiz him about his costume!" Sir Harris snapped back incredulously.

"Well, I'll know. Just say you're a pirate," Sir Andrews muttered as he crossed his arms stubbornly.

"Actually, Harris, you raise a good point. Fin, what will you do if Lady Jenoure is thoroughly sotted already?" Heather piped up, her wide eyes filled with genuine worry.

"Did you just call me Harris?"

Fin ignored the knight's mock amusement at the timid maid foregoing his title and addressed her concern.

"I doubt she will be. In a room full of royalty, it wouldn't be like her to make a scene."

"Until a short while ago, I would've said the same about you," Peter reminded dryly.

Fin blushed at the reminder of his less than appealing behavior not even a week earlier.

"She is better at maintaining her composure ... and better at drinking, for that matter."

At the last description, everyone was in complete agreement.

"Sounds good to me, but quick question ..." Sir Lewis, who was normally a quiet observer, spoke up then.

When all eyes turned to him, he gestured over his shoulder at the then-closed door.

"What are you going to do about the Troivackian knight that's been following you around?"

The room fell silent.

They'd all forgotten that there had been one of Lord Piereva's men tracking Fin's every move of every hour of every day.

"You could just stay in here afterward and sleep in front of the fire like you did before we fixed up your cottage," Sir Taylor suggested.

"Er ... well ... you see, I would normally, but we've been sweating in this kitchen all day, and I was thinking I should maybe bathe." Fin rubbed the back of his neck awkwardly.

"You do not need to try quite that hard!" Sir Harris exclaimed seriously.

"Oh no, he definitely should do that." Hannah and Heather nodded, frowning as the knights shared confused glances.

"Alright, so how are you going to go back to your cottage, bathe, and then come back in costume without being followed? Not to mention getting into the ball itself?" Peter wondered aloud.

The room was completely quiet for a full minute before a slow smile began to stretch across Sir Harris's face.

"You know ... I'd be curious to see how the Troivackian knight would respond to a little ... romantic interest being thrown his way. It might help persuade him to retire early for the night."

Hannah and Heather rounded on the auburn-haired knight with sparks in their eyes.

"Do you know how dangerous that is for us?!" Hannah exploded.

Sir Harris turned to the two women with his hands on his hips.

"Before I say anything else, I'd just like to say: Hannah, we all know that knight would be in far more danger from you than you from him if we were all nearby and Fin loaned you his pan."

Hannah continued to glower darkly up at him.

"... However, I wasn't suggesting that either of you or Heather flirt with the man."

Everyone's face morphed into confusion.

"I was wondering how suave our good friend Peter here was."

The aide's jaw dropped.

"The man could kill me!" Peter spluttered in disbelief.

"We'd be nearby in the bushes, and if he tried, you know that the king would have grounds to imprison him."

"I don't like that you aren't denying my death as a possibility," Peter narrowed his eyes at Sir Harris. "Why don't you do it?"

"Because of all of us, I am the most likely person to be killed after unintentionally infuriating someone."

"You mean you don't do it on purpose?!" Hannah remarked mortified.

Sir Harris ignored her words and clapped Peter on his slender shoulder. "Come on. Where's the daredevil, the legend of a man who ran naked around the castle?"

Peter said nothing for a moment as he continued to glare at him.

"Who here told this big-mouth about that?" Peter demanded icily. "I learned things myself about everyone that night, you know."

The rest of the knights all became fascinated with various spots on the ceiling and floor, and none of them volunteered the answer.

Exasperated, Peter let out an agitated sigh.

"Fine. I'll do it, but if I'm in trouble, you lot better get in there quickly. I'm just going to try and make him uncomfortable to the point of leaving, right?"

Sir Harris smiled brilliantly.

Fin had his mouth covered as he watched the entire scenario play out, but he could no longer stop himself from interjecting.

"Peter, I can't ask you to do this. I'll figure something else out, I promise."

Peter held up his hand without looking away from Sir Harris.

"No, Fin. Everyone here but me helped get things ready for tonight. This is my role."

"Why are you all doing this for me?" Fin asked quietly after a moment, unable to fully convey his overwhelming sense of gratitude and awe over their collective efforts.

Everyone looked at him blankly, then shared glances amongst themselves before answering.

"You helped everyone who's ever needed it, of course we'd do the same," Hannah explained, as though it should've been obvious.

Fin swallowed with great difficulty.

"Thank you, everyone. Truly, no one has ever done anything like this for me before."

There was a moment of uncomfortable silence before Sir Harris cleared his throat, unable to let the moment stay sweet and pure for long.

"Right, well ... Peter, do you own a tighter tunic by any chance?"

CHAPTER 53
CINDERFELLA

Sir Karter Dawson stood at the edge of the king's forest with his arms crossed and his finger tapping his forearm impatiently. He had hoped to join the festivities at the ball, but of course, Lord Piereva wanted to see if his threats toward the Royal Cook would make the man act out rashly. A ball with nobles flooding in from all over the continent would've been far more interesting than standing around waiting for the gangly redhead to bed down for the night ... Though, if there was to be any other late-night food for the guests, it could mean an even longer night for the cook.

Speaking of which: the door to the kitchens opened, and out filed the knights, along with at least one of the other aides.

Perhaps they're going drinking. Lucky bastards. Sir Dawson rubbed his eyes tiredly and waited for the cook to exit.

Sure enough, after a few minutes, the unmistakable tall figure of Fin exited into the night, shutting the door firmly behind himself.

As was usual, he strode purposefully to his cottage, his small black cat following him along happily.

Occasionally, Sir Dawson would hear him talk to his cat. Uncertain of the words but finding it altogether very peculiar that he would do such a thing, Sir Dawson would file it away for his report with the earl.

The cook entered his cottage, closed as tight as an ale barrel, and the sound of him conversing with his mother drifted out periodically.

Nestling his shoulder against an oak tree twice his width, Sir Dawson settled in for another long night.

"Do you always get the boring shift?"

The knight nearly leapt out of his skin. Standing behind him was one of the cook's aides, looking all too innocent in the pale moonlight of the night.

"Just out for a walk," he grunted, narrowing his gaze at the newcomer.

"Why don't I join you? You have quite muscular legs, and I wouldn't mind a pair of my own," Peter said with a wink.

Sir Dawson's face was frozen. It had to be a diversionary tactic. There was no way an aide of the cook's just "happened" to come out into the woods to express an interest in him.

"No." Sir Dawson turned his attention back to the cottage, fixing his gaze to the shuttered windows.

"If you keep stalking Fin, he will be more repulsed than interested." The pitying note in Peter's voice made the knight turn back around, a strange glint in his eyes.

"You think I'm following your cook because I desire him?"

The aide, who was a little under a decade older, smiled and pressed his hand into the trunk of the tree by Sir Dawson's head and leaned in a little bit closer.

"No need to be shy, just about everyone has had a crush on him. He's a tough slice to butter, though." Peter shook his head slowly, still smiling intently at the knight.

Sir Dawson swallowed with great difficulty.

He would not let this servant distract him.

"I have no interest in the man aside from his suspicious behavior." Sir Dawson's voice came out a growl, yet somehow the aide didn't flinch. Instead, he chuckled.

"Oh please. That dullard?" Peter raked his eyes over Sir Dawson's toned chest and bulging sleeves. "Tell me, do you have to train for hours every day to get biceps like those?" Peter had conveniently forgotten how to express shame.

"You are trying to distract me. Be gone," Sir Dawson tried again, narrowing his dark eyes even more.

"Well, you started it by strutting your business up and down that garden pathway the past few days. You need to be held accountable, you know. Besides, everyone is inside having fun or asleep. Why can't you enjoy yourself every once in a while? Or is your earl set on being a wet sock about that—what's his name again?—Lord Puny?"

Despite himself, Sir Dawson snorted.

"Ah! Would you look at that, you have me weak at the knees with a smile like that."

He tried to keep a straight face, but it was futile, he laughed again. The aide was too outrageous for words.

"Do you sweet talk your way into every bed in the castle with these distasteful compliments?" Sir Dawson blurted out before he was able to stop himself.

For a moment, he could've sworn a small look of shock crossed the aide's face, but he didn't have time to think on it, because Peter's face suddenly lit up in a smile.

"What's your first name, Sir … ?"

"Dawson. Karter Dawson."

"You know, Sir Karter Dawson, I happen to have an excellent bottle of family-made absinthe back in my quarters. Would you perhaps be interested in joining me for an hour or two?"

Sir Dawson chortled, then shook his head. Folding his arms and leaning slightly closer to the aide, he dropped his voice huskily, "I doubt your absinthe will hold up against Troivackian moonshine. I have to bring it from home so that I don't have to taste Daxaria's inferior alcohol."

"Why don't we have a taste test then, hm?"

Sir Dawson glanced over his shoulder briefly at the quiet cottage. Odds were higher that he'd be able to get more information out of the cute aide than watching the cook's home. Why not have a nice evening while getting more done?

"Very well, lead the way. We'll see if your smart mouth lives up to the standard it set."

The faintest of blushes swept across the bridge of Peter's nose as the knight pushed off from the tree and took several steps forward. "Shall we?"

There was a tense moment when Sir Dawson truly wondered if the aide had been bluffing in order to be a distraction, and some part of him felt oddly … displeased.

Then, Peter smiled again.

A strange warming sensation spread through Sir Dawson that he did not want to think any more about.

Peter took a few steps and stopped at his side.

"I'll show you the way then ... Karter."

As the two men strolled off into the night, speaking amicably, they eventually disappeared around the castle corner. The knights, huddled in a thicket of underbrush only a few yards away from where Sir Dawson had been previously standing watch, began to stir.

The men all stood up swiftly at the same time. Their jaws had dropped roughly around the time that the Troivcakian knight had flirted back with Peter, and they all remained open.

"What the hell just happened?!" Sir Taylor balked as he tried to comprehend exactly what he had just seen.

Sir Harris let out a small laugh of disbelief.

"I think our dear friend Peter might be partaking in an intimate nightcap with one of the knights close to Lord Piereva!"

"You don't think it's a trap and he's going to hurt him, do you?" Sir Lewis worried aloud as he stared after Peter with a slight frown.

The men shared uneasy glances.

"Alright. Two of us will go and try to keep an ear out to be sure that Peter isn't in any trouble," Sir Taylor announced, nodding to Sirs Andrews and Harris.

"Why us two?!"

"I'm too big to be sneaky. You're good at talking, an' Andrews has the lightest step of all of us."

No one could argue his reasoning, and so the men split up. Each group would have their own stories to share the next morning. However, both sides would have a few important differences ...

Fin stepped out of his bed chamber as his mother tilted the empty tub back into the corner of the cottage. It had been the first purchase Fin had made with his salary the day after his drunken escapade, and it had been a wise decision. The second purchase had been a pair of good black boots that would be able to pass at a noble's ball, but that he could also wear for years after.

When Katelyn Ashowan turned and took in the sight of her son, her hand moved to her chest.

"My love, you look ... noble." She grew a little teary-eyed at the sight of her handsome boy looking so poised and regal.

His hair was clean and swept to the side, and he was clad head-to-toe in fine clothes.

Fin winced in embarrassment but gave her a small smile. An action which made him look more like his usual self.

"I'll keep to the shadows best I can. Afterward, I'll be back in the kitchen for the late-night feast. The servants will come around midnight for the dishes, so I have until then. Sorry I didn't end up wearing what we worked on." Fin handed his mother the bandana and hat as he strode over to one of his kitchen chairs and seated himself so that she could tie it for him.

When he had walked into the cottage that evening, Kate hadn't said a word about her encounter with the earl. Just as she predicted, something had worked out for her son.

Focusing back on the task at hand, Kate took great care in ensuring that the black material covered every strand of his coppery locks shining after his bath.

"Do you think she'll have you then?" Kate tried to hide the warble in her voice. Her son felt like a new man to her somehow. Bigger, stronger …

"I don't know. I turned her down twice and I haven't heard from her in days, but I'll still say what I have to. I'll find out if she still wants to gamble on a stubborn ass like me."

Katelyn wrapped her arms around her boy and tried to blink back the tears, but they spilled over all the same.

"She's a fine lady. I had wondered why she seemed so glum about her suitors." She kissed the top of Fin's hidden hair and stepped back. "I have a good feeling about tonight. The Goddess must be happy about this plan—for whatever reason."

Fin chuckled and stood, carefully tying the demi-mask around his face. It was a plain, sleek black mask with no finery or ornaments, which suited his objective even better. He donned the hat last and turned to his mother one final time.

"Would you be able to recognize me?"

Frowning slightly, Kate carefully studied her son from head to toe. "The coat makes your shoulders broader, and the boots make you stand even taller. You're quite an imposing figure right now, my love. I would recognize you after looking at you for a good while, but only if I were close."

Fin let out a shaky breath and nodded gratefully. "Well then, if anyone knocks, don't answer."

Katelyn smiled and gestured to the door. "I love you, my sweet boy. Be safe."

"I love you too, mum." Then, with heavy footfalls, Fin left the cottage and disappeared into the night.

Kate let out a long breath and half-collapsed into the kitchen chair. She was in utter disbelief that the plan had gone off without a hitch, given her nasty confrontation with the earl that morning. Upon remembering the encounter, she felt her anger begin to swell again.

Turning to her own bag of belongings, Kate began rummaging around and drawing out some of her physician's instruments. She was still crafting her own personal revenge on the earl, though she needed to learn more about the brute before enacting any retaliation. As she worked, she silently chanted the same mantra over and over in her mind.

No one bullies me or my family without facing the consequences.

Fin stepped in through the east castle entrance, near the maze garden. Several masked, giggling noblewomen pulled along their equally giddy partners toward the balmy summer's eve. Some of the women that swished by gave a second glance at the impressive figure that drifted by them. The castle guards nodded to each of the respective guests, and to Fin without batting an eye. He responded as he knew he should: by ignoring them completely.

Admittedly, he was having a hard time keeping his shoulders perfectly straight. Keeping his head high and his gaze direct was another matter entirely—but his pounding heartbeat wouldn't allow him to grow complacent. He had to appear like he belonged.

As Fin strolled down the castle corridor, he did his best to melt into the shadows away from prying eyes, until the din of music and laughter reached his ears. His steps slowed, and he knew he was nearly upon the doorway to the banquet.

As he rounded the corner, the entrance to the party appeared. Massive oak doors yawned wide with intricate wrought iron hinges and handles waiting for him. Two guards stood watch, their backs pressed against the solid wood. Bright warm light gleamed into the otherwise darkened corridor, nobles donning all sorts of costumes drifting in and out of the ball. Some had discarded their masks, while others wore entire felt masks to look like animals. An impressive alligator costume stumbled past Fin as he tried not to betray his hesitancy in his step.

With an imperceptible deep breath, Fin stepped in front of the banquet hall.

Guests were beginning to surround a large table where plates and cutlery had been stacked to serve. Standing on the steps that led up to the king's table was a familiar small child. The prince looked smashing in his fiery red, black, and gold mask, with a fine red coat, snowy white tunic, and pants. The most impressive feature, however, was the wings that appeared crafted out of fabric so fine that it appeared sheer.

Fin smiled without thinking, and stepped into the room, his previous worries and anxiety momentarily forgotten.

Until he realized what was about to happen …

The cake.

He thought it had been served an hour ago.

The servants had brought it out of the kitchen but evidently had not yet served it. The last course must've run later than scheduled!

Fin quickly side-stepped out of the doorway and pressed himself against the back wall, earning him a few curious glances from the nobility. He did his best not to look away, instead giving a regal tilt of his head.

As he forced a casual stance, he began quickly searching the room for Annika. He saw several beautiful gowns that whirled with every movement, or glittered in the shifting candlelight, but Fin could tell at a glance that none of them were the black-haired beauty.

As he searched, he thought about how Annika was first and foremost a spy. If she didn't need to play the political stooge, she'd more than likely dress inconspicuously to observe the occupants of the room.

Fin changed the direction of his gaze to the perimeter of the room. Several giggling noblewomen were allowing their costumed mates for the night to paw at them, or flirt shamelessly without any reprimand. The men were thrilled. A flash of lily-white flesh in one corner, a scandalously cut gown in the other. None were Annika's naturally tanned skin.

Despite his careful scrutiny of the wall, he still nearly missed a stream of black hair flowing down an equally black billowy dress with thin silver designs along its hem and fluttering sleeves. To say the dress was underwhelming given the beauty that hid beneath it would've been a kind description.

Fin watched the smallest sway in Annika's movements while she conversed with another masked noble and came to the conclusion that his guess had been right, that she was trying to remain as unremarkable as possible in her dress.

Not that it mattered to him, however. For Fin? She glowed brighter than any candle in the entire hall, and like a wounded soldier seeing a light in the window of his home, he stepped toward the promise of warmth.

CHAPTER 54
WORDS OF A FEATHER

Fin was about to take a step farther into the room, when there was a flurry of movement from the servants, and the majority of the candles in the room were snuffed out.

Then, with his voice magically amplified, Reese Flint began to sing.

"This is for you, dear prince. Happy Birthday to you ..."

The rest of the room joined in, the exuberant voices ringing in unison. With a smile, a certain cook joined in as he watched Eric beam happily over all his guests.

It took four servants to carefully maneuver the gigantic dragon-shaped cake through the room of nobles, though once everyone saw the baked masterpiece it didn't take them long to clear a wide path.

As the final note of the song rang out, one of the servants lit the carefully rubbed bourbon on fire, and the effect was complete. A dragon wrapped around a castle (the castle was a small wooden figure Fin had made very roughly), with the fire extending out on the table-sized platter.

Everyone was awed and burst out in loud applause as the prince's jaw hung down to his chest.

Servants began relighting the room once the applause had died down, and the king gave a small nudge toward his son. Smiling fondly down at the young boy, Norman waited; it was clear that he had forgotten that, as the host, he was expected to make a speech.

Closing his mouth and blinking in the renewed lighting of the room, Eric scanned the crowd and swallowed with great difficulty.

"Th-Thank you everyone for coming to my ball. I like your costumes a lot, and I hope you all have fun." With his cheeks turning a deep crimson, Eric stepped back beside his father. It was obvious to Fin that the boy was fighting against the impulse to hide behind the king.

Everyone applauded politely, and then the music began once again.

Fin decided to take the opportunity of everyone's divided attention to start moving through the room.

He was halfway toward Annika, when a masked blond woman in a peach gown stumbled into him.

"Oh shhh— I'm soo sorry!" she slurred heavily, gripping his arms to steady herself. When the young woman looked up, she found herself staring into a very solid chest. When her eyes moved higher, she saw the set of piercing blue eyes regarding her calmly.

"Are you alright, my lady?" Fin asked in a low voice. He didn't want to draw too much attention to himself.

Her red glassy eyes peered up at him.

"Yahs."

"Glad to hear that. Pardon me." Fin gently helped right the woman, then sidestepped around her, cutting between the shoulders of guests and serving staff alike.

He realized he was beginning to draw attention with his steady pace, however, and quickly grabbed a goblet off a passing tray to sip. A couple Daxarian knights were eyeing him up and down curiously, most likely due to the fact that he was taller than the majority of the guests and staff, and Fin had to fight every nervous urge in his body to appear relaxed under their scrutiny.

He then struggled to remember what to do with his hands as he gazed around the room at all the splendor and did his best to not stare at Annika's back.

When the knights grew distracted by a buxom lady dressed as a rabbit, Fin melted even farther into the crowd until he was nearly pressed against the stone wall.

He drifted past one of the stone pillars, where an elderly lord dressed as a jester was bent down talking to a woman of a similar age who wore a matching costume. They appeared too absorbed with one another to pay him much mind.

As Fin neared Annika, he could see that she wore a black mask with a beak, and he realized then that she had dressed as a crow.

Her fluttering black dress was the perfect costume for remaining unnoticed …

It was clever and subtle. Two of her strongest qualities …

Fin watched her talk calmly with a lord dressed as a novice physician. Her posture was perfect, but he could see from the slight lean of her head she wasn't truly focused on her conversation.

The longer he watched her, the harder his heart beat. The room was fading around his vision as he waited. He wasn't even sure what he was waiting for, but at that moment he was content just to see her.

He was so lost to his own thoughts on Lady Jenoure, that he was brutally startled when there was a tug on his sleeve.

Looking over swiftly, Fin saw the drunken woman he had helped earlier peering up at him from underneath her feathered mask. He could see her cheeks were tinted pink, and that she was still quite unsteady on her feet.

"Who're you?" She gave a small hiccup as she stared at him expectantly.

"I'm a pirate of the high seas, my lady." Fin tipped his hat, though he felt horribly ridiculous doing so.

"Oh … Are you … Are you going to ask who I am?" Her bottom lip began to protrude in a pout.

"I am not. Forgive me, my lady, but …" Fin gestured with his goblet toward Annika. "I'm hoping to have a brief discussion with the crow over there." After a short nod, he partially turned away from the woman to signify the end of the conversation.

Unfortunately, the libations of the evening had whittled away the woman's social sensibility.

"That's Lady Jenoure!" The woman leaned over and whispered conspiratorially. "She's supposed to be picking a suitor after tonight!"

Fin had just opened his mouth to reply, when a cool female voice interrupted from behind him.

"It's rude to talk about other people's business."

Annika stood only a few feet away from them. Her one arm was crossed around her middle, resting her hand in the crook of the other arm that was lifting her goblet to her mouth.

The woman beside Fin squeaked and tried to slink behind him. Fin, however, felt himself smile, and lowered his hat so she couldn't see his face when he turned around.

"I'm sorry to say it is in fact my business, Lady Jenoure." He cast his voice down and gave himself a slight rasp.

He could practically feel the raised eyebrow she was giving the top of his hat. Fin felt the young damsel behind him edge away and ease back into the crowd, leaving him all alone with Annika.

"How is it your business?" Her voice was icy.

"Well, you see, I intend to offer myself as a candidate for your hand this evening." Fin bowed and offered his upturned palm, while his other tucked his goblet behind his back.

There was a beat of silence, not that he was surprised. He felt border-line giddy as he waited for her reply to his absurd declaration.

"If you would like to make a formal bid to wed me, please see His Majesty," she answered stiffly, before turning back toward the crowd.

Fin straightened, still smiling. "Your response is the only answer that matters. Though I will need to know your opinion on a very particular matter first."

He knew she wouldn't be able to resist asking.

Annika turned back around, and Fin could see from the rigidity in her back that she wanted nothing more than to clobber him.

He braced himself.

"What particular matter is that?" Her scathing derision could have cut him to pieces, but he waited to see if he would need to take her irritation to heart.

"Tell me, have you come to hate witches and stubborn cooks? If so, that might prove fatal to my cause." Despite his forced, dry tone, Fin's heart was in his throat as he slowly tipped his hat up away from his eyes and gazed down into Annika's stricken stare.

Even though she remained silent, Fin could see the color drain from the bare lower part of her face. She had realized who he was, and the knowledge appeared to have robbed her of breath.

Gradually, the shock sunk in. Annika suddenly looked him up and down carefully, as though suspecting him to be an imposter.

Fin took a tentative step closer.

"I'm afraid I might have to insist on an answer, before I commit myself to bachelorhood."

Annika opened her mouth and closed it. She was completely at a loss for words, her throat had swollen shut from emotion, and her entire body felt as though lightning had just coursed through it. She tingled all over.

As she tried to grasp for words, the beginning notes of the next song began. Feeling completely embarrassed and awkward, Fin reached out and gently took her hand. He waited, giving her the chance to pull away, but she did no such thing. He set his goblet down on a tray being carried by a passing servant, then slowly took Annika's and set it down beside his.

Nothing else existed around them as Fin pulled her into his arms, and they began to slowly step to the dance on wobbling legs.

While most of the couples had paired off on the dance floor, they proceeded to dance back farther and farther into the shadows of the room, until they neared the banquet hall's doors.

"I thought you didn't dance," Annika finally said. She felt the warmth of emotion in her cheeks as they stepped together in a perfect blend of slow, whirling black.

"I learned."

Fin knew that his dance instructor Lady Laurent would've given him the lecture of a lifetime for what he did next, but somehow, he couldn't be bothered to care.

He drew Annika closer to himself and felt everything in the world fill with goodness.

Everything was vivid, brighter, happier, hopeful …

He could smell the strange aroma of spices that always lingered around her, and found himself gently inclining his head slightly closer, as though drawn in by it.

"So when are your dancing feet going to turn cold?" Annika's voice hitched as their dancing became more of a sway in a particularly quiet corner of the banquet.

"I'll buy the best quality socks so they always stay warm."

Her grip tightened on the material of his sleeve, and Fin could feel the pain and fear coursing through her as she dared to trust his words.

He cursed himself bitterly.

"I'm sorry I was a stubborn ass. I … I don't expect you to forgive me for being a coward, but … I had to tell you … even if I'm too late. Just in case there is still a chance."

"Tell me that you'll buy better socks?" she bit back, gripping on to his coat all the tighter.

"No. That I love you."

Annika's eyes widened and a small breath escaped her lips. Fin could see that she was barely hanging on to her composure as she clenched her teeth. He knew, if he didn't keep talking, she could reject him with her next breath.

"I will trust you completely. Whatever plans you have, whatever you say you want, wherever you want us to go. I will trust you." He released one of her hands, but gently gripped the other and hid it between them so no prying eyes could see. "I know you better than I know most people, and I know you will do everything in your power to make things work out. If you will still have me … I just want to be there with you."

Annika swallowed with great difficulty and dropped her gaze. Fin didn't know what that meant, and so laid the rest of his soul out for her judgment.

"I'm not alone anymore because of you, and even if you say no and want me to bugger off into an open grave, I want you to know that you've changed my life. I—"

A trio of drunk knights passing by accidentally knocked Annika from behind, propelling her straight into Fin's chest. There was a beat of silence between the pair as they both blushed and failed to rectify the situation. It was too intoxicating to want to stop …

Closing his eyes, and using a strength he didn't know he possessed, Fin carefully took Annika by the shoulders and had her step back so she could properly see his eyes. He needed her to hear every last word.

"I don't have anything to offer other than the fact that I am capable of changing for the better, and I am trying every day. I want to someday be good enough to be your home. If you still think that you'd like to take a risk on me, I will do everything I can to make sure you never regret it for a single day."

Fin felt cold sweat building underneath the black coat as he tried not to hide his gaze, to not assume he was going to have to accept the loss and rejection. He watched her carefully, trying not to appear too awkward.

Annika didn't notice. Not that Fin knew exactly how flustered he was making her … There was no way that he could know she was dizzy.

That she wanted to say something.

Anything.

She wanted to respond to Fin's confession in the most honest way possible, to tell him everything within her that she had never showed another person. To find solace and a life of their own together.

449

Before Fin could receive the reply he so desperately needed, a great clamor began near the king's dais as the young prince ran off into the crowd. The king stood with a frown and nodded toward the guards by the party's entrance.

Without thinking, Fin lunged for the boy as he streaked by them toward the open doors.

"Let me go! I don't care if he's a cook! Fin made my cake! He worked so hard; he should be up here! I'm going to bring him up and you can't stop me!" Tears ran down Eric's face. "I want Ruby here too, and Kraken! Hannah is nice, what about my governess? This isn't fair!"

Fin stilled as the boy squirmed in his arms. Thankfully, he was no longer wearing the wings. The lad had very obviously been pushed hard that day, and all the early mornings before the ball in his dance classes, and his words made Fin love him all the more.

"Eric." Fin had clamped the boy down enough that he was able to speak directly into his ear. The nobility had cleared a path for him as he carried the prince back toward the king, and so was able to speak quietly without the risk of being overheard.

The boy stilled at being called by his first name, then peered at the side of Fin's masked face, confused.

"If you go down to the kitchens to get me, you'll get me fired. I'm glad you liked the cake." Fin kept up the appearance of a smile, while speaking through clenched teeth. He could see the prince stare at him in astonishment, right before he broke out in a smile.

"You came to my party!" he whispered excitedly.

"I did. You can't tell anyone though, promise?"

The prince didn't get a chance to answer before Fin set the boy down on the step and bowed low to the king. The disguised cook backed away toward the party, not realizing he was entering the musicians' designated corner.

The king stared sternly down at Eric, and after a few hushed words, the prince wiped his tears away with the back of his sleeve and turned to face the quieted room.

"I am sorry for my childish outburst. I am going to bed now." Eric's hands were balled into fists at his sides as his cheeks flamed in embarrassment. When he stepped woodenly down from the dais, his watery eyes drifted over to the crowd where Fin stood. Fin gave him the smallest of winks, and once again, the prince was all smiles.

The crowd remained quiet until the young boy had left the room.

"Right! Now we can properly drink!" one of the Troïvackian knights hollered out, and everyone laughed and suddenly the laughter and chatter seemed to double.

"My my. I must say, I haven't ever seen the prince be calmed by someone so easily, except by a certain Royal Cook."

Fin felt his blood freeze as he slowly turned to see the delighted expression of Reese Flint.

"Well, hello there, Captain Handsome, having fun this evening?"

CHAPTER 55
FIN'S FINALE

Fin didn't dignify Reese with an answer as he turned toward the crowd, placing his back to the man. He needed to get to Annika and hear her reply before returning to the kitchen. He could not be delayed again.

Lord Piereva strode past Fin at that moment, failing to notice him as he addressed the Troivackian knight at his side. The earl had predictably not worn a costume, and he stared at the festivities with open derision.

"... Dawson isn't at the cottage? Then I'll go check myself if that cook is where he ought to be."

Fin froze on the spot. The earl was several strides ahead of him, and he had no chance of surpassing him, even if he tried to run to the kitchen using an alternate path. His hands clenched at his sides as he tried to think despite the disaster unfolding before him.

Then, a certain bard he had already forgotten about spoke.

"Need a distraction?"

Slowly turning around, Fin felt a creeping dread settle into his stomach.

Reese Flint had his tunic unlaced to reveal part of his bare chest, and his hair was swept up and to the side. He sported brown trousers and a forest green coat cut snugly against his hardened form—frankly it looked uncomfortable to Fin. Behind the bard was an impressive ensemble of musicians that looked to their leader expectantly for their next song.

"… How much time can you buy me?"

"A single song."

"How would you—'"

"Darling, he is almost at the doors. Grant me a favor in return and you will get your head start." Reese smiled innocently as Fin turned and saw that the bard was sadly correct.

"Fine," he snapped in desperation.

Reese smiled again, closed his eyes, raised his hand in the air, and let out a long breath as he drew it down slowly back down in front of himself.

"I've dreamed of this moment."

"What the hell is wrong with you?!" Desperation layered with exasperation could be heard in Fin's voice.

"I haven't gotten to do something like this since my time with the Emperor of Zinfera."

"What?"

Reese didn't answer as he snapped his fingers, and over his shoulder shouted, "Clarisse, Angelisse, buckets! Don't even dream of being a beat early!"

He then grabbed an odd short metal cylinder with a glass orb at its top. Throwing his arm out, Reese pointed directly at …

Keith Lee.

The mage's son was standing at the opposite corner completely alone, holding a goblet. When Reese signaled him, he smiled, then drew out his wand and gave it a wave, muttering a word they were too far away to hear. A beam of bright pure white light shone out of its crystal tip as every other candle in the banquet hall was extinguished.

Reese pointed at Lord Piereva, and Keith's smile broadened as he aimed the light at the earl and the entire room fell silent.

The bard stepped forward into the light, and the crowd shifted as Lord Piereva slowly turned around. The instrumentals began as Reese began strutting slowly to the beat and swaying his hips toward the earl.

As he moved in slow body rolls, Reese would reach out to one of the adoring ladies that had flocked to the edge of the dance floor, and gently caress a lock of hair or hand. Sighs and giggles followed that confused Lord Piereva, especially when Reese's green eyes never left his face.

Reese suddenly dove to his knees at Lord Piereva's feet as two buckets of water doused him from the sides. Then he began to sing … a powerful, enticing ballad that was unapologetically … suggestive. His tunic was transparent, water droplets trickling down his body as he stared up hungrily at the stunned lord, his impassioned tones unaffected by the dampness.

Reese Flint stood and began dancing closely around the earl, before summoning the crowd of fawning noblewomen he had worked into a fervor. Unprompted, the women began twirling around the bard and earl, brushing feathers and fans against them, all while they attempted to press their bodies closer to the two men.

The king sat on his throne with his hands steepling over the tip of his nose and grinning mouth to hide his amusement. Captain Antonio at his side was on the brink of hysterics, and wasn't even trying to hide it, while Lord Fuks stood to the side of the throne and was jerking his shoulders to the beat of the song. Mr Howard watched, mortified, over the king's right shoulder.

"I wish Ashowan and Mage Lee could see this," the king called over the music, as the captain succumbed to uncontrollable laughter. They were unaware that the house witch was a mere twenty feet away and equally as delighted as them.

Annika was standing shoulder to shoulder with Lord Jiho Ryu, her jaw hanging open wide enough to catch an entire swarm of flies before she leaned over to him.

"This is the greatest night of my life."

Reese continued shimmying and dancing in a tight circle around the earl while the noblewomen continued to dance closely in their swirling silk skirts and costumes. Lord Piereva was completely hemmed in, but he was defeated more by the flashing low cut bodices and ample bosoms than the bard.

It was then that Reese managed a hasty wink in Fin's direction—a gesture that was sorely misinterpreted by the crowd of adoring noblewomen as they collectively swooned.

Fin finally snapped out of his stupor, and began to maneuver his way through the crowd, resuming his escape. He tried to see Annika, but the partygoers had shifted and without much light, Fin had no way of knowing who was where.

Hastily, he slipped through the sweltering bodies, amazed that the noblemen did not seem to mind their wives behaving so outrageously, as they were all too amused by the situation to fully care.

~~~~~~

Annika stood shaking her head as the dance came to an end and Reese Flint bowed to the wild crowd.

"Thank you everyone! A round of applause for this dashing Troivackian earl for spicing up that number. You were a terrific sport." Reese Flint bowed to the lord, whose expression darkened as the women gradually faded back into the crowd.

He stalked off purposefully with his knight, Sir Wickfield, on his heels.

"I wish there was a way to hold that event in my memory for the rest of my days." Annika chuckled as her eyes continued to scan the crowd for Fin. She had lost sight of him after he had set the prince down. It was odd that he had rushed off without hearing her reply …

Then again, what if he had changed his mind after confessing?

I have no right to be surprised if that's it. He's probably drunk and just came to wish the prince a happy birthday.

"So have you made your decision regarding your future husband?" Jiho asked breezily with his hands clasped behind his back. He surveyed the room with a serene expression behind his mask. He had come dressed as a blue jay and wore fine blue silk with swirls of cream to best bring the image home.

After doing another cursory scan of the room and seeing neither hide nor hair of a captain's hat, or black coat with gold thread, Annika felt her newfound hope withering away inside her chest.

"I suppose so," she replied bleakly. For once she didn't have to pretend to be dull—she *felt* dull. All the light in her felt as though it had a bucket of ash doused over it.

"Wonderful. I am certain we will have many brilliant children."

She turned slowly to stare at Jiho, who looked perfectly pleased with himself.

"You think I will choose you?"

"We both know I am the obvious choice."

When Annika didn't say anything in response, Jiho turned to the doors with a slight frown.

"Hmm, odd. I suspect Fin must be overwhelmed right about now."

Annika's head snapped back to stare up at him.

"What do you mean?"

"Well, my lady, he dismissed his entire staff this evening in order to prepare the late-night meal all on his own. I suspect that is why Lord

Piereva is as angry as a bear. He most likely is hungry and went to speak with him. Poor man."

Annika felt the wretched hope fill her yet again.

Had that been it? Had he come to only talk to her then needed to rush back to his duties?

"You know, sometimes the simplest explanation is the right one." Jiho's voice once again broke her thoughts.

Annika blinked several times before she turned and saw Jiho smiling down at her knowingly.

Too knowingly …

"Do me a favor, my lady?" Jiho began as Annika's eyes began to narrow. "Don't ever be afraid to give an emotional shove to that stubborn ass. Even if it's over a cliff."

Her breath caught in her throat.

"What are you—"

"He's terrible at hiding his nonsense, and I can see that his affliction is beginning to spread. I recommend that you retire straight to bed this instant to rest and avoid worsening the condition." With a wink, Jiho crossed his arms over his chest and stared back over the party.

Smiling with enough radiance to embarrass the sun, Annika went up on her tiptoes and planted a platonic kiss on Jiho's cheek.

Then she slipped out of the banquet.

Jiho leaned his head back against the wall and plucked a goblet off a nearby servant's tray.

Well Fin, try not to mess it up. We've all done all we can.

Exiting the banquet hall with a stumble, Fin took off running toward the doorway to the maze. He couldn't head straight to the kitchen, as that would be too suspicious.

By the time he reached the exit, his lungs were screaming. He mentally tried to gauge how long he would have before the song ended and the crowd cleared enough for Piereva to leave. Fin was nearly down the steps, when he screeched to a halt behind a costumed couple that were in the throes of a passionate kiss.

"Erm … I don't mean to be … could you maybe …" The couple remained oblivious to the inconvenienced figure. "Forget it."

Fin leapt the rest of the way down the steps into the soft grass and bolted down the castle wall, making sure to duck beneath windows and keep his face turned away when he would hear the occasional laugh or shout.

He rounded the corner of his kitchen, and before entering, magicked the hearth fire out. He didn't need anyone peering in.

Diving into the darkness, Fin immediately stripped out of the mask, bandana, black coat, and tunic. He yanked out his backup work tunic from under a bag of flour and pulled it over his head. He tied his apron around his waist, and with a hasty snap of his fingers, had the fire roaring again. He ceased all magical cookery that was preparing the midnight meal and dusted his apron and arms with flour for good measure. He hid his costume under several stacks of potatoes, and mentally begged Sir Taylor for forgiveness if it became ruined in any way.

He was beginning to pull a tray of brownies out of the oven, when the castle door was thrown open with great force, and in strode Lord Piereva with Sir Wickfield behind him.

The earl leveled Fin with a scathing appraisal of his appearance. Fin raised his eyebrow and glared back, still trying to catch his breath without it being noticeable.

"Lord Piereva, to what do I owe the pleasure?" he asked dryly.

"Where's my knight?" Lord Piereva barked, striding farther into the kitchen until he was in front of Fin's table.

Sighing, Fin set the pan down and placed his hands on his hips. "Well, let's retrace your steps. Where did you last leave him?"

"I'm in no mood for your smartass remarks," Lord Piereva growled while Sir Wickfield's eyes gleamed. The man was salivating over the promise of violence.

"Is the ball really so bad that you have to come harass me? Are there no noblewomen interested in your obvious need for a hug—or is it because you evidently need a doctor?" Fin leaned the tops of his fists on his table. He knew he was taking a dangerous risk in baiting Lord Piereva, but he couldn't stop the excitement of the night singing in his veins.

"The earl needs a doctor?" Sir Wickfield looked at his master worriedly. Before Lord Piereva could say anything, Fin jumped in yet again.

"Of course he does. It is unwise to leave that stick up his ass for too long—it could become infected."

Lord Piereva's hand shot out and yanked Fin up by the tunic. His eyes were wild like a boar's as his other fist came sailing down toward Fin's face.

Only he didn't hit Fin.

He hit the tray of brownies that Fin had grabbed and used to shield himself with.

Snatching his hand back with a hiss, Lord Piereva's knuckles were already growing pink from the burns that came as a result of his strike to the bottom of a hot pan. Fin set the tray on the table and tutted.

"Half a tray of brownies ruined."

"I'LL HAVE YOU FIRED, COOK! YOU HAVE MY—"

"Lord Piereva. You have harassed me and my staff, have people following me, you just physically attacked me, and while in the beginning I was cordial, there is no need for me to continue being so now. You haven't *once* gone to any of my superiors with your grievances. Which means one thing and one thing only: you will be in far greater trouble than I will be should the king find out you are acting like a tyrant in *his* castle. You are a guest here, my lord. You do not get to get away with behaving like a spoiled brat."

For several moments, Lord Piereva looked as though he were about to explode.

His face grew vermillion red, his eyes bulged almost as much as the vein in his forehead, and his hand was inching suspiciously closer to the hilt of his sword.

Sir Wickfield looked as though it were the morning of the Winter Solstice.

The door to the kitchen suddenly opened then, as servants filed in to start carrying out the trays of food for the midnight meal. At the very end of the line, Ruby appeared in the doorway, and with a single glance surmised that Fin was about to be stabbed.

"Lord Piereva, a Lady Keely Hawkins is looking for you in the banquet hall."

"Who?" Lord Piereva snapped, his vein still throbbing mightily.

"Lady Keely Hawkins? I believe she was dressed as a colorful fish this evening. Bright pink, if I recall."

Lord Piereva's attention was captured.

He cast a lone glare at Fin as he began to walk toward the door.

"We aren't finished with this conversation, cook," he snarled, all the while missing Ruby's dark expression directed at him as she slowly followed the other servants out of the kitchen. Apparently, she was satisfied that Fin's death wasn't quite as imminent.

"Have a terrific evening, my lord— Oh. You have a feather in your beard, by the way."

There was a violent snort, but the earl stormed out of the room and slammed the door shut behind him.

Fin waited several beats of silence before he walked over to the door and gave it a small tap with his finger to lock it for the night. The servants would place the dirty dishes in their banquet hall to be dealt with in the morning. The kitchen was cluttered enough.

As he turned back to his table, Fin gave a small spin with extra effort.

Next thing he knew, he was smiling and dancing to himself as he dusted flour off his hands and remembered feeling Annika in his arms whirling around the banquet.

The kitchen began to magically clean itself around him as he grew more and more exuberant in his dancing. He let himself celebrate the euphoria of the night's rousing success and couldn't stop his smile becoming an occasional burst of laughter as he gave a particularly energetic spin.

"I'm glad you saved that footwork for when you could be alone."

Fin swung around and found Lady Annika Jenoure leaning against the garden doorway with her arms crossed over her chest.

She wore men's trousers and her black cloak, and no longer wore her mask. She stared at him with an unreadable expression, but even though she was hiding it, Fin knew why she had come.

He could feel it.

"I'll have you know a very beautiful crow thought my dancing was spectacular this evening. What brings you to my kitchen, Lady Jenoure?"

He began striding toward her slowly.

"I was checking to make sure the castle was properly protected. There was a mysterious pirate at the banquet, after all."

Grinning broadly, Fin stopped in front of Annika with his hands on his hips.

"I see, and what would you say to this pirate should you find him?"

"You promise you won't have any second thoughts?" A small smile of her own was beginning to bloom on Annika's face.

"Love, you've been my first and only thought for quite some time."

Annika looked like she wanted to laugh and bicker with him more, so he did the only thing he could think of to keep such a challenging woman happy with him.

He kissed her.

As Fin drew her farther into the kitchen, the garden door swung gently closed behind them and locked.

No one would enter or leave Fin's kitchen for the rest of the night, but the two that remained in its cozy glow didn't mind one bit.

ACKNOWLEDGMENTS

A big shout-out and thanks to Kieve Svetnikov for penning the tavern song and giving it to me for the story. I wish you the best in all your endeavors!

He just wanted a decent book to read ...

Not too much to ask, is it? It was in 1935 when Allen Lane, Managing Director of Bodley Head Publishers, stood on a platform at Exeter railway station looking for something good to read on his journey back to London. His choice was limited to popular magazines and poor-quality paperbacks – the same choice faced every day by the vast majority of readers, few of whom could afford hardbacks. Lane's disappointment and subsequent anger at the range of books generally available led him to found a company – and change the world.

'We believed in the existence in this country of a vast reading public for intelligent books at a low price, and staked everything on it'
Sir Allen Lane, 1902–1970, founder of Penguin Books

The quality paperback had arrived – and not just in bookshops. Lane was adamant that his Penguins should appear in chain stores and tobacconists, and should cost no more than a packet of cigarettes.

Reading habits (and cigarette prices) have changed since 1935, but Penguin still believes in publishing the best books for everybody to enjoy. We still believe that good design costs no more than bad design, and we still believe that quality books published passionately and responsibly make the world a better place.

So wherever you see the little bird – whether it's on a piece of prize-winning literary fiction or a celebrity autobiography, political tour de force or historical masterpiece, a serial-killer thriller, reference book, world classic or a piece of pure escapism – you can bet that it represents the very best that the genre has to offer.

Whatever you like to read – trust Penguin.